PRAISE FOR
BLOOD OATH

"This action-filled debut by scriptwriter Farnsworth reads like a cross between P. N. Elrod's historical vampire adventures and Thomas Greanias's conspiracy thrillers."

—*Publishers Weekly*

"Don't think of Mr. Farnsworth's debut thriller as the umpteenth vampire knockoff on the market. Think of it as the inventive one in which a brave young White House staff member asks, 'You really expect me to believe we've got a vampire on a leash, and we can just send him after terrorists and spies whenever we want?' Multibook series and $200 million movie franchises have been built on a lot less."

—*The New York Times*

"Christopher Farnsworth's taut thriller . . . is an irresistible page-turner . . . a complex and unnervingly realistic tale in which vampire Nathaniel Cade, a Secret Service agent sworn to protect the president, is far less of a monster than his human colleagues at the CIA and FBI . . . Dazzlingly clever."

—*The Washington Post*

"Farnsworth's series debut asks the reader to set aside disbelief and buy into this premise, among other more fantastic concepts, and it's almost easily done with his adept writing style."

—*Library Journal*

"The two key elements that make *Blood Oath* an entertaining espionage paranormal thriller are the clever intermingling of history with the supernatural . . . and [a] plot [that] never takes itself seriously."

—*Alternative Worlds*

continued . . .

"*Blood Oath* is exactly how I like my Presidential thrillers. With vampires." —Brad Meltzer, author of *The Book of Lies*

"The vampire novel that finally gets it right. Christopher Farnsworth has done his homework in places where most writers wouldn't even know to look—and the result is a rollicking tale of the supernatural grounded in some of the true oddities of American history. If Dan Brown wrote a vampire thriller, this would be it."

—Mitch Horowitz, author of *Occult America*

"As someone who thinks Stoker's *Dracula* has never been bettered, and who would happily stick a stake through the heart of most modern vampire fiction, it almost pains me to say how much I enjoyed *Blood Oath*. Witty, exciting, and compulsively readable, with a central character who seems destined to become a favorite of both skeptics and true blood believers, this may just be the best debut vampire novel in many years."

—John Connolly, author of *The Whisperers*

BLOOD OATH

CHRISTOPHER FARNSWORTH

JOVE BOOKS, NEW YORK

THE BERKLEY PUBLISHING GROUP
Published by the Penguin Group
Penguin Group (USA) Inc.
375 Hudson Street, New York, New York 10014, USA
Penguin Group (Canada), 90 Eglinton Avenue East, Suite 700, Toronto, Ontario M4P 2Y3, Canada
(a division of Pearson Penguin Canada Inc.)
Penguin Books Ltd., 80 Strand, London WC2R 0RL, England
Penguin Group Ireland, 25 St. Stephen's Green, Dublin 2, Ireland
(a division of Penguin Books Ltd.)
Penguin Group (Australia), 250 Camberwell Road, Camberwell, Victoria 3124, Australia
(a division of Pearson Australia Group Pty. Ltd.)
Penguin Books India Pvt. Ltd., 11 Community Centre, Panchsheel Park, New Delhi—110 017, India
Penguin Group (NZ), 67 Apollo Drive, Rosedale, North Shore 0632, New Zealand
(a division of Pearson New Zealand Ltd.)
Penguin Books (South Africa) (Pty.) Ltd., 24 Sturdee Avenue, Rosebank, Johannesburg 2196,
South Africa

Penguin Books Ltd., Registered Offices: 80 Strand, London WC2R 0RL, England

BLOOD OATH

A Jove Book / published by arrangement with the author

PRINTING HISTORY
G. P. Putnam's Sons hardcover edition / May 2010
Jove premium edition / March 2011

ISBN: 978-0-515-14903-6

JOVE®
Jove Books are published by The Berkley Publishing Group,
a division of Penguin Group (USA) Inc.,
375 Hudson Street, New York, New York 10014.
JOVE® is a registered trademark of Penguin Group (USA) Inc.
The "J" design is a trademark of Penguin Group (USA) Inc.

PRINTED IN THE UNITED STATES OF AMERICA

10 9 8 7 6 5 4 3 2 1

To my mother and my brother,

and

to Jean,

who believed in me when I didn't believe in myself

Some time in the year 1867, a fishing smack sailed from Boston. One of the sailors was [NAME REDACTED]. Two of the crew were missing, and were searched for. The captain went into the hold. He held up his lantern, and saw the body of one of these men, in the clutches of [NAME REDACTED], who was sucking blood from it. Near by was the body of the other sailor. It was bloodless.

[NAME REDACTED] was tried, convicted, and sentenced to be hanged, but President Andrew Johnson commuted the sentence to life imprisonment.

—Charles Hoy Fort, *Wild Talents*

ONE

Republic of Kosovo

After two extended tours in Iraq, Army Specialist Wayne Denton thought he'd never be cold again.

That was before he was sent to Kosovo. He stepped off the plane and realized it was, in fact, possible for Hell to freeze over. The war in Kosovo, supposedly over for ten years, seemed to have been preserved under a thick layer of ice.

There were still bomb craters and rubble in the streets where the U.N. peacekeepers patrolled. Armed bandits still hijacked cars at night. The Russian Mafiya smuggled guns and drugs. All the while, the Serbian army waited at the border, pacing like an angry dog behind a fence.

Wayne had been at a window in an abandoned building behind his M24 sniper rifle for six hours now. The boredom he could handle—but the cold was killing him. He wasn't even allowed to use chemical hand warmers; his sergeant said the bad guys had thermal imaging capability.

They didn't look that sharp, Wayne thought. He checked them again through his scope, careful not to touch his skin to the freezing metal.

They waited in the courtyard of the bombed-out apartments, sixteen stories down from his position. Bunch of big, unibrow, Cro-Magnon SOBs, their hairlines almost meeting their beards. All wearing trench coats. The cold didn't seem to bother them at all.

They were called the Vukodlak, which was supposed to be Serbian for the Wolf Pack, or something. He hadn't been paying attention to that part of the briefing.

They looked as bored as Wayne felt. He wondered, not for the first time, why his Army Ranger unit was babysitting a bunch of former death-squad thugs. Surely the locals could handle this.

Hell, Wayne could end it right now, all by himself. The Wolf Pack was a little over a hundred yards away—point-blank range for any sniper. He could kill each man on the ground before they knew what was happening. He'd done it before.

Back home in Casper, Wyoming, Wayne was the quiet kid in the back of the class. He wasn't unpopular, he was just there. Sort of taking up space, drifting along in life.

Then 9/11 hit, and everyone in his family assumed he'd put off college and enlist, because they were at war now, and that's what kids do in a war, right? They join the army. He put his community college application away, unfinished, and signed up at a recruiting station in a mini-mall.

He was surprised to find his talent for fading into the background becoming useful for the first time. He was selected for Sniper School, then joined the Rangers.

He never thought he'd get used to the blood and death—much less delivering it. He found he could simply focus on the quiet place in himself. That was where he pulled the trigger, and that was where he stacked the bodies. Sometimes he worried about what would happen when he got home—if the bodies would all spill out into the rest of him, or if the quiet place would just sit there, untouched, and he'd go on as normal as ever, for the rest of his life.

He wasn't sure which was worse, actually. He tried not to think about it too much.

He kept his shit together. He survived. By the end of his first tour, the other guys in his unit looked at him like a veteran. They depended on him.

He was no longer just a placeholder. In fact, he was kind of a badass. After three years, he thought he'd seen it all.

Which is why he was annoyed, but not surprised, when his unit was pulled off the active hunt for an al-Qaeda cell and sent to this winter wonderland. The army had its own way of doing things. Orders were orders.

Wayne's CO had been more tight-lipped than usual, but the rumors made their way down.

When Kosovo declared independence, that didn't go

over too well with the Serb neighbors. A bunch of Serbian nationals walked past the shack that served as a border checkpoint, and immediately began rioting in front of the U.S. Embassy. Some buildings got torched, and in the confusion, someone lost something important. Something big. It turned up with the Wolf Pack, who offered it to the highest bidder. The U.S. wanted it back.

Above all, the whole thing had to be kept quiet. The Rangers were good at quiet.

After they got to Kosovo, they spent a day and a half tracking the Serbs. But when they found the Wolf Pack, they were told to stay back and wait.

All the sergeant said was, move in, set up a ring, and make sure none of the Serbs left it. Questions were met with the kind of silence that implied a court-martial in the near future.

The CO got a message from way up the chain of command. A flight came in from Ansbach in Germany, and he sent a couple of Rangers to the airfield. They came back with a duffel full of cash.

Wayne figured it out then. The U.S. might not negotiate with terrorists, but it would sure as hell bribe them. He had seen plenty of it firsthand in Iraq, with CIA spooks giving away stacks of hundred-dollar bills stuffed in the aptly named Halliburton briefcases. Just one of those stacks could have bought his parents a new house. But the funds were earmarked for the people busy shooting at their son.

The only other thing they brought back from the plane was what the army called a "transfer case." But everyone knew what it was: a casket, used to take the bodies of dead soldiers home.

It gave Wayne the creeps. He was glad to take his sniper position and get away from it.

Wayne decided he hated this James Bond crap.

But orders were orders.

The sun dipped behind the empty buildings. It would be full dark in a matter of minutes. Wayne began to worry about his toes falling off, like loose ice cubes inside his boots.

Then his radio crackled to life. "Stand ready," the CO told the unit. "We're going to open the package."

The sun vanished completely behind the horizon. The dark came down like a sudden rain.

Wayne switched his scope to night-vision and checked on the Wolf Pack again—and nearly jumped back. One of the Serbs was staring right up into the window. As if he could see him there.

Impossible. He was totally concealed. The Serb would have to be able to see in the dark. He looked back through the scope.

The Serb was still staring. Had to be a coincidence. People stare at things, look around aimlessly, when they're bored. It didn't mean anything.

Then the man made a gun with his thumb and forefinger, and pointed it directly at Wayne. And winked.

Wayne's finger twitched involuntarily on the trigger, because every instinct he had screamed to kill the man.

Despite the cold, Wayne started to sweat.

The man moved out of the range of the scope. Wayne

dialed back the magnification quickly, to get a view of the whole courtyard.

Another man was being dragged by two of the Serbs. He was dressed in all-black Special Forces fatigues, without insignia—the kind the spooks loved to wear, even in broad daylight in the desert, when the temperature got above 120 degrees. Then they bitched about how the dust and sand got all over the neat creases in their clothes.

Some covert ops cowboy, and they'd have to bail his ass out. Still, Wayne wondered—where did he come from? They had the area staked out a mile in every direction, and he'd never seen the guy arrive. Sure, he could have missed it . . . but there would have been some radio chatter. Something.

He shoved the thoughts away, along with the cold and the fear that had seized him a moment before. It all vanished as he went through his pre-shoot rituals. The world narrowed to the field of focus through his scope. It was comforting.

The Serbs kicked the operative to the ground. Wayne winced—that looked like it hurt—but the man didn't. He didn't even seem bothered. Or scared.

He was dragged up, and then kicked down again—made to kneel before the leader of the Wolf Pack. The Alpha Male, Wayne guessed. The biggest guy in the group, a wildly bearded man at least six-five, packed with muscle. He looked like he could eat everyone else in the courtyard for lunch.

Wayne heard a burst of Serbian through his earpiece.

The spook was wired with his own radio, broadcasting on the Rangers' channel.

The operative's mike picked up the sound of the Alpha's laughter, and Wayne felt cold again.

"Please don't attempt to speak in my language," the Alpha Male said. "It's insulting." Crisp, clear English.

The man shrugged. "Fine," he said. Wayne was impressed. This guy didn't sound the least bit scared. "You're the Vukodlak, then?"

"We are. But you do not appear to have what I want."

"I need to confirm that you have the object."

"Why don't you ask your soldiers? They've been here all day."

That's when the Alpha pointed up into the air—directly at Wayne, then at the positions of his fellow Rangers, all around the apartments.

Impossible, Wayne thought to himself. *Totally frigging impossible . . .*

He clicked his radio on. "Sarge, we're made—" Panic in his voice, despite his best effort.

"Shut up," the sergeant snapped back. "Maintain radio silence."

Because of this exchange, Wayne only caught the tail end of what the Alpha Male said.

"—your big plan? They would come running to your rescue? We will be chewing on their hearts before they pull their triggers."

The Serb turned back toward Wayne. This time there was no doubt. The Serb stared right at him. And smiled, with perfect teeth that glowed in the night-vision scope.

It took everything Wayne had not to get up and run.

More laughter. All the Serbs were practically howling now.

The operative spoke after the tumult died down.

"You'll get the cash, as we agreed, once I have the item." He sounded bored.

Brass balls, Wayne thought.

The Alpha considered this for a moment. Apparently he wanted the cash. He nodded, and two of his thugs went into a tent.

They emerged a second later with a metal box, marked with U.S. Army stencils. Wayne couldn't read them with the scope, but it looked like the sort of thing you didn't want to open.

The Alpha opened it.

For a moment, a light bloomed in Wayne's scope. It played hell with the optics, like the night-vision didn't know how to adjust for it. Then it cast an eerie glow around the courtyard.

Oh, Christ, Wayne thought. They have a nuke. The secrecy all made sense now. The army would do anything to keep a nuke out of the hands of terrorists. Even send a whole Ranger unit into an ambush.

He could see the weird glow reflect on the operative. He looked too young to be out in the field alone. His features were perfectly calm—way too calm. Maybe they had doped him up, so he didn't know he was going to be a sacrificial lamb.

Wayne peered intently inside the box. It seemed too small to hold a nuclear weapon, but he heard they could fit those things inside suitcases now. Maybe this was just the next generation. The glow made it hard to see, but he could have sworn the eerie light was coming from something shaped like a human hand. . . .

Whatever it was, the operative nodded, and the Serbs closed the lid. The glow switched off like a lamp, and the scope's optics went back to normal.

The operative looked at the Alpha Male. "Some things shouldn't be touched," he said.

The scorn in the Alpha's voice came through Wayne's earpiece. "Then you should have been more careful with it."

"You're right." The operative stood. "Drop it," he said into his radio.

Across the courtyard from Wayne, about ten stories down, there was movement in one of the blown-out windows. He saw a guy from his unit toss the black duffel bag.

It landed a few feet from the Serbs. One went over to it, pawed it open, and examined the contents.

He displayed the open bag to the Alpha, showing the stacks of cash.

The Alpha frowned. "We really prefer euros," he said.

"You get what I have."

The operative picked up the box by its handle, and turned to go.

Wayne couldn't believe it. It couldn't be that simple.

Of course it couldn't. The Serbs closed ranks, blocking the man's path out of the courtyard.

"I don't think so," the Alpha said, with his perfect enunciation.

The operative didn't turn around to face him. His shoulders sagged for a moment, as if he was very tired. Then he straightened up again.

"Don't be stupid."

"I promised my boys some sport. American soldiers ought to be able to hold out longer than our usual game."

The Serbs were closer to the man now. Moving in. Wayne didn't know why he was so close to panic again. This made no sense. None of them had pulled a weapon. They didn't seem to have any guns. They were covered by an armed force in a superior position. They should be the ones who were afraid.

And yet, they seemed ready to tear the operative apart with their bare hands.

"Walk away now," the operative said. His voice was stern, like he was being firm with an unruly child.

The Alpha snarled. "You don't order me around," he said. "Your teeth aren't sharp enough."

"Perhaps not," the operative admitted. Quick as a blink, he whirled and brought out a knife. It reflected silver in the moonlight. "But this is. Walk away now, and you get to live."

The Alpha took a step back. He seemed more frightened of the knife—a simple KA-BAR, from what Wayne could see—than of all the heavy artillery around him.

He still shook his head. "Only one of us gets to leave here alive tonight."

"You're right," the operative said. He put the box down.

Then they were on him.

In spite of himself, Wayne shouted, "Jesus Christ!" and prepared to fire.

The CO's voice came loud and clear over the channel. "Hold your fire!" he screamed. "Do not fire! Damn it, do not fire!"

It was insane. The Serbs were going to kill the man. They were like rabid dogs: growling, snarling, flecks of foam at their mouths.

Then the first Serb went flying out of the mob. He landed hard on a pile of rubble, his head nearly cut off by a jagged slash at his throat. Dead.

And then another, launched out of the pack like he had been fired from a cannon. He clutched a bloody stump where his hand used to be.

There were several more already on the ground, like broken dolls. Wayne could see the operative now—barely. He was a blur inside the trench coats, stopping only when he sliced one of them. Then another Serb would fall over.

Wayne noticed the Alpha Male standing back, watching. He didn't look pleased, but made no move to help his crew.

The operative ducked, and kicked, and a Serb howled with pain, holding his knee where the lower leg flopped uselessly, shattered. The howling stopped, the operative's knife blurring away from the Serb's throat, blood floating in the air in its wake.

The Alpha Male turned, the bag of cash in his hand. He was going to leave.

The operative saw this. But he was still dealing with the other Serbs, who didn't know or didn't care that their leader was about to abandon them. They threw themselves back into the scrum, even if they were missing limbs. As if they felt no pain.

The Alpha Male began to walk. He was going to get away.

The hell he was.

Wayne flipped his scope to focus solely on the Alpha.

He aimed, breathed out smoothly and pulled the trigger.

The sound of the M24 was a polite cough.

It was a beautiful shot. It should have split the Alpha's head right at the temple.

Except the Alpha Male wasn't there anymore.

Impossible. A hundred yards, a bullet traveling at twenty-eight hundred feet per second . . . he would have had to move before the noise of the shot could reach his ears. Faster than the speed of sound.

Frantically, Wayne scanned the courtyard, trying to reacquire the Alpha.

He didn't have to look far. The Serb leader stood just a few feet away. Scowling. At Wayne.

He looked seriously pissed.

Before Wayne could fire another shot—before he could even think about it—the Alpha was gone again.

Dimly, he realized his sergeant was shouting at him

over his earpiece: *"—You fucking idiot, Denton, move, move, get out of there—"*

He noticed the operative was dealing with the last two members of the Wolf Pack. The only survivors. But the operative spared a glance up at the window. He looked almost as pissed as the Alpha had.

Wayne stood, began to stow his gear. His legs were like wood. His movements were clumsy and slow.

Then he heard something in the stairwell. Something coming.

His mind shut down. He didn't care anymore that it was impossible. That no one could climb thirty-two flights of stairs in less than thirty seconds.

All he knew was the Alpha Male was coming for him.

He lurched toward the door, his legs rubbery, his rifle in one hand, the rest of his gear on the floor.

The door shattered open before he got there, flying off its hinges.

The Alpha Male stood in the doorway. His wild beard had grown, joining the fur at his chest, on his head. His shape was twisted under the long coat, his arms and legs longer than anything human. He opened his mouth, and that's when Wayne realized he was looking into a snout, filled with the sharp, jagged teeth of a dog.

No. Not a dog.

Sometimes, during firefights in Iraq, everything would slow down. Wayne would remember things. Like how an insurgent's headband had the same colors as a football team he used to play against in high school.

This time, it was something more immediate. He remembered what Vukodlak meant.

It didn't mean "wolf pack." It meant "werewolves." It was the Serbian word for werewolves.

He smelled the blood and meat on the breath of the Alpha, and realized it wasn't just a nickname.

He raised the rifle, and heard, rather than felt, his fingers break as the Alpha tore the gun away.

He was on his back, throat exposed, before he even knew how he'd gotten there.

The long teeth were above his neck, and he felt saliva dripping from the Alpha's mouth, smelled the feral stink of its excitement.

He was going to die.

There was a scrabbling noise, then movement at the window. Cold air rushed past Wayne, and the weight of the monster left him.

The Alpha was knocked across the room, slamming into the crumbling plaster wall.

Somehow, the operative was there, between the nightmare thing and Wayne.

He'd covered sixteen stories almost as quickly as the Alpha—only he hadn't used the stairs.

Struggling to find words, Wayne pointed at the gun, trying to tell the man to use it.

The operative ignored him. The Alpha got to his feet—Wayne noticed, for the first time, they were bent at an angle, like a dog's hind legs. He hesitated, growling, a long string of drool hanging from his muzzle.

He spoke, his words rough and high-pitched at the

same time. Exactly like a dog that's learned to talk, Wayne thought.

"My pack," was all he said.

The operative smiled. "You should have kept your boys on a leash."

The operative still had the knife, gleaming bright where it wasn't covered in blood.

The Alpha Male looked at it, a challenge in his eyes.

The operative nodded, and flung his weapon down. The knife thudded into the floor.

The Alpha Male released a howl that became a scream as he leaped, growling and snapping, eyes burning with rage.

The operative didn't move.

For a second, all Wayne could see was the Alpha Male's muzzle, his bright white snarl.

But somehow, the operative caught the werewolf by the neck, in midair. He held the thing there like it was a bad puppy. The Alpha thrashed and howled.

Then the operative reached with his other hand, grabbed the Alpha's lower jaw, right between those snapping teeth—and tore it clean off.

Shock and pain filled the Alpha's eyes, and it tried to howl again. But the noise was drowned by the sudden rush of blood pouring down its throat.

The operative stood, holding the Alpha off the ground, until there was no more movement.

He dropped the body to the floor. Went back to his knife and pulled it from the floor, then turned and sank it into the creature's chest.

The doglike rear legs kicked once, and didn't move again.

Wayne stared at the operative. The black fatigues were covered with blood, and torn, but the man didn't have a mark on him.

He glared at Wayne. The soldier suddenly realized he was alone with something infinitely more frightening than the Serbs.

Wayne considered leaping out the window. It had to be preferable to whatever else was coming.

Maybe the operative realized this, because the anger on his face faded.

He picked up the M24, and handed it, stock-first, back to Wayne.

Wayne took it, fumbled and nearly dropped it. That was when he remembered the fingers of his right hand were broken.

"You were ordered not to shoot for a reason," the operative said, his voice cold. "It just makes them angry."

Wayne finally found his voice. "That was—" He stopped, looked at the corpse in the room with them.

It was a man again. Missing his lower jaw and half his face, yes, but recognizably human.

"That's not possible," Wayne said. "No way that just happened. That can't be real."

"That's right," he said. "It never happened. Because if what you saw was real, you would never go home. You understand me?"

Wayne nodded.

"Good," the operative said. He turned to leave.

Wayne knew he should have stayed quiet. But the question escaped him before he could stop it, or even think about it.

"What are you?" he asked quietly.

He wasn't sure the operative heard him. But then the man stopped at the door and turned back.

He grinned in an unfunny way. "I'm on your side," he said. "That's all you need to know."

It took the other Rangers a half-hour to pile the dead bodies in the center of the courtyard. They poured gasoline. The corpses burned faster than Wayne had ever seen before.

The operative had the metal box under his arm while he watched. The unit medic was splinting Wayne's fingers when the CO approached.

The CO had his hand out for the box. "I'll take that now," he said, in his usual, don't-fuck-with-me tone of voice.

The operative made no move to let go. "No," he said. Simply, quietly. No room for argument.

"My orders—"

"You shouldn't have lost it in the first place."

The CO looked uncomfortable. "Look," he said. "I don't want to fight with you . . ."

The operative glanced at the pile of burning bodies, then back at the CO.

"That's right," he said. "You don't."

The CO wasn't used to having anyone question his orders. But he wasn't stupid. He walked off, catching Wayne's eye as he went. Wayne looked away quickly.

The operative kept the box.

Debriefing was quick, and the CO and the sergeant both made the same point as the operative: this mission never happened. None of the Rangers saw anything. Forget you were ever in Kosovo.

They were on a plane back to Iraq before morning. The box—and the casket, Wayne noticed—went back in another plane, headed for God knows where.

Wayne was more than happy to forget it. He would work at it every day for the rest of his life, in fact.

But there was one thing that stuck with him, that woke him up in a cold sweat until the day he died, no matter how much he tried to push it away.

He'd never forget what he saw when the operative grinned.

Only the man—of course, he wasn't actually a man, but it made Wayne feel better to call him that—hadn't been grinning.

He was showing the long, curved fangs in his mouth, right where his eyeteeth should have been.

And he still had the jawbone in one hand.

TWO

Politics is a blood sport.

—Aneurin Bevan

TWENTY HOURS LATER, WASHINGTON, D.C.

Griff looked at the kid sitting across from him in the White House limo. Fidgeting, nervous. Bopping his head to some inner tune.

Zach Barrows. Twenty-five years old. Volunteered on the current president's senate campaign before he could vote, rewarded with a staff job after college. Then he ran three states in the election, delivering them comfortably to his boss.

But no military experience, no time in law enforcement. Griff doubted that Zach had ever held a gun. For him, battles were fought with words and papers and backroom deals.

Ours is not to reason why, Griff reminded himself.

The kid looked away from the window, where the familiar sights of Washington, D.C., were scrolling past, and smiled at Griff.

Griff recognized the smile—a politician's grin, with the kind of animated delight reserved only for total strangers within its radius. A smile designed to win friends and influence people, so they could be used and later discarded.

"So," he said. "Where we headed?"

Griff didn't smile back. "We'll be there soon," he said.

"You can't tell me where we're going?" His voice was full of disbelief.

"Information containment," Griff said. "We tell you what you need to know when you need to know it."

The kid smirked. That was actually how Griff thought of him when the president introduced them in the Oval Office: 150-odd pounds of smirk in a suit. He leaned forward. Here it comes, Griff thought.

"Look, Agent . . . Griffin, was it?" Zach said.

"Griff is fine."

A more patronizing variety of the earlier smile. "Agent Griffin. I know you were probably wearing polyester and protesting Nixon before I was born. But I was the deputy director for White House affairs, and I'm not even thirty yet. *Washingtonian* magazine called me the next Karl Rove."

Griff kept his face bland. "Impressive."

"Thank you. So what say you quit with the spy stuff and just tell me what I want to know. I'm not here to play games."

Griff considered that for a moment.

"The way I heard it," he said, "you're here because the Secret Service caught you with the president's nineteen-year-old daughter in the Lincoln Bedroom."

He took a second to savor the look on Zach's face. Then added: "Doing something that was *definitely* not for the purpose of procreation."

Zach opened his mouth to say something, then closed it and looked out the window instead.

"Don't worry, Zach. You'll find out what's going on soon enough."

Zach didn't respond. Just kept sulking.

Griff took a small amount of pity on him, thinking of his own introduction to the job, almost forty years earlier.

"And then you'll wish you hadn't."

The limo stopped.

"We're here," Griff said, and got out.

ZACH LOOKED AT THE BUILDING lit up under the security lights as the limo pulled away.

"I've done the tour before," he said.

The older man didn't turn around, just kept walking toward the wall of the Castle, the oldest part of the Smithsonian Institution.

"We're not doing the regular tour," Griff said.

Zach was used to being the youngest guy in any room. It came with the title of boy wonder. Old guys, especially in politics, didn't want to listen to some whippersnapper with a bunch of newfangled ideas. So he'd been forced to come up with a variety of strategies for dealing with them, from flattery to outright insult. Then, once the target was unbalanced, Zach could take charge.

None of that worked with this guy. Zach couldn't

seem to throw "Griff" off his stride. From what he'd seen so far, Zach figured the older man had to be near retirement, probably FBI, or maybe Secret Service—he moved with an easy, physical confidence despite the spare tire on his big frame—but that was all he'd been able to glean so far. He simply couldn't get an angle on the guy.

It was really starting to piss him off.

For a moment, Zach thought of the only time he was ever in trouble with the law, when a cop found him and his buddies in a stolen car. He was sixteen. Zach was a fast talker even then and spun everything he had at the cop. The cop listened to the whole story, calmly and patiently.

Then he arrested them anyway.

Griff reminded him a lot of that cop.

Zach watched as Griff pressed an otherwise ordinary looking brick.

It sank a half-inch into the wall, and an old mechanism, created by master stonecutters over a century before, locked into place.

A large slab of the wall lifted and revealed a hidden staircase, worn with use. It didn't make a sound.

Zach didn't even try to hold back his laughter. Griff looked back.

"Oh, you have got to be kidding me. A secret entrance? *Seriously?*"

Griff just pointed to the stairs. "Watch your step."

Zach snorted again, but entered the passage. "When do I get my decoder ring?"

No reply.

Thirteen steps later—Zach counted—they were inside

another chamber. The lights came up automatically, once they crossed the threshold.

The carved-stone space looked, at first glance, like the museum above. The walls were lined with rows and rows of books; old, leather-bound volumes. Tables and display cases were arranged in the wide, open space between.

But these exhibits were definitely not for the general public.

Wicked, piranha-like teeth grinned at Zach from a man-sized fish head floating in a large jar. An old brass plaque identified it as SKELETAL REMAINS FROM INNSMOUTH, MASS., 1936. Pieces of cast-iron armor, like a robot made from an old woodstove, were mounted under a sign reading BRAINERD'S STEAM MAN, C. 1865. A large beetle, colored bright gold. Something blood-red and slimy in a glass case, called Allghoi Khorkhoi. Under another case sat what looked like an ordinary log: WOOD FROM THE "DEVIL TREE," BRITISH GUIANA, 1897.

Other things. A crystal skull. Stone tablets. Carved idols. A mummified monkey's paw.

Zach's attention was drawn, finally, to the coffin at the back of the room. There was no card or plaque on that.

Zach didn't know how long he'd been gaping at the exhibits when he heard Griff speak up behind him.

"Welcome to the Reliquary, Zach," Griff said.

Zach managed to close his mouth before he turned around, put the necessary sarcasm into his voice.

"Nice place. All that's missing is a giant penny."

"This isn't a joke, Zach."

"You're telling me all this stuff is real?"

Griff nodded.

Zach took a second to process that. Somehow, he knew the older man was telling the truth. There was a logical part of his brain that didn't want to accept it, but the things in here didn't look fake. They had the same undeniable, everyday reality of a chair or table. Looking at them, you just knew.

But he asked the next question anyway, to satisfy that nagging voice of reason.

"So that"—Zach pointed—"is a real alien corpse from Roswell, then?"

Griff looked over. "That one's from Dulce, actually."

"Of course it is."

This wasn't what Zach expected when the president called him into the Oval Office. Sure, the president probably knew about Zach's fumbled, drunken encounter with his daughter—but Christ, it's not like Zach was the first guy there, and she'd barely spoken to him since. Zach was a valuable part of the team. He felt sure he was going to get a promotion, maybe even chief of staff, and get that much closer to his ultimate goal. . . .

Instead, he was told he was getting a transfer. The president said something about trusting him with national security, and shook his hand. Then Griff took him to the limo.

To be perfectly honest, Zach had a little trouble listening after he didn't hear the words "chief of staff."

Now he was in a basement, looking at the castoffs from a traveling freak show. Somewhere along the line, he'd screwed up. Big-time.

"What am I doing here?" he asked quietly, mainly to himself.

Griff answered him anyway.

"You're about to learn one of the nation's oldest and most important secrets, Zach. There's no paper trail on this—none that leaves this room anyway," he said.

"If this is such a big secret, then why would you hold on to all this? First thing I learned in politics: you *always* shred the documents."

"It's more of a trophy room than anything else. He needs to keep trophies. He's a hunter. You should always remember that."

Zach gave him a long look.

"You know, just because you put words together in a series doesn't mean you're actually explaining anything. I can tell you like playing Yoda to my young Skywalker, but could you just tell me what the shit is going on here?"

Griff nodded, and leaned his bulk against a table.

"What I'm about to tell you is known only to the president, a few members of his cabinet, myself—and now you."

Zach made a face. "I'm honored."

Griff sighed heavily and continued.

"In 1867, a young man was found on a whaling vessel that had run aground outside Boston Harbor. He had apparently killed several of his crewmates. The corpses were bloodless, except the one that the young man held in his arms. He was still drinking from that one.

"They called him a vampire. He was convicted, and sentenced to be executed. But President Andrew Johnson pardoned him—spared his life. He lived out the rest of his days in an insane asylum, until 1897, when he died. At least, that was the official story.

"In fact, the young man really was a vampire. And Johnson only pardoned him so he would work for the United States. For the past hundred and forty years, it's been his job to defend this nation against the threats from the Other Side."

Zach tried not to laugh. "A presidential vampire, huh? Is he a Democrat or a Republican?"

"That's a bit like asking a shark if it wants red or white with its meal."

"Right. So why do you need me?"

"You're the vampire's new liaison for the office of the president. You will convey the president's orders and instructions, provide support and intelligence, and work with the vampire in all aspects of his operations."

Griff stopped. Zach waited for the punch line. But there wasn't one.

"Bullshit," Zach said. "I have White House clearance and I never heard anything about this."

"That was only for what you needed to know out in the daylight world. This is something else entirely."

"You really expect me to believe we've got a vampire on a leash, and we can just send him after terrorists and spies whenever we want?"

For the first time all night, Griff laughed. He seemed genuinely amused, and that pissed Zach off even more.

"What's so funny?"

"There are worse things in this world than al-Qaeda

and North Korea, Zach. And they are just waiting for their chance at us."

He gestured at the room, all the objects in it.

"These artifacts—they're all relics of their attempts to break out of the shadows and into the daylight. Into our lives.

"Humanity will not survive that. They're an infection, and they spread like Ebola. Whatever it takes, we have to keep that border between light and dark. Or we lose. Everything. Every one of us will die.

"Someone has to be there to hold the line. That's what we do. We fight every incursion they make. They invade, we repel. Forget the War on Terror, Zach. This is the War on Horror. And you've just been drafted."

The room seemed very quiet now to Zach. He asked the only question that made sense.

"What if I don't want the job?"

"Not an option, I'm afraid. There's no quitting, no transfer. You will do this until you retire. Or you get killed. Whichever comes first."

Zach wasn't sure which part of the news was making his head spin—the knowledge that vampires were real, or that his career had just come to a screeching halt.

For a moment, Zach was struck with the unfairness of it all. He'd spent his whole life working his way closer to the center of power in America. He'd given up his weekends in high school to hand out flyers and hang campaign signs. Forgot what sleep was like in a half-dozen campaigns. Ate crap food and worked for less than minimum wage, when his college friends were pulling down six figures at investment firms, all so he could get to the White House.

It was all going according to plan. Now this.

"And if I refuse?"

Griff's expression didn't change. "You really think you can just walk away? With all you've seen? With all you're going to see?"

"Is that a threat? Are you threatening me? Listen up, old man, because there's *no way in hell*—"

"It's not his job to be threatening, actually."

For a split second, Zach didn't know where the words had come from.

Then he turned and faced someone standing directly behind him. As if from nowhere.

"It's mine," he said, and smiled.

He was taller than Zach, wearing ragged black fatigues. He looked young. And pale. Very, very pale.

He stood there, perfectly calm.

Too calm, even. Unnaturally still. Almost the kind of stillness you'd only find in a casket. But just standing there.

So Zach couldn't figure out why his whole mind narrowed down to one thought, burned in capital letters across his brain: RUN.

Zach felt a stirring of instinct honed when humans huddled at the edges of campfires, terrified of the noises in the dark. He suddenly knew he was in the presence of something that stalked his kind, and had for thousands of years. Something inhuman. A predator.

There is a reason humans are genetically programmed to fear the dark. Zach was looking at it.

Then Zach saw the fangs at the edges of the smile.

He began to shake. He couldn't get his legs to move.

He tried to speak. Nothing came out.

Something warm and wet began running down his thigh.

Both he and the vampire—because that's what it was, standing right there in front of him, no doubt left anywhere in Zach—looked down.

A small puddle formed around Zach's shoe as his bladder emptied.

The vampire's smile vanished. He looked over Zach's shoulder and spoke to Griff.

"So this is the new boy?"

"Zach Barrows, this is Nathaniel Cade," Griff said. "The president's vampire."

Zach still couldn't move. Cade looked down at him again.

"Perhaps you should show him where we keep the mop," Cade said.

He walked around Zach. Zach's head swiveled to follow.

Cade paused to set a metal case on one of the tables. Then he dropped something that clattered on the wood, next to the case. It looked like the bone from some kind of animal—like a dog. Or a wolf. Lined with teeth and fur, still bloody in some places.

"Take care of that, please," he said.

Cade headed straight for the coffin and yanked it open.

Griff tried to get the vampire's attention. "Cade, we should talk about—"

"Later," Cade said, and slammed the coffin lid shut.

Griff shrugged, in a sort of apology, to Zach.

"He's been in the cargo hold of a C-130 for the past fourteen hours," Griff said. "Makes him a little cranky."

Zach stood there, his pant leg dripping. His mouth was open, but for once in his life, he had nothing to say.

THREE

6–1. General

The Army, Navy, and Air Force have established armed services mortuary facilities outside of the United States. These facilities are established to provide mortuary services for eligible deceased personnel when local commercial mortuary services are not available or cost prohibitive. Establishment or disestablishment of armed services mortuary facilities will be coordinated at the Departmental level.

—*Army Regulation 638-2, "Deceased Personnel, Care and Disposition of Remains and Disposition of Personal Effects" (Unclassified)*

ONE MONTH EARLIER, MORTUARY SERVICES DIVISION, CAMP WOLF MILITARY BASE, KUWAIT

Dylan Weeks backed the truck as close to the mortuary building as possible.

The sergeant stomped over to him before he was out of the cab, looking pissed. Here we go, Dylan thought.

"I got another complaint about you being late," she said. "The airfield is right across the damn base. You stopping for a beer on the way?"

Yeah. A beer, in Kuwait. That'd be the day. Out loud, however, all Dylan said was, "I'm going as fast as I can."

She looked at him for a moment, apparently trying to decide if he was lying or just stupid. "Get your shit together," she said, and turned away neatly on the heel of one of her combat boots.

"Yes, ma'am." Bitch, Dylan thought. Put a chick in uniform and she thinks she's a frigging general or something. She had no idea who she was screwing with. But she'd get a big surprise soon enough.

He started to load the truck.

As he struggled to hoist the transfer cases holding dead U.S. soldiers into the back, he reflected again on how unlucky he was. He never should have been put in this position. It was all going to change, but still, he never should have had to go through any of this shit in the first place.

Dylan was one of hundreds of civilian contractors working at the base in Kuwait. A year before, he was driving a vending machine route, delivering candy and snacks to office parks.

He saw both jobs as beneath him. In fact, he saw most jobs as beneath him. If his father weren't such a prick . . .

Dylan was supposed to be rich. His father had been a successful singer/songwriter, with a series of minor hits in the '80s. He was never famous himself, but he wrote and produced for people who were. He made a shitload of money. It kept coming, in the form of residual checks from car commercials and greatest hits compilations.

Dylan's parents had moved from L.A. to Orange County when he was born, in search of a more wholesome family environment.

They found it. Dylan grew up marinating in wealth and privilege with kids just like him. Vacations in Cabo, private schools, and a Porsche at sixteen.

It was something of a shock when Dylan's dad sat him down at twenty-three and said it was time to get a life.

This was just after Dylan had been kicked out of the third and last college he would attend. He majored mostly in beer-drinking and hangover recovery. While the first two schools simply flunked him, his academic career ended for good with an unsuccessful date-rape and a faceful of pepper spray.

Criminal charges were avoided with a generous settlement. That's when Dad decided it was time to talk man-to-man with his son. They sat on the patio of the house in Newport Coast as the sun set into the Pacific. It was beautiful. Father and son cracked open several beers to get over their mutual discomfort, then got down to business.

Dylan's father admitted he hadn't been around much. His marriage to Dylan's mom ended, and a series of increasingly blond, pert and young stepmothers followed. While they talked, Dylan's dad kept touching his new hair plugs, like a gardener tenderly checking new sprouts.

He asked Dylan what he wanted to do for a living.

Dylan said he'd like to go into the music business, like his father. Start a band. Maybe go on tour. It would take about fifty grand in operating capital.

Dylan's father offered the opinion that it might be a good idea to learn an instrument, and perhaps how to read music, first.

Dylan countered with the observation that his father's

music sucked, and he didn't need to read music to do better than that "dentist's-office crap."

Things deteriorated from there. Dylan's father finally threw up his hands and walked into his home office, where he smoked a joint and wondered how he'd managed to raise such a thoroughly unpleasant little shit. Twenty years of voting Republican, and for what? He blamed the schools.

Dylan found his credit cards canceled, his trust fund locked up tight until he turned forty. His mother convinced her current husband to allow him to live in the guesthouse on their property. After six months of his moping, she insisted he take a job, and her husband called in a favor from a friend, getting Dylan a truck on a vending-machine route.

It was about that time when Khaled got in touch with him again. Dylan was playing Grand Theft Auto: Vatican City online at three a.m., after another unsuccessful band practice, taking out his frustration by slaughtering his opponents with an Uzi. The instant-message window on his computer popped up.

It was Khaled, a guy he'd known back at school. Khaled had been a Saudi student living in the dorm on the same floor.

Ordinarily, Dylan would have been the first to mock and abuse a foreigner living within such close range. But Khaled was awesome. He spoke English better than Dylan, wore jeans and T-shirts, and listened to hip-hop and rap. It also didn't hurt that he had more money than God, and always scored good drugs.

They started IM'ing regularly over the next couple of months. Between rounds of virtual carnage, Khaled sympathized with Dylan's troubles. He recalled the unfortunate incident with the girl and the pepper spray. Men—men like Khaled and Dylan—were cut off from their natural role, which was to command. To be respected. That woman who maced Dylan, for instance. She should have known her place. "Whores," Khaled typed. "The world has turned all women into whores."

The world was screwed up. Anyone could see that. But Khaled actually seemed to know why. He explained to Dylan how all of his problems were a result of the forces aligned against men like them. The war in Iraq was a ploy by international bankers. Just like 9/11, the government rigged the whole thing.

Which was also why Dylan couldn't get a recording contract—the music business was completely controlled by the same people. And of course his father was hoarding his trust fund. The bankers wanted to keep it, to suck it dry.

It all fell into place. It really wasn't Dylan's fault. He wasn't quite sure how it all added up, but he liked the bottom line: he deserved better, and someone had conspired to take it from him. There had to be some reason a guy like him was stocking candy and Coke machines for a living.

Some people were meant for better things than menial labor, Khaled said. He had a plan, and Dylan could be part of it.

Khaled's father had multiple businesses contracting

with the U.S. Army. In Kuwait, Khaled promised, Dylan could be making as much as a hundred grand a year, just for driving a truck like he did now. Everyone else was profiting from the war, Khaled said. Why shouldn't Dylan get a little of the action?

Dylan knew it was time for a life change. His once toned gym muscles were going soft, and his hair was getting thin. His band had broken up. His boss had knocked his hours back, and he tried to buy a girl a drink in a bar in Newport Beach a week ago, only to find he didn't have enough in his wallet for her fourteen-dollar appletini.

What the hell, he thought. There was nothing tying him down. The closest thing he had to a relationship was a favorite stripper at Spearmint Rhino. Khaled sent him a plane ticket and an advance on the first month's paycheck.

His great adventure in Kuwait didn't start at all like he planned.

He wandered around the Kuwait City airport, jet-lagged and clueless, surrounded by men and women wearing long robes. One of the locals spotted him, broke away from a pack of his friends, and approached.

Dylan was nervous. This was just after those contractors in Baghdad were kidnapped, and he had a frightening vision of his own head rolling on the floor in some Jihadi terrorist's garage.

Then he recognized the guy behind the beard.

Khaled was wrapped in traditional robes, covered in hair. If he hadn't smiled and said Dylan's name, Dylan never would have put it together.

He embraced Dylan warmly, even though his friends

all scowled. He escorted Dylan to a new apartment, which came with the job. Khaled couldn't stay and talk—he was running his father's shipping concerns in Kuwait—but he promised they'd catch up later.

After a month, Dylan was considering chucking the whole thing and heading home.

First off, he was getting a lot less than a hundred grand a year. The big money was for the people willing to work in Baghdad and risk getting blown into stew meat. His paycheck worked out to about what he was making back in the States.

But instead of loading up candy machines, he had the worst job on the base—mortuary support. Which was a fancy name for undertaker. Dead bodies would show up all day and all night at Camp Wolf. He was responsible for taking the coffins—sorry, "transfer cases," the army called them—and stacking them, then driving them over to the airfield, where they'd be shipped back home.

Dylan realized he was in Hell. Roasting in the heat, then freezing in cold storage, surrounded by corpses every day.

When Khaled finally got back in touch, Dylan was pissed off and ready to go back to the States.

Khaled tried to soothe him. Dylan didn't want to listen. He invited Dylan to his apartment. Dylan was hesitant, until Khaled mentioned beer.

Khaled sent his Bentley for Dylan. At his massive, luxury apartment, they opened a case of contraband Coors Light and drank while Khaled explained what was happening.

Obviously, he said, things had changed since college.

Dylan, who'd slammed two beers and was working on his third, said, "No shit. What's with the outfit?"

Khaled explained: his father had found out how he was spending his time in America, and pulled him out of college. He was sent to a strict madrassa in Saudi Arabia.

"Sucks, man," Dylan said.

Anger flashed in Khaled's eyes, but it passed. "At first, I thought so," he said. "But then I learned the truth."

All of the things they'd talked about, all of the problems in the world, all of that had to change. And Khaled and his friends had the answer. They were going to make things right.

They were part of a group called Zulfiqar. They were a sword of righteousness to cut the evil out of the world.

But they needed Dylan. They needed him to step up and be a hero.

And, of course, they were willing to pay for one. Being a hero shouldn't come without rewards, Khaled said. He offered an even million dollars.

Dylan passed. A million? That was less than he had in his trust fund. He could survive until forty. Not worth it.

There was some haggling. Khaled pointed out the benefits of tax-free cash. He eventually offered $3.5 million.

Dylan said, "Cool."

The caskets were in the truck. Dylan started the engine and drove around the corner from the mortuary building.

He made sure the bitch sergeant wasn't watching him as he left.

About halfway to the airfield, Dylan pulled into a parking lot and slid his truck between two personnel carriers. He shut down the engine.

He took the small toolbox Khaled had given him and hopped out of the cab. He didn't look around as he got into the back of the truck. He'd learned one thing about the army: look like you knew what you were doing all the time. Do that, and nobody would question you; they had their own problems.

He'd made sure the casket he wanted was on top of the stacks. PFC MANUEL CASTILLO, THOUSAND PALMS, CALIF. He unstrapped it, quickly pulled the flag off like he was unwrapping a gift and snipped the fastener seal with wire cutters.

The remains inside were covered in plastic garbage bags full of ice. It didn't matter much—PFC Castillo was headed to a closed-casket funeral. He'd been thrown from his Humvee by an explosion that tore through the bottom of his seat; they probably shoveled him into the body bag.

That's why Dylan had picked him.

Dylan tossed the ice packs to the floor of the truck and unzipped the bag. Half the poor bastard's head was sheared off, all the way to the collarbone; he'd been shot straight up, like an ejector seat, into the frame of the vehicle.

But his right leg was still intact, from the hip down.

Dylan checked his list, just to be sure. RIGHT LEG—

followed by five boxes. Four of them had check marks. He took out a pen, crossed off the last empty spot.

Then he opened the toolbox and got to work.

The circular saw was remarkably compact. It was almost smaller than a cordless drill, and when it revved up, it cut through skin and bone like tofu. Dylan was glad, once again, these guys weren't shipped home in their uniforms. That was all done at the other end, at Dover Air Force Base, after they'd been embalmed. He didn't think he could handle stripping a corpse down to its underpants.

He checked the joint where the hip met the leg. He didn't have to be precise, but Khaled bitched at him when he shaved off too much.

He leaned back as he pressed the power button on the saw. The first time he did this, he'd gotten a faceful of gore by hunching too close to the cadaver. He only had to learn that lesson once.

The blade sliced through the dead flesh and bone. A couple strands of skin snapped like rubber bands when he lifted the leg out of the body bag.

This was the way Khaled explained it to him. Nobody would ever miss a few body parts. The army morticians in the States certainly wouldn't question it, because it wasn't like they got an invoice of all the arms and legs a corpse was supposed to have upon delivery. The families back home were told their soldiers had been blown to pieces. They were expecting an incomplete package, if they even bothered to look. With all the car bombs and shrapnel and IEDs in Iraq, there were plenty of guys going home short a few limbs.

The only downside: Khaled wanted the heads of the soldiers, but Dylan's best picks were all guys who didn't have much left above the neck. It was a sore spot. Khaled had finally told Dylan to forget it, he'd make other arrangements.

Dylan turned off the saw and unfurled his own special plastic sack from the toolbox. There was some kind of chemical coating inside that kept the leg cold; it activated as soon as the sack was peeled open. Cold vapor curled in the air around him.

He crammed the leg inside, struggling with it like a side of beef.

Sweating, Dylan zipped up the body bag and repacked the corpse with ice, stuffing the bags around the casket. He latched it shut and used a tiny, battery-powered soldering iron to reseal the fasteners. Then he slung the sack with PFC Castillo's leg over his shoulder.

He tossed the leg on the floor of the passenger seat and started the truck. It only took him a short while to clear the gate at the airport. He unloaded the coffins into a hangar, where they waited for the next flight out.

Nobody wanted to look at the flag-draped boxes. Nobody wanted to think about what was inside. Dylan was grateful for that.

He took the truck back out the gate. He slowed near the fence line, as he hefted the sack with the leg off the floor of the cab. With one smooth motion, he opened his door and dropped it onto the side of the road.

One of Khaled's guys was waiting, as usual. He saw the dark figure scurry out of a ditch and pick up the bag.

Dylan smiled. He wasn't sure if he believed everything Khaled was selling. Most of the time, he didn't care one way or the other. But he definitely liked the idea of getting some payback from the world that had mistreated him. And getting paid at the same time.

Dylan could handle this shit job for a little while longer. He was undercover. Like James Bond.

Pretty soon, everyone who underestimated him and disrespected him would get a big lesson. Dylan would be rich, living the good life on a beach somewhere.

That would show his dad. And everyone else. They could all just blow him.

FOUR

Subject: Cade is functionally immortal. That is to say, his cells do not undergo regular cell death, or even aging or degradation, as long as the subject has a regular supply of fresh blood. Cell repairs are nearly perfect—any cells destroyed by an outside force (see Appendix: "Subject's Resistance to Knife and Bullet Wounds") are replaced with indistinguishable copies. Subject can heal from any wound short of massive bodily trauma in a matter of minutes, although his rate of recovery will vary depending on the amount of fresh blood in his system.

—BRIEFING BOOK: CODENAME: NIGHTMARE PET ***(Eyes Only/Classified/Above Top Secret per Executive Order 13292)***

Something landed near Zach's head, jarring him awake.

He was facedown in the briefing book, his cheek resting in a lake of his own drool.

He looked around blearily, realized he was sitting at one of the tables in the basement of the Smithsonian.

And he wasn't wearing his own pants.

"Oh good," Zach said. "It wasn't all just a wonderful dream."

He'd fallen asleep reading the briefing book. It was hundreds of pages, and they were written like the owner's manual for a microwave. He noticed the volume he'd been given was number five. He had a lot more to look forward to.

Griff loomed above him, holding the gym bag he'd thumped down on the table a second before.

"Brought you some clothes. You should move some things here from your apartment."

Zach yawned and stood, then had to hike up the sweatpants—stenciled PROP. SMITHSONIAN INST.—that Griff had given him after he'd soiled himself last night.

He checked his watch. Almost noon. "Hey," he said. "Why am I up? I thought he slept during the day."

"It's only midnight."

Zach checked his watch again. It wasn't noon. There was no natural light down here. He yawned again.

Griff looked at the drool-soaked page of the book on the table. "How far did you get in that?"

"I skimmed it."

"Right," Griff said. "Here's the Cliffs Notes version. Cade can operate during the day, just not in direct sunlight. He's awake for days at a time. You'll have to sleep when you can."

"What if he gets hungry? Am I a convenient snack-pack?"

"He doesn't feed on humans."

"Seriously?"

Griff nodded.

"Why not?"

"Ask him."

"Terrific."

Zach began looking through the gym bag.

Jeans. T-shirts. Sweatshirt. Cross-trainers. Griff had gone through his bottom drawer, where he kept his rarely used workout gear.

"What is this?"

"You're going out in the field. You need to be able to move."

"You're wearing a suit."

"Old habits. I was FBI. We weren't allowed to wear anything else."

"What am I, the gardener? I've worn a suit to work every day since my first campaign, when I was fourteen. I'm not about to change that."

Griff shrugged. "Fair enough. Your pants ought to be dry by now."

He handed Zach a mug of coffee.

Zach took it, and his sweatpants nearly fell to his knees again.

He could have sworn Griff was trying not to laugh. Then he was distracted by the mobile phone Griff pulled from his suit jacket.

It looked like a touch-screen model, only slightly thicker, with a jutting antenna at the top.

"I know you wanted a decoder ring, but I got you this instead," Griff said as he handed it to Zach. "Satellite-enabled, GPS tracking system, Internet access, camera, motion detector, emergency beacon, and a few other options you get to use after you've got more experience."

"Nice," Zach said. "Who pays for all this stuff? I've never seen an appropriation bill for vampires."

"The White House dentist's budget is surprisingly large."

"Funny." Zach kept fiddling with the phone. "Does this play MP3s?"

"Just learn to use it. It can save your life."

"Do I get a gun, too?"

"Maybe when you hit puberty."

Zach hiked up his pants with as much dignity as he could manage. If this was his job now, he was going to make the best showing possible. "Is there someplace I can shower? Or do you expect me to hose off outside?"

Griff pointed toward a wooden door on the opposite side of the room. "Help yourself."

Zach grunted and headed through the door.

GRIFF CHECKED HIS WATCH and busied himself taking a waxed-paper carton—the size of a half-gallon container of milk—out of a small fridge under the coffeemaker. He shook it, then placed it in the microwave. When the timer beeped, he took it out and placed it on the nearest table.

Two minutes later, the coffin opened and Cade emerged, completely alert. His eyes made a quick scan of the room, as they did every time he woke up. He saw the carton, but ignored it.

Instead, he stripped out of his ragged military fatigues and stood on the cold stone floor naked. Griff had gotten used to this: Cade didn't care about a lot of human niceties anymore.

Cade changed into a cheap button-down shirt and

black suit hanging from a nearby hook. It was the kind of off-the-rack special any bureaucrat would buy on a government salary. The only difference was Cade didn't wear a tie. Too many times, someone or something tried to use it to pull his head off. So now he looked like an accountant on casual Friday.

Except for the cross. Made of old, tarnished metal, it rested on a leather cord in the hollow of Cade's throat. No matter what else Cade wore, he never removed the cross. If it weren't so rough and weathered, it might be something a rock star would wear. Instead, it looked more like the museum pieces upstairs.

Once dressed, Cade continued to ignore the carton. He stepped over to a computer terminal, the only concession to the twenty-first century in the entire place.

Unlike Griff, Cade had no problem with computers. Given time, he could learn to use any tool. He had to, if his kind was going to hunt an endlessly inventive race of tool-using apes. Anything a man could build, he had to be able to master. Anything a man could learn, he had to learn it faster.

It might surprise some people that Griff looked at Cade as the product of evolution. But he'd watched Cade, and to him, it was obvious: he was looking at an apex predator. He was human once, but that was a long time ago. Now he just carried the shape, which enabled him to move among his prey. Everything else was engineered to make him—and all the creatures like him—the most efficient hunter of Homo sapiens possible. What they called, in a different age, a man-eater.

But it wasn't a matter of belief or disbelief for him. Griff had been with Cade as he fought—and killed—demons, vampires, werewolves, invisible men, aliens, creatures that had no names, and even one thing that called itself a god.

Most of those things had ended up on any number of government autopsy slabs, and he'd seen the results. And whatever else they were, they were solid. They existed in this world. And whatever put them together had to use the same toolbox of physics and biology that governed every other creature on the planet.

Sure, some of those hard-and-fast rules of science got bent pretty badly. There was a lot Griff didn't understand, and a lot the government's teams of eggheads couldn't explain. Like Cade's aversion to crosses and other religious symbols. Or the magic that bound Cade as securely as iron to the will of the president.

But no one had ever been able to explain quantum mechanics to Griff's satisfaction, either. It didn't make the science wrong. He just didn't have the math.

Some things you just had to take on faith.

"You send the boy home already?" Cade asked, typing away.

"He's in the shower," Griff said. "Getting ready for his first day on the job."

"Did you warn him?" The shower facilities had been built in what was once a lockup for prisoners who needed to be kept in secret. Some of them seemed to like the place enough to remain after their deaths. Occasionally the shower ran red with blood, and skeletal faces appeared in the mirrors, behind the steam.

"It didn't come up," Griff said.

Cade's mouth twitched. You had to watch for it; it was usually the only way you knew he was amused. His fingers flew over the keys, entering his report on the Kosovo incident.

"You locked up the artifact?" he asked.

"It's secure," Griff said. He pointed to the carton. "You should eat something."

"I'm fine."

"When was the last time you fed?"

"Few days ago."

"Cade. Eat."

"Is that an order?" Cade's tone was sharp.

Griff sighed. "It's advice."

Cade turned away from the computer, and picked up the container and opened it. It was filled with dark red blood, still steaming from the microwave. A mixture of cow and pig, from livestock kept in a CDC testing facility near McLean, Virginia.

Cade drained it in one long gulp, not spilling a drop.

The effect was immediate. He stood taller. His muscles corded and flexed, and his pale skin flushed before the blood settled down into him.

"Thank you," Cade said, and threw the carton into the trash from across the room, without looking. He went back to the keyboard.

"So. What do you think of the kid?"

"Bit of an oilcan," Cade said.

Griff waited. Sometimes Cade used expressions long out of date. It was a side effect of fourteen decades of slang crammed into his head, and slowing down his thought processes for normal conversation.

But it took only a second for him to realize he'd slipped. "A fake. A politician."

"Maybe the president figures you need that more than you need a field agent. That's probably why they sent him over earlier than expected."

Then, with a deep breath, Griff decided to tell him. "And the cancer's back."

Cade's fingers hesitated on the keyboard for a fraction of a second.

"I know," he said, the clatter of the typing picking up again.

He knew. Of course he knew. He probably knew before Griff did. But he didn't say anything; he was waiting for Griff to let him in on the secret. His version of courtesy. Of friendship.

"What did the doctors say?" Cade asked.

"Inoperable."

Cade looked back down at the computer and finished entering the case into the log. He probably knew that, too.

"I'm sorry," he said.

Everyone around him dies, Griff thought. Sooner or later. But not him.

Griff worried what would happen once he was gone.

Griff was the closest thing Cade had to a friend. Over thirty years, he had only seen the gulf widen between Cade and everyone else. Without some kind of connection, Cade might forget what it meant to be human completely.

Griff wondered how dangerous that might be.

And remembered that whatever happened, he wouldn't be around to see it.

THE KID CAME out of the bathroom, breaking up what could have been an awkward moment. His hair was still wet, and he was trying to smooth the wrinkles out of his shirt.

He froze when he saw Cade at the computer.

Griff stood up and guided Zach over to the table.

"Relax," he said. "He won't bite."

"You're. Not. Funny." Zach was breathing hard.

"Show him your papers."

"What?" Zach was shaking. He wouldn't take his eyes off Cade. Griff couldn't really blame him—he remembered the first time he'd encountered Cade, and he'd had a lot more training, with physical combat under his belt. It was a little like waking up and finding a cobra coiled on the next pillow.

Cade was doing his best to ignore this, to spare Zach any further embarrassment. Still, they had work to do, so Griff carefully reached into the jacket pocket of Zach's suit and took out the envelope there.

"Show him your orders from the president," Griff told Zach. "Go on. Do it."

Zach took the envelope back from Griff, and stepped forward to hand it to Cade. As soon as it touched the vampire's fingertips, Zach jumped back again.

Cade opened the envelope and read aloud: "'I hereby

invest Zachary Taylor Barrows with the powers of liaison for the Office of the President of these United States, with all rights, privileges and duties pertaining to that position. . . .'"

Cade finished reading the letter silently, then nodded. "Welcome aboard," he said, folding it into the envelope again. "You are now a designated officer of the President of the United States. You are under my protection."

Zach's breathing began to slow. A little. "What? What does that mean?"

"That means he can't hurt you. Even if he wanted to," Griff said. "He's bound to follow your lawful orders, and keep you from harm."

Zach looked back and forth between them. "What is that, like a magic spell?"

"Actually," Cade said, "it was a blood oath."

FIVE

1867, Fort Warren,
Georges Island, Massachusetts

Cold water stung him, a wet slap against his face.

He woke up, not knowing how long he had been asleep.

For one blessed instant, he thought it had all been a nightmare.

Then he felt the chains on his wrists, and it came back with terrifying clarity.

He was in a dank stone cell, the floor covered with the shit and filth of other men. His arms were locked in heavy manacles above his head. There was a dull ache in his chest, and he remembered being shot.

He looked down, and saw the bullet wounds healing on his chest and abdomen. But he couldn't imagine how that was possible.

A second later, his mind caught up with his senses. He was aware of other men in the room.

Four soldiers with rifles, wearing the blue uniforms of the Union, watched him. One held a bucket, still dripping with the cold water he'd thrown to wake Cade.

Sitting on a stool between them, an older man. Barrel-shaped, with a greasy forelock of hair over his thick brow and nose. He wore a good suit and expensive boots.

Cade realized, with some horror, that he could smell the man, just like he'd smelled the corpses on the boat, and it seemed completely natural to him now. Like he'd grown a fifth limb without questioning it.

He smelled talcum powder, the pomade holding the forelock in place, and above all of that, whiskey. The man seemed to be sweating it.

The man in the suit turned to Cade and smiled.

"No, no," he said. "Don't get up." Then he wheezed at his own joke. Cade would have been able to smell the whiskey on his breath even without his new senses.

Cade caught a whiff of the soldiers, too. Sweat-damp wool, and the already familiar stink of fear. It was just as vivid to him as the images from his eyes.

The man on the stool spoke again, to one of the soldiers.

"What's it called, Corporal?"

"Cade, sir. Nathaniel Cade."

"Cade, is it? Did you know that means 'a pet of unknown origin or species' in Old English?"

"No, sir. I did not."

"I never had a proper education, you know, but I have

done a great deal of reading. Never stop trying to improve yourself, Corporal."

"Yes, sir. Thank you, sir."

The man looked at Cade again, eyes narrowed.

"I suppose you are my pet now, Cade. I pardoned you. Spared your life."

"What happened?" Cade asked.

"You've been asleep for nearly three days," Johnson said. "You missed the trial. They intended to hang you at dawn. While I doubt the hanging would have killed you, the dawn most certainly would have."

Cade looked at him, baffled.

"Who are you?"

The man in the suit laughed and then coughed. He took out a flask and uncapped it. The whiskey scent blotted everything else as he tipped it back.

"I'm Andrew Johnson, President of these United States since the death of Abraham Lincoln two years ago."

As keen as his ears were now, Cade wasn't sure he'd heard any of that right.

"The president is dead?"

"Don't you listen? I'm the president. I'm alive and well. But, yes, while you were out at sea, someone put a bullet into poor old Abe's brain. This bullet, in point of fact."

He fished a handkerchief from his vest pocket. He unwrapped it and revealed a round lead ball, stained with rust-brown powder.

Cade smelled it immediately: blood. Old and dried but unmistakable.

His mouth watered.

"Please," he begged. "Please. Let them kill me." He searched for the words. "You don't know—you don't know what I am."

Johnson laughed, but there was no mirth in it. "If I didn't know what you were, you'd be dead already."

That seemed incomprehensible to Cade. "You *know*?"

Johnson nodded.

Cade was shocked. "For the love of God, why didn't you let them kill me?"

The drunkenness seemed to slide off Johnson, and his voice was quiet and dark when he spoke.

"There are other nations in this world. Nations that don't have names, or borders, but they exist all the same. And make no mistake—we are at war with them. They would wipe us from the face of the Earth quicker than any foreign army. Unless we find a way to strike at them before they gain a foothold inside our own country."

Cade barely listened, panic rising inside him. He was beginning to feel the thirst again. The wounds in his chest throbbed. He started to see the blood pulsing in the men in the cell, just beneath their skin.

Cade struggled to lean forward. He had to make the man see.

"You don't understand, *you have to kill me* . . ."

His chains rattled and pulled taut.

The soldier smashed his rifle butt into Cade's face, putting him back onto the floor.

Johnson looked annoyed.

"You owe your life to me, creature," Johnson said.

"And you're going to spend the rest of it paying off the debt."

He took another swig and then nodded to the corporal. The soldier ducked outside the cell and returned with a different bucket. This one was smaller, and stained with red.

"I hate to drink alone," Johnson said. "Join me."

The aroma nearly made Cade pass out. It was not exactly right—not what the thirst really craved—but it was blood. He was close to choking on his saliva now, and he felt his canines growing.

Carefully, the soldier placed the bucket on the floor in front of Cade, and stepped back quickly.

Pig's blood. Cade could see it was already starting to thicken in the cool of the cell.

It took everything he had to clamp his mouth shut.

They would not make him do this. He might be an abomination, but that didn't mean he had to accept it.

He didn't trust his voice, so he simply shook his head at Johnson.

"It's from the finest butcher in Boston. You should be honored. What's wrong? Had your fill on the boat?"

Cade shook his head again.

Johnson laughed, belched, and put away his flask. "You have no say in this, creature." He turned to the corporal. "Make sure he drinks all of that. He's not going to starve. I have plans for him."

Johnson exited, and the soldiers turned to Cade. They regarded him fearfully, but they followed their orders. They beat him with their rifle butts until he stopped thrashing and then rolled him onto his back. One man plugged his nostrils, and they held him down as they emptied the bucket of pig's blood into his throat.

And despite all his efforts to resist, Cade shuddered with pleasure as he drank.

JOHNSON RETURNED SIX DAYS LATER.

Cade watched him enter. He was stronger now. The soldiers had forced buckets of pig's blood into him. Until two days ago, when he learned he didn't need to breathe anymore. They couldn't choke him, so he didn't have to swallow. Still, he'd already fed, whether he wanted to or not, and the change was working in him.

Johnson apparently wanted him presentable. With their bayonets fixed at his throat, the soldiers had watched Cade while the garrison's barber groomed him. It didn't take much effort. The hair sloughed off almost by itself. His hair came back, but his beard had not regrown since. The soldiers washed him by dumping buckets of icy water over and over until the last of the blood and grime was gone. Then they tossed him a freshly laundered prison uniform and watched him dress at gunpoint. He noticed something: aside from the aroma of soap, he had no scent. His body had stopped sweating—nothing was left to interfere with his ability to sniff out prey.

After that, he began to hear the other prisoners in their cells, despite the stone walls.

This morning, the soldiers couldn't hold him down. He shook them off like fleas. The last scab flaked off his chest where the bullet holes had healed, revealing fresh, unmarked skin.

Cade figured that in another day, two at most, he could pull the chains out of the wall. If he wanted, he could feed on the soldiers when they came.

But he wouldn't. The fact that he even considered it told him what course of action he had to take. He would do the only sane thing: he'd end his own life.

He was considering how he'd accomplish this when the door opened.

Johnson was not alone. In addition to the blue-uniformed guards, he had a Negro woman with him.

No, not Negro, Cade realized. Mixed race. Her eyes were almond-shaped, her skin the color of dark gold. She carried a cloth bag and wore a headscarf, both dyed in bright colors that shone in the murk of the cell.

Two things struck Cade: he couldn't tell how old she was. She could have been anywhere from twenty to fifty years old.

And she didn't look the slightest bit afraid of him.

Cade inhaled, and could name each soldier by his odor. He smelled Johnson's hangover like a cloud around the president's head.

The woman smelled like nothing he could name. Some exotic flowers, perhaps. Or a kind of spice he'd never tasted.

"He's just a boy," she said. Cade knew she meant him.

"He was a boy," Johnson corrected her. "Now he's something other."

Cade tried to ignore this, as he had the soldiers' insults

and the sounds beyond his own walls. But he was intrigued. He looked at Johnson.

"Cade, this is the Widow Paris, Mme. Marie Laveau of New Orleans. I had to go to some expense to bring her to you."

The woman—Laveau—had not taken her eyes off Cade yet.

"You're certain your Negro hoodoo will be able to do this?" Johnson asked her.

"It's called *vodou*, Mr. President, and I am Creole," she said, something of a schoolmarm in her tone. "It will work."

Johnson nodded and handed her a piece of paper. "These are the words. Exactly these, do you understand?"

She nodded.

"You can read, correct?"

She gave him a withering look.

Johnson looked away, almost sheepish.

"You brought it?" Laveau asked him.

Johnson nodded. "It's never left my side. Though I still don't see why you need this."

"There is a great deal you don't see, Mr. President. Please."

She held out her hand.

Johnson reached into his waistcoat and came out with the handkerchief, still wrapped around the bullet that killed Lincoln.

"As you asked," Johnson said. "Just as it came out of his skull."

Mme. Laveau took the bullet and held it in her palm. She turned away from the president and his guards.

"You need to leave," she said. "All of you."

"Impossible," Johnson said. "We don't know what he will do—"

"I do," she said. "Go."

Johnson hesitated and then nodded to the soldiers. "Very well, then."

They left the cell, and Cade was alone with Mme. Laveau.

She set her bag on the ground and began taking things from it. A small leather pouch. Some bones, and plants. And then, finally, a long knife.

"Do it," Cade said.

She looked at him, a question on her face.

"Use the knife. You can end this."

"That's not why I'm here," she said. She was starting a very small fire, lighting the green plants so they smoked on the floor of the cell.

"But you could," Cade insisted. He tried to keep his voice even. "Please."

Before he could say anything else, she had the knife in her hand and pointed at his throat. She had covered the distance between them too quickly for even Cade, with his new senses, to see.

Cade flinched back involuntarily.

"Do you really want to die?" she asked.

Suddenly the question was no longer a far-off possibility. It was right there, at the point of the blade.

"Yes," Cade said, after hesitating a moment.

"You a Christian, child?" she asked.

He nodded. Carefully. The knife hadn't moved.

"What makes you think God wants a thing like you?"

That stopped Cade. He hadn't considered that. But it made sense. There was no place in Heaven for what he had become. His soul was damned. It had to be.

"You still want to die?" she asked.

This time, Cade couldn't open his mouth. Still, there was only one answer. Even if he was condemning himself to Hell, he could not go on. Not like this.

He nodded.

Mme. Laveau looked disappointed. "You are a coward, then."

Some remnant of pride surfaced in Cade. "I am not a coward."

"It's easier to die than fight," she said. "There is much good you could do, even now."

"I'm damned," Cade said. "You just said—"

"Yes, you are damned. There is no chance of redemption for you. You are a vampire, and you drank the blood of an innocent. You are an abomination before God."

"Then what hope is there for me?"

"For you? None," she said. "But you can still do good in this world. This man, your president, will ask you to fight. You are lost to the darkness, but you can still save others from it."

"What do you mean?"

Mme. Laveau sat back. "I could use the *bokor* paste, and make you a slave. That's what he wants." She nodded back at the door Johnson had exited. "But without free will—without your mind, your spirit—you would be little more than a club, and you would fail at any job that required more than simple battering. I don't think this world can afford that. You have to be better than that."

She paused, an odd look on her face. "Besides," she added, "I find the idea of slavery . . . distasteful."

Cade got the idea they were bargaining, but he didn't know what for.

"There is another way," she said. "The *gris-gris.* It ties into you, becomes part of you. But then, the magic is only as strong as the thing it's tied to."

She pointed. While they were talking, she had put the leather pouch, open, on the floor between them. The herbs were like a nest for the bullet that had killed President Lincoln. It sat there, still crusted with his blood.

Cade looked at her, curiosity overcoming his fear for the first time in days. "What do you want?" he asked.

"I need to know how strong you are."

Cade didn't know what to say. To live like this, with no chance of redemption . . . he didn't know if he could take it.

"You don't know what this is like," Cade said. "This hunger, this thirst . . ."

"Is it stronger than your faith?"

Cade had always believed. Always. He learned to read from the family Bible. He knew that this world didn't matter, not the poverty, or the work, or the pain. It was a test on the path to salvation.

But it was easy for that boy. Those tests were nothing,

that pain barely registered. That boy hadn't been turned into this thing. He hadn't fed on the blood of his friends.

That boy was dead. Cade was all that was left. But he wouldn't turn his back on everything he was. He refused.

In the end, there was only one answer.

"No," he said. "It's not."

She looked into his eyes—seemed to look even deeper than that—and took something from the folds of her dress.

Cade looked at it, and winced. It was a small, rough cross of some base metal, covered in silver.

It felt like needles in his skin, in his eyes.

She placed it in his hand. Agony shot through his fingers.

But he didn't drop it.

She nodded, as if he'd passed some test.

She struck a wooden match on the stone floor and lit the herbs.

Then she slashed quickly with the knife.

It stung, but the pain of the cross drowned it out. He saw that she had sliced deeply into his cheek and cut a chunk of his hair out in one stroke.

His blood pooled in the leather pouch, right where she had placed it.

It hissed as it extinguished the burning herbs. Then his blood covered the assassin's bullet, briefly turning the brown crust fresh and red.

Mme. Laveau took his hair and knotted it, expertly, into a tiny doll—arms, legs and head, like a straw man.

Then she waved it through the smoldering herbs, chanting some language Cade didn't understand.

When she looked back at him, her eyes were glassy, and she dragged the hair-doll through his cut—wiping up his blood, soaking it into the hair.

He noticed that the cell had seemed to shrink, down to just the two of them. The air thickened with smoke, and something else, something unnamable. It felt as if there were another world, crowding in around the edges of his vision, trying to get his attention.

She spoke in a voice that wasn't quite her own, without looking at the paper Johnson had given her, but just holding it:

"By this blood, you are bound," she intoned. *"To the President of the United States; and to the orders of the officers appointed by him; to support and defend the nation and its citizens against all enemies, foreign and domestic; and to serve it faithfully for all the days you walk the Earth."*

More of the strange language, then the hair-doll was used to crush out the smoldering embers of the herbs. She gathered the bloody, sooty doll into the leather pouch, along with the bullet, and cinched it tightly shut.

Cade could feel the cut on his cheek healing already. And he felt something else. Like a new spine, growing down his back. A certainty that had not been there before. He knew what he had to do. He knew what his unnatural life was for, now: to protect and to serve.

The smoke dissipated and the cell seemed to snap back to its normal size.

Mme. Laveau rose and gathered her things, as matter-of-fact as a woman picking up her knitting.

He still had the cross in his hand. It still hurt. But the pain helped him focus. Helped him see clearly. It gave him something other than the thirst.

"What did you do?" he asked, not sure he wanted to know.

"About your hunger? Nothing," she told him. "You will have many chances to take human blood, if you want. Your president will give you that. But the choice is always yours."

She leaned down again, took the cross gently from his hand. The pain stopped, but Cade found he wanted it back.

She took a length of cord and looped it through a ring on the cross, then tied it around his neck.

She held his gaze for a long moment.

"You are bound to this man now, and all the ones who will follow him. You will fight the dark forces. You will have to fight.

"But you are not a slave," she said, holding his hands in her own. "Remember that: no man is a slave."

She stood quickly and picked up her bag. The leather pouch was in her other hand.

She knocked on the door, and Johnson and a soldier reappeared as it opened.

"It's done," she said, and gave the pouch to Johnson. "You may remove those chains."

"You're certain?" Johnson asked.

She gave him the same scowl as before. Johnson gestured to the soldiers to unlock Cade.

Mme. Laveau looked at Cade one last time before she walked out the door. Her eyes were full of pity.

"I can see your road, child," she said. "It is not easy. You might have been better off dead."

SIX

There is no known physiological reason for the pain Cade experiences when exposed to the sight or touch of a cross, or other religious paraphernalia. While there are no lasting effects, a cross can be enough to keep a vampire at bay.

It appears that prolonged and repeated exposure can build a resistance, or at least, an accommodation with this pain. Unlike other vampires, our subject wears a cross around his neck. (He claims the pain helps him focus on beating his thirst for human blood.) Some in the research group have suggested that the pain is psychosomatic, an abreaction to the vampire's disgust and self-loathing at his or her transformation. However, this does not explain why religious symbols affect all vampires more or less equally, without regard for the individual's religious background.

—BRIEFING BOOK: CODENAME: NIGHTMARE PET

Zach sipped his coffee and grimaced. It was awful. The only stuff he'd ever had that was worse had been in the mess of an aircraft carrier, during a visit with the president. But a single cup kept him awake for twenty hours.

He looked at Cade, then Griff.

"Okay," he said. "So he has to do what I say?"

Cade's face didn't move, but Zach got the distinct feeling he didn't like the question.

"Not exactly," Griff said. "He will follow the orders you pass on from the president. But for now, you should learn the ropes from us."

Zach shrugged. He supposed he had no choice but to see where this ride would go.

"Where do we start?"

Griff handed a sheet of paper to Cade.

"This is what I tried to tell you about before you stormed off to bed," Griff said.

Zach laughed at that, then turned it into a cough when Cade looked at him.

"ICE has found something in a container off a ship at the Port of Baltimore. Their report triggered our flags in the system," Griff said to Zach. "When we get an alert like that, you'll call and tell their superiors to seal off the scene until you and Cade can get there. We have priority commands for every branch of the federal government."

Zach suddenly felt like he was in grade school again. He could have sworn Griff was talking slower than normal for his benefit.

"What did they find?"

"We'll see for ourselves," Cade said. There was no change in his tone, but again, Zach caught a distinct undercurrent of impatience.

Cade crossed the room. Even walking, the vampire moved impossibly fast. Zach hurried to follow.

Cade hit a stone in the wall at the far end of the Reliquary. The concrete slid back as if on wheels, and revealed another hidden door.

"How many of these things do you have in here?"

"I've never counted," Cade said, and slipped into the passage.

Zach looked back at Griff. "What, that's it? That's all the training and orientation? Now you just expect me to go after him?"

"Nature of the job," Griff said. "You hit the ground running."

"Fantastic. Any advice, then?" Zach said it with heavy sarcasm, but Griff appeared thoughtful before he answered.

"He's smarter than you, stronger than you, and he was eating people over a century before you were born," Griff said. "He'll try to dominate you. It's nothing personal. Just how he sees us. Don't let him."

"Don't let him?"

"He can't touch you, Zach. It's his job to keep you safe. Push back."

Griff returned to the papers in front of him.

"That's a big help," Zach muttered. Then he followed the vampire into the dark.

THE TUNNEL SMELLED like a YMCA locker room. Small electric bulbs wired to the ceiling provided dim light. Zach had never thought of himself as claustrophobic, but the roof was barely over his head, and he and Cade had to walk single file to get through.

"Where the hell are we?"

"You don't know? You worked for the White House."

"You learn something new every day. Apparently."

"Washington, D.C., was designed by a Masonic architect, Pierre-Charles L'Enfant, at the direction of Thomas Jefferson and Alexander Hamilton. They included a series of secret tunnels, which have been updated every few decades, ever since. We can get into the Metro from here—even all the way down to Virginia."

"Masons?" Zach snorted. "Please don't tell me you think there's a conspiracy to take over the U.S. government."

"Eight."

"What?"

"At last count, there were eight allied groups of conspirators working to assume control of the U.S. government," Cade said. "Those are just the major players, of course."

"Oh, of course."

There was a scrabbling in the corner of the tunnel. Zach made a face. "Jesus Christ. A master's in public policy, and I'm walking around the sewers with rats."

Zach kept talking, if for no other reason than to drown out the sound of little feet. "So. You're a good vampire. How'd that happen?"

"There is no such thing as a good vampire, Mr. Barrows," Cade said.

"But you're—"

"Trust me on that."

Whatever, Zach thought. Out loud, he tried a different tack. "Have you really been doing this for a hundred and forty years?"

"Yes."

Zach waited. Nothing else.

"What does that make me, your manservant? Should I pop down to the animal shelter and pick up a cat for dinner?"

Cade moved.

One moment a step ahead of Zach, the next a dozen feet away.

In a flash, Zach realized why people believed vampires could turn to mist.

Cade faced Zach. In his hand, a rat struggled.

Cade brought it to his mouth, fangs bared, and snapped his jaws shut. Blood spurted, and he sucked on the writhing animal like a kid with a milk shake.

Zach tasted lunch at the back of his throat. He swallowed hard.

Cade tossed the dead rat away and wiped his mouth. "I get my own meals," he said.

Cade turned and walked down the tunnel again.

Zach shoved down the bile in his throat. *He can't touch you,* Griff said. *Push back.*

"What, you don't offer me some?" he called after Cade. "Nice manners, dude."

Cade kept walking, silent. But Zach felt like he'd won a major victory anyway. He hurried to keep up.

AFTER ANOTHER twenty yards or so, the passage opened into a much wider tunnel—like a freeway underpass. Sitting on a cobblestone floor was an anonymous, late-model government sedan. Zach could have requisitioned it from the White House motor pool.

It was comforting, with all the deep weirdness he'd already experienced. But he still had to make a comment. "Not exactly an Aston Martin, is it?"

"We don't want to attract attention," Cade said.

"Does it at least have a smoke screen?"

"It has specially treated windows that block all UVA and UVB rays, and certain wavelengths of the visible spectrum."

"Wow. Sexy."

"Get in the car, Mr. Barrows."

Inside, Cade waited for Zach to put on his seat belt before he started the engine.

"You know, you can call me Zach."

"I'll keep that in mind."

"Have I done something to offend you?" Zach asked.

"No," Cade said. The sedan made its way down the tunnel, headlights on.

"You just seem like you don't like me."

"I don't know you."

Zach felt compelled to defend himself. He thought he'd already been judged and found wanting. "Look, we're going to be stuck together, so we might as well get along."

Cade shook his head ever so slightly. "We might not be stuck with each other long."

"What's that supposed to mean?"

"If you're not careful, you'll be dead in a matter of days."

Zach thought about that for a few seconds. "You're nothing but rainbows and lollipops, aren't you?"

Cade didn't reply.

They emerged from a maintenance tunnel for the Metro, not far from the Mall. Cade steered them onto I-295, toward Baltimore.

After a few more minutes of nothing but the sound of tires on the road, Zach decided to try wedging open the conversation again.

"I guess crosses don't really work on you guys, do they?"

"What do you mean?"

"Well . . . that's just something from the movies, right?"

"No," Cade said. "They hurt."

"But you're wearing one. Around your neck."

"Yes. I am."

"I thought you said they hurt vampires."

"I did. They do."

Zach waited. Nothing else.

"Christ," Zach said, under his breath.

Cade heard. "Don't blaspheme. Please."

Somehow the "please" made it more irritating.

"You religious or something?"

"Yes."

Long pause. "But you're a—"

"Yes, we established that. Someone has to protect the meek until they can inherit the Earth."

"You know, you're not explaining a whole hell of a lot here."

A slight pause. "It will help considerably if you listen the first time," Cade said.

"Ah, bite me." Then Zach remembered who he was talking to. "That was a joke," he said quickly.

Cade ignored that. "There's a whole secret history to this country, Mr. Barrows. Believe me when I say you don't know the first thing about it."

Something in Cade's tone really rankled Zach. So he decided to ask the question that had been bouncing around in the back of his head all night.

"In that case, where were you on 9/11?" he asked. "Seems like someone with your talents should have been able to stop a bunch of guys with box cutters."

Cade stared at Zach from the driver's seat, really looking at him for the first time since the Reliquary. In the reflected light from the road, his face looked like a skull.

VAMPIRE RECALL IS PERFECT. Unlike human memory, every experience—every sight, sound, feeling or smell—is recorded exactly as it happened. There is no circuit breaker, like the one in the human brain that prevents people from recalling pain or severe trauma. For a vampire, the memory of an injury is just as fresh as the actual wound.

Which is why Cade could still remember the agony of the early morning of September 11, 2001. He had trailed his target into the parking garage of a vacant building.

Then the man vanished. The next thing he saw was a sword—literally, a flaming sword—fire actually dancing on the blade—pierce the darkness and slam through his gut.

Something stopped him instantly, and he was pinned. The sword, still burning, rammed right through him and deep into the steel-reinforced concrete pillar behind him.

His feet dangled from the floor. His blood began to pool under him.

His target stood a mere five feet away. An impossibly handsome man, his face a mask of contempt. He appeared to consider Cade, to measure the danger he posed against the effort of finishing him off.

With a smirk, he turned away and walked off. The message was clear: Cade wasn't worth another moment.

Cade was trapped. He couldn't call Griff for help: the sat-phone was useless this far underground. There was only one thing he could do. He grabbed the blade and began pulling.

It took him nine hours of slicing and burning his hands, writhing and struggling, before he could finally dislodge the sword from the pillar.

As soon as the blade hit the concrete floor, the flames went out, like they were never there.

At least another thirty minutes passed before he could gather enough strength to get up and find the stairwell.

Still bleeding heavily, he made his way to the lobby of the building.

A TV was at the reception desk, left on by a security guard or whoever had abandoned it.

The sound was off. A news anchor was talking fast, his

face strained. Then a shot of the Manhattan skyline. Smoke. And something missing.

His phone rang. Griff. Screaming at him, with rage and frustration.

Cade wasn't paying attention. He realized what was missing.

The towers were gone. They'd been gone for hours by then.

THE LOOK ON CADE'S FACE made Zach very aware that he was trapped in a metal box going seventy miles an hour with a creature that could eat him.

He wondered if he'd gone too far, and how much it would hurt if he threw himself out of the car.

Cade's mouth twitched. He seemed to take pity on Zach.

"I was hung up," Cade said.

The tension drained out of the air between them. Zach said, "Part of the secret history, I guess."

"That's right," Cade replied.

They drove in silence after that.

SEVEN

The commonly held belief that vampires are capable of mesmerizing their prey does not appear to be true, at least with Cade. But there is a very real—if not easily measured—psychological and biological response triggered in humans by Cade. Researchers meeting him for the first time reported extreme anxiety, verging on panic attacks. (The fear response is probably heightened by the person's encounter with a species long assumed to be mythical.) This can cause a person to "freeze," much like a mouse will stop all movement when stalked by a snake. However, like the mouse, this is not because the person is hypnotized. It seems to be a result of an ingrained human reaction to a predatory species, rather than any inherent ability on Cade's part. The response grows weaker upon repeated encounters with Cade, settling down eventually to a generalized unease in his presence.

—BRIEFING BOOK: CODENAME: NIGHTMARE PET

PORT OF BALTIMORE, BALTIMORE, MARYLAND

The two ICE agents, a man and a woman, had clearly been waiting for a while. And they were not happy about it.

Employees of ICE—Immigration and Customs Enforcement, the catchall investigative arm of Homeland

Security—tended to be a little surly anyway. After 9/11, every agency in the country got swept into new, terrorist-fighting duties, with the plum assignments going to the big names at the CIA and FBI. Customs got new stationery and all the leftovers. They were responsible for everything from transferring prisoners to building security to searching cargo.

The last job was the least glamorous, and it was the reason they were here tonight.

They stood outside the giant metal shipping container, arms crossed, scowling, as Cade and Zach ducked under the crime-scene tape. The male agent moved to intercept them. Like his partner, he was dressed in a dark windbreaker with ICE stenciled in yellow on the back, and had a SIG Sauer P229 9mm in a holster on his hip. He looked like he wanted an excuse to shoot them right there.

Cade either didn't notice or didn't care. "I'm Agent Cushing. This is Agent Lee," he said, holding up the credentials he'd pulled from the glove box of the sedan. Zach fumbled in his pocket and came up with his own billfold, which somehow already had his photo above the phony name. It occurred to him that someone had been planning his transfer for a while.

The male agent scanned their IDs, unimpressed.

"Agent Cusick," he said, and then tipped his head toward his partner. "That's Hagan."

He had to raise his voice over the sound of the docks, which Zach was surprised to see were still busy, even this late at night. Cranes dipped down into giant tankers and freighters, and came out with containers that they stacked in big, rusting piles on the concrete docks. Semi trucks ground gears and waited in lines to pick up their shipments.

The container they were here to see was cordoned off by the tape, and a wide space on every side. There was no one else nearby, and DHS had set up floodlights. It made the metal box look like it was on display.

Cade looked at the container, its doors locked and sealed. He turned to Cusick.

"Is there some reason you're waiting to give me your report?" he asked.

Cusick's face curled into a snarl, but Hagan jumped in to answer before he could damage his career. Zach figured it was a pattern with the two of them.

"The refrigeration on this unit apparently failed, and the smell attracted the attention of the inspectors," she said. "They looked inside, called us. Then our boss got a call, and we were told to secure the scene and wait for you."

"Which we've been doing for seven hours and forty-nine minutes," Cusick said, making a show of checking his watch. "Thanks so much for hurrying."

"You're welcome," Cade said. "Where's the driver?"

"Truckers here show up with their rigs and line up for cargo," Hagan said. "We pulled him out of line and stuck him in the harbormaster's office. He says he had no idea what was in the box."

"So what's inside?" Zach asked.

Cusick scowled. "You don't know? Christ, that's great."

"Open it, and we'll see for ourselves," Cade said.

Cusick spun around, turning his back on Zach. "Hey, screw you, pal," he said. "We're not here to be your servants. I know you guys like to think we're just rent-a-cops down at this level—"

"Kirk," Hagan said, a warning in her voice.

"No, damn it, Ann, I'm sick of this shit—"

Zach recognized the tone. It was the career government employee at the end of his patience. Fortunately, he had some experience with that.

"Hey. Us too, buddy," Zach said. "We're all just doing what we're told. The guys making the decisions are safe in their soft, warm beds."

Cusick snorted. That was progress.

"None of us want to be here," Zach said. "But if you just let us into the container, maybe we can get this done before daybreak, okay?"

Cusick dialed back his anger. "Yeah," he said. "Sorry. Been a long night."

"Nothing to apologize for," Zach said. They walked over to the container. Cusick broke the evidence seals and unlocked the doors.

Cusick looked back at Zach and Cade. "Might want to hold your breath now," he said.

Zach didn't know what he meant by that. Then they swung open the doors, and the stench rolled out over them all.

Zach turned and threw up his coffee, stomach acid burning in his nose and throat. Cusick and Hagan both stepped back, gagging.

Only Cade didn't retch.

Hagan walked over to Zach, handed him a Kleenex from her jacket.

"Thanks," he croaked, wiping his mouth.

"You never get used to the smell, do you?" Cusick said. Looking right at Cade.

Cade looked right back. "No," he said. "You never do."

Cusick gave his partner a look like, *Can you believe this guy?*

Meanwhile, Zach got a good look in the container.

Inside, hanging on hooks, like a cannibal's meat locker, were rows and rows of body parts. Legs. Arms. Torsos. A chain full of hands, another of feet.

All of them going purple and green with decay, buzzing with flies and maggots in the enclosed heat of the container.

"So," Cusick said. "I hope to Christ you know what this is about. Because I've never seen anything like it."

Cade didn't answer him. Instead, he said, "Let's talk to the driver."

It wasn't a request.

THEY ENTERED the harbormaster's building, a collection of small offices and what looked like an employee lounge, with vending machines for soda and candy.

They stood by the machines while Hagan gave them the trucker's story.

"He's in there," she said, pointing to a small office off the main hallway. The door was closed. "Guy named Andrew Reese. From Jersey. Said he was hired by a referral agency to make a pick-up here. And he says that's all he knows."

She unlocked the door and they entered. Reese didn't fit Zach's image of a truck driver—an old guy, like a side of beef, in a flannel shirt and mesh-back cap. Instead, the trucker was about his age, wire-thin and wearing an OFFSPRING T-shirt. He glared at them from eyes that looked bruised from a lack of sleep.

"About fucking time," he snapped. "Do I get my cargo or what?"

"Your cargo has been impounded," Cusick said. "These gentlemen are the federal agents we were telling you about. Maybe you'd like to explain what we found to them."

Reese leaned back in his chair, unimpressed. "I already told you: I don't have a clue what was in the container. I was hired to pick it up. Whatever's on the manifest, that's what I know about it."

"You just pick up whatever you're told?"

Reese shrugged. "A job's a job."

Cusick got in his face. "And we're supposed to believe you don't know why we're here? This is all just a huge mistake to you, right?"

Reese stared back. "You know, I'm a good citizen and all. I want to help fight the War on Terror like anyone else. But I've had enough of this shit. You either arrest me, or I'm getting the hell out of here."

He stood, nearly bumping Cusick on his way up. Cusick shoved him back in his seat.

Reese smiled. "Nice," he said. "Now I can sue you for brutality. I could use a new big-screen TV."

"Shut up," Cusick snapped. "Or we'll test your blood for meth."

Reese's smile vanished. "I want to talk to a lawyer. Right fucking now."

Cusick was about to say something else, but Cade interrupted. "I think we need to take a moment. Don't you, Agent Cusick?"

They all trooped out of the room again, behind Cade.

"Hey! What about my lawyer?" Reese yelled. No one answered him.

They stood outside the door for a moment, not saying anything.

"He doesn't seem very cooperative," Cade said.

"Screw you," Cusick shot back. "If you'd been here earlier, we might have had more luck."

Cade ignored him, again. "I'd like to talk to him alone."

Cusick was instantly suspicious. "Why?"

Cade's expression didn't change. "Because I'd like to talk to him alone."

Cusick gritted his teeth and stepped back with exaggerated courtesy. "Of course. Excuse the hell out of me."

"Don't worry about it," Cade said, and went back into the room.

Zach heard Reese talking, muffled through the door. He didn't know what to say to the ICE agents, so he smiled.

They looked at him like he was retarded.

"Who the hell are you with again?" Cusick asked.

Zach blanked. He couldn't remember which division of the government was written on his fake ID.

Then the screaming started.

Zach had never heard anything like it. It came from inside the small office. It sounded like an animal caught in a trap.

It was Reese.

Cusick moved before his partner did. He lifted his foot, prepared to kick the door down—

Just as Cade swung it open gently.

They rushed in together. Cade stood back.

"What the *fuck*—" Cusick said. Zach looked down, noticed that Cusick had his gun drawn.

"He wasn't hired by a referral agency," Cade said. "He got a call from a shipping company. KSM Holdings. Otherwise, he's telling the truth. You can release him."

In the room, Reese wasn't screaming anymore. He was trembling, and trying like hell to hide in the corner, as far away as he could from Cade.

A stain spread at his crotch. The tiny office was thick with the smell of fresh shit.

"What did you do to him?" Cusick demanded.

"Nothing," Cade said mildly.

"*Nothing*? Bullshit. Look at him," Cusick said. "What do you call that?"

Hagan tried to reach over to Reese, to calm him down. He shrieked and huddled down even farther.

"Enhanced interrogation techniques," Cade said. His mouth twitched as he said it.

"*Enhanced?*" Cusick looked like he could spit. "I don't

know how you do it, but we don't allow that kind of Jack Bauer torture shit here—"

"The United States doesn't torture," Cade said.

"That's it," Cusick said. "I'm putting you under arrest, pal."

Zach noticed that Cusick still had his gun out.

Cade's expression never changed, but Zach wondered if Cade's oath to protect the citizenry of the U.S. would prevent him from putting Cusick through a wall.

He decided not to take the chance.

"Whoa, whoa, whoa there, Tex, wait a second," he said, holding up his hands.

Cusick spun back around to him, his face red.

"Come on. We're all on the same side here, right?"

Cusick nodded, a little. Like moving his head would cost money.

"Let's just . . . step outside and discuss this."

Another fractional nod. Then, pointing at Cade: "But he gets the hell out of here."

Cusick told Hagan to look after Reese. They stepped out of the office.

Zach and Cusick moved to one side, to talk. Cusick, thankfully, put his Sig back in its holster.

Cade seemed profoundly uninterested in whatever they had to say.

"I'll be at the container," he told Zach. "Join me when you're done here."

"Asshole," Cusick said, loud enough so Cade, walking away, couldn't miss it.

Cade didn't turn around as he went through the outer door.

Once he was gone, Zach lowered his voice and leaned in. Cusick did the same, in order to hear.

"Look, I gotta apologize for my partner. He's a little . . . intense."

"He's fucking psychotic."

"Point taken," Zach said. "Look. Do you really want to make a thing of this? You really want to get your career wrapped up in whatever god-awful mess we've got here?"

Cusick gave Zach a look. "So I should just go along like a good boy, is that it?"

"If I could just walk away from this, I would," Zach said, meaning it. "Believe me."

The office door opened and Hagan came out. "How is he?" Cusick asked her.

"He's fine." She saw his face. "No, really. Not a mark on him. Just whatever that guy said . . . scared the shit out of him. Literally, I'm afraid."

Cusick couldn't accept it. "He didn't touch him?"

Hagan shook her head. "Guy doesn't want to press charges or anything. Just wants out of here."

Cusick and Hagan looked at each other, then at Zach.

"So what now?" Cusick asked.

"Go home," Zach said, trying not to make it sound like a guess. "We'll take it from here."

"What do we put in our report?" Cusick asked. The look of suspicion was back.

Even Zach knew the answer to that. "Nothing."

"Nothing?"

"Not a thing. Classified. Nobody ever hears a word about this."

"We can handle sensitive information," Cusick insisted.

"We're counting on it," Zach said. "Something like this gets out, causes a panic . . . then, next week, we've got congressional hearings, and we're both out of work. You know how it is."

The agents nodded. Like Zach, they knew how the Washington blame game worked. Someone had to be a scapegoat, and it was usually the person dumb enough to have his name written down somewhere.

They got Reese out of the office, sent him to a bathroom and then escorted him to the door. His legs were still shaking, but he walked away under his own power. Hagan and Cusick each shook Zach's hand and left. Cusick looked over his shoulder once. Hagan didn't.

As soon as they were out of sight, Zach sucked in a deep breath and headed back to the container.

Even though he really, really didn't want to.

ZACH FOUND CADE near the back of the container. It was almost too dark to see. Cade wasn't having any trouble, though.

Zach was trying like hell not to touch any of the body parts. He stayed as close as he could to the wall.

"That was good," Cade said, without looking up from what he was doing. "You got them out of here, and you kept them from getting too suspicious."

Zach was surprised. "It's nothing. Just standard government bureaucrat mentality."

"You handled it well," Cade said. "I'm not always good at dealing with people."

"No. You must be joking," Zach said, deadpan.

Silence.

"So what did you do to the trucker?" Zach asked.

More silence. Then Cade asked, "You have your phone?"

"Yeah," Zach said.

"It has a camera function. Get a photo of this. Close as you can."

Zach pulled his phone out of his pocket, stabbed at buttons until the camera function appeared.

Meanwhile, Cade peered intently at the shoulder joint of an arm, swinging on one of the chains.

Zach squinted, trying to see what was so interesting to Cade. Then Cade moved, and light from the floods outside reached the arm.

At the shoulder, glinting slightly, was a metal fitting, somehow welded into the flesh and bone. It almost looked organic itself. And it appeared to have ridges and slots.

Zach realized where he'd seen stuff like that before. On computers, and office equipment. Metal joints, used to snap things together, Tab A to Slot B.

"What the hell . . . ?"

"Photos," Cade reminded him.

Zach pointed and shot. The camera came with its own flash, which lit up the interior of the container like day.

That was when he saw the other thing on the arm that Cade was looking at: a tattoo.

AIRBORNE FIRST BATTALION, it said, with the squad's mascot just underneath: 508TH RED DEVILS.

This was the arm of an American soldier.

Zach suddenly felt like vomiting again, but his mouth was dry.

"Jesus Christ, what is this?"

Cade walked out of the container. "Come along."

Zach got out of the container as fast as he could, without touching anything hanging from the chains.

As soon as Zach was out, Cade took the handles of the doors in his hands and slammed them shut.

"Call Griff. It's the first number in your phone book. Tell him we need a dental appointment."

"That's really cute, but—"

"Do it. *Now.*"

The vampire's placid expression was gone. He looked *pissed.*

That scared Zach, even as he fumbled with the phone to make the call.

"Cade. *What the hell is this?*"

He thought he was being ignored again. Then Cade spoke.

"This is quite a week for you, Mr. Barrows," he said. "First you meet a real vampire. Now you're going to meet Frankenstein."

EIGHT

In addition to his greatly amplified motor neuron transmission, subject's IQ, particularly in strategic and problem-solving functions, ranges from exceptionally gifted to genius level (161 to 174, Stanford-Binet scale). MRI and CAT scans suggest his neural function has become more efficient over time—with greater and greater communication throughout his cortex enabled by increased folds and wrinkles through the brain matter, causing more connectivity between neurons. It has been theorized that this enables the subject to "parallel-process," which is to say, work several angles of a problem at once, greatly reducing the time required for a solution.

—BRIEFING BOOK: CODENAME: NIGHTMARE PET

Dylan had no trouble clearing Customs. His shipment remained one of the 97 percent of freight containers not inspected on their way into the U.S.

Dylan only knew this because Khaled knew this and repeated it endlessly to reassure him.

It didn't work. Dylan picked up his cargo and soaked through his shirt with flop sweat. Once he'd cleared the gates of the shipyard, he took the truck out on the highway in a blind panic. Every five seconds, he checked his rearview for Delta Force commandos about to drop out of the sky and shoot him dead.

He was a hundred miles away from the port by the time he realized that no one was looking for him. No one cared.

Khaled would have said this was God's way of testing him, of preparing him for the holy mission they were about to undertake.

Dylan was sick of hearing it. He had already done way too much work for Khaled's science project. He wanted to get paid. But there was always just one more thing, just one more thing.

At first, it was nothing too demanding. Khaled had him make a little trip. A short hop on a plane to Dubai. During a weekend stay at a super-luxury hotel, Dylan delivered a briefcase full of cash to some other Arab guys. No big deal. When he got back, he found out the money was for the widows and orphans of the "brave warriors killed in the struggle against the Zionist occupation," but Dylan wasn't stupid. He knew what that meant: the cash went to pay guys to strap on suicide belts and blow themselves up.

Dylan had no real problem with that. It was like a video game, in some ways. Pick a character, send him out to do battle, and once he dies, pick another one. Simple.

But Dylan increasingly resented risking his ass to do grunt work. The trips grew more frequent. Pretty soon he was going to Dubai or Riyadh or Tel Aviv every other week. Dylan knew why he was chosen. Khaled was on too many watch lists. Dylan was a perfect, blank face.

A perfect, white, *American* face.

It didn't seem like hero's work. And he still hadn't been paid.

Then, a month ago, Khaled had called him over to the apartment. He gave Dylan another plane ticket.

Dylan unloaded his list of complaints on Khaled. He was sick of the stink of dead bodies. He was tired of using his free time to run Khaled's errands.

Dylan gave his ultimatum. He was ready to get out. He wanted his money. He was done being Khaled's flunky.

Khaled had listened patiently. Then he asked, "Are you finished?"

Dylan nodded.

Khaled hit him.

Dylan found himself flat on his back, bleeding from his nose. He'd never been struck in his life. Not even as a child.

Khaled stood above him. He tried to sit up, but Khaled put his foot on Dylan's throat and forced him back down. Dylan started choking. Khaled didn't lessen the pressure a bit.

"There's only one way out of Zulfiqar," Khaled told him. "And that is either to a martyr's Heaven or to a traitor's Hell."

Dylan wanted to ask, You're serious about that? Then all he wanted to do was breathe.

"What do you want? Do you want out?" Khaled asked.

Dylan shook his head. Unh-uh. No sir. Team player, right here.

"You're prepared to continue your mission?" Khaled asked.

Dylan nodded like a bobble-head doll.

Khaled lifted his foot, a big smile back on his face. He embraced Dylan like a brother. And he gave him the ticket again.

Dylan decided he'd stick with Khaled's plan for a while. Until he could figure out a way to quit that wouldn't make Khaled quite so mad.

So he took the trip to Los Angeles.

He met with a guy with a German name and great hair, who explained what the corpses would be used for.

Dylan didn't quite believe it, but Khaled did. That was all that mattered.

He went back to Kuwait. There were more errands, more trips to the U.S. to check the progress of the German guy. Each time, Dylan wondered if he would finally get his money and get out.

Then Khaled had told him they were ready. The plan was almost finished.

There was just one more thing Dylan had to do. Of course.

He had to pick up a cargo shipment and drive it to a new destination. It couldn't arrive at the target site—that would be taking too much of a chance.

But then, as soon as he made the delivery, Khaled promised, Dylan would get his reward.

The night before he flew to the States, Dylan met with Khaled and his friends at the apartment. They drank and toasted Dylan's courage—even the hard-line Muslim guys, who never drank anything but grape juice.

Things were getting pretty rowdy, but right before the prostitutes showed up, Khaled called for silence.

"You have renounced your country to do what is right," Khaled said to Dylan. The others nodded. "You must have a new name, to signify your new life as a warrior."

He appeared to think hard, then beamed at Dylan. "From now on, you are Ayir al-Kelba."

Khaled's friends smiled just as widely at him. Dylan felt pride swelling inside him. "Ayir . . . What does that mean?"

"It means 'great leader,'" Khaled said.

Maybe it was the booze, but Dylan got a little choked up. Even the stone-faced Saudis looked like they were struggling to contain themselves.

That was when Dylan decided he was doing the right thing. The world had to change. Khaled was right about that. And he'd chosen Dylan to help.

It all became clear: those guys really understood his potential. For the first time, he felt like someone had given him a name to match his inner greatness. They believed in him. So he would believe in them.

Dylan hung on to that moment, and to the promises Khaled made.

It helped him forget what was in the back of the truck, as he drove into the night.

NINE

Sustained exposure to high-temperature flame (propane blowtorch, approx. 600°F) causes the same damage as would be expected on normal human tissue. It's theorized that high heat may cause the same protein "shut-off" as UV exposure, though we have not yet verified this. Aside from sunlight and fire, subject has virtually no other vulnerabilities. Tests of garlic, silver and other materials mentioned in folklore had no discernable effect. In order to kill the subject, it would be necessary to completely destroy his cardiac function—through massive damage to the heart—or sever his head completely from his body. This is, perhaps, why earlier cultures decapitated corpses and staked them through the heart, in an effort to prevent vampiric outbreaks.

—BRIEFING BOOK: CODENAME: NIGHTMARE PET

New York Public Library,
Humanities and Social Sciences Division,
New York, New York

Tania entered the library just as the tolling bell sounded to announce fifteen minutes to closing. She gave the security guard a brilliant smile, and he was happy to let the pretty girl sneak past, despite the rules.

She made her way through the crowds of people to the genealogy room, one of the most popular spots in the whole building. Tania had no trouble getting to the stacks she wanted; people got out of her way without even realizing it.

The section contained records going back to when the streets of New York were filled with horseshit, and clean water was a luxury item. There were plenty of family historians, academics and homeless people still in their seats, waiting for someone to kick them out, so they could scrounge just a little more data or a little more warmth. Tania disappeared into a long row of old, leather-bound volumes—fewer and fewer of these books every year, as computers ate their knowledge and took their space. It was hard to argue with the decision, however: almost no one came to peruse the old city directories, phone books and municipal records. Lists and lists of names of people long dead. A roll call that no one would ever answer, and no one would care.

Tania wasn't looking for those names anyway. She needed fresher information.

Flipping through pages of an old citywide social register, seemingly at random, she stopped wherever some vandal had marked the book in ballpoint ink.

Circles and checks. Random words. She found the freshest ink—she could smell it—and began assembling the words together, in her head.

"Doctor" was the first new word circled. Then "commission."

She had been out of town and out of touch for a while.

And while her kind was definitely not social, they'd recognized the necessity of maintaining lines of communication. An Internet chat room wasn't going to cut it for many of them. They needed something a little less ephemeral than digital code on a screen.

Fortunately, humans were ridiculously sentimental creatures, and they hung on to everything.

Tania kept flipping, a frown marring her perfect, pale skin. "Removal," "extermination," "pest control."

Eventually, this building and all the books it held would be destroyed, plowed over by people as they rebuilt the world again. But some of the outposts of the past would remain. Look at Stonehenge. It was still around, even if it was useless as a way to deliver messages anymore.

Tania didn't like the way this message was shaping up. Not at all. "Compensation," "more," "disposal," "time," "soon," "president," "pet."

Then a series of numbers. Not a phone number, but a cipher, leading anyone who knew it and had the ability to memorize a series of sixteen-digit strings to a place where communication would continue.

Tania had seen enough, however. She slammed the book shut.

A librarian at the end of the stack looked at her with disapproval. He was the sort of man who looked, on the outside, like he'd been born in tweed.

Actually, in his off hours, he was quite fond of leather and bondage. But he liked playing the part of the nerdy scholar at work. And in both his lives, he was a stickler for the rules.

"We're closing," he reminded her. "You're running out of time."

She almost smiled at that. "Not me," she said. "But someone is, yes."

Why do we get all the freaks, the librarian thought.

She fixed him with a glare, as if she heard inside his head.

Then she swept past him. She was very attractive, but none of the librarian's usual fantasies about strapping her down filled his head. He didn't even watch her pass to get a better look. He just wanted to make sure she was gone.

As she went out the door, he felt strangely relieved, like he'd narrowly escaped something awful. Maybe he'd have to talk to his therapist about adjusting his dosage.

TEN

HALDEMAN: Point is, we'll have a harder time keeping it [unintelligible] or contained. We can ignore one paper, call it a vendetta, but if anyone else follows the story—

PRESIDENT: What about Cade?

HALDEMAN: What about him?

PRESIDENT: What if he were to talk to those two from the *Post*? Woodson, and what's the other one, something Birnbaum?

HALDEMAN: Bernstein. I don't think—

PRESIDENT: That would shut them up.

HALDEMAN: Cade won't do anything against innocent citizens.

PRESIDENT: Innocent. [Laughter]

HALDEMAN: Part of the thing. His oath. Can't touch them.

PRESIDENT: Well, that's my luck. A [expletive deleted] vampire with a conscience.

—*Partial transcript of the so-called 18½ minute gap in the tape of a meeting between H. R. Haldeman and President Richard M. Nixon, June 20, 1972*

The White House, Washington, D.C.

Nobody goes into the Oval Office expecting to get a lot of sleep on the job. Samuel Curtis's aides woke him in the middle of the night two or three times a week, minimum.

A year into his presidency, Curtis had gotten used to it. He could switch off like a light now. Order an air strike, back to sleep. No problem.

Except when Cade was involved.

The last time Cade asked for a meeting, a little girl in Nevada was saying terrible things in a dead language. Less than a week later, Curtis had to order an entire town sterilized—burning every house and building to the ground, along with anyone and anything inside.

That still kept him up some nights.

Curtis had been in politics his whole adult life before he ran for president. He'd seen every variety of human need, greed and weakness. He thought he was beyond surprise.

Then, on his inauguration day, he met with his predecessor, an overgrown frat boy with a mile-wide mean streak.

"I've got something to give you," the former president had said. Privately, Curtis thought two wars in the Middle East and an economy that resembled a bounced check were enough. There was no affection between the two men. It had been an ugly campaign. Curtis had been compared to the Antichrist. More than once.

But he kept his mouth shut as his predecessor passed

him a folded piece of paper: the daily launch codes for America's nuclear missiles. A seemingly random set of numbers that could end all life on Earth if spoken, like magic words. Curtis put them in his suit jacket pocket. He could have sworn he felt them there after he took his hand away.

Curtis watched as the former president opened a small safe behind a portrait of Kennedy on the wall. Inside was a wooden box. He took a key from a lanyard around his neck and opened it.

Inside the box was a small, leather satchel, worn and shiny with age. He showed it to Curtis, then handed him the key.

"You don't want to lose either of those," his predecessor said. He seemed more relieved to be rid of the key than the nuclear codes.

Curtis met Cade in person later that night, and realized why.

President Curtis thought of that moment now, as he checked the clock. 3:17 a.m.

Nuclear war, the president could comprehend. As awful as it was, it fit within the horrors he could accept. He could rationalize it.

What Cade brought him from out of the dark . . . there was nothing there to bargain with, nothing to negotiate. It was, for the most part, entirely out of his control.

That frightened him, every time.

You wanted the job, the president told himself. So get to work.

EACH PRESIDENT DEALT with Cade differently—brought a different group inside the knowledge of his existence. FDR didn't bother telling Truman, but Harry Hopkins, the head of the WPA, sat in on every meeting. JFK had Cade communicate through his brother, and a few other trusted aides. LBJ met with him alone, but he was the exception. More and more, it was an entire committee who sat with the president when he met with Cade. Curtis's group was called the Special Security Council.

They met in the Presidential Emergency Operations Center under the East Wing of the White House. Most people knew it by the name made famous in spy movies and on TV: the Bunker. But that was the movies. In the White House, everyone called it by its acronym: PEOC, or P-OCK.

After 9/11, P-OCK was retrofitted—dug deeper into the earth, made more spacious and wired with high-capacity communications lines.

But one thing didn't change: a hidden door that led to a tunnel called a "disused gas main" on the White House's Environmental Impact Statement. The tunnel led all the way back to the Reliquary. It had been Cade's pathway to the White House since 1960.

Only the president, his liaison and Cade knew about that tunnel. To the Secret Service, it always looked like Cade and his handlers were simply there when the president arrived. Privately, it drove them nuts.

Inside, P-OCK didn't look too dramatic. The main chamber was a regular-sized conference room, just like you'd find in a better hotel.

Still, Zach was in awe as soon as he emerged from the tunnel.

Griff noticed. "You might want to close your mouth before you start catching flies," he said as he sat down heavily in a chair.

Zach shrugged, trying to recapture a little cool. "I've never been in here before," he said.

Griff only grunted in response. Zach thought he looked a bit grayer than usual. Probably past his bedtime.

The double doors opened, and a man wearing a black suit and an earpiece came in. He scowled at the three of them, but waved an all-clear.

President Curtis entered. He was tall and slim. Despite the hour, he was fully dressed and shaved. Zach knew the protection detail had code-named him "Sinatra," because he always seemed to be wearing a tux, no matter what his actual outfit, no matter what the time of day. It was one reason Zach always insisted on wearing a suit.

Curtis was followed by another agent, the chairman of the Joint Chiefs of Staff, and, finally, by Vice President Lester Wyman—a small, pale Smurf of a man. Wyman was already scowling. This didn't surprise Zach. Wyman was always pissed off about something.

The veep was selected as a concession to the values voters. He'd been in the Senate for years before Sam Curtis—most of that time railing about profanity in movies and violent video games—and was the freshman senator's mentor. Then his protégé shot out of nowhere and became the most powerful man in the world.

Still, nobody took Wyman too seriously, even when he got the VP spot, mainly because no one could imagine an American president named Les.

But the president listened to him. Wyman was a true, down-and-dirty political type—smiling for the crowds, then carving up his friends and enemies in the back room. Every president needed a hatchet man like that.

The president sat. Everyone else in the room followed. Zach felt oddly excited. He had no idea what was going on—neither Cade nor Griff had explained anything to him—but it had to be important.

"Well, gentlemen, you've got us here," the president said. "What's the latest nightmare?"

Griff stood and went to the laptop and projector at the head of the room. Zach tried not to grin. Some things never changed. In a government meeting, even a vampire's handler had to use PowerPoint.

Griff clicked on the laptop, and Zach's photos lit up a screen at the back of the room.

"ICE intercepted this container earlier tonight," Griff said. "What you're seeing are modified human limbs."

He stopped on the photo of the soldier's tattoo on the severed arm.

"They're from U.S. servicemen."

"God above," someone whispered.

"What does it mean?" the president asked.

Griff pressed another button, and more corpses appeared on the screen. Zach drew in a sharp breath.

The images were from Dachau. He'd seen them in history class, but those were the least offensive, the ones let out for public consumption. Nothing this graphic. Dead bodies in row after row after row. Bulldozers pushing them into mass graves already filled to the brim.

Griff looked at Cade. Cade uncoiled from his position, as if finally interested.

"Unmenschsoldaten," Cade said.

"What?" Curtis asked.

"Nineteen forty-three. The Nazis had a number of occult projects within the concentration camps," Cade said.

He talks about it like he was there, Zach thought. Then he realized, he probably was.

"At that time, we discovered a scientist who was trying to create what he called *Unmenschsoldaten*—soldiers built from the parts of corpses."

Cade looked directly at the president. "Someone has started that process again. These limbs were modified to be assembled into *Unmenschsoldaten.*"

He paused, as if to let it sink in. Everyone looked grim. Zach, on the other hand, sensed a chance to reset the agenda. He knew it was a risk, but hey, he didn't get ahead without taking a few chances, and getting noticed. . . .

So he raised his hand.

The president noticed. "You don't have to wait to be called on, Zach. Go ahead."

"I know I'm new to this," Zach said, "but . . . so what?"

Everyone in the room stared at Zach like his mother dropped him on his head. A lot.

"'So what?'" Griff repeated.

"Well . . . yeah," Zach said. "Maybe this is just thinking outside the box, but who cares if someone digs up some corpses and puts them back together? I mean, sure, that's insane, and even kind of impressive, but we're talking about a corpse here."

Cade looked at him. Zach's mouth went dry, but he managed to look back.

"Living humans can walk away from car wrecks, falls, even gunshots," Cade said to him. "Now imagine a human body with all the human weakness removed. A corpse doesn't feel pain. Doesn't get hungry. Doesn't suffer shock, or exhaustion, or remorse."

"But it's still just a dead body—" Zach insisted.

"All they remember how to do is kill," Cade said. "Shoot them, they keep going. Burn them, they keep going. They do not stop. They do not rest. Given a day, an *Unmenschsoldat* can murder a thousand people with its bare hands. A dozen *Unmenschsoldaten* could quadruple that body count. A platoon—or an entire battalion—could increase that number exponentially."

The smirk faded from Zach's face. But Cade wasn't about to let him off the hook.

"Do you understand? This is a weapon that literally *kills cities*—one person at a time."

Silence.

"Is that far enough 'outside the box' for you, Zach?" Griff asked.

Zach looked down at the table.

"That will do," the president said.

"How do we even know there's more of these things?" Wyman piped up. "You only found the one container, right? Did you hit the panic button for nothing, Cade?"

The contempt in Wyman's voice almost made Zach's jaw drop. Didn't he know what he was dealing with? He had to, if he was here—but he still talked to Cade as if he were any other subordinate, when the sane response would be to run screaming for the door.

Maybe that's how vampires had lived so long, Zach thought, despite all the warnings in legends and folklore: the endless inability of humans to see past their own noses, to face what was right in front of them.

Griff spoke up. "Actually, sir, the same billing code was used for shipments that have already been in the U.S. for a while. A couple came through Baltimore, one through Long Beach, and then another one came to Los Angeles just last week. It looks like the one ICE intercepted was almost the last."

"Which was the last?"

"That would be the one headed for Los Angeles right now. On another container ship. Due to arrive at the port in two days," Griff said.

"That doesn't prove anything," Wyman said. "Could be a coincidence. Could be nothing."

Griff looked at Wyman with disbelief.

"I think what the vice president is asking is, do we have any idea who's behind this?" the president asked. "Or are we just guessing at the intent here?"

"We don't know. The container was shipped out of

Kuwait City," Griff said. "We're assuming an Islamic Jihad splinter group or sleeper cell."

"Still seems pretty far-fetched to me," Wyman said.

"Who did it is irrelevant," Cade said. "There's only one person who actually knows the secrets necessary to create the *Unmenschsoldat*," Cade said. "Dr. Johann Konrad. I would like to bring him in."

"Wait," Zach said. "This guy is still alive?"

The president looked at Griff. "Didn't you give him the briefing book?"

"He says he skimmed it," Griff said.

"Do you have any direct evidence Konrad is involved?"

Cade shrugged. "No."

"He's the only man who could be doing this," Griff said.

The president looked at his file. "According to this, that's not strictly true, is it? Other people have used Konrad's discoveries, haven't they?" The president read from the page. "Evans City, Pennsylvania, 1967. Camden, New Jersey, 1957 . . ."

"We couldn't prove Konrad was involved in those, but we suspected him," Griff said.

"We made him a deal," the president said, still looking at the folder. "Full pardon. Full citizenship. We may not like it, but I am bound to honor my predecessor's wishes, based on that favor he did for us in 1981."

"That was no favor," Griff said.

"You might feel differently if it was your life on the line, Agent Griffin," the president said sharply.

"He's still our best lead," Griff insisted.

The president thought for a moment. Wyman used the pause as a chance to jump in again.

"I have a question," he said. "Why didn't we know about this before?"

"We only made this discovery a few hours ago," Griff said.

"That's not what I meant," Wyman snapped. "Soldiers who don't need to eat, don't need body armor and can't be stopped. Why aren't we using this technology ourselves?"

Zach was pretty sure Wyman didn't see the president's look of annoyance.

"CEO Number Thirty-Seven," Cade said, his voice flat. "Signed by President Eisenhower in 1958. Expressly forbids the use of any of Konrad's discoveries by any agency of the U.S. government."

Zach finally recognized something Cade was talking about; he'd gotten that far in the briefing book. The CEOs—Classified Executive Orders—were how the presidents left instructions for their successors after they had been introduced to the big secrets, including the existence of Cade. The formal numbering only began with Roosevelt, during World War II. Before then, the presidents had merely written things down in a leather-bound journal that stayed in a safe in the Oval Office.

Wyman waved Cade off. "That was a long time ago," he said. "I'm sure Ike didn't know all the threats we'd have to face in the twenty-first century. He probably didn't intend to tie our hands like that."

"Actually, he did," Cade said. "I was there."

Wyman's scowl deepened, and he turned to the president.

"This is exactly what I was talking about before," he said, his voice creeping close to a whine. "When I see these things just going to waste, under glass in that little secret hideaway he sits in . . . These aren't artifacts. These are *weapons.* We should use them."

Griff made a noise, deep in his throat.

"Something to say, Agent Griffin?" Wyman asked.

Zach hadn't seen Griff's face like this before. The veep had done something Zach hadn't managed with all his needling. He'd pissed the old guy off.

"Yes, sir," Griff said. "Are you out of your fucking mind?"

Wyman's mouth dropped open. The president suppressed a smile.

"You are out of line, Agent Griffin," Wyman hissed.

"I'm not finished," Griff said. "Haven't you been *listening*? Those things aren't weapons. That's just the promise they dangle in front of the people stupid enough to use them. They're keys, and they open a door that has to be kept closed, at any cost. This isn't a policy debate. You haven't a fucking clue as to what I've seen, and you damn sure don't want it walking the Earth. *Sir.*"

Wyman's face went red. "We've already let evil inside," he said, looking at Cade. "Some might say we've let it get far too close."

Griff looked ready to fire back, but the president held up his hand.

"That's enough, Agent Griffin," he said.

"What about a missile strike?" the chairman of the Joint Chiefs asked. "Conventional or nuclear, those bastards can't walk away from that."

"No, they can't," Griff agreed. "Neither will anyone else in the target area."

The chairman made a face. "In other words, the only way to stop them from killing thousands of people is by dropping a bomb that will kill thousands of people."

"Maybe we could get some Predator drones into the air," the director of the CIA suggested.

"In domestic airspace?" Wyman shot back. "Are you insane?"

"And who would be at the trigger?" the chairman asked. "CIA or DOD?"

The men began talking over one another. Cade walked away from the table. The president noticed.

"Are we boring you, Cade?"

"Yes," he said.

A short, shocked laugh from someone. "Unbelievable," Wyman muttered.

"You have something to add, let's hear it," President Curtis said.

Cade looked at the ceiling, then back down at the men at the table. "Very well. Small words. If we are right, there will be dead soldiers walking down the street of an American city. Killing everything they find. Made of the pieces of men who died to protect this country. Mothers will see their dead sons' faces on television, doing horrible things.

And people will believe in the things in the dark again. Every time this happens, the Other Side gains ground. Its borders expand with fear. It feeds on our pain. And every corpse that is piled in the street will tell the world you failed to protect this nation."

That shut everyone up. Even Wyman.

The president looked at the photo of the tattoo, still on the screen.

"So what are our options?"

"We stop them before they are activated," Cade said. "That is the only option."

Zach knew he probably shouldn't say anything. But now he was scared, too. "Maybe it's too late for that," he said. "How do we know they haven't been fired up already?"

"Because no one is dead yet," Cade said.

THE PRESIDENT DIDN'T TAKE long to reach a decision after that. He ordered Griffin to stay in Washington and find out where the shipment came from and who sent it. Cade, he ordered to talk to Konrad, to treat him as a suspect, but not to do anything without proof.

"Like it or not, the man is a citizen now," he said. "You hear me, Cade?"

Cade nodded.

"Zach, you'll go with Cade," the president said. "Nothing like starting in the deep end."

He closed the folder and left the room, the Secret

Service men right behind him. Wyman was up like a jack-in-the-box, already complaining as they walked to the elevator up to the White House.

Without a word to Griff or Cade, Zach hurried out the door after them.

CADE AND GRIFF WATCHED them go. Griff, still seated, let out a huge puff of air; to Cade, his breath smelled of frustration.

"You know we should bring him in," he said.

"No," Cade said. "I should have killed him years ago."

Griff nodded. "But we have our orders," he said.

"We have our orders," Cade agreed. He was busy wiping the hard drive of the laptop, running a program that would scour it to the bare metal. No records of these meetings were ever kept, and the digital images from Zach's phone could never be allowed out of the P-OCK.

"What was that, with Wyman?" Cade asked.

"It's not like I'm worried about losing my pension."

Another uncomfortable silence. Cade really thought he'd be better at watching people die by now.

Griff nodded in the direction of the door. "Looks like the kid is going to try to quit."

Cade gave Griff his ghost of a smile. "I wish him luck."

ZACH CAUGHT UP with the president and Wyman at the elevator doors. The Secret Service stepped forward slightly. For a split second, Zach was flattered that they considered him a threat. Hanging with a vampire was raising his street cred.

The president made a small gesture, and they stepped back again. He shook Zach's hand.

"Zach," he said. "How do you like the job so far?"

You bastard, Zach thought. Out loud, he said, "Sir, I think you've made a mistake."

"I gave you my orders, Zach. You and Cade will question the doctor—"

"That's not what I meant, sir." Ordinarily, Zach would never interrupt the president, but he had to talk fast. The elevator down into the P-OCK took a while, and that was all the time he'd get. "I don't think I'm right for this job."

"I disagree," the president said.

"Sir, with all due respect, you're wrong. Unbelievably wrong. I am not the guy for this. You need a Navy SEAL or someone from the CIA. For God's sake"—Zach lowered his voice here—"when I met Cade *I wet my pants.*"

"He has that effect on people," the president said.

"Sir, please, if you want me to say I'm sorry about your daughter—"

The president took Zach around the shoulders and walked him away from the others. "Zach—you really think you're here because of what you did with Candace? I know you're smarter than that."

"Then why?"

The president looked him in the eye. "Because you *are* smart. You're resourceful. And you're loyal. Those are qualities that are hard to come by these days."

Zach might have imagined it, but he thought the president glanced back at Wyman.

"Believe me, Zach," the president said, "this is the most important job you could possibly have in my administration. Trust me when I say I need you to do this."

The elevator chimed softly. The president turned, and he and Wyman and the agents got on board. He looked at Zach. Then the SOB actually *winked* at him.

Zach just stared dumbly back as the doors closed.

ELEVEN

1967—So-called Night of the Living Dead incident, Evans City, Pennsylvania—Unintentional release of experimental compound based on the work of Dr. Johann Konrad (see "Baron von Frankenstein") causes recently deceased humans to regain metabolic function, i.e., "return to life." Revived humans attacked a farmhouse where non-affected residents of the area sought safety. The compound broke down after approximately eight hours, and the deceased "died" once again. No survivors.

—BRIEFING BOOK: CODENAME: NIGHTMARE PET

The next few hours were strangely dull for Zach—the usual hurry-up-and-wait of preparing for a trip. They took the car to Andrews Air Force Base. A man in a suit took the keys from them after they parked, and drove off fast in the direction of the runways.

Zach didn't have time to ask what that was about. The sky was getting light. He had to hurry to keep up with Cade as he entered a small hangar marked EVERGREEN AVIATION.

Inside, the space was mostly empty, aside from a few spare tires for landing gear, and a long, aluminum case.

Cade got inside the case and snapped the lid shut, without a word to Zach.

Zach didn't know what to do. He waited.

Everything that had happened in the past twenty-four hours began to pile up. He tried to assimilate all he'd learned by holding an imaginary press briefing in his head. He'd done a few while at the White House, and he found nothing focused his thoughts like fending off the jackals of the media.

Q: Mr. Barrows, you say you've been selected to assist a vampire? Are you quite sure you haven't had a psychotic break with reality?

A: Well, when I see him, my guts turn to water, and I have to clench everything I have just to keep from screaming in raw panic. And he's got fangs. So, yeah, I'm going to go with vampire.

Q: Does he feed on human beings?

A: He says not.

Q: And you believe that?

A: I've got no reason to doubt him. So far. Yes, Helen?

Q: What other supernatural elements is the U.S. government employing? Are there werewolves at the State Department?

A: You'd have to ask them. For all I know, they've got zombies at the IRS. All I can tell you about is the vampire.

Q: The material you handed out says he's vulnerable to sunlight and fire. What about garlic? Or silver?

A: Search me. I haven't bought him any pizza or jewelry yet.

[Laughter]

Q: This *Unmenschsoldat* threat—it sounds like a lot of people could die if you screw up.

A: That's not a question.

Q: What's this "Other Side" we keep hearing about?

A: I'm afraid that's classified.

Q: You mean you don't know.

A: And that's all we have time for.

Q: Mr. Barrows, is this really what you wanted to do with your life?

A: Thank you all for coming.

Zach thought it over. He was stuck. The president had made that clear. But maybe there was a way back into a real power position. If he did the job, went along with this madness . . . maybe he could get promoted. Or a transfer.

Two maintenance personnel entered wearing grease-stained coveralls. They picked up the case and walked out with it. Zach figured he was supposed to follow.

They loaded the case into a jeep and then drove out to a runway where a C-130 cargo plane was waiting, engines idling.

Inside the huge mouth of the plane, Zach saw the sedan parked, with more men in jumpsuits strapping it into place.

The maintenance men hopped out of the jeep, grabbed the case, and hustled it on board. Zach jogged after them.

The pilot—who wore coveralls without any insignia or patches—waited by the car. The plane was as big inside as an elementary school gym. He yelled something Zach couldn't hear over the engines, and turned for the head of the plane.

Up in the cockpit, the copilot was already seated. He pointed to a free pair of headphones. Zach put them on.

"—welcome to sit here, or in the back with your luggage," Zach heard, the words suddenly synching up with the man's moving lips.

The pilot flipped levers. Zach heard a bunch of terms he didn't understand through the headphones as the men went through the preflight. Stuff about deltas and niners and headers. Zach walked back into the cargo hold again.

In the back, the maintenance crew ran off the plane quickly, both the sedan and the case strapped down.

The plane lurched forward. Zach hurried to a seat near Cade's coffin. He felt like that's where he belonged.

Suddenly, the pilot was talking to Zach again. "Hey, you like Zep?"

"Uh . . . sure," Zach said.

He fastened his seat belt as the sounds of Jimmy Page's guitar began to wail through his headphones.

Maybe there really are werewolves in the State Department, he thought.

Then, despite the music and the roar of the engines, Zach fell asleep.

TWELVE

With the capture of the specimen by Operative Cade, actual physical examination reveals *A. Khorkhoi* to be a tentacle, the only visible part of a much larger creature. However, like a starfish, the tentacles are capable of detaching if seized, and can then grow another full-sized version of the creature. This may be the creature's only method of reproduction, and it is quite laborious and slow. The *Khorkhoi*'s lifespan measures on a scale similar to tortoises and trees. It's possible the same creature has existed since the time seawater covered the Mongolian desert, splitting off and forming new bodies as years and centuries pass.

—Notes of Dr. Peterson Sloane, Sanction V Research Group

THE RELIQUARY, WASHINGTON, D.C.

Griff felt a draft. The papers on the desk in front of him rustled slightly.

The only way that could have happened was if someone opened the hidden door, which no one else was supposed to know about.

It shouldn't have been possible, but he'd been at this too long to waste time on disbelief. Instead, he reached below the desk and put his hand around the stock of the modified Protecta Street Sweeper mounted there. The semiautomatic shotgun was designed to clear riots.

At the bottom of the stairs, he saw curly hair framing the cheerful, open face of a young woman barely into her twenties, almost a girl.

Tania. Thirty-three years ago, when she was still twenty-one and human, Cade had promised to save her. He'd failed.

Griff had been there. He saw it all happen. He never knew if she held a grudge against him.

Griff supposed he shouldn't have been surprised that she could find the secret entrance to the Reliquary. He suspected Cade had given her access once when he wasn't around.

She gave him her usual bright smile, like a cheerleader on meth. Vampires shouldn't be cute little strawberry blondes, Griff thought. It was just too disturbing.

"Where is he?" she asked.

"Nice to see you, too," Griff said.

Tania smirked. "Let's not be tiresome. I want to know where Cade is."

"He's working."

"Where?"

"Classified."

"You think I'm going to hurt him?"

"I don't know what you want, Tania. All I'm telling you is, he's not here."

"He's in danger. I need to speak with him. To warn him."

"I can take a message."

Tania's smile became a grim line. "Are you going to be difficult about this?"

He cocked the shotgun's lever back as quietly as he could. She still heard.

She looked at him a little more closely. "That thing between your legs won't stop me," she said.

Griff smiled back at her. "Doesn't mean I can't—" Griff said, and then couldn't speak.

She was behind him, her arm around his windpipe, the cool flesh of her cheek against his ear.

"Let's not fight, Griff. You know how Cade hates it when we fight."

She added a little pressure. Griff couldn't breathe. While he still had the strength, he shook his head.

A little more pressure. Spots danced before his eyes. Then, as suddenly as she was there, she was gone again.

Griff sucked down a huge lungful of air.

"Stubborn," she said, now back across the room. "So damn stubborn. No wonder Cade tolerates you." She sniffed. "Then again, it's not like you'd have a lot to lose if I did snap your neck."

Griff eyed her warily. "Everyone's so concerned about my health these days." He reached for the drawer that contained the holy water—something he should have done the moment he saw her.

She saw his hand move and took an exaggerated step back.

"I'm going. No need to be such a nervous Nellie. I guess you'll just have to live with it if anything happens to Cade."

"Cade can take care of himself."

"You better hope so."

She turned, and was gone up the stairs in a second.

Griff took out the vial of holy water just in case. It wasn't like Tania to give up on something she wanted. She was a pain in the ass that way even when she was human. Without the restraints of mortality, she was a feeding frenzy on two legs.

Then Griff looked down and realized why she'd left without a fight.

He'd been checking the cargo plane's flight schedule. It was right there in front of him, on the desk. Along with Cade's destination: Los Angeles.

So Cade was going to have someone tagging along.

For a moment, Griff considered going out after Tania. She wasn't as unstoppable as she liked to believe. He could have slowed her down. Or, if he didn't want to put in that much effort, he could have run her latest current aliases through the computer, in case she tried to fly commercial.

But for some reason, he decided to simply let her go. Maybe it was just his own troubles, but Griff had the feeling something bad was coming. Cade might need someone to watch his back. Sure, she was evil, inhuman and had a body count in the triple digits. But Griff had to admit, Tania was a hell of a lot more capable than Zach.

THIRTEEN

Edwards Air Force Base is probably best known from the movie *The Right Stuff* as the place where Chuck Yeager first broke the sound barrier in the X-1. Or you might know it from the stock footage of the landing of the first Space Shuttle.

But the base's real purpose—at least according to conspiracy theorists—is to test top secret aircraft designs based on technology reverse-engineered from the wreckage of intergalactic spaceships. If you believe the reports, these alien hybrid craft make a stealth bomber look like a balsa-wood glider with a rubber-band propeller . . .

—Secret America: A Guide to Deep Weirdness in the U.S.

They landed at Edwards Air Force Base, ninety miles outside of L.A., a couple hours before sunset. Zach woke with a start as the wheels hit the tarmac.

Cade popped out of his coffin just like the vampires in the movies, standing straight up as they landed. It was, like everything else so far, way creepier to see it in real life.

Cade got into the car before they opened the cargo doors, and stayed in the passenger seat even as the crew unstrapped the sedan.

If the pilots noticed the additional passenger, they didn't say anything.

Zach got behind the wheel.

"You sure you don't want to drive? I don't know—"

"I'm sure. Time is wasting. Let's go, twenty-three skidoo."

Zach smiled. "Twenty-three skidoo?"

Cade might have looked embarrassed. "I said, let's go."

Zach kept smiling. "Whatever you say, Grandpa Munster."

He drove down the ramp and off the runway, Cade directing him the whole way.

They passed the main gate at Edwards—Zach noticed the motto TOWARD THE UNEXPLORED on a sign—and got onto Highway 14, headed south.

They hit the evening rush hour. The highway looked like a giant parking lot.

Zach felt covered with a crust of grime; he was hungry and half deaf from the flight, and sore from sleeping in the cargo seat.

He sniffed the air. Something smelled. Zach wondered if vampires stank. Then he took off his jacket and realized the odor was coming from him.

"Hey, this suit is really getting ripe," he said to Cade. "I didn't get a chance to pack a bag. If it's okay by you, we'll stop at a mall, get something to wear—"

"No," Cade said.

"What?"

"You're not on vacation, Mr. Barrows. We have work."

"Dude, I'm really starting to stink."

"Yes. I know."

Nothing else. Zach thought about what he'd learned earlier.

"What if I ordered you?" he asked.

Cade looked at him. "Try it."

There was no change in Cade's tone or facial expression. But somehow, Zach got the unmistakable sensation that the vampire was threatening him.

"You know what?" Zach said, after a moment. "I'm fine."

"Good," Cade said.

At least Cade didn't seem comfortable, either. Despite the shaded windows, he fidgeted in his seat.

That was unusual. In the short time they'd spent together, Zach had noticed: Cade didn't move. Most people twitch, they tap their feet, swallow, turn their heads. They move around.

Cade didn't. He was perfectly still, until he wasn't. Then he made nothing but smooth, precise movements. Like the hands on a very expensive watch.

But he was flinching now.

"You doing all right?"

"I'll be fine."

Another long silence. Zach tried again.

"I bet you don't get out here much. California. Three hundred days of sunshine a year."

"I think that's part of the reason he chose to relocate out here."

Konrad. "So you know this guy?"

"It's a long story."

Zach waited. And waited. Traffic moved like an IV drip.

"Hey, you know what?"

Cade looked at him.

"You're the strong, silent type, I get that, I'm sure the ladies love it," Zach said. "And I know you think I'm nothing but a useless douche-nozzle. But I'm here. I am doing this job. So maybe you could talk to me like a frigging grown-up, huh?"

Cade was silent for the time it took to move forward two car-lengths. Then he started talking.

"In 1693, an alchemist in Germany named Johann Konrad Dippel was searching for the Elixir of Life—the key to immortality. Even returning the dead to life. He was rumored to be digging up corpses, experimenting on animals. You have to understand, just a few decades before, Galileo was arrested for saying the Earth went around the Sun. This was much, much worse. But he was nobility—a baron—and nobody could touch him."

"Diplomatic immunity."

"Something like that. The Baron lived a long time, especially in those days. People thought he'd found the Elixir. He went into seclusion. Nobody saw him for years. Then, one night in 1734, one of his creations got loose. The records are spotty, but it's supposed to have killed dozens before they brought it down. Then you had the mob scene. Another thing the movies got right. Villagers, torches, storming the castle. Only the Baron was gone. Again, there's not a lot of detail, but they found horrible things, in cages. Strange equipment. They destroyed it all. About a hundred years later, a writer named Mary

Shelley was on vacation, visited the village and the castle. Which was still named for the Baron's hereditary title—Castle Frankenstein."

Cade stopped. That was apparently the end. Zach needed a little clarification, however.

"Wait. You mean this guy is the inspiration for the story. He's *the* Baron Frankenstein?"

Cade nodded.

"You're telling me he's immortal?"

Cade considered that. "When you come right down to it, 'immortal' simply means someone who hasn't died yet," he said. "If you were to, say, pull out his spine and show it to him, he'd die like anyone else."

Zach shuddered. Maybe it was the A/C. Maybe it was Cade's tone. "So, there's some kind of history between you two?"

"Yes," Cade said. "Too much."

FOURTEEN

1970, Port Harcourt Province, Southern Nigeria Disputed Territory of Republic of Biafra

Cade walked ahead of Agent Griffin through the deserted streets. The town was behind enemy lines, and anyone who could manage to leave had fled. They'd heard what the Nigerian soldiers did to prisoners.

The war was close to an end. Everyone knew it. The Nigerians had run through the breakaway republic like knives through a piece of cloth. The Nigerians had MiGs and Kalashnikovs supplied by the Soviets, and money from the British to buy anything else. The Biafran army—what was left of it—went into the field with thirty rounds of ammunition and bolt-action rifles.

There were some who couldn't run, of course. Cade saw the child watching them, hollow-eyed and wasted, from an open doorway.

No food or medical supplies had been allowed inside Biafra for almost six months. Even Red Cross planes were fired upon. Millions of people were left scrounging in the bush for food.

They weren't very good at it. The Biafrans were shopkeepers, doctors, teachers and lawyers. They weren't prepared to play Tarzan, any more than the Duluth Chamber of Commerce.

The whole country was starving to death.

A second later, Griffin saw the child, too.

"Jesus Christ," he said.

"We've talked about that, Agent Griffin," Cade said. Griffin had been his liaison with the president for almost nine months now, fresh from the FBI, and before that, two tours of covert operations with the army. He was a strapping young man who used his brain like his muscles: apply enough force, problem gets solved. The only real change he'd made since taking the job was to let his hair grow. The shaggy sideburns he wore now reminded Cade of the last time they were fashionable, just before 1900.

"Sorry, I forgot your delicate sensibilities for a second," Griffin said. "The kid looks like a skeleton."

"You were in Vietnam," Cade said.

"So what? This is different," Griffin shot back.

Cade said nothing.

"You disagree, I take it?"

"Nothing humans do looks very different to me," Cade said.

They walked in silence to the town center after that.

The United States was officially neutral in the Nigerian

conflict. Nixon had no desire to get into another proxy battle with the Reds while still struggling to extricate America from Vietnam.

So Biafra was dying.

But Cade and Griffin went in anyway—taken by sub off the coast, then escorted by a navy team to the shoreline under cover of darkness.

They'd heard reports of something going on in the captured Biafran territory—something they couldn't stay neutral about.

The town was the last outpost of the Biafran government. Only their contact waited for them, sitting behind the wheel of a jeep parked in the center of the main square.

They came closer. The man was asleep. Air strikes had hit the town just a few hours earlier.

Griffin tapped the man on the shoulder. His eyes flew open. He saw their faces—their white faces—and relaxed, as much as he could.

"Apologies," he mumbled, wiping the exhaustion from his eyes. Like everyone else they had seen so far, he spoke English beautifully. It was the official language of Biafra. Cade wondered, for a moment, if that was meant to engender sympathy from America. If so, it didn't work.

The man sat up, extended his hand toward Cade. "My name is Joseph—"

He stopped abruptly and drew his hand back as if scalded.

Cade saw it in his eyes. Joseph knew. Somehow, he knew what Cade was.

Cade didn't care. "Where is he?" he demanded.

Joseph simply shook his head and got out of the jeep. He backed away slowly, never taking his eyes off Cade.

Griffin tried to get his attention. "Joseph, I'm Griff. We're here to help."

Joseph shook his head again. "No." He turned and began walking quickly away from them.

Griffin sighed. "Bring him back," he said.

Cade shifted, ever so slightly. Joseph was ten feet away—less than a hop for Cade. Suddenly he was in front of the Biafran man, who stopped, his shoulders sagging.

"You plan to kill me?" he asked.

"Not why we're here," Cade said.

"You called us, Joseph," Griffin reminded him, as he crossed the distance between them. "You know what's going on out there. You comfortable with letting it continue?"

Joseph glared back at Griffin. "You were comfortable with letting this happen to my country," he said. "You let all of this happen."

"Not our job," Griffin said.

Joseph's shoulders sagged even lower. For a moment, he looked ready to sleep, right there, on his feet. "No," he said. "Of course not."

He walked back toward the jeep without Cade or Griffin forcing him. He appeared resigned as he started the engine.

"Get in," he said. "I will take you there."

Cade sat in the back. Griffin took the front seat.

"How did you know about Cade?" Griffin asked.

"We're closer to the truth here."

Cade understood what he meant. Griffin didn't. "You some kind of witch doctor?" he asked.

Joseph gave him a weak smile. "I have a degree in economics," he said. "I was the deputy minister of finance."

They drove for an hour, the open country surrounding them on all sides. The jeep ran without a hiccup. Even without food, the Biafrans had gasoline. Their nation sat over a vast pool of oil, and as the war ground on, the refineries never stopped.

Griffin checked his watch. Sunrise would be coming in six hours.

Joseph read the gesture and understood. "We are almost there," he said. "Unfortunately, we're never far from the latest atrocity."

He cranked the wheel of the jeep to the left, and stopped. They were suddenly looking over a long trench.

Corpses. Dozens. Hundreds. Men, women and children. Cade's eyes fixed on a pair of tiny feet, jutting from under a woman's torso. Perhaps she had tried to shield the infant with her body. Perhaps she had just fallen that way.

He leaped out of the jeep and began checking the bodies.

It didn't take him long to find what he was looking for.

He lifted the evidence for Griffin to see: one of the bodies, its limbs neatly severed with surgical precision at the places where the arms and legs terminated in the air.

"It's him," Cade said. Then he looked at Joseph.

"There is a camp," Joseph said. "A few more miles. He should still be there."

"How many men?" Griffin asked.

Joseph looked amused. Something had finally struck him as funny.

"They won't be expecting a fight. Don't you see? They've already won."

They left the jeep a mile from the camp and continued on foot, taking great care not to make any noise.

But Joseph was right; the Nigerian troops were celebrating. They were gathered in a circle around a bonfire, electric lanterns casting harsh light on the center of their camp. A diesel generator churned in the background, blotting out most of their laughter.

Griffin and Cade watched as the Nigerians passed a bottle around.

The soldiers stood by a large metal trailer, a portable Russian field headquarters. The door opened, and a pale man with neatly combed white hair appeared. He wiped his hands on a towel stained dark with blood.

Cade recognized him from the last moment he had seen the man, wearing an SS uniform twenty-five years earlier. He had not aged a day.

Konrad.

Griffin took out his sidearm, checked the magazine. "Remember," he said to Cade. "We take him alive."

"What?" Joseph hissed.

"We have our orders," Griffin said, giving the man an apologetic shrug.

"After everything he has done, you will—"

"Quiet," Cade said, and they both shut up.

Two men in Soviet fatigues followed Konrad out the

door. Military advisers. Or more likely, bodyguards. Konrad was a valuable asset.

Unlike the Nigerian soldiers, they were not drunk. They looked alert and competent.

"I didn't bring you here to let him escape punishment," Joseph said to Griffin.

Griffin's voice held the last thread of patience, threatening to fray. "Look. I'm sorry your country got a shit deal, okay? But we have our job to do. And our job is to bring Konrad back alive, even if that means—"

"Agent Griffin. Look."

It had taken Cade a moment to see it. Fire was not his friend, and he unconsciously avoided it.

But as he pointed, it became clear even to Griffin and Joseph what Cade had seen.

The bonfire wasn't made of logs. It was constructed of old tires.

And the bodies of at least three people.

One of the Nigerian soldiers came from the bush, dragging another starved body. This one looked fresh. He hurled it onto the fire. Impossible to tell, in the firelight, if it had been a woman or a child, even for Cade's night-vision.

The soldier took a metal can from near the trailer and poured more gas on the fire. A huge ball of oily smoke went up into the air, along with a cheer from the other soldiers.

Biafra had no food, but there was still plenty of gasoline.

"Cade . . ." Griffin said. Cade realized he was emitting a low growl.

The skin was almost gone from the corpses. White bone burned to black.

"Cade . . . Konrad is the priority," Griffin said, his tone almost pleading. "I know it stinks on ice, but he could be finishing his weapon right now. He's got the parts. Cade, are you listening? Cade . . ."

Griffin said something else. Cade pretended not to hear it. He was already gone.

The hot, still air parted in front of him. He hit the men in the camp like a scythe.

Only Konrad moved, running back into the trailer and locking the door. The Russians were too shocked. The Nigerians didn't have time.

Out in the bush, he heard Joseph whisper, "My God."

Then it was over.

Cade turned to the Russians, who were still gaping at him. One raised a pistol, arm shaking badly.

"Cade, damn it, stop!" Griffin yelled. He was panting. He'd run from the bush. His .45 was up, and he had the Russians covered.

Cade edged forward.

"That is an *order*, Cade," Griffin said, his voice and the gun shaking. "We can't touch the advisers. The last thing we need is another incident with the Soviets."

Cade turned to him. "That's the last thing? Really?"

Without waiting for a reply, Cade moved to the trailer and tore the metal door from its hinges.

Inside was what looked like an army field hospital, but one turned 180 degrees from saving lives. Blood leaked off a steel gurney from mismatched pieces of human flesh. A large, complex machine stood in one corner, shielded from the dust by long plastic surgical tubes trailing from tanks and pumps.

They led to a row of chairs, lined up against the trailer's far side. In the chairs were young men—boys, really. Captured refugees from the war.

They were all dead. Desiccated. As if something vital had been sucked from all of them.

Whatever it was, it wasn't enough to spark life in the horror still on the table.

Konrad stood calmly by his aborted creation, hands in the air.

"You're here for me, I assume," he said.

Griffin had entered behind Cade. He looked around.

Konrad shrugged at the corpses. "Another failure. I thought they were healthy enough," he said. "But starvation has its drawbacks."

"You sick fuck," Griffin said.

"Oh, do not judge me so harshly," Konrad said. "After all, how different am I from your pet there?"

Cade wanted, very badly, to do what his orders forbid him from doing. "I am," he said, "nothing like you."

"Really?" Konrad smirked as he looked past Cade and Griffin, at the scene around the campfire. Bodies everywhere. Torn open, like burst sacks of blood. A mirror image to the carnage inside the trailer, the bodies like deflated balloons.

"You'd be hard-pressed to prove it," Konrad said.

Griffin took a pair of handcuffs from his belt and locked Konrad to Cade's wrist. "Don't push it," he said. "We could always make it look like an accident."

The Russians only watched as they dragged Konrad out. "*Dosvidaniya*, comrades," Griffin said.

Joseph drove them back all the way to the coastline. They arrived in plenty of time to rendezvous with the navy squad.

Griffin was speaking to the crew when Joseph approached Cade.

"What were you trying to prove back there?"

He meant the camp. Cade said, "I should have thought you'd want to see those men dead."

"I did, yes. But this isn't your country, or your war, remember?"

"I didn't do it for you."

"No," Joseph said. "You wouldn't have, would you?" He pointed at Konrad, who was being shackled by the sailors and loaded into the boat. "What will happen to him?"

"I don't know," Cade said. He had no reason to lie.

"You should learn. Because it's your responsibility now."

Cade was, for once, caught off guard. "What does that mean?"

"The boy"—he meant Griffin, who couldn't have been more than ten years younger than Joseph—"doesn't understand what you did here tonight. He has the same disease as all Americans. He believes the world can be made to behave, provided one is strong enough. He believes in the lesser evil for the greater good. He believes monsters can be tamed."

Cade couldn't argue with that.

"But you know better. You know what will happen if he's ever given the chance."

"Why would I know that?"

Joseph gave him the same sad smile as before. "Because you know yourself."

Griffin called to Cade then. The sub was waiting. Without another word to Joseph, he turned away and joined the others on the raft.

The air strikes began again as they paddled back to the sub.

Cade watched Joseph sit on the beach, as explosions in the distance tore the last of his country apart.

FIFTEEN

Subject's body does not produce fatigue poisons, and processes blood with a far higher efficiency than human digestion. Virtually all of the metabolic energy in the subject's blood meals is available for immediate use, or can be stored without conversion or loss of energy in the deep capillary beds in the subject's chest and abdomen. Subject will only grow "tired" after several days of consistent effort, and can be rejuvenated simply by feeding.

—BRIEFING BOOK: CODENAME: NIGHTMARE PET

LAS VEGAS, NEVADA

Dylan woke on the hotel bedspread. He'd heard that you weren't supposed to remember anything after a drunken bender. It wasn't true.

The room spun around him, yes, but he remembered everything. Stopping at the hotel. Just to rest, he told himself. He wasn't going to screw up now. Khaled was checking on him every few hours.

But he was bored. Nothing on TV interested him. He went for a walk. Not on the Strip. Too much temptation. He used to love the five-hour drive to Vegas, arriving at the tables, spending obscene amounts of cash and then drinking at the clubs.

But across the parking lot from his hotel, he found a dingy little strip club. He told himself he was just going in for a pack of cigarettes.

When he saw the naked women onstage, writhing around, humping the metal pole, he realized how much he'd missed tits and ass while in Kuwait. Burqas everywhere, covering everything. He'd almost forgotten what naked chicks looked like.

He sat down and ordered a beer. The waitress leaned over, breasts wobbling in his face, and asked if he wanted to open a tab. Without thinking about it, he handed over the credit card that Khaled had given him.

He ended up having another beer. Then another. The girls loved him. They sat on his lap, crowded around him and rubbed themselves all over him. He signed credit card slips. A lot of them.

Much later, he staggered back to his hotel, his shirt pulled out over his stained pants.

His face still hurt from grinning so much.

He found the strength to roll over, and thanked God that Khaled had not been around to see this. It was the first time in months Dylan had had any fun at all.

He finally got his feet on the floor and checked out of the hotel room. He started toward the large asphalt lot in back of the hotel, where he had parked his truck. It was in the same direction as the strip club, which made him smile again. His phone rang. He checked the number. Khaled. Just what he needed.

He answered, knowing it would only cause trouble if he didn't.

Khaled screamed at him in Arabic, then in English. Dylan had never heard him so angry. Demanding to know why the credit card they'd secured in a fake name for him was maxed out.

"I had some expenses," Dylan replied when Khaled paused for breath.

"What is 'Wild J's Lounge'?" Khaled fired back. "Did you forget I could see your charges on the Internet?" Before Dylan could respond, Khaled was questioning his intelligence, his ancestry, his devotion. . . .

Dylan quit listening. Screw Khaled. Self-righteous virgin. Let him come out here and do the hard work. So far, Dylan was the one taking all the risks. Let Khaled put his ass on the line for a change, and he could—

Dylan stopped in his tracks. The sound of Khaled's voice became very distant in his ears.

"I'll have to call you back," he said, and snapped his phone shut.

The truck was gone.

IT TOOK DYLAN an hour of standing at the front desk, talking to the fat, gum-chewing desk clerk—in slow, loud sentences—just to figure out what happened.

He cursed his luck again. How was he supposed to know that the lot where he'd parked was off-limits to trucks? He had to keep his mouth shut and stifle the urge to scream at every slack-jawed employee of the hotel. He couldn't draw any more attention to himself.

It wasn't easy. The clerk took another forty minutes to

find someone who knew where the truck had been towed. The city impound lot, halfway across town. A search through the phone book gave him a number, and a maddening voice-mail menu finally—after two disconnects—told him what he had to do. Show up, in person, with proof of ownership of his vehicle, and six hundred fifty dollars. Cash.

The recorded voice droned on, "Business hours are Monday through Friday, nine-thirty a.m. to five-thirty p.m. . . ."

Dylan felt his stomach clench again. He checked the time on his watch, just to confirm.

It was 5:34 p.m. He was stuck here until morning. At least.

His phone kept ringing in his pocket. He didn't answer.

SIXTEEN

As a result, at night, when fully nourished, subject has the strength of 20 men (bench press = 4,000 lbs.); can run at speeds up to 75 mph, and leap from a standing position roughly 24 feet into the air. Subject does not need to breathe, as long as he has fed recently. He can store oxygen in the blood he consumes for later use. In one test, subject stayed submerged underwater for over an hour.

—BRIEFING BOOK: CODENAME: NIGHTMARE PET

The doctor's offices looked like an enormous Art Deco mausoleum. Cade and Zach walked through glass doors that swung between the statuesque legs of an idealized, sexless human form that was molded into the building's façade. Tasteful pewter letters spelled out THE PROMETHEAN CLINIC—DR. JOHANN KONRAD, M.D.

The lobby was empty, except for the high-gloss slab of a reception desk and the sculpted blonde behind it. She smiled at them as they approached.

"Can I help you?" she asked.

"We need to see Dr. Konrad."

Her smile disappeared at Cade's tone.

"I'll have to see if he's in, Mr. . . . ?" She let the question hang there.

Cade flipped out the wallet with the DHS creds.

She only gave them a glance, then handed them back.

"I'm sorry," she said. "These could be faked. We can't let just anyone back into the offices. We have a problem with the paparazzi, you know."

Cade leaned closer to her. It was only a slight movement, but the receptionist rolled her chair back from him, her eyes widening.

Zach decided it was time to play good cop. "We thought it might be more convenient for him if we talked to him now," he said. "You know. After business hours."

That didn't help. "Actually, we're fully booked," she said.

Zach looked around the empty lobby. "Right now?"

She nodded. "Dr. Konrad's patients appreciate a certain flexibility in his schedule. Many people are still very judgmental about aesthetic enhancement."

"You mean plastic surgery?"

She relaxed a little. "As the doctor always says, we don't perform surgery on plastic. We allow human beings to reach their full potential."

Zach gave her his best aw-shucks grin. "Well, clearly the doctor did his best work on you."

Her eyes narrowed. "Actually, I've never been a client."

"Oh." Zach didn't know what else to say.

"Thank you both for stopping by," she said. "If you gentlemen would like to call and make an appointment—"

"Enough," Cade said. "Get him out here. Now."

Again, Cade barely raised his voice, but she pushed her chair back even farther.

"Just one moment," she said, and hurried through a door behind her desk.

"Smooth," Zach said, as they stood there. "Couldn't you hypnotize her or something?"

"It doesn't work like that."

"I thought vampires were all sex gods with the ladies."

Cade looked at him. "What gave you that idea?"

"Uh . . . late-night TV, mostly . . ."

"Humans are our food. Do you want to have sex with a cow?"

"Touché. So what do we do now?"

"We wait."

The door opened again. The receptionist was back, flanked by a massive escort wearing a dark suit over a T-shirt. Security.

"They showed me some phony badges," she said, pointing at Cade and Zach. "Get them the hell out of here."

The huge man came around the desk. Zach moved out of his way. Cade didn't.

He looked down at Cade. He was nearly a head taller, and built like the door of a bank vault.

Cade glanced at the man's hands. Knuckles distended. Layers of scar tissue. Mallet fingers, the third joint flopping dead and nerveless, the result of too many bad breaks.

The man was a boxer. A brawler. He was already half into his fighter's crouch, ready to bring his dukes up and go ten rounds.

He was no threat.

"Time to go, little man," he said, putting a hand on the vampire's shoulder to march him out the door.

Zach blinked, so he missed it.

Cade reached over and gave an effortless tug, and suddenly, the goon was on the floor, screaming in pain, his shoulder dislocated and twisted.

Cade looked back at the receptionist. "Dr. Konrad. Please."

Zach turned to see the big man get up on one knee, his face now full of rage.

"Stay down," Cade said, without looking.

The man reached inside his jacket pocket, gripped something there. Cade still wasn't looking, and Zach figured it out—

He was about to say the word "gun" when Cade moved. Zach saw it this time.

A casual sweep of Cade's hand before the weapon could clear the man's holster.

The plateglass window, shattering as the big man flew through it.

The receptionist screamed, but she was late to the party. Cade stood calmly. The big man was an inert lump on the pavement outside. Her wail died away almost comically. There was only the sound of the broken glass falling out of its frame.

The receptionist huddled against the door.

"I'll call the police," she said, nearly shrieking.

"That's not what your master instructed you to do, is it?" Cade said.

She looked at him, and Zach recognized the panic in

her eyes. He'd felt it himself. She was about to start gibbering and crying.

The intercom on her phone beeped to life. A voice—deep, cultured, very slightly accented—came through the tiny speaker.

"That's enough, I think," it said. "Laura, please show our guests back to my office."

Cade looked around, then up. Zach saw what he was looking at: a camera, set into the corner of the ceiling.

"Hello, Konrad," Cade said.

"Good evening, Cade," the voice on the intercom replied. "You could have called first."

THEY LEFT the security man outside. The receptionist led them back into the clinic, casting nervous glances over her shoulder.

They passed a number of doors to private exam rooms.

"How did you know he was here?" Zach asked.

"I could smell him."

Ask a stupid question, Zach thought.

They were at a set of double doors at the end of the hall. The receptionist opened them and hurried out of their way.

Konrad sat behind a steel slab of a desk with nothing on its surface but a computer that looked like a sculpture.

Despite snow-white hair, he didn't look much older than Zach, with handsome features set in a welcoming smile.

If he was nervous about them being here, he didn't show it.

The receptionist, however, danced from foot to foot like she had to go to the bathroom.

"You can go, Laura," Konrad said. "Please have someone fix the window. Tonight. Thank you."

She rushed out, pulling the doors closed behind her hard enough to slam them.

Konrad shook his head. "I hope this was necessary. You frightened the poor girl half to death."

"I have questions for you, Konrad."

The doctor rolled his eyes and smiled at Zach. "He's always like this. No social graces whatsoever. I am Johann Konrad. A pleasure to meet you."

He stepped from behind the desk, hand extended to Zach.

Zach moved to take it, more reflex than anything else. Cade blocked him.

"You don't need to know his name," he said to Konrad. He turned to Zach. "And you should know the first time we met, Konrad was working for the Nazis, spreading a fatal variant of the flu virus by handshake."

Zach put his hands behind his back. Konrad laughed.

"What can I say? I was young and impressionable." He looked at Zach. "We all make mistakes."

"Oh, sure," Zach said. "You were just experimenting with Nazism."

Konrad's smile faded.

"What do you want?" Konrad asked, returning to his seat.

"Unmenschsoldaten," Cade said. "Have you been working on them again?"

Konrad looked genuinely surprised. "What? No, of course not. You know the terms of my agreement. I am forbidden from . . . 'experimenting' anymore, as your friend puts it."

"You haven't been approached by anyone for the methods?"

"Absolutely not."

"No one has accessed your records here at the clinic, or spoken to you about the process?"

"I don't even keep those records anymore. The only place they exist is with your government. And we both know that's not as secure as it should be. What was the name of that man in 1957? Carlton?"

"We dealt with him," Cade said. "Who else has access to your files?"

Konrad laughed. "Who doesn't? This is the age of the Internet, Cade. There are no secrets anymore. I have seen all of the Nazi archives displayed on conspiracy sites. It's only the public's disbelief that keeps any first-year medical student from reproducing my work."

"That's not true," Cade said. "Your creations only really work with the Elixir. Which only you know how to create."

"We're going in circles here. I gave the formula to your government as part of our agreement. You know this."

"And you still know how to make it."

Konrad looked frustrated. "But I wouldn't. That's my

point. I have not broken our deal. I am a man of my word."

Cade looked at him for a long moment. Stalemate. Even Zach could see it. They had no way of disproving anything Konrad said.

"I can hear your heartbeat, you know," Cade finally said. "It's pounding like you just ran a marathon. Ever since I walked into the room."

Konrad's face flushed. His urbane demeanor dissolved into a scowl.

"That's very impressive, Cade. And I should care . . . why?"

"Just to let you know I can hear your heart, Konrad. And I could end that sound without too much effort at all."

Cade turned and started for the door. Zach guessed they were finished.

"Cade," Konrad said. "Whatever else you think of me, you should know I am grateful for my new life. This is the land of second chances, after all."

"It wasn't up to me," Cade said. "I wanted to kill you."

Konrad smiled at Zach, seemingly calm again. "You see what I mean about him having no social graces? Honestly, who says things like that?"

Cade turned and faced the doctor.

"I know you," he said. "I know that whatever else you say, you will never give up playing God. You don't even want to. Someday, you're going to overplay your hand. And I will be there."

Konrad gave Cade the ugliest look Zach had ever seen.

"It must be so frustrating for you," Konrad said. "To always be sent on these little errands. And to know they will never let you touch me."

Cade didn't respond. Zach followed him out the door.

SEVENTEEN

**1981, Lee Federal Penitentiary,
Jonesville, Virginia**

Cade stalked down the corridors of the penitentiary. Ordinarily, the presence of a visitor would have brought shouts, catcalls, even feces and flaming toilet paper from the cells. Not this time. This time, the prisoners simply watched until Cade passed by, and then they breathed a sigh of relief.

The guards escorting Cade gave him a wide berth as well. There was no outward sign of his anger. But you could feel it, coming off him like heat.

In the pocket of his coat, orders for a full pardon. Immediate release, citizenship privileges and a sizable check drawn on the U.S. Treasury.

Everything the prisoner had asked for, in other words.

A few hours earlier, Cade had watched it happen from a TV screen. He saw the gap in the Secret Service's line, the perfect angle for the camera. The president used to be an actor. He could never resist a good shot.

Leaving an opening for the cameras also left him open to a bullet. He never thought it would happen.

You could see the surprise on his face, captured on video, as the firecracker sound of the little handgun snapped away.

Six shots. At least one direct hit. Out there in broad daylight, where Cade was useless. It was 1963 all over again.

Before long, the phone rang in the Reliquary. It was still an old-fashioned landline then, directly wired to the Oval Office.

The president's chief of staff was on the other end. The bullets were Devastator rounds. Lead azide, designed to explode on impact. The press secretary was standing nearby, and half his head was gone. "One was right next to the president's heart," the man said.

He had an assignment for Cade.

Cade was flown to Jonesville in a special Air Force transport and then driven in a limo with specially tinted windows.

The press had heard the president was in bad shape. The White House got a lock on that, spun a story about the man joking with the surgeons. "I hope you're all Republicans."

In the meantime, Cade retrieved the only man who could repair the damage—who could bring dead tissue back to life.

Konrad was imprisoned in Jonesville. If he'd been in

any other facility, there would have been no hope. No way to get him to the hospital in time.

Jonesville was no better and no worse than any other high-security federal prison. Rape, drugs, murder. Cade honestly had not thought about it when they deposited Konrad there.

But when he got to the cell, he saw Konrad had sampled every one of the facility's offerings.

His face was scarred. There was a fresh bruise on his temple. Kept from his equipment and his potions, Konrad had even aged—his flawless skin beginning to pucker and warp.

Still, he stood with as much dignity as he could manage; his dirty hair combed with water from the toilet and swept back. He looked down at Cade, a baron in his mind if nowhere else.

A day later, the president was back on TV. Smiling. Joking. The Devastator rounds failed to explode, the press was told. Collapsed lung, nothing more. An inch from the heart. The president was a lucky man.

His mind never really recovered from the long period of clinical death, even though his body went on for years after. Toward the end of his second term, he would sit in his bedroom all day, still in his pajamas.

Cade remembered the look of triumph on Konrad's face when he arrived at the door of the doctor's cell. He smiled, revealing several missing teeth. But he looked no less happy.

"I told you, Cade," he said. "There will always be someone willing to pay for my services."

EIGHTEEN

There is a long list of individuals who have claimed immortality. It's easy enough to disprove the boasts of many simply by waiting around 40 or 50 years. However, if we are pressed for time, a search of the historical records will have to do. Leaving aside those who have been granted extremely long and durable lives by supernatural means—like our good friend Mr. Cade—there are at least nine individuals who appear to have been around for centuries, and have been verifiably sighted by different historians, at intervals as great as 500 years apart. Of those nine, several may play a role in U.S. interests. There is the Comte St. Germain, of course, who visited the White House not too long ago. . . . But we have recently been apprised of another one of these blessed (or cursed) beings, who is supposedly also the inspiration for the popular novel written by Mrs. Shelley about a scientist who discovers the secret of life through robbing graves. He's said to have offered his talents in the service of the German empire.

—Letter to President Theodore Roosevelt, dated 1903, signed only "HH" (Classified)

Konrad waited a full five minutes after Cade left, taking the time to get his breathing back under control. Over sixty years, and the hate was still there, rushing back to the surface.

There were times Konrad simply wanted to talk to Cade. He remembered an absurd burst of joy when he first learned of Cade's existence. He'd known about vampires before that, of course—he had been acquainted with the Other Side for a long time, because of his studies.

But with Cade, he thought he might have finally found someone who could understand. Other vampires abandoned the human world almost immediately, except to feed. Cade insisted on dressing and acting and talking like a person. He was still tethered to humanity, as much as Konrad was, but like Konrad, was above it.

Of course, Cade was much younger. And disappointingly moralistic, even priggish. Konrad had to abandon his fantasy of the two of them sitting down like civilized beings, perhaps over cards or chess, and discussing what they had learned in their long lives.

Cade hated him. Had from the moment he first saw Konrad. Konrad knew why, of course. He spent enough time with Sigmund, back in Vienna, to make a simple diagnosis. (Sigmund found him distasteful—probably for reasons even the analyst could not explain, or would ever care to plumb. But he was bound by the rules of polite society, of gentility, to converse with a man of Konrad's wealth and stature.) In Konrad, Cade saw a parasite feeding off the life of others. He despised that.

It was only a reflection. Konrad was just the surface on which Cade projected his own self-loathing.

Konrad was forced to conclude that Cade was too sentimental. He did not recognize what he was, how he was greater than the common mass of humanity.

It also kept him from recognizing Konrad's position, as far above Cade as Cade was from the common herd. That was why Cade would always fail. He did not know his place, Konrad decided. He was incapable of recognizing his superiors.

At last, it was time to remedy that.

He picked up his phone and dialed. It took a moment to connect; the encryption was always a bit slow.

"It's me," he said to the voice that picked up. "The president's pet bloodhound was just here."

A slight pause. "What did he want?"

"That's not the right answer," Konrad said.

Another pause, longer this time. "We'll handle it," the voice replied.

"Yes. I thought that was what you meant."

"There's no need to be snide, Doctor." Even through the electronic masking, Konrad could hear the wounded pride. "I simply wondered what you'd done to attract the president's attention."

"It doesn't matter."

"Are you sure about that?"

"Yes," Konrad said. "It doesn't impact our agreement. You don't need to know."

"You sound frightened, Doctor." Now there was a slightly mocking tone.

Konrad took another moment to compose himself. "Do you really think you're in a position to push me?"

Another pause. "I understand."

"No, you don't," Konrad said. "But you will."

NINETEEN

The subject's blood itself is filled with previously unidentified hormones, enzymes and antibodies. These compounds, which we continue to study, may explain the subject's immunity to our test-panel of diseases. Attempts to inoculate the subject with everything from the common cold (Rhinovirus) to AIDS (HIV) failed completely. Within an hour, no trace of any viral or bacterial contaminants could be found in the subject's blood. Similar efforts with bioweapons (powdered anthrax), nerve agents and gases were also unsuccessful.

—BRIEFING BOOK: CODENAME: NIGHTMARE PET

Zach followed Cade to the parking garage attached to the clinic, headed for the sedan.

"What did you think of him?" Cade asked.

"Give me some credit," Zach said. "Guy's more full of shit than a duck pond."

Cade's mouth twitched at the corner before settling into its usual stony calm.

Cade opened the trunk, and retrieved a black nylon case. He unzipped it, and revealed an array of electronic gizmos held by Velcro straps.

Zach grinned. "Sweet. Finally some superspy tech."

Cade resisted the urge to sigh. He turned on the small, battery-powered GPS tracker. A signal lit up on his sat-phone.

Then he found Konrad's parking space, Zach trailing along behind.

The doctor's Ferrari was parked under his RESERVED sign. Cade looked around for cameras and then ducked under the rear wheel. The rare-earth magnet on the tracer stuck to the axle like glue.

Zach watched, still grinning. "So what do we do now?"

"Now, you wait here. Konrad has several cars. Tomorrow morning, you do the same thing I just did if he comes to work in a different one."

Zach's face fell. "That's it?"

"For the time being, yes."

Zach stewed all the way back to the sedan. Cade figured the tantrum would come before they exited the garage. Zach didn't even make it inside the car.

"You know, I'm getting a little bit sick of this," he said. He stared at Cade over the roof of the sedan. "You're supposed to take orders from me, remember?"

It suddenly occurred to Cade why Zach annoyed him. He was completely convinced that he knew the shape of the world, and resisted every attempt to knock him out of that certainty. Cade had not dealt with anyone like that for decades.

In short, he was young, and he made Cade feel *old*. That was a human feeling—one he hadn't had before. Not ever.

He wasn't sure what to make of it.

He knew Zach was frustrated and acting out, trying to assert control over an arguably insane situation.

It didn't make him any less irritating, however.

Cade buried the feelings. "It doesn't quite work like that."

Zach wasn't going to be put off. "So how does it work? Tell me. What happens if I give an order and you don't follow it?"

"You don't want to know."

Zach rolled his eyes, then reached inside his jacket and came out with a small silver flask.

"Actually, I do."

Cade couldn't sniff the contents of the flask—it was sealed tight. "What is that?"

Zach looked inordinately pleased with himself. "About twelve ounces of type O negative, I think."

"What? Where did you get that?"

"I swiped it from the doctor's fridge, when I told you I was looking for the restroom."

Cade stepped back from the car. His hands were shaking, and despite his best efforts, they would not stop.

"Why would you—why?"

"Because I want to know, Cade. What kind of vampire doesn't drink human blood?"

"I won't do it."

"Sure you will. I'm following the rules. I just gave you a lawful order. And I'm the president's representative. As far as you're concerned, that's the same as coming straight from him." Zach's smug look was just about unbearable now. "So drink up."

Cade felt his right foot move, as if on its own, back toward the car. The first step to taking the flask and downing it, all in one long, easy gulp . . .

His mouth was full of saliva. He found it difficult to talk. "Please," he said. "I'm begging you."

Zach laughed. "Begging me? I thought you were the guy in charge, Cade—"

He didn't say anything else, or Cade didn't hear it, because that's when the seizures started.

His right hand reached out for the flask, so he drove it into the door of the car instead. The panel crumpled under the impact. The force under all his thoughts shoved its way to the front of his mind, telling him to just pick up the flask and follow the order. He stood in front of it like a man before a tidal wave on the beach, trying desperately to keep his footing in the sand.

His body thrashed away from him. Pain, overriding his nervous system. Punishment. His legs kicked out, and vaguely, he noticed a fender torn off the driver's side of the car.

Mme. Laveau's voice came back to him, bigger than anything, softer than silk. *"By this blood, you are bound,"* it told him, *". . . to the orders of the officers appointed by him . . ."*

He screamed, to drown it out. Because even if it left him in ruins, he swore, *never again*, not one drop, no matter what.

He thought back to a ship, the last night he had been human. He remembered how he had failed to stand against the darkness. And how easy it would be to just give in to it again.

No. Never again. No matter what.

Then he heard another scream, a different voice. The sound of sheer panic. It took him a moment to recognize the voice. To connect it with a name.

Zach. "—Jesus Christ, Cade, I'm sorry, I'm sorry, I take it back, I take the order back—"

A lawful order, from an officer of the president.

The pain vanished. The certainty moved back to its normal place, in the back of his mind.

The gray cleared from his vision, and he noticed he was on the floor. His fingers had carved small furrows in the concrete.

Zach was next to him, worry and fear on his face.

Cade had bitten through his lip. He pulled his fangs back in, and shifted to a sitting position. He leaned against the door of the sedan. He didn't think he could manage standing just yet.

Zach had never stopped talking. Of course.

"—I didn't know, I swear, I mean, holy shit, holy *shit*, Cade, I'm sorry, I really didn't know, I just—"

"You just wanted to find out how far you could push," Cade said. His voice was a croak, strangely distant in his own ears.

Zach kneeled down closer to him. The flask was in his hand.

"Please," Cade said. "Get that away from me."

"What? Oh, this?" Zach opened the flask, and the smell touched Cade like a burn.

Zach took a quick swig.

"Whiskey," he said. "Graduation gift from my dad. I

carry it around everywhere. I figured by the time I actually opened it, it would be twelve-year-old Scotch, instead of the cheap crap he put in there."

Cade stared at him for a long moment.

Zach finally looked away. If he wasn't ashamed, he was doing a good job imitating it.

"I'm sorry," he said. "I wanted to know."

"Now you do," Cade said.

Slowly, he got to his feet. He looked at the car. The rear driver's-side door was wrecked. The window had cracked, but not shattered. The right front fender had been sent across the garage. There were scratches in the paint Cade didn't remember making, and a fist-shaped dent in the roof.

Zach tried to help him up. With more force than he intended—maybe—Cade shook him off.

"Cade. Seriously, man. I'm sorry."

"Stay here," Cade said. "Wait for Konrad to leave, then call me. If I don't answer, call Griff. He'll tell you how to activate the tracker on my phone."

Zach looked worried. "You're leaving me here? Where are you going?"

Cade walked over to the side of the garage. They were on the fourth story. The parking structure was open to the air. He breathed in deeply, smelling the night-blooming jasmine, the heavy metals in the smog.

His hands were still shaking.

"Let me give you a word of advice," Cade said to Zach. "I'm not human. Don't make the mistake of treating me like one."

“What’s that supposed to mean?”

“You remember that magician in Las Vegas? The one who was mauled by the tiger he’d used in his act for years?”

Zach nodded.

“You can bring it inside, put it on a leash and dress it up, but a wild animal never really loses the taste for blood,” Cade said. “You might want to consider that before you test me again.”

Cade leaped over the side, and was gone.

TWENTY

In spite of its famous name, Frankenstein Castle is little more than a pile of rubble south of Darmstadt today. But in the 17th century, it was the home of Johann Konrad Dippel. Born in 1673, Konrad eventually entered the seminary, where his teachers and fellow-students alike admired his quick mind. But the adulation may have been too much, combined with his natural arrogance. Konrad was said to question the Catechism at age 9, and while in school, also practiced palmistry, read the Tarot, and discovered what would become his abiding passion, alchemy. His obsession with mortality is evident in the title of his 1693 master's thesis, *De Morte (On Death).*

—*Chapman and Ainsworth,* Lives of the Alchemists

Konrad wanted relaxation after this pig's ear of a day. He pressed his intercom. Laura told him the contractor was just finishing with the new window. He told her to go home. Then he checked his watch. He had some time to kill.

Konrad moved into the next room, an opulent lounge complete with wet bar, where he would entertain celebrity clients who preferred leather chairs to paper-covered exam tables. He poured himself a drink and checked his reflection in the mirror above the bar.

No one could say he looked his age. But there was a slight sagging to the jowl he didn't like, and there, a slight thinning at the crown . . .

He took out his mobile and called Nikki. She was more than happy to come over to his office, despite the time.

Nikki was a beautiful girl, raised by adoring parents, pursued by handsome boys in a pain-free suburb of Chicago, where she did modeling for catalogs and believed everyone who told her she should be in movies. Los Angeles came after a degree in communications. She thought she would be an actress, or at least an anchorwoman.

Two months in, she was working for a "modeling agency" that specialized in providing pretty, available girls in the right situations. She moved into Konrad's orbit after a party where she'd been hired to dress up the scenery by serving as a human sushi platter. Naked under carefully placed salmon and unagi rolls, she'd smiled at him.

She came when he called, and always left with money and gifts. She would have slapped anyone who called her a whore.

Konrad was getting bored with her, but she was reliable.

Within the hour, she arrived. No one saw her enter, because she used the door that opened into the adjacent alley, another service Konrad offered his famous patients.

She entered the lounge, pink and warm from a recent shower, her tight young body bound up in expensive gym clothes. Konrad smiled and pretended to care about her difficulty with the rush-hour traffic.

She was going on about something else while he stood

behind the bar, fixing her a drink. Predictably, she loved icy, frothy concoctions that required him to use the blender.

That gave him an idea.

He cut her off mid-sentence and called her behind the bar.

"How would you like to compete in a little game show?" he asked.

She came to his side, smiling.

"Well, I don't know. Is it network or cable?"

"It's right here," he said, dumping the pink mess out of the blender, revealing the stainless steel blades. "It's called 'Trust.'"

She giggled. It was her response whenever she didn't know what was going on, like a cat grooming itself.

"I will give you—*give* you—twenty-five thousand dollars. Cash. I will pay your rent for the next three months. I will even throw in the lease on a new Mercedes SL"—and here, he pitched his voice like a TV announcer—"that's right, *a brand-new car.*"

Nikki stood there, her smile going rigid. "What do I have to do?"

"Almost nothing," Konrad said, smiling himself now. "You just have to trust me."

He took her hand in his own and placed it in the blender. It was delicate and small, and fit easily.

She jerked back, but he held her there. "That's the game, dear. Do you trust me?"

She looked into his eyes. He took his hand away. And she kept her hand where it was.

Konrad nodded. And then he hit the button marked PURÉE.

Her screams were mixed with the sound of the blades spinning.

She tried to pull away again, but this time he grabbed her wrist and wouldn't let go.

Blood was spattered over both of their faces when he released the button and her wrist, at the same time. She curled into a ball, clutching her mangled fingers to her chest, shrieking.

Konrad let out a deep sigh, savoring it. His windows were soundproofed, of course.

"You win," he told her.

"THERE, THERE," KONRAD SAID, his tone soothing as he escorted her into the exam rooms. "It's going to be fine."

Nikki sniffled, tears running down her face, her mangled hand clutched to her chest. It was bleeding through the bar towel Konrad had wrapped around it.

"You can really fix it?" she asked, for what seemed like the hundredth time.

Amazing, he thought. Not even a hint of anger. Just pleading with him to make it better.

At moments like this, Konrad thought he might as well have been from another world. When he was a boy, everyone was an enemy. His father had taught him that. Everything his father had, he had because he had taken it, and killed anyone who would take it away. Death was everywhere, waiting patiently. Germany was still a collection of principalities devastated by the Thirty Years' War. His father could remember the armies of mercenaries that scoured the land clean, spreading famine and disease. The greatest treasure of all was life, he would often say. It had to be guarded, constantly.

Centuries later, Konrad still couldn't fathom these children who grew up surrounded by abundance, unable to comprehend hunger or desperation. Who put their trust in strangers. Who expected to be safe as they skipped merrily from their homes and playgrounds.

Girls like Nikki were so alienated from the idea that anyone would hurt them, they couldn't believe it was real, even when it happened. No matter what their age, they seemed like infants to him.

"Of course, I'll fix it," Konrad said. "You won't even know the difference when I'm done."

It wasn't entirely untrue.

Konrad took her back into his private operating room, the one where he did his real work. No patient was ever allowed to see this part of the clinic.

"Why do you have those animals in cages?" she asked.

"Testing," he said. "An unfortunate reality of medicine. We can't test on humans."

"What's wrong with that one?"

She shivered. It wasn't shock, or blood loss. He had to move.

"Please," he said. "We have to hurry. Lie down."

She hesitated, biting her lip. Her tears had erased most of her makeup. She looked like a child now.

"I think you did it on purpose," she said.

Konrad tried not to sigh or roll his eyes. "No," he insisted. "It was an accident. My finger slipped. I told you before."

"Maybe we should just go to the emergency room," she said.

"All they will do is stitch you up," Konrad said. "I'll make you beautiful again. Flawless."

Nikki waited a moment more, then nodded. She got on the steel table, on her back.

Konrad took a syringe out of a drawer and shot Nikki up with a combination sedative and paralytic. She began to doze off immediately, her eyes fluttering.

Konrad went into the corner and took a heavy sheet off a piece of equipment.

Nikki's eyes snapped open again when he wheeled the machine into view. Of course by then she couldn't move.

Her breathing quickened. "What is that thing?" she asked, struggling to raise her head. "Why can't I move?"

"Shhhhh," he said, stroking her hair. "It will all be over soon."

Again, not entirely untrue.

"What are you doing?" Her voice was little more than a whisper now.

"I'm sorry, Nikki," Konrad said. He kissed her forehead. "I need something from you."

She tried to scream, but the drugs would barely allow

her to breathe. He had to get started. He needed her alive for this procedure.

Konrad maneuvered the machine into place. It looked like an industrial press mated with a Portuguese man-of-war: tubes unrolled from the main body of the machine, slithering over her body. He flipped a switch and the tentacles came to life, writhing over her skin, seeking purchase. Flat disks at the end crawled into position, on her arms, legs, neck and chest. Then, with a sudden snap, they burrowed in.

Nikki felt it, despite the drugs. He could tell by the widening of her eyes.

The machine began to drink. The tendrils began drawing her life, her actual essence, from her, along with all the cells and vital fluids that carried it.

Nikki's arm hung limply off the table. The bar towel had come unwrapped, and her blood dripped onto the tile floor.

The machine kept working. In less than a minute, the blood slowed to a trickle, then stopped completely.

Konrad watched the dials and monitors as the vials within his machine filled. Another process was already starting, which would concentrate the harvest down into its purest form.

Konrad had what he needed. But there was still plenty left. He never believed in wasting anything.

From the center of the tentacles, another hatch opened. The machine sprouted a bouquet of gleaming steel: scalpels, saws and blades, each on its own mechanical arm, arranged in a circle.

They whirred to life, almost merrily, as they lowered to the body and began slicing.

The skin, which came off in great strips, could be reduced to slurry and made into collagen filler to plump up sagging body parts for his patients, to restore lips to the fullness of youth, or even inflate a man's penis to the size he thought he deserved.

The bone, chipped away and captured by the extended probes, would be used to rebuild noses, chins and jawlines. The meat of the muscle and cartilage could repair ruined joints and tendons. And of course, there was a booming market in organ replacement for those who didn't want to wait on a transplant list.

The machine carved it all away and collected every piece, sucking it away to vacuum-sealed jars and plastic containers for freezing.

Konrad didn't have to watch. The machine did everything almost by itself now. He'd been at this for years, perfecting its mechanisms. He could have gotten himself a coffee.

But he enjoyed the show.

A small light—dignified, restrained, Konrad thought—signaled that the fluid had been processed. While his marvelous machine stored away Nikki's tissues and organs, he prepared a syringe.

The vital fluid filled less than 2 cc's. Still, it was enough. He loaded the life-essence into the needle, then injected it into his veins.

He shuddered. Felt hair growing on his scalp. Felt skin tighten, the paunch at his belly flatten out.

Konrad had wrested the secret of eternal life from corpses, stolen from their graves centuries before.

Eternal *youth*, however . . . that required something a little . . . fresher.

Konrad disposed of the needle in a sharps container, put on his jacket and walked to the door. He glanced back at his machine, just before he switched out the lights. The steel table gleamed as if nothing had ever been there.

AT ABOUT SEVEN P.M., Zach watched from the sedan as Konrad left the elevator and strolled to his car. The Ferrari sounded like a jet fighter about to take off. Konrad slid out of the parking space as if greased, and the car vanished down the ramp.

The GPS locator on Zach's phone began blinking immediately, showing a red dot moving away on a grid, farther from his position.

The thing was idiot-proof. He could follow Konrad all over town if he wanted.

And really, why shouldn't he?

He wasn't Cade's sidekick or errand boy. He was an officer of the President of the United States, and he was damn sure going to act like it.

He started the engine of the sedan—the fender Cade had kicked rattled loudly—and then took off after Konrad.

ZACH'S CAR HIT THE STREET. A black car waited in a metered space half a block away.

Its windows were tinted, and from outside, it looked as if it were filled with a liquid darkness, blacker than ink, deeper than oil.

When Zach turned the corner, the black car merged into traffic and followed.

TWENTY-ONE

Research (see "Vampire King" file) indicates most vampires of Cade's age would be much stronger, and faster, with a range of abilities Cade does not possess. But unlike other vampires, this subject sustains himself with animal blood. He refuses to drink the blood of a human, even though human blood is what his vampiric body is designed mainly to consume and metabolize. (He refuses to drink even transfused human blood, viewing it much the same way an alcoholic views liquor.) If there were some way to overcome the subject's squeamishness in this regard, there is no telling how effective an agent he might become.

—BRIEFING BOOK: CODENAME: NIGHTMARE PET

Neon Hangul characters glowed above the entrance of the place where the AA meeting was held, a rundown auditorium near Koreatown. The lobby was plastered with posters for get-rich-quick seminars, and the interior was filled with rows of salvaged theater seats. Cade took one near the back.

He had been going to AA since shortly after World War II. The war had not been easy for him. He was certain, at many times, that he was on the losing side, that the darkness was winning against the light. Even aside from the otherworldly evil that Hitler's occultists summoned up, the merely human brutality was almost too much to bear: Auschwitz and Dachau, Bataan, even the internment camps in the U.S. Many times, he was tempted to start drinking from the fountains of blood that seemed to spring up all around him.

The thirst didn't go away after V-E Day. Coming back to the States, he found his faith almost undone. Winning hadn't solved that. He thought they were lucky.

Everyone said they had saved the world. He didn't believe that. Worse, he was no longer sure it deserved to be saved.

One night in 1947, he'd stumbled into a church in New York. It hurt—any house of worship did, even more than the cross he still wore around his neck. But it was better than the thirst.

He was surprised to find people there. They were telling stories—how they had struggled, and often failed, to control their own need for a strong drink. And yet, they kept struggling. Kept fighting.

He listened for as long as they talked and then came back again the next night. Then he would find a meeting whenever he could.

The people never asked him to say anything, or even introduce himself. He was careful, over the years, to vary his patterns, so no one would notice that alone, out of all the drinkers, he never aged. Even so, the people at the meetings always respected his privacy.

It wasn't the same thirst. He knew that. But it helped. He wasn't sure exactly how, but it helped.

He needed to hear that right now. The taste of his own blood was bitter in his mouth, and he didn't like thinking how much he had wanted to give in to Zach's order—to drain the flask and then keep drinking, to drown in oceans of blood if he could.

Someone up front was talking about receiving his one-year chip when a man sat down next to Cade in the back.

He was dressed in expensive but casual clothes, munching one of the free doughnuts, a cup from Starbucks in the other hand.

"What's up?" he asked Cade, not bothering to lower his voice. A few people turned in their seats and looked back, but he didn't notice.

Cade didn't respond, which didn't make a difference. The man kept talking, without a pause for breath.

"You new? I'm new. I mean, to this place. I've been to other meetings. But a friend of mine said this is where Robert Downey, Jr., comes. You seen him?"

Cade gave the man a look, then pointed at the speaker.

The man nodded, smiled and went a whole three seconds before talking again. "See, confidentially, I don't really have a problem with alcohol. I mean, aside from when it's last call and they cut me off, know what I'm saying? It's just, I hear this is such a great place to network."

The man didn't smell of booze. Cade couldn't believe it, but he was drunk on nothing more than his own fumes.

"Frankly, you don't look like one of these other losers. I mean, if you have a problem, I don't mean to offend ya. You look like you've got it under control. I'm Brad. Brad

Lawrence," he said, polishing off his doughnut and offering his hand in one move.

Cade stared back. For the first time, Brad seemed to actually notice him. He gulped.

"So . . . uh . . . how long has it been for you? Since your last drink, I mean."

Cade decided to answer him. "Fifty-one thousand, nine hundred and sixty-eight days," he said quietly.

Brad did the math in his head. Then he gave Cade a strange look and moved to another seat.

Cade felt something like amusement, or as close as he got. His humanity was long gone, and he would never get it back. He was beyond redemption. He knew that. But these meetings reminded him what humanity was—both how small and how great.

It reminded him of what he'd lost, and that was important. Aside from the cross around his neck, it was the closest thing to an article of faith Cade had left.

TWENTY-TWO

The term "vampire king" isn't strictly accurate, in that it doesn't refer to a leader of the Vampire Nation, as we've come to call them. Vampires, from what we've seen, are obsessively territorial and isolationist, much like any other apex predator, with limited social interaction. If a human were to exhibit these same tendencies, we'd call them sociopathic. But like other apex predators, they respect strength, and the "vampire king" is roughly the equivalent of a bull elephant—the biggest, most powerful member of its species. Of the few hundred vampires believed to exist worldwide, there are perhaps two or three vampire kings—maybe as few as two or three in the entire species' history. These king vampires do not seem to exercise any authority over the rest of the Vampire Nation other than the rights allowed by brute force. Any vampire who does not yield to a king vampire will probably find its unnatural existence put to a quick end.

—Notes of Dr. William Kavanaugh, Sanction V Research Group

Cade stood outside as the meeting broke up, taking a moment to absorb the noise and scent of the people as they left. They talked about their jobs, traffic, the unbelievably crappy streak the Lakers were on. They lit cigarettes, jangled their keys in their hands, or walked away without looking at anyone else. More than anything else, this is what he needed here.

"You are such a masochist, Nathaniel."

The voice came from behind him. She wrinkled her nose at him and giggled. As always, when he saw her, Cade thought of a song popular during World War II, about a girl who wouldn't sit with anyone else under the apple tree.

Then she smiled a little wider, showing her fangs, and ruined it, like she did every time.

"Hello, Tania," he said. "What are you doing here?"

She looked at the crowd as it broke up, and her eyes danced again. "I knew I'd find you at a place like this. Really, Cade, you're such a martyr."

"What do you want?"

"Oh, don't be like that. Can't a girl say hello to an old friend?"

Several men stared at Tania as they moved down the sidewalk. She sized them up in return, like a lion watching gazelles.

"Are we still friends?"

"We must be. I'm here to give you a little advice," she said. "Konrad has placed a contract on your life. He's put out inquiries. He wants you dead. Truly dead. Head or heart. Then ashes."

Cade noticed that not one person passing by turned their heads, even though Tania made no attempt to be quiet. That was, perhaps, the only quality he enjoyed about L.A. No matter what you said, people simply assumed you were talking about a movie.

"Interesting," Cade said.

Tania waited. Cade didn't speak.

"Is that it? Aren't you going to do something?"

"What would you have me do?"

"Kill him."

"I can't. I've been given orders. And it's not a crime to try to kill me. I'm not even alive."

"Idiot," she said. "I don't know why I bother."

She turned to go, but Cade grabbed her arm. He put just enough pressure in his grip to let her know he was serious.

"Why do you bother, Tania? You were in New York. Why would you come all this way?"

She stepped closer to him, getting into his personal space. Even in heels, she had to look up at him.

"Believe it or not," she said, "I still care about you."

"Interesting."

"What's that?"

"I would have thought a murderer would be a better liar."

She scowled and stepped back. "Funny. That was almost funny."

"I've spent time with a comedian lately."

She made a face. "Another one of them?" Nodding at the people going by. "Why do you do it? I will never understand why you spend so much time socializing with the stock."

The stock. As in livestock. His kind's term for humans. The first time he heard it, he realized how perfectly it summed up their contempt for people: an undifferentiated mass of food. It didn't surprise him at all that Tania used the name every chance she got.

"Maybe I'm trying to make up for old mistakes," he said.

"Oh, God," she moaned, and almost sounded like a teenager again. "Do *not* try to put this on me, Cade. I have told you, over and over. You tried to save me from eternal youth and godlike power. I'm happy you didn't."

Cade's self-control broke, and the anguish shone on his face.

"Don't do that," she said. "You look like I just killed a puppy."

"This isn't life, Tania."

"Talk to me in another hundred years. If you live that long. You know what happens if you don't feed on the stock?"

Cade made a face. "You're going to tell me the others like us view me as a traitor. I've heard it before. And everyone who made that threat is—"

She cut him off, rolling her eyes. "Yes, yes, I know how frightfully tough you are, dear. That's not what I was asking. Do you know what will happen to you if you don't drink?"

Cade just looked at her.

"It's like putting kerosene in an engine meant to run only on premium unleaded," she said. "Already, you're less than you should be. Keep denying your body what it needs, and it will just get worse. You'll be less resilient, less able to process damage, less efficient. You'll get tired. You'll get *old*."

"I'm not afraid of dying."

"Who said anything about dying? The change will keep you alive—but your body will wear down. Eventually, you'll be decrepit. Feeble. An old man, forever. No one will even bother to put you out of your misery."

"You're right," he said.

That stopped her cold. "I am?"

Cade smiled. "I'm older than you. I may not get invited to the family gatherings, but I've seen what happens to those of us who don't feed on humans."

Cade had seen a vampire at the end of the cycle—starved of human blood, left to feed on whatever vermin he could find, as a punishment.

It wasn't pretty, even for their kind.

He remembered the starving vampire's parchment skin, crisscrossed with deep lines. His joints frozen with disuse. Tumors swelling his abdomen. And his eyes, screaming with pain, begging for release.

It was an object lesson. One he had chosen to ignore.

Tania asked him, "And your purity is worth that much to you?"

He did something he didn't do very often. He laughed. At her.

"I'm not pure," he said. "And yes. It is."

"Idiot," she said again. There was no teasing in her voice this time.

Cade's phone buzzed in his jacket. ZACHARY BARROWS, the display read.

"I have to go," he told her.

"Don't let me keep you," she said, her voice light and

mocking. "I was headed over to the Christian women's college for a bite to eat anyway."

He was already walking away, his back to her. She'd find him again. She always did.

Cade had other priorities right now.

TWENTY-THREE

Likewise, some vampiric abilities we can regard as mere myth. Cade has not proven capable of changing into a bat, or fog, or a wolf. These stories no doubt rose from accounts of vampires' actual speed and strength, which are impressive enough. But we can safely say that for all the power Cade has displayed, vampires cannot fly, or change shape.

—BRIEFING BOOK: CODENAME: NIGHTMARE PET

Tania wanted to hit Cade in the back of the head as he walked away. She didn't know why she bothered. It was like spraying graffiti on a wall and expecting the wall to learn English.

She'd even had herself shipped FedEx for him. In a *crate*. She hated to do that.

Tania didn't know how Cade could stand at the edge of a never-ending feast, a buffet that stretched for eternity, and not join in. She didn't know what he had inside him that replaced the need.

And when she was honest with herself, she really didn't care.

She turned and walked in the opposite direction, headed west on Wilshire.

She checked her watch. It was auto-synched with sunset and sunrise in every time zone she entered, and beeped a series of alarms as they approached. It cost about as much as a used car.

Well. If Cade wouldn't do what was necessary, she would. She had plenty of time, if she didn't bother with traffic.

Fortunately, this part of the city had tall buildings. Not skyscrapers, really—but tall enough.

She slid into a crowd clotted around the entrance to the Wiltern Theatre, waiting impatiently for the doors to open, some band she'd never heard of. She made a mental note to check them on iTunes.

She took a brief, heady sniff of the crowd scents—the hair gel, the perfumes, the slightly sexual anticipation, and the blood underneath. She didn't have time to pull any sheep from the flock, but she still liked the aroma.

She cut ahead of one young man, gym-muscled, dressed in expensive rags, stinking of creatine and protein supplements and Polo by Ralph Lauren. He was about to protest, but she gave him a smile, and the fight went out of him.

She slid on by, her hand brushing his chest, and then followed the building around to the alley. Behind her, she heard the young man's girlfriend say, "Hey!" and punch him—hard.

She grinned. Then stifled it. Maybe Cade's remark about her age bothered her more than she wanted to admit.

She shook it off as she found the fire escape in the

alley. Rust-eaten ironwork, only used for smoke breaks by people in the offices above the Wiltern. But it would do.

She hopped up, and was at the second story. Another leap, and she swung forward easily onto the roof.

She took a moment to orient herself, laying the map in her head, memorized with a glance earlier that night, over the real-life grid of the city lights.

There. Her destination was that way.

She stilled herself, prepared for the shift.

It would have been easier if she had eaten. But then, she would have missed Cade entirely.

She wondered, not for the first time, why she remained so attached to him.

She remembered feeling something for him. Fierce and hot and bright, like the sun.

But like the sun, she couldn't see it anymore.

It was the memory of the feeling that kept her coming back. She wasn't sure she would like it if she forgot that sensation.

Plus, over a century old, and Cade was still sexy as hell. That helped a lot.

She slipped out of her dress, wearing nothing underneath.

She folded the dress into a neat square, then slipped the dress and her shoes into her bag. She slung the strap of the purse around her neck.

For a moment, she just savored the cool night air on her bare skin. She imagined someone in the nearby buildings, a guy working late maybe, glancing out of his window, unable to believe his eyes when he saw her.

She tilted her head back, ran her hands over her neck, her breasts, her flat stomach. Imagined her watcher watching this, getting excited. Hoping she would touch herself some more.

Then she grinned. This ought to wither his erection.

And she started to change.

She shoved all thought out of her mind. Pushed her mass to her center. Lengthened her tendons, stretching herself, feeling joints pop into new positions. Sucked marrow from the inside of her bones, stored it elsewhere.

Distantly, she heard the cracking noises as her skeleton set into its new position. She reached inside herself, as if withdrawing arms inside her sleeves, and pushed outward, pulling the skin away from her ribs, forming a great wing of flesh on each side.

Then she stopped thinking rationally, as her skull flattened at the cranial sutures, giving her a more aerodynamic profile.

She would operate mainly on instinct now, heading toward her destination, which shone in her mind like light through a keyhole in a dark closet.

She stepped off the roof. The wind rising off the street caught her, and she began gliding across the night sky.

TWENTY-FOUR

Part of this high resistance to damage is due to the altered physiology observed in subject's full-body MRI and X rays (see Appendix: "Medical Imaging"). Subject's muscle density is roughly the same as aramid fibers (Kevlar = 1.50 g/ml), or nearly 50 percent higher than standard human muscle (1.06 g/ml). His bones have a tensile strength more than twice that of an average human (300 MPa vs. 150 MPa).

—BRIEFING BOOK: CODENAME: NIGHTMARE PET

It took Zach a while to notice the black car following him. All his attention was on Konrad's Ferrari and the unfamiliar L.A. streets.

Then, with a burst of acceleration, the Ferrari sped through a red light. Zach slammed on his brakes as a delivery truck swept through, horn blaring.

Konrad's Ferrari was gone, and Zach had left a burnt-rubber trail to the middle of the intersection. He put the car in reverse, to get out of the oncoming traffic.

That's where he saw the black car for the first time, back at the light.

The tinted windows revealed nothing. Both cars just sat there, as if waiting for the starting flag in a race.

Zach checked the streets around him, checked the in-dash navigation system and realized something else. He was almost in downtown L.A., and he had no idea how he'd gotten there.

The light turned green. Zach didn't move. Neither did the other car.

Not a good sign, Zach thought.

Zach wasn't completely stupid. He took his phone out of his pocket, and hit the button on the touch screen marked CADE.

Cade answered immediately.

"Is Konrad moving?"

"Oh, we've got a *lot* of catching up to do," Zach said.

"Where are you?"

"Not sure. I tried to follow Konrad . . ."

"And?"

"Sorry, I thought you were going to yell at me there."

"I assume you already know that was a bad idea."

Zach looked at the black car, still just sitting there, next to him.

"You could say that. There's someone after me. Black car."

"You're sure?"

Another driver behind the two cars honked. Zach, startled, hit the gas. The black car took off a few seconds after he did, and maintained a steady pace a car length behind.

"Cade, they're right here."

"Don't panic. I'll be there soon."

"I don't know where I am."

"I'll find you."

"Cade?"

"What?"

"You sure this car doesn't have a rocket launcher?"

"Just keep driving. I'll find you."

There was a click, and Cade was off the phone.

Zach made a wild left turn, realized he was going the wrong way down a one-way street.

The black car followed him, keeping its distance.

Definitely not a good sign, Zach decided.

CADE TOUCHED ANOTHER BUTTON on his phone's screen, and a map of Los Angeles popped up. Zach's GPS beacon showed him on the edge of downtown—about five miles from where Cade was standing.

Wilshire was bumper-to-bumper with Friday-night traffic.

Cade began to run.

A few people gave him looks, but he reached a side street before he really started to move.

At the end of two blocks, he was sprinting. He stayed in the center of the road, his feet making a sound like a continuous drumroll. In one of the pocket neighborhoods behind the Miracle Mile, a car ran a stop sign, right in front of him.

Cade vaulted it easily. The driver never saw a thing.

Cade kept running.

ZACH WATCHED the rearview mirror, rather than the road. Before he knew it, he was lost. He didn't even know Los Angeles had railroad tracks, but he'd crossed them several times. Freeway overpasses, offering the promise of escape, were above his head, but he couldn't seem to find any on-ramps. He'd look up, grinding his teeth, wondering why the hell anyone ever said this city was easy to drive around.

Through it all, the black car stuck to his tail like grim death.

He'd managed to find himself in an almost totally deserted section of town, concrete on all sides, and a bridge—bridge? Since when did L.A. have a river?—in front of him.

A streetlight above went dark. As if that was a signal, the black car revved its engine and closed the gap between them. Its headlights grew huge in the mirror.

The car tapped his bumper.

He slammed on the gas, and the sedan nearly leaped off the road, pushing him back in the seat.

Whatever special government engine he had under the hood, his pursuer had something better. The black car closed the gap, tapping his bumper harder this time.

Zach's phone started beeping. Not really a good time to take a call, he thought.

CADE PUT HIS PHONE AWAY, with a small amount of frustration. The boy wasn't answering. That would make this slightly more difficult.

As he thought this, he was running at about forty-five miles an hour on the overpass, not yet breathing hard.

The phone's GPS tracker put the boy right below him.

He saw both of them—the sedan, driving wildly, and the black car behind it, smoothly accelerating to follow.

Slightly more difficult, but not too bad, he decided.

Without breaking stride, Cade jumped over the concrete barrier, out into the empty air.

ZACH SWERVED AROUND A CORNER—and slammed on his brakes.

Dead end. The only thing between him and a concrete drainage canal was a chain-link fence, topped with razor wire.

He didn't have a lot of time to consider his options. The black car appeared at the end of the street, then accelerated toward him.

CADE STOOD IN THE ALLEY where he'd landed. Zach had raced by a second before. Cade heard the screech of brakes that told him Zach had just discovered the dead end.

Cade put both hands on the edge of the dumpster, filled with metal parts from the machine shop out front.

The pursuit car's engine told him it had found Zach. He heard it rev and then peel rubber.

He waited, for just a second, calculating the time it

would take for the black car to reach the end of the street, for him to reach the end of the alley.

Then Cade put his legs into it and started running, pushing the dumpster along in front of him.

ZACH BRACED FOR IMPACT and wondered if it was going to hurt when he was knocked over the edge.

He couldn't take his eyes off the rearview mirror. The headlights got bigger again, the sound of the engine roaring—

Something hit the car, knocking it clean off the road. The headlights jerked out of view so fast it was like they were shut off.

Zach turned around in the seat, not believing it.

A dumpster had come out of the alley like a missile, T-boning the black car at the driver's door.

The dumpster rolled away, crushed from the impact. The black car, crumpled up on one side, rested against a row of parking meters, some of them bent and snapped.

Zach felt eyes on the back of his neck, and turned in the other direction.

Standing in the street, in the sudden burst of steam from the black car's smashed radiator, was Cade.

Cade walked over to the car.

A thick man in a suit stumbled out of the ruined driver's-side door, fumbling for a gun in a shoulder rig.

Cade knocked him to the pavement. Then he grabbed the edge of the crushed door, pulling it right off its hinges, and flung it away.

He dragged the passenger out. Zach caught a glimpse of bright blond hair as Cade deposited her on the ground by her companion.

Zach got out and ran to Cade's side.

Cade examined him. "Are you all right?"

Zach got a really good look at the side of the car now. It was totaled. The wheels were bent off the axle.

"Yeah—I just—holy shit, Cade, how did you do that?"

The blonde shook herself and tried to stand.

Cade moved between her and Zach. She staggered a little on her high heels.

Zach felt a little ridiculous, being protected from a 105-pound girl. He stepped forward, brandishing his fake creds like a shield.

"You're in big trouble, lady," he shouted. "We're with the Department of Homeland Security."

She focused on his badge. Then she laughed and stood up straight.

At first glance, you could have mistaken her for a corporate lawyer, or maybe even a TV reporter. She had that kind of brassy, too-perfect attractiveness.

"No, you're not," she said, as she brushed the broken safety glass from her blouse. "*We* are."

She flipped out her own badge.

"Helen Holt," she said. "Special liaison to DHS."

Zach stood there looking at it for what seemed like a long time. Cade didn't say anything.

Zach looked at the blonde again. She gave him a smile that would put any spokesmodel to shame.

"Well . . . crap," Zach said.

TWENTY-FIVE

1957—"Teenage Monster" incident, Camden, New Jersey—Another experiment with Konrad's work leads to a local doctor, last name Carlton or Karlton, assembling a creature from the parts of several deceased teenage athletes. After the creature murdered several people, Operative Cade dealt with the doctor and his experiment.

—BRIEFING BOOK: CODENAME: NIGHTMARE PET

The other man got up off the pavement.

He was limping, but didn't say anything about it. He showed Cade his own badge, which ID'd him as Reyes, also with DHS.

"Mind if I pick that up?" he asked. He pointed to his gun, still on the ground.

"I wouldn't," Cade said.

Reyes grimaced, puffed up his chest. Looking to salvage some scrap of his pride. "You going to stop me?"

"Yes," Cade said. Matter-of-fact. No bluff in it. Reyes considered his options and then wisely chose to join Helen, leaning against the car.

"So you guys going to give us a ride, or what?" she asked.

Cade ignored the question. "Why were you following him?"

"Your colleague was stalking one of our assets," Helen said. "That caught our attention, you might say."

"You're protecting Konrad? Why?"

"I'm afraid that's classified," she said. "Let's just say Konrad is vital to national security interests that don't concern you."

"I don't suppose the president knows about these interests."

"Oh, do grow up. Plausible deniability. Ever heard of it? The politicians can't be trusted with the hard facts. You should know that by now."

Cade stepped closer to her, radiating menace now.

"Perhaps you want to let me in on the secret."

Zach could feel Cade's anger. Even Reyes flinched a little.

Helen stood there, serene. "I'm not afraid of you," she said.

Cade evaluated her for a moment. "No," he said. "You're not. You're taking all of this quite well."

"Come now, Mr. Cade. You don't really think you're the only extra-normal operative working for the government, do you?"

Cade's mouth twitched. "Extra-normal. Clever."

She shrugged. "Government jargon. What are you going to do?" Still looking amused, she didn't seem willing to offer any more information.

Abruptly, Cade turned away and put his phone to his ear.

Which left Zach standing there, talking to the two agents alone.

Reyes glared. But Helen looked him over, sizing him up.

"How do you like the new job, Zach?" she asked.

That caught him off guard. "Do I know you?"

"Nope." Still smiling. "But I know you."

Christ. More mind games. Like he hadn't had enough of those today. "Whatever you say."

"You should listen to me, Zach," she said, still infuriatingly calm, as if someone—some *thing*—hadn't just broken her car nearly in half.

"Why is that?"

She gave him another million-watt smile. "Because we're the good guys, of course."

Zach laughed. "Yeah. I can tell."

Her expression changed to pity. "You can't. You've been fed a pack of lies. You joined the wrong team. I mean, really, would the good guys have a vampire working for them?"

Zach looked away from her, over to where Cade stood, phone still to his ear.

She kept pushing. "Ask him a question: how many people has he killed? Not in the line of duty. How many innocent people has he killed, just so he can feed?"

"He doesn't feed on people," Zach said.

"And you believe that?"

Zach didn't have an answer.

She laughed at him. "Poor Zach," she said. "You don't know who to trust."

CADE HIT THE BUTTON for Griff. It took the man a moment to answer. His voice sounded rough.

"Yeah?"

"We've run into some people from the Agency."

"You sure?"

Cade listened to the woman as she worked to turn Zach against him.

"Fairly certain, yes. What should I do with them?"

"They look dangerous to you?"

Cade almost smiled. "They never do."

Griff thought about it for a moment. "Just get out of there. You don't need the Agency on your ass."

Cade looked back at Helen and Reyes. Saw the troubled look on Zach's face. The woman was talking to him, and he was listening.

"It might already be too late," Cade said.

He hung up, got Zach and got back in the car.

HELEN WATCHED Cade and the boy leave. She knew Zach was looking back at her. She smiled and waved.

As soon as their car turned the corner, her big smile shut off.

She checked her watch. Past three a.m. Sunrise in a little more than four hours. Cade would have to go to ground soon.

Reyes was on his phone already, calling for backup. He was bent over with pain now. He'd put up a good front, but Cade had hurt him. Helen wouldn't have been surprised if he had broken bones.

Not her problem. Helen crossed her arms and leaned back against the trunk of the car again.

Reyes snapped his phone shut. "We'll have a ride in five minutes."

She sighed irritably. That would have to do. She still had another meeting tonight. She wasn't looking forward to it, but she wanted to get it over with.

God, she hated to wait.

TWENTY-SIX

And you thought all we had to worry about were earthquakes. According to mining engineer G. Warren Shufelt, Los Angeles sits above a lost city filled with golden treasures and mysterious inventions left by a race of Lizard People with intellects far in advance of our own. Shufelt says he found records of this reptile race in the ancient legends of the Hopi Indians, and is presently raising funds to drive a shaft 250 feet under the ground beneath Downtown.

—Los Angeles Daily Tribune, *January 29, 1934*

Zach kept looking through the back window as they drove away.

"We're just going to leave them there?"

"Yes."

Zach watched them through the back window until Cade turned down another street.

"Yeah, I suppose they can call DHS for a tow truck."

"They weren't from Homeland Security," Cade said.

"How do you know? Were the badges fake?"

"Not the badges. The names. There are no employees of DHS named Helen Holt or Augusto Reyes."

"How can you be so sure? You know the name of every Homeland Security employee?"

Cade didn't respond.

"You know the name of every Homeland Security employee, don't you?"

"And their positions," Cade said. "Those two, whoever they are—they don't exist."

Zach wondered what that meant. Before he could ask, Cade spoke again. "I would have expected better driving from a car thief."

Zach looked over at him, stunned. Nobody knew about that.

"I never—" Zach started. Then decided fuck it, no use lying.

"That was a long time ago."

"It was nine years."

"Right, I forgot. That's like waiting in line for a latte to you, isn't it? What do you care anyway?"

"I'm wondering how you ever got away with it."

"Well, I didn't, obviously. I got caught."

"Only once," Cade said.

"Once was enough."

At first, Zach told himself it was little more than a practical joke. People in his hometown still left their cars unlocked. If they didn't, Zach had figured out a way to pop open most doors. If he couldn't bust the lock, he'd learned that a spark plug, tossed just so, would shatter a car's window instantly, with barely a sound. He taught himself how to hot-wire from a schematic he found on the Net.

It was a challenge. And it was dangerous—miles away

from the hours in class where he was the predictably bright student, the kid who got along with everyone, who always said and did the right things.

The money didn't hurt, either. Tyler, one of Zach's buddies, was pretty much aimed at prison from the moment he came out of his mother's womb. Absent father, abuse from Mom's boyfriends, too little money and too much time on his hands.

He and Zach were friends in grade school, before either knew they shouldn't be. Both latchkey kids, with single moms. Tyler came over to his house after school. They stuck together, like some bad movie version of themselves, the tough guy and the brain. If he stopped to think about it, Zach knew Tyler counted on him for stability. And he knew that once he went off to college, he'd never see Tyler again.

In the meantime, Tyler knew a guy who was willing to pay them for the cars they brought him. Laughably small amounts, really. But Zach wasn't exactly rich himself. He needed cash for that Ivy League escape he'd planned.

So, while he spent time after school and weekends doing Mock Legislature, Poli-Sci Club and volunteering for campaigns, Zach also ran around a few nights every month stealing cars.

Then they were caught.

The cop who wouldn't buy into Zach's bullshit—the one Griff resembled so much—also figured out this was the reason for the recent rash of auto thefts. He and the prosecutor gave Zach a choice—go to juvie or turn in Tyler and his buyer.

Zach, sitting in a grimy conference room in the courthouse, didn't have to think about it long. He saw his whole future turning to dust. He asked for only one condition: that his arrest record remain sealed.

Tyler went to juvie. His buyer went to prison. Zach made his escape.

And this was where it got him. He tried to settle back into his seat.

"You're not as different as you think, Zach," Cade said. "Everyone has secrets. You'll see."

Zach wasn't sure what that meant. He wondered if Cade had heard Helen's conversation with him. Then he yawned so hard he nearly passed out. He looked at his watch and wondered when he'd get any sleep.

"Almost sunrise," Cade said, as if in answer. "We're going to the safe house."

TWENTY-SEVEN

While many of the subject's organs have shrunk from lack of use—most notably the stomach and intestines—other organs have shifted, enlarged, and re-purposed. His lungs have filled with dense "stacks" of blood vessels that draw liquid blood directly from the esophagus upon feeding. These stacks have also expanded to fill the empty abdominal space left by the shriveled digestive organs. They store the subject's liquid meals, and release the blood when it is required by other organs or muscle. Kidneys and liver have enlarged as well, and appear to filter the subject's blood for foreign particles down to 15 microns.

—BRIEFING BOOK: CODENAME: NIGHTMARE PET

Konrad entered his home in the Hollywood Hills. It had a beautiful view of the city, a chef's kitchen, clean lines—and a vampire waiting in the living room.

Tania sat on the edge of the couch, swinging her legs.

Konrad bit back a curse. This was really getting to be too much for one day.

"Shouldn't you wait for an invitation?" he asked, walking to the entry table. She'd already deactivated the alarm. How thoughtful.

"You know that's just superstition," she said.

"But it would at least be good manners. I assume you're here for the bounty on Nathaniel Cade."

Her smile only widened. "I am. But not quite how you think. I'm going to make sure you never bother Cade again."

He stopped sorting the mail on the entry table. "Interesting," he said. "You must be Tania."

"You know me?"

He nodded. "In our little world, you're known as the girl who will do anything for money. And there are always errands that need to be done. You've created quite an industry for yourself. I would think you would be happy to take my commission. Can I ask why not?"

"The reasons don't matter."

"The reasons always matter," Konrad said. "I'm offering blood, money and even limited ability to travel in the day. All of that is well within my abilities. So what is Cade to you that you'd pass over a substantial reward?"

Tania dropped her smile. "Cade is mine," she said. It was almost a growl. "You don't threaten what's mine."

Konrad nodded. It made sense now. "Yes. I see. You're not much for feelings, but you are very proprietary, aren't you? Territoriality. Ownership."

She looked bored. "You can stall if you want. You know how this conversation ends."

Tania took a step toward Konrad. He didn't look worried.

"I've lived a very long time. And I didn't survive this long without taking measures against parasites like you."

Quicker than Tania thought possible, Konrad's hand stabbed what looked like a light switch.

The bulbs above flared to life, and the pain brought her to her knees.

Ultraviolets. Full-spectrum. And intense. Thousands of watts. Enough to light up a small stadium.

It wasn't like true daylight—it would not kill her—but it delivered a stunning amount of agony all the same.

Before she could shake it off, Konrad was standing over her. She swept one arm at him, but she was still dizzy. Her aim was off. He snapped something around her neck. She heard a lock click, and then there was a new weight at her throat.

She stood. The glare was still awful, but she could handle it now. She opened her eyes and prepared to leap at Konrad.

"One moment, please," he said. In one hand, he had a remote. "You're now wearing six ounces of C-4 plastic explosive. It's not much of a fashion accessory, I admit. But it's more than enough to blow your head clean off your body."

She touched the collar. Decapitation. One of two sure ways to kill a vampire. Head or heart.

"I've got your attention," Konrad said. "Good." He shut down the lights. "I can activate the collar with this remote. If I press a button, you die. It also includes a proximity sensor. Attempt to get near me, and you die. And the collar has a GPS sensor, so I can program it to limit you to a specific area. Attempt to leave that area, you die. Are you quite clear on the rules?"

Tania nodded, her jaw clenched tight.

"Good," he said.

She tensed. Her reactions were faster than his, if she could just . . .

Suddenly, her nerves were on fire. Every muscle in her body went into spasm. She hit the floor like a rag doll tossed by a fickle child.

Dimly, she heard Konrad speak again. "The collar is also capable of delivering electrical shocks in the range of eight amps. That's more than an electric chair. As you may have noticed."

She lifted her head to glare at him. It felt like she was swimming in wet cement.

"Do you understand your situation now?"

Tania nodded.

Konrad kneeled to look her in the eyes. "I won't insult you by pretending this little training collar would be enough to make you kill Cade. I have someone else for that. However, there are quite a few errands you can run for me. I've got a lot to do in the next few days."

"What do you want?" Tania asked, biting off each word.

"You'll see," Konrad said, rising again, straightening his shirt and tie. "For now, I want you to get in the closet downstairs and shut up."

Tania couldn't help looking puzzled.

"Not that it's any of your business, but I have a date," Konrad explained.

TWENTY-EIGHT

Subject's senses are augmented as well, due to several changes in brain structure and chemistry, as well as physiological changes apparently sustained since the incident. Subject's hearing is acute enough to detect the heartbeat of another person (3 dB) within 100 yards, while baseline human hearing can only detect around 10–12 dB. Subject has developed a third structure, in addition to the rods and cones normally found in the human eye; this cube-shaped light receptor is able to detect and distinguish near-infrared parts of the spectrum. Subject's eyes also possess the reflective layer (*tapetum lucidum*) found in many animals, which assists night-vision. Starlight would appear almost as clear as broad daylight to the subject. Subject's sense of smell is on par with a canine, and he was able, in repeated tests, to detect particulate emissions as low as a few parts per billion.

—BRIEFING BOOK: CODENAME: NIGHTMARE PET

It was almost dawn by the time Helen got to the house. She opened the door with her key, then she rubbed her eyes and yawned as she entered the foyer.

Konrad waited on the couch. One side effect of his long life—he rarely needed to sleep. Somehow, he even looked younger than when she last saw him. Bastard.

"Tired?" he asked.

"Long day," she said.

"It's not over yet."

She was exhausted, but that didn't mean anything. She still had work to do.

She dropped her bag and began to strip. First the suit jacket, then the blouse, then the skirt and the panty hose. She did it without any flourish. He liked it as mechanical as possible.

Then, naked, she went to him and bent over the arm of the couch.

Konrad stood. He dropped his pants. Kept his shirt on.

He hummed Wagner. It was the only sound he ever made.

AFTERWARD, IN KONRAD'S BATHROOM, she surveyed herself, checking her face carefully in the mirror. Another line, faint but undeniably there, at the corner of her right eye. The price she had to pay for staying up this late.

She rummaged in her makeup bag and came out with a vial of her collagen-enhanced anti-wrinkle cream. She ground it into her skin viciously, knowing it wouldn't really help.

She was aging. There was nothing she could do about it. Thirty-six years old, and there was no way she could turn back the clock.

But Konrad could.

He entered the room behind her, stood looking at the both of them in the mirror. He moved her blond hair off her neck, a gesture that could be mistaken for tenderness.

She knew better. He was inspecting her, like a specimen under a microscope.

"Another little crow's-foot," he said.

Bastard. "I know."

"You should take better care of yourself, Helen."

Helen tried not to smirk at that.

"You could do something about it," she said.

"I never pay in advance. We've had this discussion."

She turned to face him. "You know how much I've risked for you?"

"You know what they say about great risk. It's the only way to great rewards."

"Haven't I done enough?"

"No," he said. "Not yet."

"You keep saying that." She tried to keep the anger, the pain, out of her voice. "How do I know you'll ever give me what I want?"

"I give you my word," he said calmly. "You'll never age another day. Once Cade is truly dead."

He removed her hands from the front of his robe and left her in the bathroom.

She checked herself in the mirror again. No gray hairs. Nothing showing at her roots. No visible sagging, no other lines.

He had to come through for her. Because every day that he put her off, dangled the promise of eternal youth in front of her, that was another day on the wrong side of the calendar.

Time was ticking away. She had to get Konrad's secret soon.

Living forever wouldn't mean a damn thing if she had to become an old woman first.

TWENTY-NINE

You have no doubt heard about the incident at Hanover. . . . One must wonder why the Leeds creature was near a place so vital to the defense of our nation. It seems the border between our land and Hell is not stable, and, like any other border with a hostile power, we must fortify it. No matter how outlandish it seems. . . . If the Devil is afield in our nation, we have to defend ourselves against Demons.

—Commodore Stephen Decatur, U.S. Naval Commissioner, letter to President Thomas Jefferson, 1804 (Classified)

The safe house turned out to be a windowless space in an office park near LAX with few other tenants. They parked in a garage in the back, a heavy steel door closing behind them.

Inside, it was like a garage attached to a cheap hotel room. The car sat on bare concrete, which ran right up to thin carpet, with a bed, table and a corner bathroom.

Another steel door was placed in the center of the wall. While Cade unloaded equipment, Zach wandered over and opened it. Cade didn't say anything, or stop him. It opened into a fake office—a reception desk with a plastic palm tree. On the other side of the frosted glass was the front parking lot.

Zach went back into the room. There were toiletries in the closet-sized bathroom, including toothbrushes and toothpaste. The White House dental budget. Bigger than you'd expect, Griff said.

The phone rang.

"You expecting a call?" Zach asked.

Cade picked up the handset. "What?"

"Put me on speaker, the kid needs to hear this, too," Griff said. He was used to Cade's way of answering the phone.

Cade hit the button, and Griff's voice, tired and rough, filled the room. Zach checked his watch, still set to D.C. time. Just before seven a.m. there, and it didn't sound like Griff had spent any time sleeping.

"Here's what we've got: the container was shipped by KSM Holdings, a Kuwaiti front company for a Saudi national."

"Super," Zach said. "Let's send the CIA or someone to go talk to that guy."

"Unfortunately, it's never that simple," Griff said. "The Saudi national is Mahmoud al-Attar."

"Crap," Zach said. Zach knew exactly who that was. Cousin of the current ruling family. Massively invested in Western businesses. Occasional visitor to the U.S., including diplomatic missions on behalf of his relatives. There was probably more than one photo of him shaking hands with the president.

"Yeah. Exactly."

"It doesn't matter," Cade said. "If he's involved, he should be punished."

"Slow down there, Cade, there's more," Griff said. "The front company—a shipping concern—is run by one of al-Attar's sons. Kid is from the second or third wife, I forget which. Name's Khaled al-Attar. Apparently he and his father aren't close."

"Then we can send the CIA to talk to him, right?" Zach asked.

"Oh, they'd like to. They've been looking for him for some time. Khaled has been a big contributor to Hamas, Islamic Jihad . . . basically anyone willing to strap on a suicide belt and run into a crowd. Here's the problem: he's off the map. Last intel report I can find says Khaled was getting impatient with the lack of progress in killing the infidel. He began moving toward a more mystic interpretation of Islam, including following Iblis."

"Who's Iblis?"

"The Devil," Cade said. "In Islam, Iblis is the name of the Devil before he fell and became Shaitan."

"According to our last report, Khaled felt that maybe this world belonged to Iblis, because it was so corrupt," Griff said. "And the only way to cure that corruption would be to bring about the final battle between good and evil. It seems like he formed a group called Zulfiqar—named for a magic sword used at the battle of something or other. From there, he got deeper into black magic, rituals summoning demons, that sort of thing. This led our guys over there to label Khaled a whack job. They think he went off to a monastery to study religion or something."

"And that's when they lost track of him, I bet," Zach said.

"Good guess."

"Then we'll find him ourselves. When he comes to Konrad," Cade said.

Zach frowned. "Wait a second. Something about this doesn't make sense. Konrad is a mad genius. Right? Emphasis on *genius.* Sending a container that can be so easily traced back to the source doesn't sound all that smart to me."

For a moment, the only sound was the static over the line on the speakerphone.

"Kid's got a point," Griff said.

Cade was unimpressed. "Are you suggesting Konrad has been framed somehow?"

"I'm not suggesting anything," Zach said. "You guys have your history, and that's something, sure. But you might want to look into this a little deeper. Maybe we need to change our focus."

"No," Cade said flatly. "Konrad is involved. He's the only one who can make the *Unmenschsoldat* process work."

"That's not what he said."

"It's a waste of time, Mr. Barrows."

Cade seemed to think that ended it. Zach didn't.

Zach rolled his eyes. "Get over yourself, will you? I can't believe I'm telling the vampire and the secret agent this, but things aren't always what they seem."

Griff made a noise, over the speakerphone. "Might be worth considering the alternatives, Cade."

"Where is that last shipment from KSM Holdings?" Cade demanded.

"Should arrive in L.A. tomorrow night," Griff said.

"There's no time for alternatives. Without Konrad, there will be no way for Khaled to use the creatures. This is the most direct solution."

Griff paused. "I think Cade's right," he said.

"Whatever," Zach said. "You're the big frightening monster killers. You don't need me, I'm going to get something to eat."

Zach stalked away from the phone to the front of the garage.

"Take me off speaker, Cade."

Zach went to the other side of the safe house. Cade put the phone to his ear.

"He's really growing on you, isn't he?" Griff said. Cade looked at his knuckles, still slightly bruised from where he'd punched dents in the car while seizing.

"He's smarter than he appears," Cade admitted. "What's going on there?"

A heavy sigh over the line. "Wyman's office called. He wants to see me. I get the impression he's angry about the investigation, but I couldn't tell you why," Griff said.

"That's another thing that doesn't make sense," Cade said. "The agents watching Konrad. Now Wyman wants to talk. Why are so many people so anxious to help Konrad?"

"I'll look into it. In all my free time."

Cade waited.

"I said I'll look into it," Griff said. "Don't stand there with that creepy look on your face. I know you."

"You're in pain," Cade said. "I need this information. Especially now that we're looking at the possibility of an imminent attack. If you are not able to do this—"

"Don't lecture me. I've got it under control. You just watch yourself and my replacement."

Silence.

"He's not replacing you," Cade said.

Griff paused. "Oh, for God's sake. Don't get all cuddly on me now, Cade."

He hung up.

Cade forgot his brief moment of sentimentality by the time the phone was back on the hook.

Zach walked back over to the phone, munching dry cereal out of the box.

"You think any more about what I said?"

"No," Cade said. "We have a long day tomorrow. You should sleep."

"Whatever." Zach shrugged, and headed back for the hotel-room section of the safe house. He stopped, and faced Cade again.

"Hey," he said. "If these things really are on their way here—I mean, you've fought them before?"

"One. I only fought one."

"But you could take a group of them, right? I mean, that's what you do. You could beat them, if it came to that."

Cade didn't reply.

"Cade?"

"It's late, Mr. Barrows," Cade said. "Get some sleep."

THIRTY

Before he became president, General George Washington was said to have warned his countrymen about a great menace to its freedom in the coming years. A "shadowy angel" allegedly visited Washington at Valley Forge, and told him of a "dark cloud" that would envelop "America in its murky folds. Sharp flashes of lightning passed through it at intervals, and I heard the smothered groans and cries of the American people." The omen is generally meant to warn Americans that the country can never be defeated by outside threats, but could be destroyed by an enemy within.

—Presidential Secrets: Offbeat Facts About America's Founding Fathers

Helen got to work at nine, red-eyed and surly. She passed through the regular corridors of the Federal Building on Wilshire, on her way to the conference room. People smiled vaguely at her, like any coworker they only sort of recognized. She'd been based here for a year, but was still invisible.

Her creds said DHS, but her agency had long ago dropped off any official organization chart or government budget. The highest-ranking official in the building didn't even approach her security clearance. With a phone call, she could order anything short of a nuclear strike.

Cade thought she was CIA. That was true, a long time ago. Now she was something else entirely.

She'd heard rumors about an agency behind the Agency, doing the jobs that couldn't be exposed to the light. Black-budget, black ops.

But she had no idea of the size or scope.

When the CIA fought the Cold War, Helen's employer ran guns and drugs and laundered money to pay for it. Nazi scientists got safe passage in exchange for their discoveries. Mouthy foreign leaders ended up dead, and friendly dictators were installed.

The official leaders of the CIA appeared before congressional committees and denied any knowledge of assassinations, torture or bribes. The president could hold his head up high while he defended the United States.

In the meantime, her bosses did the real work, the stuff that could never be exposed, and descended further and further into the dark. Even the conspiracy theorists would have been stunned to realize what the Company had actually done over the years. All those half-baked ideas about JFK and Roswell and AIDS were nothing compared to the truth.

In time, her employer had evolved into something else, like those fish turned into eyeless horrors by centuries in underground rivers. It grew new appendages, developed different organs and, eventually, became totally separate from its daylight ancestors. It no longer answered to any elected official. It made its own calls, and forged alliances with other things, out there in the night. . . .

Until it stood tall on its own legs, and started carrying out its own agenda. The Company still believed in American supremacy, but only as long as it didn't interfere with the Company's supremacy. The War on Terror was the perfect cover. Operatives who hadn't been seen in years were suddenly back in their old offices, giving orders and taking names.

But, like Helen, no one really knew who was in charge.

It had no official name, but everyone called it the Shadow Company. Helen liked it. It fit.

They were simply there, right next to the other government agencies, using them as cover, always in step. Just like a shadow.

SHE ENTERED the conference room, then unstrapped her 9mm SIG Sauer pistol and set it on the table.

"What do we have?" she asked.

Her two Shadow Company operatives looked back at her from across the table. Shadow Company units operated like terrorist cells—small and mobile, hidden within the larger structure of other organizations.

To her right was Ken. He was as blandly handsome as the doll that shared his name. He'd joined the CIA at the same time she did, went through training with her. She'd been recruited to the Shadow Company long before him, but when she was given a chance to bring him aboard, she didn't hesitate. She knew he'd do anything she told him.

She remembered back at the Farm, the CIA training program, someone had called them Ken and Barbie the first time they were paired for an exercise. During hand-to-hand practice, she punched that guy so hard he lost a tooth. The nickname didn't catch on.

The other was assigned to her without her input. The Company, she was reminded repeatedly, was not big on democracy. They gave her Reyes because they wanted her to have someone who knew the area.

Pushing forty now, he was local, a former cop who had been bounced out for massive corruption. Raised in East L.A., it turned out he'd never given up his gang affiliation when he put on LAPD's uniform. You could see the beginning of a prison tat under the collar of his button-down shirt.

"How are you feeling?" she asked him. His arm was in a sling, a souvenir from last night's encounter with Cade.

"Fine," Reyes said.

That was the limit of her concern for Reyes. "And we delivered the package to the new address?" she asked.

The men looked at each other. By some unseen referendum, Ken was elected to speak.

"We had some concerns about that," he said carefully.

Helen frowned. Both men held their breath. She was not someone you wanted angry.

"What concerns?"

"This is going to cause some blowback. Are we prepared for that? We're risking some exposure."

Helen's face grew tight with rage, but her voice was still controlled. "Are you telling me we did not deliver the package?"

"No, no, that's not what I said. Not at all," Ken said. "The package was delivered. Checked everything twice. It's in place. Ready to go."

"You're sure?" Helen asked.

Furious nodding.

"Okay," she said. "As long as it was delivered." The anger drained away, and the men relaxed.

"You can go," she said. "I have things to do."

They rose and moved to the door. "Keep an eye on Konrad," she said. "I don't want him left unguarded."

"But . . . it's daytime," Ken said.

"Thanks for the update," Helen said. "Tomorrow we'll work on basic math. Until I say otherwise, you stay on Konrad."

The door closed. Helen savored the peace and quiet that only came in the complete absence of stupid questions.

HELEN HOLT'S CIA training officer said this in her final evaluation: "If I had just a dozen more recruits with balls like Holt's, we could rule the world again."

She would have had that framed, if it wasn't classified.

The CIA put her out in the field almost immediately. She excelled out there. She was smart and ambitious. Nobody really knew how ambitious. Or even how smart.

Helen had flown past all the usual checks and balances for a CIA operative. She knew the right answers to give on the personality tests, had in fact taken the MMPI until she could deliver whatever score she wanted. The CIA likes a little viciousness in its recruits, but just the right amount. She was within all the right tolerances.

It wasn't until two years into her career, when she came back alone from a four-man mission in Montreal, that she raised any warning flags for anyone in the system. The other three operatives on her team—all senior to her—had been killed while watching a radical Muslim cleric believed to be a recruiter for al-Qaeda.

They put her in guest quarters at Langley—not a prisoner, not exactly—while they debriefed her. Different men questioned her, over and over and over, checking her story for holes.

She wasn't afraid. She told herself this was standard agency procedure whenever anyone died in the field. But it was exhausting. Fifteen, twenty-hour sessions, the same mind-numbing interrogation the entire time. Fifteen minutes here and there for a break. Then back to the questions.

That night, like every other night, she was out as soon as her head hit the pillow in her antiseptic dorm room.

And then she was standing, naked, in a pool of harsh light in a dark room.

She could barely see anything outside the glare of the uncovered bulb over her head, but she knew someone was out there. In the shadows just a few feet away, a group sat behind desks. Watching her. Examining her body in a curious, sexless way.

It had the unreal quality of a similar dream, the one

where you show up at school for finals, only you're not wearing anything, and you haven't studied, and you can't find your classes.

But this was worse somehow. Her feet were cold. She wanted to retreat from the light, to cover herself, but she couldn't move. She looked down and saw she was standing in a circle of painted lines on the stone floor. It was made up of odd symbols—like an alphabet of a language she'd never seen before.

One of the people in the shadows spoke to her. "We're considering you for a very special program, Helen," he said. She was pretty sure it was a he. She still couldn't make out faces, but when he leaned forward, she saw the dull white of the collar and cuffs of his oxford shirt, underneath his black suit and tie. Dim light reflected off his wire-rimmed glasses.

"We're impressed with what we've seen so far," he said. "But we need to ask you a few questions."

"Who are you? What's going on?"

She heard paper rustling. The man in the shadows continued as if she'd never spoken.

"When you were four years old," he said, "you stayed with your grandmother. She had a bird she named—rather unimaginatively—Petey. What happened to Petey?"

Helen laughed. This had to be anxiety, mixed with too much fast food and coffee. She didn't remember any damn—

And then she did. It came back to her as vividly as daylight.

"I don't know," she said.

Her right arm suddenly sang with pain, like a razor blade slicing cleanly up to her shoulder. She gasped for air, and would have dropped to her knees, but something held her in place. It didn't stop the tears from rolling out of her eyes.

You weren't supposed to be able to feel pain in your dreams, Helen thought. She was sure of that.

"Please don't lie to us again," the man said mildly. "Now. What happened to the bird?"

"I killed it," Helen said, and it all came blurting out. "She loved that goddamn thing more than me. It bit me, and all I wanted to do was pet it, it *bit* me, and she wouldn't do anything about it, so I got one of the little green pellets out of the rat poison box, and the greedy little shit took *that* right out of my hand—"

He cut her off. "Thank you. That'll do."

But the memory stuck in Helen's mind: the stiff little body of the bird on the bottom of the cage, her grandmother's tears, her mother taking her home early.

Her grandmother never had her to stay again.

"Next," the man said, and the images vanished. "What happened to your first lover?"

Helen didn't try to lie this time. In fact, she was still a little proud of how she'd handled herself back then.

She was a freshman in college, saving herself for the right guy, he was a TA, and it was all so predictable. She was in love, she thought, or something close to it, until she saw him exit another dorm room one morning, still wearing yesterday's clothes. She went to a lawyer, the dean and the department head, in that order. In the space of two days, he was fired and expelled, and facing the threat of criminal charges. She didn't have to pay another dime in tuition.

"Thank you, Helen," the man said, stopping her again. "I meant, what happened to him after that?"

"He killed himself. Pills."

"Are you at all sorry?"

"No," Helen said, and felt the same flush of triumph she did when she'd heard the news years before. "He was weak."

"I see." The sound of a pen, scratching notes. "So, what really happened in Montreal?"

Helen knew she couldn't tell the truth. Not to this one.

As if sensing her reluctance, her arm began to throb with pain again.

Helen's mouth was dry. She swallowed hard. "Start at the beginning," the man prompted.

"We were there to watch a target named Khalil Haj-Imad. He's gotten a little following in the past couple years. Young Muslims. Kids, really. Six months ago, some former members of his mosque turned up in pieces in Iraq, after they strapped on suicide vests and tried to get inside the Green Zone—"

"Yes, yes." Impatient now. "So what did you do?"

"I wasn't given much to do," Helen said, unable to keep the resentment from creeping into her voice. "I maintained communications while the senior members of the team"—arrogant pricks, she thought—"tracked the target's movements and evaluated the chances of removing him from the field for questioning."

"You disagreed with that?"

"I felt I could convince him one-on-one. He liked blondes."

"I see. Continue."

"Then our cover was blown. All three of the other field agents were killed."

The images came back to her, in brilliant detail. Corman, the lead operative, half his head blown away, his brains all over a wall in a coffeehouse. Marta, her throat slit, her body found in an alley ten blocks from the mosque. And David—whom she kind of liked, actually—dragged from the wheel of his van, later found beaten to death on a back road.

They didn't get her, because she was safe in their rented room, behind a wall of computers and surveillance equipment. She was on a flight out of Canada, back to the U.S., when her team failed to check in. The worst she'd had to face was a cranky Customs inspector.

"How was their cover blown?"

"I don't know . . ." she began, and this time the pain did drop her to her knees.

She woke a second later—she'd never passed out in a dream before—with drool strung from her mouth.

"Strike two, Helen," the man in the dark said. "There won't be a third. Do I need to repeat the question?"

"I did it," Helen said. It almost felt like a relief to get

it out there. "I was sick of being stuck in the background. I thought I could move out front if Marta's cover was compromised."

"How did you do it without your superiors finding out?"

"That was the easy part." A stupid surge of pride here. "I snapped a quick shot of her in the street with a disposable cell phone that had a camera. Uploaded that in an Internet café on a lunch break. Sent it through an anonymizer in Finland, bounced it back and forth through some message boards, and then made sure a Jihadi website picked it up. She was blown. Never even knew it."

"Why would you risk another operative's life like that?"

Helen considered lying again and then decided fuck it, it's just a dream, right? And it would feel good to say it out loud, finally.

"I hated that bitch," she said, her lips pulled back in a snarl. "Just because she had dark skin, they put her in the mosque, make her out like she's Marta *Fucking* Hari and had me answering the phones, for Christ's sake. I knew I could have gotten him. We'd seen him go to the strip clubs. He would have followed me anywhere."

"So you got her killed."

"I didn't think the entire team would get blown."

"Still. They did. Three people dead. Because you felt . . . what? Professionally slighted?"

She looked down, feeling the eyes on her again. "Yes."

"Last question, then," the man said. "Are you sorry?"

She looked up, defiant. "No," she said. "They should

have listened to me. None of it would have happened if they had just done what I said."

Another image flashed in her mind. Helen herself. In junior high. Alone, as she was every day, despite her clothes, her hair, her family's money, her shiny good looks. As if the others could sense the hole inside her, and they stayed well clear, afraid to fall.

The man looked at the other figures in the gloom, then nodded. "Thanks for your time," he said. "We'll be in touch."

Helen woke up immediately, still in her bed in Langley.

She turned on the light and examined her arm. There wasn't a mark on it, but it hurt like hell.

They came for her the next morning, right after the final Board of Inquiry. The man with the wire-rimmed glasses, the one she would come to call Control, gave her a new set of credentials.

Then her training began for real. Her new job turned out to be far more demanding than the CIA. And far more rewarding.

It only took her a little while to realize what happened in Montreal wasn't a black mark to her new employers. Far from it.

The Shadow Company liked survivors. That was really the only reason they recruited her. They didn't care about her schoolgirl crush on fascism, or the twigged brain chemistry that made her believe other human beings were expendable. Those were bonuses, yes, but they weren't essential.

Bottom line, they wanted Helen on their side because she would do anything to gain what she wanted. And she hated—absolutely hated—anyone or anything who got in her way.

They could use that.

THIRTY-ONE

Dylan stood in line at the impound lot. Everyone waiting with him seemed just as hung over, sweaty and tired as he felt. The man ahead of him had a burst blood vessel in one eye and a large bandage around his head.

When he'd discovered the truck was gone, he had stifled the urge to catch a cab to the airport and run like hell. He still had a chance, as long as no one looked inside the truck. . . .

He had spent the night before locked inside his hotel room, too scared to even look at his cell phone. He knew it was Khaled, every time. He didn't need that stress on top of everything else. He opened the door only for room service and then only after checking through the peep-hole. He was sure he was screwed. There was no way his truck could be impounded without anyone checking the cargo.

When morning finally came without a knock on the

door from any cops, Dylan steeled himself. Then he ran to the bathroom and puked out room-service Jack Daniel's. He went downstairs and found a place in the casino that would give him the cash advance. That was the easiest thing he'd done since the trip started.

Next, an insufferable cab ride with an old driver who smelled like the inside of a coffin, a long wait in the wrong line, followed by a longer wait in this line.

Dylan looked up and saw the CCTV cameras in the corners of the room, wondered who was watching. The longer he waited, the more he became convinced that this was all a ploy to stall for time as they examined the truck.

He played it out in his head, saw it happening right now. One of the pricks would look at him through the lens and say, "That's him. That's the sick bastard."

Would they understand what was inside the truck? Or would they simply assume he was dangerous and had to be killed?

Dylan knew what he would do in their position.

When he reached the front of the line, he was certain that at any moment black-suited thugs from Homeland Security would appear from nowhere and gun him down in a hail of bullets from their automatic weapons. Or torture him first. He heard that happened a lot.

The impound clerk, looking supremely bored behind the glass window, waved him over.

Dylan swallowed. He handed the man his receipt and his proof of registration.

"Where are you from?"

"Orange County," Dylan said. Khaled had coached

him: keep the cover story simple and as close to the truth as possible. "I'm heading back to college." He looked the part: short hair, jeans and a T-shirt with fraternity letters on it. He wondered if that last bit was too much.

"Says this truck is a rental."

"Yeah," Dylan said, still smiling. "I'm taking my stuff back to school."

A frown from the clerk. "Sort of a big truck for that."

Dylan shrugged, trying not to panic. "It was all they had at the rental lot."

The clerk just stared.

Dylan added, as casually as he could, "I'm bringing a hot tub to the frat house."

The clerk looked incredulous for a moment, then broke into a wide grin. "No shit?" he said. "Damn, you really know how to party, buddy. Wish I'd thought of that when I was in school."

The clerk stamped his paperwork.

"Take that to the guy out back, he'll get your truck."

Dylan took the paper, grateful, but the clerk didn't let go of it. He leaned close. Dylan did the same.

"I know what's going on here," he said, a leer on his face.

Dylan nearly wept. He'd gotten so close. . . .

"You went a little overboard at one of the clubs last night, didn't you?"

He laughed again, and Dylan laughed loudly with him. "Yeah," he said, feeling the anxiety flush out of him. "I guess so."

"Hey, I been there. You get away from those girls with your wallet, you're lucky. Travel safe."

"Thanks," Dylan said, feeling the sweat roll from under his arms. "You too. I mean, uh . . ."

But the clerk had already called up the next person in line.

Dylan walked down a corridor, handed his papers over to another person and, twenty minutes later, was behind the wheel of the truck again.

Twenty minutes after that, he was back on the highway. He could still make the rendezvous. If he hurried.

He couldn't believe his luck. Maybe Khaled knew something after all. Maybe Dylan really was on a mission from God. Someone certainly seemed to be looking out for him.

THIRTY-TWO

Wyman sat behind his desk, wearing a plain shirt and jeans. Griff knew without looking that the VP had moccasins on his feet—a throwback to his days as a pot-smoking, Vietnam-protesting hippie. He wore them whenever he came in on the weekend. It was his trademark now, with several prominent mentions in profiles in newspapers and magazines. Of course, these days, he'd discovered the virtues of clean living and a good war, particularly now that he wasn't eligible for the draft.

Griff stood, hands behind his back.

"Have a seat, Griff," Wyman said.

"No thank you, sir."

"Suit yourself." He passed Griff a single sheet of paper. "What is this?"

Griff picked it up off the desk.

It was a copy of an approval for an arms sale—$2 billion worth of planes, guns and missiles—to Kuwait.

"Looks like a done deal to me, sir."

"You'd think so, wouldn't you? But then I've heard that there's a former FBI agent—who works for a department that doesn't actually *exist*, by the way—kicking up all kinds of crap with our Kuwaiti friends. Then I find that agent is asking questions about a good friend of this administration, a respected diplomat—"

"Mahmoud al-Attar," Griff cut him off. "Yeah. I know. His holding company was the one that sent the shipment with the pieces of our soldiers in it. His son, Khaled, has links to—"

"I don't care. Mahmoud al-Attar is a friend. And his companies are helping to broker this deal."

"That's not really my problem, sir."

"I know you don't like me, Agent Griffin. And I don't like you."

"Your opinion means a great deal to me, sir."

"But try to be reasonable," Wyman continued. "It's the biggest shipping company in Kuwait. Millions of tons move through it every day. You have any actual proof this is connected to your little problem?"

"That's what I'm trying to find out—"

"No. You don't. And what has your friend Cade found out in L.A.?"

"He's still investigating."

"In other words, nothing. We need every friend we have in the Middle East, especially this one, to get supplies to our troops. And you're jeopardizing that. For what? Nothing. Pure speculation."

"I'll be happy to discuss it with the president when he returns, sir."

"We're discussing it right now," Wyman snapped. "The last thing this administration needs is to be connected in any way to a scandal. I'm ordering you to leave it alone."

Griff had to smile at that. "I'm sorry, sir?"

"Don't look so amused, Griffin," Wyman said. "I mean it. I'm ordering you to leave the al-Attar family alone."

"No," Griff said.

"What?"

"You heard me, sir."

Wyman's face went bright red. "I gave you a direct order, Agent Griffin."

Griff leaned forward, his fists on Wyman's desk. He wasn't feeling great, and he had no patience for a bureaucratic ass-chewing. "And I said no. What are you going to do about it?"

Wyman's mouth worked a moment before sound came out. "The president is out of town until tomorrow. That makes me the head of the Special Security Council in his absence. You are legally bound to follow my—"

"What do you think this is, Mr. Vice President?" Griff asked, still looming over the smaller man. "You think this is the scene in the movie where the detective gets ordered off the case? You're wrong. It's not that part of the movie. You want me to stop doing my job? Call the president. Otherwise, shut the fuck up and quit wasting my time."

Wyman sat back in his chair, eyes mean as a snake's.

"Get out," he said.

"Thank you, sir," Griff said. He turned and walked to the door.

"You know, someday I might be sitting in the Oval Office, Griffin. You should remember that."

Griff paused, his hand on the knob. "And you might want to remember you're the seventh vice president I've worked under."

"What's that supposed to mean?" Wyman asked.

"Seems likely you'll be out of here before I am, sir."

Griff closed the office door before Wyman could reply.

As soon as Griffin was out the door, Wyman opened a desk drawer, pulled out a cheap pay-per-minute mobile and dialed.

The encryption took a moment, like it always did. Then, as soon as the person on the other end picked up, Wyman started talking.

"It's me," he said. "I talked to Griffin. He won't listen to me. He's going to continue investigating the Kuwaiti connection."

He listened.

"No. That would draw far too much attention. Things are tense enough here as it is."

He waited again, looking angrier by the second.

"No," he snapped. "That's not my problem. I've met my end of the bargain. I gave you the information you wanted. I told you where Cade's safe house is located.

And I've given you a clear shot on . . . on the other thing. What you do with it—that's your business. I can't afford to do any more."

The tone of the voice on the other end raised several notches.

"Hey, I did my best," Wyman said. "How am I supposed to scare the guy? He spends all day in a basement with a vampire, for God's sake. It's up to you now."

He pressed a button, ending the call.

Across the country, in her office in L.A., Helen slammed her phone down. Unbelievable, she thought. Wyman didn't even have the balls to handle an over-the-hill FBI agent. Christ, I have to do *everything* myself.

THIRTY-THREE

Helen couldn't believe Wyman had hung up on her. With that same phone, she could order anything from a tax audit to a cruise missile strike. But she couldn't make Wyman pay for his insult. It was necessary to have a man on the inside. Unfortunately, they always seemed to be such worms.

The door to her office opened. No knock. Helen grinned, thankful for someone stupid enough to interrupt her while she was in a mood like this—

Then she saw the man at the door and she froze.

He wasn't a scary individual on the surface. Far from it. Balding, average height, round glasses that made him look like a small-town librarian.

But the power that Helen used all flowed through him. She called him Control. It was his title. It was his role in her life, as well.

He stepped in to keep tabs on her, offered the occasional instruction. He could find her anywhere, simply showing up like this, unannounced and unscheduled. He knew every detail of her life. She didn't even know his real name.

But she knew he could kill her, and would, without a second's hesitation, if he thought it necessary.

Helen was powerful, but Control—Control was God.

Helen checked her fear and gave him her best smile. "What do you need, sir?"

Control looked back at her, his face as placid as ever.

"Agent Holt," he said. "A word, please?"

She gestured to a chair.

He looked up at the ceiling, the walls. "Not in here," he said.

He went out into the hall. Whatever he had to say, he didn't want the office's recording gear to pick it up.

Her hand shook slightly as she grabbed the handle and followed.

Control leaned against the wall in the corridor. "What are you doing, Helen?" he asked.

"What?"

He sighed. "Why are you antagonizing Cade?"

Helen's fear vanished as the anger welled up inside her. "He was stalking one of our primary subjects—"

"So?"

Helen's mouth worked for a second before she could come up with a reply. "We need Konrad. We can't afford to lose him—"

"Why would we lose him?"

That stopped Helen short.

"Because—you know their history," she stammered. "We can't allow Cade to be this close."

He looked annoyed. "Please. If Cade wanted to kill Konrad, he could have done it five times already. He hasn't. What does that tell you?"

"The president hasn't authorized him to take any action," she said. Reluctantly.

"Correct," he said, a teacher rewarding a slow pupil. "So why are you threatening your cover by involving the White House?"

His face revealed nothing more than idle curiosity. Another federal office drone walked between them in the hall, giving them an apologetic look. Helen waited until she was gone.

"Konrad wanted us to do something," she said.

He took off his glasses and wiped them on his tie. "Do you take orders from Konrad now?"

She flushed. "No, sir."

"And there's no reason to believe Konrad is involved in anything that would jeopardize him—or the Company," he said. "Is there?"

"No, of course not," she said, too quickly. She tried to keep her face—and her mind—as blank as possible.

He waited for her to say something else, but she kept her mouth shut. He put his glasses back on and nodded at her.

"Then we have nothing to worry about."

"Cade is screwing with what's ours," she snapped. "We ought to put a stake in his heart. Or that kid with him. Just to send a message."

"We're not prepared for that kind of fallout."

Helen sensed a weakness here, and she did what she always did: she pounced on it.

"Maybe *you're* not," she said.

He looked at her for a long moment. Long enough that Helen started to get nervous again.

"You think you can handle Cade?"

She opened her mouth, but he raised his hand. "You weren't with us the last time we killed someone in Cade's operation," he said. "The president set Cade out like a mad dog. What do you think would happen if Cade were to tell the president his former aide turned up dead in Los Angeles? We had to cut loose a lot of people to cover our tracks. A lot of people. They found out the hard way they weren't as valuable as they thought."

"Is that a threat?"

Her controller looked disappointed. The slow student had taken a step back.

"Of course it's a threat, you stupid twat."

She looked away. "I'm sorry," she said.

He turned away and headed for the elevator. He was done with this conversation.

"What am I supposed to do?" she asked.

"You said Konrad isn't doing anything, right?" her controller said, pressing the button for the elevator. "Then it's simple. Cade has no reason to be here, once you stop provoking him."

"Yes, sir," she said.

"Good girl." He got inside and the doors closed. Helen knew he'd disappear once he walked out of the lobby.

She bent over, feeling nauseous. Helen was very grateful Konrad was going to make her immortal. Because she was going to betray the Shadow Company, and it had punishments that only started at death. From there, they got much worse.

She took a deep breath and considered her options.

Control suspected her of something, but didn't know. If he knew, she'd already be dead.

He was watching now. But he was a busy man. She wasn't the only agent he had to track. The Company would give her plenty of rope to hang herself.

She had to move fast, though.

She went back into her office and hit the intercom.

"Ken," she said. "I need the activation code for the package."

"Uh . . . okay," he said. "Are you sure about this?"

Helen gritted her teeth. Was *everyone* going to give her shit today?

"I just got confirmation," she said, voice steady and clear. "The Company wants Cade off the board. He's not supposed to be here. The White House will take care of any fallout. They'll have to."

Nothing but silence from Ken. Helen rolled her eyes.

"Oh, don't be such a wuss," she said. "How many people get a chance to put 'vampire slayer' on their résumé?"

THIRTY-FOUR

The belief that sunlight will cause a vampire to immediately disintegrate, or burst into flames, appears to have originated with the film *Nosferatu* (1922). It should be noted that this idea does not appear in the folklore of vampires until after the film. Rather, vampires in folklore were vastly weakened during the day—and a full day of exposure to direct sunlight was often considered the way to kill a vampire. Our own investigations bear out that hypothesis. Direct sunlight debilitates the subject, causing him great pain and increasing weakness. (Simulated UV lights will weaken but not completely incapacitate him.) The proteins in the subject's cells that ordinarily repair damage appear to switch off, and prolonged exposure would most likely result in subject's blood and tissues desiccating and breaking down completely, causing coma, total bodily shutdown and irreversible death. However, even out of direct sunlight, subject's abilities are reduced during the day. His strength wanes to that of five men (bench press = 1,000 lbs.), and his reflexes are only twice as fast as an average human's. In addition, if he does not rest in a comalike state in complete darkness for at least 12 hours roughly every seven days, he will grow steadily weaker.

—BRIEFING BOOK: CODENAME: NIGHTMARE PET

Zach woke on the bed. He hadn't reset his watch since D.C., so he had no idea of the time.

He rolled over—and saw Cade standing there. He snapped up, limbs flailing. "Jesus Christ!"

"We've talked about that," Cade said.

Zach eased himself back to the bed. "Maybe it would help if you didn't loom over my bed while I'm sleeping."

"I heard you wake up. Your breathing changed."

"Well. That makes it all better. What time is it?"

"Daytime. Let me know when you're dressed," Cade said. "You'll need to get to the clinic and watch Konrad again."

"Yes, sir," Zach muttered.

Zach squinted at his watch again, did the math . . . it was barely past ten a.m. He'd been asleep for less than four hours.

With a grunt, he heaved himself out of the bed.

The phone rang. Cade picked up. "What?"

It wasn't Griff. "Nice manners," the female voice said. "Rude much?"

The not-DHS agent from the night before: Holt.

"I wasn't expecting your call," Cade said.

"Don't tell me: you're an old-fashioned guy. You don't think the girl should call so soon after the first date." Cade could hear the pride in her voice. No one was supposed to have this number. Her resources surprised him. Again.

But he wasn't about to rise to the bait. He waited.

"Who is that?" Zach asked. He wandered closer to the phone, grazing from the cereal box again.

Cade gave him a look.

"Fine, sorry, never mind." He went away.

"Tough room," Holt said, when it became apparent Cade wouldn't answer. "I guess I should get to the point. Leave the doctor alone. He belongs to us."

"And who are you?" Cade said. "You're not CIA. You're not Homeland Security."

"Need-to-know basis, and you are not among the needy. This is about keeping America safe. Surely you can understand that."

"I've heard it before. Usually just before a lot of people die."

Holt snorted. "You should be more worried about yourself."

Cade was bored. Sometimes it seemed ridiculous, talking to humans. Their slow thought processes, their short, fragile lives.

"This no longer interests me," he said. "You said you know me. Then you know I won't stop. Whatever you're going to do, you might as well do it."

"Yeah," Holt said. "I figured as much."

Cade heard a tone in the background. The noise of a plastic button being pressed.

He dropped the phone in the same second he realized what was happening. Stupid. Calling during the day. When he was slower. Weaker. When his senses were dulled, down almost to human levels.

When he was less likely to hear a detonator being triggered by a radio signal.

He was moving now, too slow. The phone hung in

midair. Zach appeared before him, standing in the doorway. His face registered surprise.

The cereal box dropped out of Zach's hand, flakes falling in a comet's tail after it.

"What—" Zach said, before Cade tackled him, picking him up.

He felt a rib in Zach's chest crack with the impact. Still too slow.

The explosion began at the far wall, sending the concrete ahead of it. Cade could see each piece of rubble break free and take flight.

The steel entry door was locked. No time to open it. No time at all. He kicked it down.

The explosion was at his back now, the blast wave like a giant fist swinging for him. He accelerated. The glass door of the entrance dissolved into fragments.

Blazing daylight, and his speed and strength vanished. The heat caught him on the side, as he did his best to shield Zach.

He felt the blast lift them both, the fist of the explosion connecting, knocking them out onto the pavement of the parking lot, and a sound like a jet engine hit them just after that.

Zach was no longer in his arms. The light was burning him, and his head felt too heavy to move ever again, and all Cade could think was, *Too slow.*

THIRTY-FIVE

Helen smiled and hung up the phone. She took the sudden burst of static on the other end as a very good sign.

She felt a glow of pride, but not surprise. Vampire or not, he was an obstacle. Helen took obstacles quite personally.

And, now that she was thinking of it: Griff.

That nimrod Wyman was right about one thing. She would have liked to send a black-ops team after Griffin, but that would have been too much. It might alert the president.

Besides, she didn't need anything that obvious to end a man's life. She turned to her computer instead.

Like everything else in her office, the PC was a little more than standard government issue.

She held still while a thin red laser scanned her retina, and entered a series of passwords and keys.

In less time than it took for Windows to boot up, she was deep inside BASKETBALL, the software behind the Total Information Awareness Program.

It never failed to amuse her when Americans got indignant about the idea of someone eavesdropping on their dreary little lives. The fact was, everyone in America was already under surveillance.

Giant computers at Fort Meade scanned billions of phone calls, e-mails and faxes every day, searching for key words like "terrorist," "bomb" or "Allah." If one of those messages hit statistically determined criteria, it was forwarded on to a live analyst, who would check it while pulling up the credit report, criminal history and tax records of whoever sent the message.

Most of the time, it didn't mean dick. Pointless little conversations between people discussing a movie or a TV show, usually.

BASKETBALL was the code name for the program that made it all happen. It was the mother of all search engines; the geeks who built Google would have wept if they could have stolen a look at its algorithms. Entire rooms of computer servers made up its brain. It could find anything, any scrap of data, anywhere in the world, as long as it crossed an electronic line somewhere, at some time.

But what Helen really loved about BASKETBALL wasn't that it could retrieve any private conversation or database in the country. No, what was amazing about the software was that it could leave evidence behind as well.

Agent William H. Griffin's private info was locked

down better than a civilian's. He was, after all, a secret agent with classified access, who answered directly to the president.

But in some ways, that just made it easier for Helen. Nobody really expected the government to start spying on itself. The same protocols that opened tax returns and phone bills also let her insert anything she wanted.

She looked over her work, satisfied. The only thing really missing was a motive. Griffin had been a loyal soldier his whole life. Why would he sell out now?

Then she peeked into his medical file and cross-checked his doctor's billing codes.

Helen smiled when she saw the diagnosis: cancer. Griffin was dying.

Bad news for him. But, really, perfect for her.

THIRTY-SIX

For a moment, Zach thought he'd been in a plane crash. It would explain a lot: the dust and smoke and noise. And the pain. His chest hurt worst, like someone was stabbing him with an iron poker with every breath.

Then his last memory pushed its way forward again. He'd heard the phone ring and was walking down the short hallway when something launched him like a human cannonball.

His legs, flailing wildly behind him, struck the side of the reception desk, but he was moving too fast for the pain to catch up. Then there was glass everywhere, stinging his face and neck like snow.

And then the parking lot was in the sky, and it came down to meet him—hard.

He shook his head, trying to clear it, and realized he couldn't hear anything over the ringing in his ears.

Zach flopped over. The stabbing in his chest subsided.

Less than a dozen yards away, the building was a

smoking wreck. Rubble was scattered all over the lot. Car alarms shrieked as if in pain from their broken windshields.

A bomb. Someone had tried to blow them up. And Cade had saved him.

Blinking, Zach sat up, and felt the poker in his side again. It hurt like hell. His face stung. He wiped at it, found tiny bits of glass stuck in his fingers.

Cade was a couple feet away, facedown, like something left for the trash.

Zach blinked again, feeling sleepy and slow. He looked up at the sun.

The sun.

"Shit," Zach said, and suddenly his head cleared. He scrambled over to Cade.

Cade's arm was a mess, a sleeve of ground beef up to the shoulder. Blood pooled under him.

Zach had never seen much blood before, but it looked wrong—black and thick. But what was worse, Cade's face, where it was turned to the sun was—well, it was dying. There was no other way to say it. It was shriveling and cracking, veins and furrows growing more pronounced every second.

Zach had to get him out of here. As the ringing in his ears faded, another sound was rising. Sirens.

Zach rifled through Cade's pockets, found the keys and hit the remote to unlock the sedan's doors.

Nothing. Then he remembered—the car was in the garage, which was nothing but a pile of crumbled cinder blocks now.

"Shit shit shit," Zach said. He wasn't a spy. Maybe Griff would know what to do now, but Zach didn't have a clue.

He looked down at Cade again. He'd aged even more in a few seconds. His skin had pulled back from his teeth, revealing his fangs.

People started to emerge from their cars, from other nearby buildings, gawking. Any minute now, they'd see him and Cade, and Zach didn't think that was the way you kept a 140-year-old national secret.

He saw a Honda Accord parked in the last row, well away from the blast. There was a piece of concrete from the rubble, about as big as his fist.

Five seconds later, he was sweeping safety glass out of the driver's seat and hoping like hell he could remember how to do this.

He twisted wires together, his fingers shaking. Nothing. He pulled them apart and tried another pair. The engine turned over.

He sighed with relief and thought of how hard he'd worked to hide his one youthful indiscretion. Now his juvenile record was the best thing on his résumé.

Cade was a lot heavier than he looked, but Zach had adrenaline going. He flung Cade into the backseat, covered him as best he could with his suit jacket.

A crowd was milling about now, getting closer. Someone was watching Zach with interest. "Hey," the guy called. "You all right?"

Zach didn't reply. He hopped behind the wheel and jammed the Honda into gear.

The crowd was between him and the exit from the lot.

Another man had joined the first guy in staring at Zach. He looked surprised, then angry.

"Hey . . . hey . . . *that's my car!*"

Zach floored the pedal, and the Honda leaped over the sidewalk, landing heavily in the street.

He heard horns and a screech of tires. The sirens were almost on top of him now.

Zach took the first right turn he could and lost a hubcap as he skinned the curb. He wiped sweat from his face, came away with a few more glass fragments.

He sucked down deep breaths, trying to stay calm. He had to get away. Someone was trying to kill them.

He chanced a look into the back. The sharp turn had caused his jacket to slide off Cade, exposing his face again.

Cade groaned in pain. The sound was nearly as frightening to Zach as the explosion. He hadn't heard anything like that from anyone. Ever.

Zach fumbled in his jacket, found his phone. He scrolled through the numbers, looking for the entry for Griff.

Griff would know what to do. Zach pressed a button, which made a loud beep.

Cade's hand reached over the seat and grabbed Zach's wrist.

Zach nearly turned into the oncoming lane of traffic.

He managed to pull his hand away. Cade remained sitting up. Barely. He looked twenty years older already. "Don't call anyone. Compromised."

Zach's brain began working again. Cade meant that

someone had found them, had just blown up *a top secret safe house*. He could use his phone, call Griff, but if they were supposed to be safe in there, then whoever was after them could get them *anywhere*.

They were alone.

"We've got to hide," Cade said.

First things first. They needed cash.

From the backseat, Cade assessed their situation: Zach's wallet had less than a hundred dollars inside. Anything Cade had was smoldering in the wreckage of the safe house.

Following Cade's instructions, Zach pulled their stolen car up to an ATM on the sidewalk.

It was early enough that the sun had not yet burned completely through the L.A. haze of smog and cloud. But Cade still looked like someone was pouring acid over him.

"Stay here," he grunted, and popped the door.

Zach didn't think he'd be able to get out of the car, but Cade stood, one arm hanging like meat from a hook.

Zach checked around nervously. No pedestrians. Cars flew past on the street.

Cade paid no attention. He walked up to the ATM set in the bank's concrete wall. Using his undamaged hand, he punched the ATM. First, smashing the camera above the keypad. Then he punched it again, driving his fist into the steel.

He pulled it back like foil, and a stack of twenties spilled out.

Cade took the pile still in the machine and turned back to the car.

Cade dumped the money into the front seat and then collapsed inside.

"What are you doing?" Zach screeched.

"Drive." Skin fell from Cade's face in long strips where the sun touched him. There was no blood, just a red-brown dust.

An alarm began to ring. Zach slammed on the gas, leaping into traffic, forcing another car to swerve.

"Slowly," Cade said, curling up on the seat, getting as low as he could.

Zach forced himself to drop to the speed limit. The twenties were scattered all over the front seat.

"You might want to put those in your pockets," Cade said.

Zach grabbed a wad of the cash. "What the hell was that?"

"Operating capital."

"Jesus Christ . . . Someone tried to kill us, and you make us bank robbers now, too?"

"The mission takes priority. Above all else."

"What do we say to the cops if they catch us? Huh? You think of that? Jesus Christ, Jesus Christ, Jesus *Fucking* Christ—"

"Enough," Cade barked. The word was as sharp as a slap across Zach's face. Zach shut up.

Cade's face was dark with anger and pain. His eyes bored into Zach.

"Enough," Cade said again. His voice sounded like it was coming from another place. "This is for the mission. That's all that matters. Best you remember that, boy."

Zach's panic was gone, replaced by fear. As freaked as he was by the bomb, Cade was still scarier.

Fortunately, that outburst seemed to sap the last of Cade's energy. He slid down in the seat. His eyes fluttered closed.

There was no question about it now: the sun was cooking him, killing him every second it shone through the windows. The haze was peeling back, revealing another beautiful day.

Zach considered parking the car on the side of the street, and calling a cab for the airport. He almost believed he could fly back to his old life.

But how long before they came looking for him? Whoever did this, they knew him now.

And Cade . . . Despite everything, Zach would be a wet spot under the rubble if it weren't for Cade.

Zach only knew two things for certain now: He was a target. And the only one who could get him out of this alive was dying, right next to him in the car.

THIRTY-SEVEN

The clerk at the cash-only motel hadn't cared about the blood on Zach's face. Behind the bulletproof Plexiglas, he didn't even look up.

The room looked like the last guests had built a meth lab inside, but the curtains were thick and blocked out the daylight, except for a small crack.

Zach hobbled under Cade's weight and dropped him on the far bed. He tried not to think about the sound Cade's arm made when the burned flesh broke.

Out of the sun, Cade was able to move on his own again. He still looked like hell, but he managed to turn over and straighten his legs.

The effort seemed to exhaust him. Zach was about done, too. For a moment, they sat there, just breathing.

When Cade spoke, it sounded like his throat was filled with dust.

"Where are we?"

Zach ran a hand through his hair. More glass shook out. "Uh. I don't really know, actually. Maybe five, six miles from the airport."

Cade grimaced, either in frustration or in pain, Zach wasn't sure.

"Don't call Griff."

"I won't. I mean, I haven't."

"Right. You've done well."

Cade lapsed into silence again. With his eyes closed, and his new, deeply aged face, he could have been a corpse. Zach was about to touch him, see if he was awake, when Cade spoke up again.

"I'm sorry," he said. "I'll need you to get something."

"Cade, what's going on? Was it those guys, the ones you said were—"

Cade hissed out a breath, and Zach shut up.

"We'll get to that. But you have to do this first."

"What do you need?"

Cade's eyes finally opened, and he looked right at Zach.

"Blood," he said.

ZACH NEARLY wet himself again before Cade explained.

Then he cleaned up as best he could, covered Cade with the bedspread, and got in the car. He headed to the area Cade told him: Pico-Fairfax, home to a large part of L.A.'s Orthodox Jewish community.

And at least four or five kosher butcher shops.

Several of the men in the bloody aprons behind the counters wouldn't help him. They either said no or refused to talk to him once he said what he wanted.

But in the fourth place, a butcher shrugged and took Zach's stolen cash for a bucket full of stuff he was just going to throw out anyway.

Getting the bucket back to the hotel room was almost harder than buying it. At every corner, he was sure it was going to spill and then he'd have to explain a stolen car full of blood to the cop who would inevitably pull him over.

But an hour and a half later, he made it back to the room.

Cade didn't look any better when Zach pulled the bedspread off. He was still breathing, but the charred arm was oozing, and his skin was still drawn back on his skull.

He managed to get Cade awake by slapping him pretty hard.

Cade's eyes snapped open and fixed on Zach. His pupils had filled the whites, turning them black. His lips pulled back, and he lurched up.

Zach went backward, over the other bed. He stumbled to his feet, prepared to throw the curtains open, bring the sun into the room.

Cade was still seated. He was looking down, his face a mask of agony.

"I'm sorry," he whispered. "I didn't mean to—I wouldn't—"

"I know," Zach said. "I know. It's okay. What do we do now?"

"Bathroom," Cade said, through gritted teeth.

IT WAS PROBABLY NOT the first time blood had been spilled in the filthy little tub. But it had to be the largest amount.

With Zach's help, Cade peeled off the burnt remains of his shirt. It stuck to the skin in places, which came away like wet tissue paper.

Then Cade slid into the blood-filled tub, hunching so the liquid came up to his chin, his ruined arm covered completely.

His skin began to flush and loosen again. Zach stood back in awe as very small ripples appeared in the blood near the arm.

The level of blood lowered, and Zach saw the veins snaking out of Cade's charred skin. Writhing like eels as they drank.

Cade looked up at him from the tub, eyes filled with red. He didn't seem to really see Zach.

Zach stumbled backward. "I'll . . . uh . . . I'll just go now."

He closed the door behind him as fast as possible.

TWENTY MINUTES LATER, the sound of the shower woke Zach up. He couldn't believe it. He'd fallen asleep sitting on the bed. His side was on fire now. Carefully, he unbuttoned his shirt and looked at his chest. His skin was mottled with deep bruises already.

He decided to check on Cade.

The tub was empty, except for a dirty red ring.

Cade stood by, completely restored. His eyes were clear, and his arm was healed.

He was also naked. Muscles corded and bulged under new, pale skin. He looked like a marble statue stolen from a museum.

For an instant, Zach considered going to the gym more often. Then he concentrated on looking anywhere else.

"You'll need to make another shopping trip," Cade said. "If you can manage it, Mr. Barrows."

"Are clothes on the list?"

"Yes."

"I had a hunch."

ASIDE FROM CLOTHES, Zach bought duct tape, and plenty of it.

Several yards went to secure the curtains to the walls, so the sun wouldn't come in. Then Cade used half a roll to tape Zach's ribs.

"You'll be fine," Cade said, tearing the last strip on Zach's torso.

Zach felt the wrappings gingerly. Zach wasn't convinced it would work, but he had to admit the pain subsided and he could breathe again.

"That helps," he said.

"I've done this before," Cade said.

Zach smirked at him. He couldn't help it.

It was a lot harder to take Cade seriously as a creature of the night. The drugstore where he'd bought the supplies had a limited clothing selection. As a result, Cade was decked out in drawstring pants and a Lakers jersey, with flip-flops on his feet.

Cade caught the look. "What?"

"Nothing."

Cade looked down at himself, then back at Zach. "You're sure this was all they had?"

"You look fine."

Cade almost said something else. Zach could see it. The big bad vampire cared about his appearance.

Somehow, Zach felt better about that than he did about surviving the explosion.

He checked the time on his spy phone—about the only thing he and Cade both managed to get out of the explosion intact. Almost six hours until sunset.

He stretched out on the other bed. "We've got some time," he said. His eyes fluttered almost immediately. "I think I'm gonna . . . catch a few z's . . ."

Cade poked him in the side, not gently. Zach's eyes flew open and he sat straight up.

"What the hell did you do that for?"

"You might be concussed. It's not advisable to sleep now."

"Well, it's not exactly advisable to nap next to a blood-sucking fiend, either, but I'm tired," Zach said. "Fine. I'm awake. Probably safer that way, anyhow."

"We've been over this before. You have nothing to fear from me," Cade said.

"Yeah. You keep saying that. Guess I should just take your word."

Cade was silent for a moment. "Something on your mind, Mr. Barrows?"

Zach shifted uncomfortably.

"How many people have you killed?"

Cade looked away, unwilling to meet Zach's eyes. "I've killed in the line of duty. Some of it is classified."

"Not what I meant, and you know that," Zach said. "How many people have you killed?"

"You ask like a man who already knows the answer."

"That woman told me you're evil. A murderer," Zach said. "Griff said you killed those people on a boat."

Cade nodded.

"They're both right," he said simply. "I am a killer. I am evil."

Zach waited for more, but that was it.

"That's all you have to say?"

"What else do you want? I am damned. I am a horrific thing that deserves to burn. Nothing else I do will ever change that."

"So you're only doing this because you've been forced. You're a slave. If it were up to you, you'd be out drinking blood every night. Is that it?"

"Believe what you want. You couldn't possibly understand," Cade said.

"God." Zach stood up quickly, waving his arms at Cade despite the pain in his side. "You are such a fucking *whiner*. It's always 'Oh, poor me, I'm a vampire.' Well, it doesn't seem like that bad a deal, Cade. You're superhumanly strong and fast, you can walk off a fatal injury and you get to live forever. And all you have to do is drink some blood. Sounds pretty fair. You're going to be around long after I'm six feet under, and, I'm sorry, but skipping a suntan seems like a small price to pay. If I could do what you do . . ."

Zach noticed Cade was quiet. Painfully quiet. He stopped ranting.

From the expression on Cade's face, Zach suddenly believed the vampire couldn't lay a finger on him. No one looked like that without considering murder.

"You . . ." Cade seemed to search for a word large enough to contain his contempt. "You . . . *people*," he finally spat out. "You think you know me. You think you know *anything*. Less than seventy-two hours ago, you didn't believe I could exist, and now you think you know what I am. But you are right about one thing, Mr. Barrows: you will die long before I do. And if you are lucky, you will never know what a blessing that is."

A long silence. Behind the taped-down curtains, the sun shifted a little farther west.

"Maybe you're right," Zach said. "Maybe I don't know. Enlighten me."

"What?"

"Tell me what it's like." Zach waved his arms at the hotel room, the cheap furniture. "We've got time," he said. "What else am I going to do?"

Cade turned away again, dismissing him.

"I'm serious, Cade. Tell me about what you are."

Cade thought about it. Then he nodded and started talking.

"It was 1867," he said. "I was twenty years old."

THIRTY-EIGHT

1867, Whaling Grounds, Indian Ocean

Cade was slightly ashamed that, all these years later, he couldn't really remember much of the voyage, before it went bad.

His mind played tricks on him sometimes.

There were days he thought he recalled William's face, or the sound of Jonas's voice. Or the taste of the food slopped out by the cook.

Some days, Cade could remember looking out over the rail, into the painfully blue waters of the Atlantic.

None of it was true. Those were only illusions. When he was honest with himself, Cade had to admit he only really remembered the blood.

Hundreds of gallons of it. Every whale was filled with blood, spilling everywhere from the wounds made by harpoons and lances, raining down on him as they hauled the carcasses onto the deck, pouring out in sheets as they ran blades along the bodies, slicing open great slabs of blubber.

He would, at times, wake from dreams of those days with his mouth full of saliva. Hungry.

Everything else belonged to his human memory, which was as fallible and weak as he had been.

But the vampire in him latched on to the image of all that blood.

At times like that, he wondered how much of himself was left—how fully the curse and the old witch's tricks had wormed their way inside and replaced the boy who was a sailor in Boston more than a hundred and forty years ago. He wondered if that boy wanted anything else in his life, or if he'd even remember.

And always, he decided it didn't matter. That boy was dead.

IT WAS ONLY his second whaling trip, he told Zach. He'd been a shipkeeper—basically a deckhand—on his first, which lasted four years.

He was more experienced when he signed on to a new ship, the *Charlotte*, a two-hundred-ninety-ton whaling bark with a crew of thirty men, not counting the captain and the first mate. But he didn't fool himself. He knew the reason he was hired was because of his friend William.

During the four years that he and Cade and another boy, named Jonas, had served as shipkeepers, William had grown into a massive, heavily muscled young man. Anyone who looked at him could see he'd be useful. Cade was able to go without rest for what seemed like days, and Jonas was smart enough to fix anything that broke on a boat. But these weren't obvious gifts. It was William who got them on board.

The *Charlotte*'s planned route would take them down around the tip of South America and then out into the Pacific and the whaling grounds there. But the War Between the States interfered. Several whalers had been blown out of the water by Confederate battleships.

The captain decided to head for the whaling grounds in the Indian Ocean. It would take longer, but it was better than being sunk.

From then on, the trip was uneventful—almost pleasant. The weather was calm. The days were filled with the usual mind-numbing routine of hard work and empty hours.

THEY ROUNDED the Cape of Africa six months after they left Boston, and made their destination three months after that.

Then there was nothing but the urgency of the hunt.

The men had worried that these grounds were done, that the whales had moved on. But they found more whales than they could possibly chase or slaughter. They began the long journey back several weeks ahead of schedule, the ship packed tight with oil and ivory.

They had just made the open Atlantic, still thousands

of miles from home. There was no port they could reach. Nothing on any side of them but water. It would be weeks before they saw land again.

That's when the first man went missing.

Cade later realized this wasn't a coincidence.

A ship is never quiet, even at night. Cade had learned to sleep despite the sounds of the waves and wind, the creaking of the timbers, the farting and snoring and groaning of every other sailor above and below him in the forecastle.

But he would swear on his life he heard something that night.

A sound like an ax being driven into wood, even through the thickness of the hull. Half asleep, he considered getting out of his bunk to see if something had hit the ship.

Then there was the sound of a splash, like a wave hitting the deck. He decided this was normal. None of the other men were up. He didn't want to be the one to panic, to mark himself as a fool and a coward at the same time.

Besides, Cade would be out on deck soon enough—his shift was next on the watch. He listened carefully, but he must have dropped off to sleep again.

Because the next thing he knew, Adams, the ship's first mate, was shaking him violently, yelling questions at him.

He barely had his eyes open when Adams clouted him hard across the face. The words coming from the mate's mouth finally made sense to Cade.

"Where is he?" Adams demanded. "Damn you, answer me. Where is he?"

Cade managed to stammer out the truth: that he'd never been woken for his shift on the watch; he must have slept through the night.

Adams hit him a few more times and then pushed him out onto the deck. The other sailors followed behind.

The light of day was just breaking the horizon. The captain stood at the rail, his face set like he was trying to keep his food down.

There was no one else on deck. Cade was confused. Then he realized *that* was what they wanted him to see. There was no one else on deck.

The man who stood the night watch was missing. Vanished, as if he'd simply dropped off into the sea.

CADE TOLD THE CAPTAIN and the mate everything he knew, which wasn't much. After a few hours of yelling at him—and occasionally beating him again—they decided he was telling the truth.

It didn't answer the question of where the man—his name was Talbot—had gone, in the middle of the night, in the middle of the ocean.

They called Talbot a suicide. It happened, more often than anyone liked to admit. Drowning was considered a pleasant way to go. Cade heard it was like going to sleep, once the water began to fill your lungs.

So they stopped talking about Talbot, and the crew was down to twenty-nine.

But everyone looked a bit strangely at Cade. Even his two closest friends, Jonas and William.

Whatever had happened to Talbot, it had just missed Cade. No one was sure if that made him lucky or simply next in line.

THE NEXT FEW DAYS were quiet. The ship continued its slow passage. Within a month, Talbot was forgotten, and everyone began talking again about how he planned to spend his pay when they returned to Boston.

Then it happened again.

Two more crewmen went missing in the night. Long, the man on watch, and Ellery, a cooper who had chosen to sleep on deck.

There was no way to hide it, but for some reason the captain and Adams refused to address it.

Without any more whales to kill, the crew had nothing but time. And they talked. Rumors infected the entire ship.

Some of the men said that the man on watch had been acting strangely around the cooper, that there was a matter of money owed in a card game.

That didn't satisfy many in the crew for long. Someone else said that maybe the captain and Adams were killing them all, to keep all the profits for themselves. No one laughed at him. The sailors began to take their knives with them into their bunks.

Eventually, Talbot's name came up again. So did Cade's. Cade noticed the whispering stopped whenever he got near.

TWO MORE WEEKS PASSED. The captain stayed in his cabin with the door locked most of the time. Adams carried a club with him wherever he went and used it whenever he heard anyone breathe so much as a word about the disappearances.

The uneasy peace held until they found the body on deck.

Another man on the night watch. Owens this time. But instead of vanishing into thin air or the deep blue sea, whatever had killed him left him out like a trophy.

Cade could remember the scream when another sailor found Owens—a high, almost childlike noise. Then he and the rest of the crew crowded around, despite Adams's best efforts to push them back.

Owens's throat had been torn out; his head was attached to his body by a few strings of gristle.

In spite of the massive wound, there wasn't a single drop of blood on the deck. Not anywhere.

Owens's corpse was as pale as if he'd spent the last month on the bottom of the sea.

Cade wasn't sure who said it first. But he heard it as clearly as the other men: "Vampire," someone whispered.

And within a moment, everyone was repeating it, over and over, in all their different accents and voices. "Vampire. Vampire. Vampire."

They were looking at Cade when they said it.

It took only half a second for the crowd to become a mob. Cade had been spared that first night, so now he was the only suspect, the only target.

Adams shouted orders, but no one listened. He went

scurrying off toward the captain's cabin, where the only guns were kept.

It would be too late to do Cade any good. The men were a wall around him, closing in, determined to do something—anything—to deal with the horror that was living with them on the boat.

A strong hand took Cade by the arm, and he reached for his knife. He would at least go down fighting.

But then he was moved back, toward the forecastle wall, and William and Jonas stood in front of him. William had a harpoon and he held it out so it almost touched the first man in the crowd.

"Stop it," William said. He wasn't so brave that his voice didn't shake. But the harpoon didn't tremble. "This is Nathaniel, damn you. He's one of us."

The sailors looked at Cade, and he stared back at them. And something in them broke. They saw him and knew William was right. Cade was just as frightened and just as bewildered as all of them.

The man with William's harpoon at his chest looked down and stepped back. The suspicion of the other men subsided—like the sun gone behind a cloud.

Adams and the captain were there by then, waving pistols and shouting, but the mob was gone, replaced by the men Cade had lived and worked with for over a year.

Owens's corpse went into the sea. Adams and the captain ordered more chores and brought out the whip for anyone who hesitated even slightly to carry out his duties. The captain took to wearing his pistol in his belt, just as a reminder.

They clamped the lid back on the ship, just barely. William and Jonas stuck close to Cade after that. They never said it, but they were afraid for him.

And perhaps just a little afraid of him.

AFTER THE NEAR MUTINY, it was regular as clockwork.

The sailors tried to stay awake all night, but eventually, exhaustion overtook them. The extra chores didn't help, and Adams was whipping them all to get every bit of speed out of the sluggish old whaler.

But the closer they got to home port, the more men vanished. Every few days, the morning would find the crew's numbers reduced. If two men were on watch, both would be missing. Sometimes a body was left for all to see; most of the time, there wasn't a trace.

The word "vampire" was still going around. Cade heard arguments about the creature—disagreements about its abilities and powers, depending on where each man came from. Stavros, a Greek, called it a *vrykolakas*, and insisted it took the form of a young woman. The Portuguese cook said it could fly and was preying on them from above like a hawk. It was supposed to have amazing strength and did not need air or water, as long as it had enough blood.

No one knew why it had chosen the *Charlotte*, or even how it had joined them. But they all agreed: they were only safe in daylight.

The captain never left his quarters now, day or night, and for all intents and purposes Adams was in charge. And they learned fast not to use the word "vampire" around him. He'd respond with a club or a whip. He was certain his men were deserting him, drowning themselves to escape the ghosts and phantoms of their imagination. He was trying to stop it, the only way he knew how.

Looking back, Cade could almost understand the mate's thinking. Sailors were wildly superstitious, even for the time. If word got back to land that the *Charlotte* was haunted by something supernatural, it would be the end of the captain's and the mate's days of running a ship. No sailor would ever follow them back out to sea, and no company would hire a captain who couldn't hire a crew.

Adams probably didn't want to starve. He was a rational man.

He never really believed in the vampire. Not until the very end.

THEY WERE LESS THAN a week away from port when Samuel, a shipkeeper—a boy, really, not much more than sixteen—lost his mind.

He had spent the last day huddled on his bunk, refusing food, refusing water, refusing to move even when Adams brought the club down on him.

Cade, who remembered what it was like to be a shipkeeper, brought the boy a cup from the freshwater keg on deck.

Samuel took it, gratefully, and then clutched at Cade's arm when he turned to go.

"Nathaniel," he said, his voice low and urgent. "We have to get off this boat, we have to."

Cade didn't know what to do. Samuel's hand felt like an iron cuff around his wrist.

"We're almost home," he said. "Just a few more days."

"No," Samuel said. "We have to get off this boat right now. There's no more time."

"We're almost home," Cade said again, trying to pull away.

Samuel sat up in his bunk and pulled Cade's face closer. "No," he hissed. "You don't understand. I was out on the deck last night. I was out there—and I saw it."

His eyes were filled with panic.

"It was just standing there," Samuel said. "Like it owned the whole ship, looking out over the rail. It looked like a man, but I saw—I saw it!"

Cade pulled away from the boy, trying to find something comforting to say. "We'll tell Adams," he said. "We'll let him know, and—"

He got no further. With a shriek, Samuel knocked him over and ran out onto the deck.

Cade took off after him. When he reached the door, he saw Samuel, already standing at the rail.

The rest of the crew was frozen, watching him with the same attention they would have given a shark.

"We have to get off this boat!" he screamed at them. "All of you! We have to!"

"Easy, boy," one of the other sailors—Quinn, Cade remembered—said to Samuel.

"You don't understand!" Sam screamed, tears running down his face now. "I saw it! *I saw it!*"

And then he leaped. Everyone rushed to the rail, but there was no trace of him in the water below.

He sank like a stone.

Cade, standing there with the others, realized they were looking at him.

Then Adams broke the silence.

"Sun's going down," he said. "I think we should get ready."

THERE WAS NEVER any shortage of sharp edges on a whaling vessel. What was left of the crew armed themselves with harpoon heads, lances, knives and grapnels.

Each man was given a lantern or a torch. Two barrels of whale oil were put into the tryworks, the brick ovens on deck used to render the whale blubber. Now they were just being used to throw as much light as possible. Thick, greasy smoke filled the air.

Cade held his torch in one hand and a double-flue iron in the other. The crew—down to sixteen, with Samuel's abrupt exit—seemed calm. Even confident. The night was falling fast, but now they were taking arms against the invader. Perhaps they were going to die. But this way, they would die like men, on their feet, rather than like cattle selected from the herd and slaughtered.

Then the captain announced he'd be leaving.

He would take one of the whaleboats under full sail

and head for Georges Island in Boston Harbor, and the military fort there. He would return to the ship with soldiers and guns.

They were less than a day away. It was the best plan, he said.

The men said nothing, because the captain had his gun drawn. He didn't put it back in his belt until he was well away from the *Charlotte.*

From the rail of the ship, they all watched him go.

Adams decided that they should search the ship.

They lashed the wheel into place, on course for Georges Island, and split up.

As newer men on the crew, William, Cade and Jonas often got the worst jobs. This was no different. They were sent into the hold, to find whatever was hiding there.

THE HOLD HAD NEVER seemed quite so big before. He should have been able to search it alone. Three of them should have been able to find anything in there.

But the silence yawned around Cade like a chasm, and his lantern barely seemed to touch the dark.

He gripped the harpoon iron tight in his right hand and took another step forward.

He heard something, like a sigh, and spun around a stack of barrels.

The thing was still feeding on Jonas. In that half-second while it was occupied, Cade got a glimpse of what had stalked them for days.

It was taller than Cade, even hunched over. Its body seemed distorted, its head too long for its neck, its elbows bent the wrong way.

Cade's eyes fixed on the long, tapered claws at the end of its arms, the ones that held Jonas.

Cade didn't have much of an imagination back then. He never had time for it, with the hours of labor and the struggle just to stay fed.

But he had the first and only flash of intuition in his life looking at those claws. He remembered the sound of something digging into the hull, as if it were clawing its way from the water and onto the boat.

He realized that's exactly what had happened. The creature had never been on the boat. But where else would a thing that hated daylight hide? A thing that didn't need to breathe? It had latched to the underside of the ship, waiting for them to reach the open sea. Until it was too late to turn back. Every sunrise, it went back down under the waterline, safe from the sun, until it got hungry again.

Cade was trembling. The creature's claws worked Jonas's chest like a bellows, pumping every last drop of blood out of the wound on his neck.

It was the teeth that snapped Cade from his paralysis—revulsion at those long, needlelike fangs.

Pure reflex took over. Cade remembered the harpoon iron in his hand, and screamed as he launched himself at the vampire.

He didn't even see Jonas after that, his friend's body hanging on those strangely bent arms like meat on a rack. He just slashed blindly at the thing holding him.

The vampire plucked him from the air and held him at arm's length while it finished draining Jonas.

It had known he was there the whole time. He was no threat.

Cade struggled. He hacked wildly with the iron. The blade struck something.

Then the vampire was gone. It moved too fast for him to see. Jonas sat on the floor, a great cavity carved out where his neck once met his shoulders.

His eyes still seemed to plead with Cade.

Cade no longer cared. His mind finally caught up with his body, and he wanted nothing more than to run.

It was already too late.

There was a whisper near him, and he was flying across the hold. He hit a barrel hard enough to crack it open.

Another slight whisper in the air, and he was flying again. This time he landed on the rough planks face-first.

The blade was gone. Dimly, he realized he was bleeding, two bloody gashes up and down his chest.

The thing was right on top of him now. He felt himself lifted again, but only to its mouth. The breath on his neck was cool and rank, the smell of an open sewer in the rain.

His head tipped back far enough to see that the thing had been scratched slightly across one side of its distorted face.

A thin trickle of blood ran from the scratch, hung at the edge of its jaw—and then dripped onto Cade.

He hadn't even hurt it. But he could feel its rage, like the heat off a stove. Somehow, he knew it was the indignity of being touched that sparked the creature's anger. It toyed with him, rather than simply gutting him.

All those thoughts were retreating into the distance, getting further and further away. He knew not much time had passed, but his legs and arms were numb. He felt cold.

Two things saved him.

First, another light: far off, maybe a million miles away. Some last part of him knew it was William, coming back for him. He was running as fast as he could, but it was all so slow to Cade.

The vampire had to shift, slightly, to meet William's attack.

Then, the second thing: the ship ran aground on the rocks near Georges Island. The entire hold jerked and shuddered, and the thing at his neck was thrown away by the impact.

He landed somewhere in a corner, the sounds of the ship's timbers groaning under the insult of the crash. He tried to get his feet under him again. Couldn't.

The darkness took him then. He thought he was dead. Some small part of him was glad, because it meant he would no longer have to live in a world where things like that existed.

He had never been so wrong.

•

EVERYTHING HURT. The whole world was the edge of a razor blade, slashing at Cade, as he opened his eyes.

He'd never before felt the millions of tiny frays in the threads of his clothes, but now they were tearing at his skin like thorns. The wooden floor of the hold was as jagged as rocks where it touched his face. His bones felt too heavy, as if they would rip through his skin like paper.

Everything hurt. The stink of the sea just outside, as it filled his nostrils like acid. The light, where it sliced through the chinking in the hull. The air, a lead weight on his skull, in his lungs.

But all of it was nothing compared to the emptiness at his core.

The words "thirst" and "hunger" were far too small for what Cade felt. Too human. Even words like "lust" or "starvation" couldn't begin to describe the emptiness, the raging need, when he woke. He had gone hungry before—his family was poor, which was how he ended up apprenticed to a whaling vessel at sixteen. And he had known thirst, when the water supplies on the ship were down to the damp wood of the barrel.

None of it was even close to what he felt then. It was as if he was collapsing in on himself—burning down to a finer, harder point that was somehow also larger than anything else in the world.

He could feel himself vanishing, disappearing into the void inside. He clung to whatever remained, but his body screamed in pain, and he lacked the strength to hold on.

His heart no longer beat—it oozed. Slowly shifting the blood in his body, dripping out every precious drop. He could feel it.

Other scents reached him. His sense of smell seemed just as acute as his vision now. Dimly, he managed to connect the various flavors and varieties of the scents with memories of people he'd known. It seemed like a very long time ago.

There was Quinn, who chewed tobacco leaf constantly, until it flavored his whole body with a slight tang. There was Avery, who was already dying of the pox, but didn't know it yet, didn't feel the little animals munching on his brain, which stood out in the scent like a worm in an apple. Adams, the ship's mate, a musk like salted jerky.

And then, closer, more familiar, William. He knew that name. And Jonas. Random images. Sitting with them, talking, wandering the streets of Boston, looking for women and drink, with a lust that seemed almost quaint by comparison. Scenes curiously dead of any emotional resonance.

A new, overpowering scent reached him. A rich, coppery tang in the air.

It smelled delicious.

All the memories vanished then, washed out in the pure, clean scent of their blood.

He leaped across the hold, his muscles pulsing with new power. Jonas and William were piled there, like they were packages waiting for him to open.

Jonas was dead—his blood was already slightly tainted, slightly old—beginning to turn rank. But the thing that had fed on him had left enough for another meal. And it was still warm enough.

His canines shoved their way out of his mouth, and he tore open the flesh of his prey.

He buried his face in the blood. It tasted wonderful.

He drank deep, and every cell in his body screamed with something too cold, too dark, to be called joy.

Jonas was empty too quickly. He tossed the corpse aside, turned to the other body.

Then he heard something. A flutter of a pulse, weak but still there.

He stooped down to William's throat. Saw William's eyes open, heard him say a name with his last ounce of strength: "Nathaniel . . ."

He knew that name from somewhere. He just didn't care anymore.

He drank the living blood, and this was even better. He felt his own wounds knitting, felt structures shift inside himself, and knew he was taking the last steps away from what he had been.

He knew. He just didn't care.

There was a noise above him. He ignored that, too. He felt, rather than heard, the leather boots on the ladder of the hold. Intruders.

He wasn't afraid. They were slow, and they were no real threat, his new senses told him.

They were men. They were prey.

He realized his mistake when he heard the gasp. They were already on top of him. Guns drawn. Frightened and ready to shoot.

He smelled their fear, along with the rankness of their sweat, under the gunpowder and oil of their rifles.

He dropped the body, now empty, to the floor of the hold. Already he had forgotten its name. He turned to face the men.

Perhaps if he had been just a few minutes older in his new life, he would have sprung on them quicker. Perhaps he would have gotten farther and torn them apart, and he would have started his new life free of any semblance of humanity.

But they were prepared, and he was too slow. They fired.

He felt the pressure in his chest—not pain, but pressure—as the hail of bullets knocked him back.

He saw his own blood, pumping out of the new holes in his skin. He struggled to stand and could not.

He looked up at the man in the lead of the intruders. Saw the hate and disgust in his eyes. Saw himself there.

Suddenly, he remembered who he was.

Mercifully, that was when the man clubbed him with the butt of the rifle, and everything went black.

"WHEN I WOKE UP AGAIN, I was in a cell. I met President Andrew Johnson. That's where my second life began."

Zach sat on the floor, with his back to the wall. Most of the time, he hadn't even looked at Cade. Just listened.

"Cade," he said, his voice quiet. "I'm sorry."

"Don't be," Cade said, angry now. "You were right. The point of the story isn't that I am a good person underneath everything. I was a person. But now I'm not."

"That's not true. You're fighting it. You're trying—"

"Mr. Barrows," Cade said patiently, "I killed my best friend to feed myself. And I felt nothing. I am a vampire and a murderer. Whatever else I do in this world, nothing will change that. I can fight on the side of the angels until doomsday, but I'm still damned."

"Then why do it? Why bother?"

Cade's face was entirely in shadow now, so Zach couldn't see his expression when he spoke again.

"Because," Cade said, "it's worth fighting for. That's all that matters."

Zach thought about that for a long moment. But he had to admit: "I don't get it."

"Maybe you will," Cade said. "Someday."

THIRTY-NINE

Neither Cade nor Zach spoke for a long time. Cade checked his watch again. The light from outside was gone.

"Sunset," he said. "Let's find Konrad."

Zach hesitated when they reached the car. Cade was in the driver's seat, but Zach wouldn't get inside.

Cade got out again and looked at Zach over the roof. "What?" he asked.

Zach looked troubled. "Why are we going after Konrad?"

"Nothing has changed. He's still the priority."

"You're sure about that?"

"Yes," Cade said simply.

Zach scowled. "Ask a stupid question . . ." He stepped away from the car door.

Cade wanted to get back on the trail. Get back to the hunt. But he bit back his impatience. "I know you're not used to speaking directly. But you need to start."

"I think maybe we should get back to D.C. Regroup. Consult with the president."

"There's no time," Cade said.

"Someone tried to blow us up, Cade," Zach said. "You don't think maybe we should pause and reconsider strategy?"

"No."

"So that's it? You're just right and I'm just wrong? You ever think that this vendetta you have against Konrad is clouding your judgment?"

"He has the answers we need. It's that simple."

"He didn't plant that bomb, Cade. Holt did. You told me that. So why is the CIA trying to kill us?"

While one part of his brain talked to Zach, Cade was forced to pause and reconsider. Not his course of action—Zach was wrong there—but he had been too focused on his prey. He hadn't considered another threat.

"You're right," Cade said, interrupting whatever snide remark Zach was making. "Get in the car."

Zach looked confused. "I am? Wait, what?"

Cade started the engine. Zach got in the passenger side.

They drove to the site of the safe house. Now it was abandoned, cordoned off by police tape. Nothing but rubble.

Cade got out of the car and walked around.

Zach followed. "What are we looking for?"

"I don't know," Cade admitted.

How had Holt managed to plant the bomb? There was no way anyone could have followed them to the safe house. He would have noticed. Vampires had been returning to their lairs for centuries—not one would have survived if it were possible for humans to track them unnoticed.

The only answer: a traitor. And not just any traitor. Someone with access to the highest levels of the White House. Someone who knew the location of the safe house, of all Cade's safe houses, who knew all his secrets.

He hated to admit it, even to himself, but Zach was right. The hunt was far more complex—and dangerous—than he'd allowed himself to think.

Worse, Cade couldn't protect the boy. Not until he knew what he was facing.

There was only one thing to do.

"I don't need you here," he said to Zach. "Go home."

"Excuse me?"

He reached into his pocket and took out the rest of the money. He tossed the wad of bills to Zach.

"Take this. Go to the airport. Go home."

Zach caught the cash one-handed. But he still looked baffled. "Wait, what are you going to do?"

"I've still got work here."

"Then I do too."

"No soap," Cade said.

Zach looked at him. "'No soap'? What does that even mean?"

"Sorry. It's an old expression, meaning—"

"I don't give a shit. Talk to me, Cade. You can't just send me away like I'm the errand boy. I'm supposed to help you—"

"You can't," Cade said simply. "You were right. You are not ready for this. Go back to Griff. Give him the report. Tell him I will be in contact as soon as possible."

Zach looked hurt. "I wasn't trying to . . . I mean, I didn't mean I wanted to quit . . ."

Cade turned away.

"Go home, Zach," he said.

He was already working out his strategy. It was a new kind of prey. A new hunt.

Cade ran across the street, leaving Zach standing by the car. He was gone in seconds.

He needed information. He was sure he knew where he could get it.

FORTY

She was kept in an atrium at the center of the building—high ceiling, skylight with retractable cover and a decorative indoor fountain. He called it his Zen garden, a place for meditation.

She could have made the skylight with one easy leap, but the collar's range extended to the roof as well. She would be dead before she touched open air.

Most of the time, she sat. She could be very, very quiet and still. But she was starting to get hungry. She was used to regular meals.

The noise of the water in the fountain was enough to baffle her hearing much of the time. (Honestly, how could anyone think with that racket? It didn't seem very meditative.) But she caught some conversations here and there. Konrad on the phone, making dinner reservations. Konrad with a patient, reassuring her that her breasts had never looked better. Konrad ordering a nurse to inject Botox.

Tania heard all this and filed it away in her perfect

memory without really listening to it. She was bored out of her mind.

She was sitting like a statue when the door to the atrium clicked open.

A voice echoed from speakers set in the ceiling.

"I've opened a pathway from the garden to the first operating room," Konrad said over the intercom. "Please join me there."

A click, then his voice was back again. "I'm sure I don't have to tell you what happens if you stray from the path." Another click, then silence.

Tania thought about disobeying, but that would only bring a shock from the collar. There was no way Konrad would try to retrieve her himself.

She had underestimated him. That was obvious from the new jewelry she was sporting. Her mistake was treating him as if he were human. She should have known better.

So she got up and walked down the hall, directly to the first operating room.

The operating room was lit up like a Vegas casino. All the overheads were at full intensity, and several more surgical lamps had been dragged into the room. There wasn't so much as a single shadow in a corner.

Tania winced, still sensitive from the UV burn he'd given her the previous night. "Does it have to be so goddamn bright in here?"

Konrad sat on a stool by the operating table. He gave her a distracted smile. "Yes."

There were parts on the table. Some looked organic.

Others looked metallic. And several looked like a horrible fusion of both.

"I've been thinking about you. And Cade. Well, your entire species, actually."

"I'm sure we're all honored."

"There's something very infantile about the vampire," Konrad said. "The liquid diet. The suckling. Just like a baby. And the childlike belief that death will never come. It makes you arrogant. Rather careless. Immortality came to you as a fluke. You have no idea how precious a gift it is, and so you waste it."

"You didn't just want an audience tonight, did you? Because if that's the case, I might want you to press that button."

He put down his scalpel and probe, then picked up the remote. "I'm going to assume you're being sarcastic, rather than suicidal."

"You're going to kill me eventually."

"True. But later is better than sooner, isn't it? No reason to rush it."

Tania looked down. "No. There isn't."

"Exactly," Konrad said. "As a matter of fact, I do have an errand for you. I need you to get some human bones for me. From consecrated ground. A complete skeleton, if possible. I'd go myself, but you know how that ends up. You rob one grave, then before you know it, mobs are lined up outside your home with torches . . ."

Tania's expression indicated she didn't find Konrad as amusing as he did. She waited for him to clear a path to the exit, but Konrad wasn't done with his lecture.

"This actually brings me back to my point. You don't need anything but blood and yet you acquire money. Lots of it. I find that curious. Why would something like you bother with all the trappings of being human? You don't need to move in the daylight world at all. Do you know what I think?"

"I think you're going to tell me."

He gave her the distracted smile again. "I think you still cling to the human world. Because Cade moves in that world. You stay attached to it, and you stay attached to him. It's fascinating, really," he said. "I've never seen one of you capable of this level of self-delusion. Not even Cade."

"What do you mean by that?" Tania was suddenly interested.

"I've lived a long time," Konrad said. "Everything always comes down to three things. Love and money are the first two. You wouldn't take my money, but you're not actually capable of love. So that only leaves the third."

"And what's that?"

"Fear," Konrad said. "You're scared of him. You're trying to appease him with your pretend affection. But part of you hopes I do manage to kill him. Because someday, he's going to come for you, Tania. Just like all the rest of your kind."

Tania's face betrayed no emotion at all. "Maybe that's true," she said. "Maybe Cade will kill me. But you won't live to see it."

"Another threat? I should think you would have realized by now, you're not going to win."

Tania ignored that. "I had a therapist once," she said. "He tasted bitter. But before he died, he told me some things about projection. That's where you imagine other people have the feelings you're having. You talk so much about me being scared of Cade. I think you're afraid of him."

Konrad snorted. "This is a rather transparent attempt to insult me."

"Maybe. But if you're so smart and you want Cade dead, why not do it yourself? Why put the commission out there? Why boss around your government friends?"

"Cade is an insect. I don't need to dirty my hands with that kind of work."

"And yet, you had that whole setup in your house. Lights, this collar. Like you planned it for him. You know what I think? I think you're a coward. You want him dead more than anything, but you're terrified of him."

Konrad's face darkened. He picked up the remote, and, for a moment, Tania thought she'd gone too far.

For a second, Tania savored the novelty of being scared.

He turned his back, dismissing her. "Go," he said. "If you're not back in an hour, I press the button. Be a good girl and you'll get a pint of blood when you get back."

"Which door?" she asked.

Konrad pointed at a back door.

"Feel free to use the alley. You should feel right at home."

Tania walked toward the door. But Konrad had to get in the last word.

"The trap was never meant for Cade," he said. "For

one thing, he'd never have been stupid enough to let it happen to him."

Biting back a reply, Tania left. Konrad wasn't going to simply kill her now; he was going to avenge the insult. It was going to be long and painful. She considered going past the one-hour deadline, just for an easier way out.

But she had to admit he was right: there was no reason to rush it.

FORTY-ONE

The truth is more sinister. In 1978, a team of government engineers was drilling through rock to expand the giant secret underground base at Dulce, New Mexico, when they opened into a cavern containing dozens of the Greys. A firefight ensued, with sixty-six Secret Service and FBI agents killed before a "high-level government operative," supposedly answering only to the president himself, managed to restore order (according to my sources). Some "alien experts" or "paranormal investigators" will tell you the Greys, like the Reptilians, are actually aliens, sent here to colonize and subdue the planet Earth. *This is disinformation.* As their presence underground indicates, they are actually the ancient adversaries of man who have plagued us for generations. That the U.S. government has reached accord with these things tells us all we need to know about who is actually in charge.

—Anonymous website

Zach sat in the car in long-term parking at LAX. The smart thing to do would be to follow Cade's advice and go home. He never wanted this job. It wasn't in the plan. He had spent so much time planning and maneuvering, getting into exactly the right position.

And it wasn't like he was running away. Cade *told* him to go. He'd done his best. His ribs hurt like hell. He still smelled smoke and concrete dust from the explosion. People were trying to kill him. That definitely wasn't part of the plan.

He checked his phone. Still plenty of time to catch the red-eye to D.C.

So now that he had an escape hatch, why was he hesitating to use it?

Maybe because something rankled in the way Cade had dismissed him. Zach had never been fired from any job. He'd never failed at a task before. He didn't like the idea that this was too much for him—even if it was painfully true.

He got out of the car, one hand clutching the wad of cash. In the car window, he caught a murky glimpse of himself. He looked like hammered crap. Zach focused on the idea of a hot shower and a fresh suit. Even the idea of stretching out in a business-class seat with a cold beer sounded like pure luxury. That helped quell his misgivings.

Sure, he might get some strange looks from airport security, but he had his government ID. He could talk his way through any questions.

He started for the terminal. Then stopped again.

What if this really was part of the plan? What if he was supposed to be here? If he could help nail Konrad, even when he'd been told to quit, then he could probably name his job in the White House. Maybe Cade was testing him, seeing if he'd quit when things got rough.

Then again, maybe he was just stubborn.

He got back in the car and took out his sat-phone. With a tap of his finger, he lit up the GPS screen. Konrad's address was easy to find. The phone even offered him turn-by-turn directions.

Zach twisted the wires and started the car again. He wasn't done yet. He was going to show Cade, and everyone else, that he wasn't just baggage on this trip.

Zach was going to prove he could be a hero after all.

FORTY-TWO

Helen dropped her keys on the entry table and entered her apartment. It was like an operating room: clean and sterile. Not so much as a family photo or a pile of dirty laundry. Nothing to make it personal. In that way, it was the perfect reflection of her.

Helen reached for the alarm panel and punched in the security code.

Her place was wired with a system that could detect motion, changes in temperature, even differences in the composition of the ambient air in the room. The Company looked after its human capital.

Despite all that, she was careful. Something must have been out of place. Something tipped her. Or she was just paranoid.

She gripped the pistol concealed in her handbag, came out with it in a two-handed shooting stance—

Nothing.

She shook herself and lowered the gun.

Helen crossed the room to her sofa and clicked on the TV. The gun went on the end table, where the remote had been. She rubbed her eyes. Yawned.

A cold voice whispered in her ear: "Ms. Holt."

To her credit, she didn't scream. She went for the gun.

Cade threw her over the breakfast bar, into the kitchen. She bounced off the fridge and hit the floor.

Cade stood over her before she'd caught her breath. She looked up at him, disbelief etched in her eyes.

"You're dead," she blurted.

Cade hauled her to her feet and pushed her back against the counter. "And have been for some time," he said.

"How—?"

"I can find anyone," he said. "You each have a unique scent. City of ten million people, it just takes a little longer."

Actually, Cade had simply trailed her from work. But it never hurt to add to the reputation.

Not that she would get a chance to tell anyone.

He could see the effort it cost as she wiped the shock from her face. She leaned back, wincing at the pain, and crossed her arms. "Did I at least kill your annoying little buddy?"

Cade stepped closer again. "You should be more concerned about your own chances of survival, Ms. Holt."

There. He saw it. The atavistic fear, crawling up from some deep part of her brain, notifying her of the threat. Cade tried not to take joy in it, but the predator in him loved this. The pure fright of the trapped prey, with no chance at either fight or flight.

He watched as she tamped down the panic, struggled to breathe deeply. Her eyes darted around the room. The closest alarm pad was on the other side of the kitchen. Same with the phone. Her emergency beeper was in her bag, out in the hall. He'd effectively blocked her from any way to call for help.

She noticed his clothes.

"You look ridiculous," she said. "Been shopping in the clearance aisle?"

He felt another stab of admiration. Trying to buy time. Get him talking.

Cade took another step, and her composure collapsed. He was just a foot away from her now. "Do you want to live, Ms. Holt?"

She swallowed hard.

"Yes," she said, voice hoarse.

"Then tell me something I can use."

"I am a citizen, and an officer of the United States government," she hissed. "You can't touch me."

That surprised him. She knew about the oath, if not exactly how it worked.

"Where did you hear that?"

A smirk, despite the fear. "We know a lot more about you than you do about us."

She had that right, at least. Still, he reached over and gently prodded her with a finger.

"My oath to protect does not extend to traitors," he said. "You'd be surprised what I can do to traitors."

That got a response. Her eyes flashed with anger. "I'm not a traitor," she snapped.

"Of course you are. You're shielding Konrad. What I don't know is why."

"I don't make policy. The higher-ups said to watch him. I'm just doing my job."

"Just following orders? I was there when that defense was invented. It didn't work then, either."

"Don't get self-righteous with me. I've seen your file. You've done a lot of monstrous things in the name of God and country. We're just like you, Cade. We get our hands dirty."

Cade was tempted to laugh in her face. "You think you're like me?"

"I know what you've done."

"You have no idea what I've done. I have been on this planet a hundred and sixty-three years. I have filled whole graveyards with bodies. Watched Hell erupt on Earth a dozen times. Killed beings older than mankind. You're right, I have done monstrous things. Because I am a monster. While you—you are merely human."

He stepped closer again. Now he was only inches from her face. She started to tremble.

"Why are you protecting Konrad? What's he offering you?"

"I can't tell you," she said. "You can call me a traitor, you can kill me—"

"I could, yes. But I want to know: why?"

"I can't, I can't—"

Cade let his voice drop to a whisper. "Then there's nothing else to say, is there?"

Helen's eyes widened as she realized what that meant. She made her decision fast.

"I told you before," she said. "He's a valuable asset. You don't seem to understand, Cade, we're fighting the same war. We just refuse to fight it unarmed."

Cade knew what she was selling. Pitching herself as another soldier. At the mercy of forces greater than her, trying to do what was right in an insane world.

Of course, he also saw her palm a steak knife out of the drawer behind her.

"He can give us tools we need. He's still brilliant. We can use him."

"That's not what I asked," Cade said. "What I want to know is, what is he offering *you*?"

She tried to look confused. Failed. "I don't understand."

"You've gone too far, Helen. You tried to kill me. Whoever you work for, I don't think that was their idea. I can only think of one person that would serve: Konrad."

"No, you're wrong, I'm not—"

Cade let his voice drop to a growl. "Don't lie to me again. Last chance: what has Konrad offered you?"

She looked torn. Calculating. For a second, he thought he saw the real her, underneath all the shifting façades.

Abruptly, she reached up and tore open her collar at the throat.

"Bite me," she said.

Cade was genuinely surprised. He took a step back.

"What?"

"Make me like you." Her voice was pleading. "Please. Do it. I'll do anything you want, tell you all of it—but you have to give me this."

"It's not—it doesn't always work," Cade said, the truth stumbling out of him. The change didn't take in every victim of a bite. Most people simply died. Some rose again. He didn't know why.

Her eyes were crazed as she looked at him. Now she stepped closer to him, and he retreated again. "I know the chances. You think I don't know? I want this. I want it."

"No," he said, no longer uncertain. It was a simple fact, embedded in him like bedrock: he would never spread the disease.

"I can make you do it," she said.

He didn't bother to reply to that. It was simply too absurd.

Then he heard something from the TV.

"—to Jennifer Espinoza in Culver City," the anchor with the sandblasted face was saying.

The screen switched to a shot of an attractive young woman standing in front of what looked like a park.

"Roger, I'm standing here at Holy Cross Cemetery, where someone displayed a sick sense of humor by robbing the grave of famous horror actor Bela Lugosi. Police say someone took all the remains of Lugosi, best known for playing Dracula in the classic movie—"

Cade turned his head, like a dog on point.

"Lugosi was buried in one of the many capes he wore in his most famous role, Roger, so police are monitoring eBay and other auction sites in case someone tries—"

Cade was momentarily baffled. Konrad would never be so obvious. It would almost be like sending him a message.

Helen thought he was distracted. She whipped the steak knife from behind her back.

Cade didn't care. She couldn't hurt him. She gave him a hard smile.

He figured it out a second too late. She already had the serrated tip at her throat.

With a quick slash, she laid open her own jugular.

Blood sprayed down the front of her blouse, out onto the kitchen floor.

Cade froze.

Her blood was everywhere. All over her. The stink of it, rich and fresh and warm.

Still smiling, Helen sagged to the floor as her life poured out of her.

"Come on," she whispered. "Do it."

Cade felt his fangs push their way out of his mouth, unbidden.

He turned and ran. Nearly knocked the door off its hinges on his way out of the apartment.

His inhuman hearing picked up a small chuckle from the back of her throat. "Pansy," she said.

FORTY-THREE

In Europe in the Middle Ages, and even later, witches were known to be notorious grave thieves. Their dissection of corpses for parts of the body needed in the "witches brew" is famous in folklore. . . . Not too many years ago, the only way for medical students and medical schools to obtain corpses for dissection and study was to hire grave robbers. Sometimes when students were unable to hire others to do the gruesome job, they were obliged to do it themselves.

—*Claudia De Lys,* A Treasury of American Superstitions

Konrad heard the back door of the clinic open. He checked his Patek Philippe. Right on time.

Tania entered the room, a contractor-grade trash bag slung over her shoulder.

Konrad couldn't help smiling. She looked like an elf, carrying presents for a psychopathic Santa.

She dumped the bag on the operating table. Konrad winced a little, even though the condition of the remains didn't matter.

"I got what you wanted," she said.

"Well done," he said. "You get your treat. It's over there."

He pointed. A bag of type O rested on the counter.

Tania, hating herself for her eagerness, rushed over to it and tore it open with her teeth. It slid down her throat in two smooth gulps.

Konrad was busy pulling the remains from the bag. The body was mostly decomposed, with long strings of dead tissue here and there. The rest was bone.

"You can use that?" Tania asked.

"Oh, yes," he said. "It was so difficult, so long ago. When I was looking for the Elixir of Life. When I was still a mere alchemist."

Konrad's eyes grew soft and warm as he tore the remaining flesh from the bone. "It was like the heavens opened when I finally learned the secret. Death is, you see, paradoxically, fundamental to survival. Our bodies are in a constant state of flux. Cells must die in order to be replaced. To halt this process, to freeze it in place, is to turn living tissue into a corpselike state."

He used a bone saw to cut the limbs into smaller chunks. Grit and dust flew into the air.

"Death itself held the secret to eternal life. I soon learned what your kind has always known, on a cellular level. The process can be halted, but only if one is willing to become a living corpse."

Tania made a face. "We're both in pretty good shape for corpses."

Konrad began digging into the bone with a metal pick, scraping something out. "Because we sup regularly at the fountain of youth, my dear. We know that immortality and rejuvenation are not the same thing."

Konrad hit a button on the wall, and his machine lowered itself from the ceiling. Even Tania found that thing disturbing.

Konrad placed the scrapings lovingly into one of the collection arms of the device. Then he activated it, and the bits of bone and marrow went into a cup, where they began to be soaked in some kind of fluid.

"Life requires death," Konrad said, his face rapt. "And death consumes life."

Konrad began scraping more bone, Tania seemingly forgotten.

She wondered if she could make the door while he was playing with the corpse.

He looked up at her then, seeming to wake up.

"You don't understand," he said. "It came to you as an accident. But I had to stalk it and hunt it down, and make it mine. This is why my prize is so much purer than yours."

Tania just stared. She'd seen all variety of human emotion reflected through the eyes. Whoever said they were the windows to the soul was right. She'd seen her prey stare back at her with fear, with hate, rage, disbelief, even love.

But there was something she'd never seen in Konrad's eyes. She wondered if she was seeing true madness for the first time.

He shook his head, as if pitying her.

"You don't understand. No. Come. Let's put you back in your cage."

Remote in hand, he walked her back to the atrium at the building's center.

She was nervous. She had the feeling that the trip to the cemetery was the last thing he needed. But Konrad seemed so happy now. Calmed by touching death.

Perhaps he wasn't going to take his revenge on her after all.

She walked into the atrium and sat by the fountain. He waited at the door, smiling.

Something was off. She sensed it immediately. She looked up.

The screen over the skylight had been drawn back. She could see the stars. Eyes wide with realization, she looked at Konrad.

"Sunrise will be in a few hours," he said. "Perhaps you can learn something new about fear in that time."

"You son of a bitch," she said, looking around frantically for something that would shield her from daylight when it came.

Nothing. The room was as empty as ever.

"There's nothing you can do," Konrad confirmed. "I haven't left a secret passage for you, or anything to torture you by raising your hopes. I'm not really the mustache-twirling type, I'm afraid. It's enough for me that you will spend your last moments in utter despair. You will die."

He closed the door.

Tania stood there, waiting. If she felt she had the right, she would pray that Cade would find her. She had drawn enough attention to her errand for Konrad. It had to work. He was her only chance.

The door opened again, Konrad smiling.

"I thought you should know: Cade is already dead. My associates saw to it this morning."

Tania sat down, numb. The noisy fountain seemed to chuckle behind her.

FORTY-FOUR

Konrad went home. He began packing. The game was almost over. Now it was time to fulfill his final obligations and depart this sad, sprawling mess of a city.

Cade was dead. Odd, it didn't feel more like a triumph to him. Perhaps it was because, as the female vampire said, he did not do it with his own hands. But that was ridiculous. He'd engineered Cade's demise. He'd killed thousands over the years. He supposed his lack of joy was simply due to the fact that Cade was, in the end, no more of an obstacle than any of the others who'd come up against him.

He put a few of his best clothes into a garment bag, a treasured copy of *Mein Kampf* into his briefcase, along with a stack of cash in dollars and euros. So many things he had to leave behind. But he'd done it before. And there were plenty of shops in Europe where he could restock his closet and bookshelves. He'd left other homes with less preparation. At least this time, there were no peasants at the gate.

There was a heavy pounding at his front door. He sighed. Perhaps he'd spoken too soon.

The young man at the door didn't wait to be invited in. No great surprise there. He looked like a typical product of the American system: muscled and overfed, healthy and attractive despite his obvious pig-eyed stupidity. He wore a sweatshirt with the name of some inferior university on it, in the same way that small children need notes pinned to their jackets.

"Where is she?" he demanded as he shoved his way past Konrad.

"Where's who?"

"Don't. Just fucking don't," he said, waving a warning finger at Konrad. "Where is Nikki?"

Nikki. How utterly predictable.

"And you would be . . . ?"

"Dude, I'm her boyfriend."

"You had an open relationship, I take it."

The young man stepped closer, into Konrad's personal space. "You looking for an ass-kicking, pal?"

Konrad smiled. "I'm simply saying, she never mentioned a boyfriend."

He smirked. "Oh, yeah. You thought she was in love with you? That she was getting all she needs here? Wake up, Gramps. You've been paying our rent for a while."

"Ah," Konrad said. "So you're her pimp."

The young man pushed him, hard. "Told you to watch your mouth, old man."

"Yes. Yes, you did."

"Now. Where is she?"

"I wish I could help you. But I haven't seen her since I last fucked her."

The boyfriend/pimp scowled at that. He stepped past Konrad, shoulder checking him out of the way.

"Asked you a question, dude. Where is she?"

"And I told you: I don't know."

"Bullshit. You called. She came. I come back to the apartment today, she's not there."

"Perhaps I'm not her only client." A smile played on Konrad's lips. "Or perhaps she's not, as you put it, 'getting all she needs' at home?"

The pimp raised his fist, ready to strike Konrad, then stopped. It took him a moment, but he beamed when he figured it out.

"You did something to her, didn't you?"

"I don't know what you're talking about," he said tightly.

Smugness oozed from the pimp. "Sure you don't. And I bet that's what you'd tell the cops, too."

"Which is where you're going, I assume," Konrad said. "Because you're so worried about your lady love."

The pimp nodded. "Afraid so, dude. Unless . . ."

He let it hang there. Konrad winced at the ham-fistedness of it, the crassness of the approach. But the little hangnail was right: he couldn't afford a visit from the police right now.

"How much?" Konrad asked.

"Ten grand," the pimp blurted. When he saw that Konrad didn't react to the figure, he added, "Just to start. Then we'll see."

Amateur, Konrad thought. Well. Whatever it took to get him out of the way.

Konrad gave him a curt nod, then headed into the main room. He opened a wall safe concealed behind an original watercolor from prewar Vienna.

He took out an envelope, made a show of checking the currency within and extended it to the pimp.

"Here you are," he said. "I hope this quells your anxiety over Nikki."

The pimp grabbed the envelope. "We'll see," he said, with the same smug look. He put his hand inside and began to count the money.

He dropped it suddenly, as if bitten.

"Ow! Damn, man, what the hell?"

He brought his fingers, bleeding, up to his mouth.

The bills had spilled on the floor. A small metal razor glinted from between them.

Konrad looked appropriately contrite. "Oh, I am sorry. Please. Do accept my apologies."

The pimp was already breathing heavily. "Is that some kind of sick joke?"

"Are you feeling all right?" Konrad asked.

The pimp shook his head, unsteady on his feet. He reached under his shirt and pulled out a gun. He pointed it in Konrad's direction, but his eyes were glassy and unfocused.

"What the hell did you do to me?"

"Try to calm down," Konrad said, his voice soothing. "I can help. I'm a doctor."

There were, of course, fast-acting chemical agents that would have stopped the man's nervous system from sending or receiving any signals, causing his body to spasm and his skin to slough off. But Konrad rejected those. Something synthetic and inelegant about them. As always, he was more interested in seeing what the human body would provide.

Cade had mentioned the flu variant Konrad built during the war. Now it looked like a child's plaything to him. The Führer had wanted to fill shells with it and fire them at England, but Konrad ultimately rejected the whole thing. It spread uncontrollably, and might have even turned back on its creator. Unacceptable.

He didn't fault his own knowledge, of course. Konrad had been manipulating DNA for decades before Watson and Crick discovered the double helix, but the advances in the equipment in the past fifty years—scanning-tunneling microscopes, genetic sequencers, computers—gave him a new level of precision and finesse. With those tools, he could create a menu of infinite choice and novelty.

For the pimp, he'd decided on a new little variant he'd been toying with for a while. He'd seen a television program, of all things, about a very rare genetic defect that caused its sufferer to have no immunity whatsoever against the human papilloma virus. One cut, even a scratch, and the skin would begin piling up warts.

It was ugly, but not fatal. Konrad reviewed the literature. He decided he could fix that.

He prepared an emergency envelope, with a sharp blade

secreted in a pile of bills, for demands like the pimp's. The pathogen smeared on the blade only needed a small cut to enter the body, and once inside, spread quickly.

He checked his watch. Thirty seconds and counting.

The pimp's gun started to shake. Tremors in the extremities.

"I said, what the hell did you do, you prick?" the pimp demanded. Eyes rolling now. Sweat running down his forehead. Konrad wondered if the man would have enough muscle control to pull the trigger.

The pimp gagged violently, dropping the pistol. No, apparently not.

Panic filled his eyes. "What did you—?"

That was all he got out before the eruptions began.

He clawed at his throat, trying to breathe. Konrad had a good view of the first growths on the man's neck and chin. They spread like a nest of spiders, racing across his skin.

The pimp couldn't see those, but he saw the ones on his hands. He stared at them as if they belonged to someone else, mouth open in mute horror.

The growths bubbled up, one after another, filling every patch of smooth skin, replacing it with hard, horn-like scales. (A boost in the keratin content of each cell, thanks to the virus.) Spirals of skin, twisting like snail shells, turning and growing out and upward.

When they had colonized the entire skin surface, they began to build on top of one another, extending feeding tubes downward below the subcutaneous level. Muscle, intestine and fat—all more fuel for the tiny viral engines, churning away.

Konrad imagined that was incredibly painful.

Not that the pimp could say anything about it. His mouth was filled with rootlike structures spitting out of his throat, as the growths filled any empty space they found.

He fell to the deep-pile carpet, alongside his gun. One hand tried to reach for it. His fingers were more or less gone, however, fused into something like a hoof.

One eye fixed on Konrad from a well of rioting flesh. The other was sealed up already.

The hair drew back inside the scalp as the viral loads consumed more and more skin cells, accumulating in layers like tree bark. Within a moment, the last strands were sucked into the swelling mass. The ears were now only tiny slits on the side of his skull.

The pimp's shoes snapped at the laces as his feet ballooned. His body was just about used up. Inside, his bones would have been tapped and converted into more food for the growths.

He stopped twitching. The growths slowed, then stopped.

Konrad waited. Five seconds.

The pimp's T-shirt ripped open, and the roots leaped out of the chest cavity, casting about for any new flesh, a last grasp for survival.

Nothing was within reach, however. The roots waved feebly about for another second and then drooped. Dead.

What was left on the floor looked more like a fungus than a man.

Konrad checked his watch again. Five minutes thirty-nine seconds.

Not bad at all. Almost totally useless as a weapon, of course. It required direct insertion into the subject's bloodstream, and wouldn't spread beyond a single carrier. But the process was fascinating, nonetheless. Complete conversion of the human biomass into a nonviable form, rebuilding the entire genetic structure in mere minutes.

This was what his patrons never understood, from the Führer to the Soviets, and now the Arabs. They always pestered him for bioweapons or anthrax or some kind of plague. What Konrad did was not science. It was alchemy. And alchemy was all about nonrepeatable results. It was what made him unique—irreplaceable. He wouldn't give anyone a weapon they could easily duplicate without him.

Konrad smiled to himself. And to think, they called him mad.

ZACH SAW EVERYTHING. The windows of Konrad's place framed everything like a plasma-screen TV. He didn't bother to close the blinds; he probably never thought anyone would be watching from the bushes.

But Zach saw it all. When Konrad's victim began to change, to transform into that plantlike thing, he almost screamed. Instead, he lost his footing on the steep slope and slid about twenty feet into a chain-link fence below.

That sick son of a bitch, he thought. He was struggling to get up. The shock was gone. All he wanted now was to punish Konrad. He'd do it with his bare hands if he had to. That son of a bitch wouldn't get away with this.

Zach started climbing the hill like he was a soldier running for enemy lines.

Five minutes later, he managed to clutch one of the struts supporting the house on the hill, sweating and panting. He'd made about ten feet. He was not in shape. Cade was right. He wasn't prepared for this.

But Cade was. Cade would probably be overjoyed to hear that the good doctor had finally committed a crime punishable by death.

Zach fumbled his phone out of his jacket and hit Cade's number on the speed dial.

It took a second to connect. He started talking right away.

"Cade, listen, I'm at Konrad's place—"

That was as much as he got out when he realized two things.

The first was that he had dialed wrong. He was talking to Griff's answering machine. Not even his mobile phone. He'd gotten the agent's home number by mistake.

The second was that someone put an arm around his neck. It felt strong enough to twist his head right off his body. He couldn't move.

Then, from behind, he heard the voice of the heavyset Latin guy from the night before. Laughing at him.

"You're hilarious," Reyes said. "I was almost willing to let you get inside for the laugh factor alone."

Zach wanted to make some kind of witty remark to save his dignity, as Reyes's hand reached out and took his phone away.

But he couldn't breathe. Nothing came out of his mouth as the pressure around his neck increased. The darkness claimed him then, and the cold was all he felt.

FORTY-FIVE

Dylan rubbed his eyes and drank more coffee. It didn't help. He was falling asleep in the booth of the truck stop.

He'd driven as long and as hard as he could, but he could only get so many miles per hour out of the truck. He wasn't going to make the rendezvous. All he wanted to do was curl up in a ball on the vinyl seat and close his eyes.

He was not going to make it. Khaled would kill him.

Even worse, he wouldn't get paid.

He was so out of it, he didn't know when the man sat down across the table from him.

"You look tired," he said when Dylan finally noticed him.

Dylan jumped in his seat, even though the man looked harmless enough. Cheap suit, white shirt and black tie. Wire-rimmed glasses.

"Yeah. I'm pretty wiped," Dylan said cautiously. Maybe

this was just some accountant, looking for anonymous sex in a truck-stop restroom. Dylan had heard stories.

"I can help with that," the man said.

Definitely a perv. Dylan's face curled into a look of disgust.

The man smiled. "I'm not coming on to you, Dylan. Or should I call you Ayir al-Kelba?"

The guy knew his name. The guy knew his secret name. Now Dylan knew he should run. But fear kept him rooted in his seat.

Before Dylan could make up his mind, the man passed him a plain paper envelope.

"What's that?"

"Open it."

Dylan was suspicious. If this was a trick, it made no sense. If this guy was from the government, he already had to know enough to arrest him. Why would he bother to set him up?

The man's eyes betrayed a hint of impatience behind his glasses. "I'm not trying to entrap you. I think you've watched too much TV. Just open the envelope."

Dylan did as he was told.

Pills. Yellow tablets, with no markings.

"What are these?"

"A little something to help you stay awake. Keep driving." The man stood. "Don't worry. No one will stop you. Just keep your eyes on the road."

Dylan looked at the pills, then at the man as he walked toward the door.

"Who are you?" he hissed, trying not to attract the attention of the other customers.

"A friend," the man said. "Drive safe."

He left, walking into the light of the false dawn, the glow reflected over the horizon that appears long before the sun actually rises.

Dylan looked back at the pills in his hand.

Oh, why not, he decided. He swallowed all of them with his coffee.

Before he knew it, he was back on the road, driving steadily, his exhaustion a distant memory. He felt like he could take on the world.

He had no idea who that guy was, but this was great shit. He wished he'd said thanks.

FORTY-SIX

The call from the White House came just before eight a.m. The president wanted to see Griff. Immediately.

Curtis looked grim when he arrived. Wyman looked ready to burst into song.

This isn't good, Griff thought. He was concerned he'd pushed too hard on the Kuwaiti connection. Maybe overstepped some diplomatic boundary. But Wyman . . . Wyman looked too happy.

"Where are Cade and Zach Barrows?" the president asked quietly.

"I haven't checked in with them yet today, sir."

The president chewed on that like a stick of gum. He nodded to one of the Secret Service men. "Show him."

The agent turned a video screen on a rolling cart to face Griff. It displayed a bombed-out building, shattered concrete and broken glass spewed all over a parking lot.

"What is that?" Griff asked.

"That," the president said, "is what's left of the Los Angeles safe house."

Griff pushed down the panic. Cade was all right. He could survive worse than that. But if it happened in the day . . .

"We covered it as a gas explosion with the locals," Wyman said. "We didn't find any bodies."

Relief washed over Griff. Then something else worked its way to the front of his thoughts.

"Why wasn't I told about this?"

"We figured you already knew," Wyman said. He threw a thick folder at Griff. "Read that."

Griff did.

Phone records. Calls, back and forth. All from Griff to the Promethean Clinic, in Los Angeles.

Then a copy of an electronic flight reservation, made in Griff's name, for a flight to L.A. next week.

And finally, in the back of the folder, his medical history. Including the latest round of tests, which confirmed the recurrence of his cancer.

Griff felt something plummet in the pit of his stomach.

Griff looked at President Curtis. There was pity in his eyes.

"No one is above temptation," he said. "Especially when they're facing a death sentence."

"None of this is true. These are faked."

"Sure they are," Wyman mumbled.

It all became clear to Griff at that moment. They thought he had sold out, for a taste of whatever miracle cure Konrad could offer.

Griff tried to think straight. But it was hard, with the blinding rage pouring through him.

"After all I've done—"

"How did this happen, Griff?"

"—I can still see some of the things, when I close my eyes, the things I've had to face to keep this country safe—"

"Griff, you have to admit, it doesn't look good—"

"—children torn to pieces, bodies stacked up on shelves in a supermarket, things that don't even have names, and, after all that, the shit I have waded through, you have the stones to accuse me—"

"Agent Griffin!" The president was shouting now.

Griff realized he was standing, with his fists clenched. He took a deep breath and sat down again.

"I'm sorry, sir," he said.

The president scowled. "You say this isn't true," he said, pointing to the folder. "You say you don't know where Cade and Zach are, or even what happened to them. I'm not sure, but I'd almost rather you were lying about that."

"Sir, I will find them. Cade has probably gone underground. It's standard procedure when there's been a security breach."

Wyman snorted. "You're the security breach, you dumb bastard. You think we're going to let you cover your tracks now?"

Griff clenched his jaw and tried to ignore him. "Sir," he said, directly to the president, "I'm not stupid enough to leave a trail like that. And if Cade and Zach are in danger—"

"We're all in danger," the president said. "We still have a threat out there, and our efforts to find it have literally blown up in our faces. Maybe next week we can sit down and sort out this mess. If nobody's dead. But right now, I have thousands—maybe millions—of people in danger. Right now, your problem shouldn't be what's on my desk. Do you understand me?"

Griff hung his head. "Yes, sir."

Curtis took a deep breath. "Do I really need to tell you what happens next?"

"No, sir."

The president looked sick and angry. "Get out."

Griff stood and turned for the door.

He didn't look at Wyman. At that moment, the VP's face would have been more than he could take.

GRIFF WAS ALMOST out of the White House when security at the gate told him to wait. He wondered if they were going to arrest him after all.

A few moments later, Wyman strolled out a side exit, three Secret Service agents trailing behind. Great, Griff thought. He wants to gloat.

He stepped over to Griff and tried to look solemn. "Agent Griffin," he said. "I'm sorry it had to come to this."

They had not taken his gun. Griff thought about that. He could probably get it clear of the holster before the Secret Service reacted. He could shoot at least once before they brought him down.

Wyman waited for a reply.

"Is that all?" Griff asked.

Wyman looked torn. He seemed genuinely curious about something.

"Will you walk with me a moment, Agent Griffin?"

Griff considered that. He wondered if Wyman needed to die. If he wasn't just greedy and incompetent and corrupt. If he was genuinely evil.

Maybe someone like that shouldn't be that close to the presidency. Maybe this was supposed to be Griff's last act on Earth.

"Depends," Griff said. "You need the entourage?"

Wyman turned to the agents. "Give us a little room, please."

The lead agent nodded, and Wyman's detail dropped back a few dozen feet as he and Griff walked toward the Rose Garden.

The day was turning warm. Spring arriving early this year. Griff wanted to see the cherry blossoms. He'd have enough time to do that.

Provided he didn't die in a hail of bullets right here.

He and the vice president walked side by side easily enough. Neither man said anything until Wyman spoke up.

"Why are you doing this?" he asked.

Griff turned, surprised. "Doing what?"

Wyman's eyes searched Griff's. "Dying. You don't have to."

Griff laughed. "We all have to." His hand was in his pocket. His suit coat flared out, covering his motions. He could easily reach to his holster.

"No," Wyman insisted. "You don't. Let's cut the bullshit, okay? I know you're not involved with Konrad."

He hissed the last part, in case the Secret Service was eavesdropping.

Griff almost went for the gun right there.

"But what I don't understand is, why aren't you? He could cure you. He could save you. Hell, he could make you immortal."

Wyman was right. Griff had read the files. Konrad could reset the clock on his body, could wipe out the cancer like a spill on a countertop.

"You really don't understand a damn thing," he told Wyman.

"I don't understand why you wouldn't use something that could save your life."

Griff looked at Wyman—really tried to see the man beneath it all.

"Don't you have something you wouldn't trade? Not for anything?"

Wyman stared back blankly. "I don't follow you."

Griff gave up. It was like trying to teach algebra to a slug. He suddenly felt tired. No, more than tired. Done. Done with all of this. He wasn't sure if this was some other angle Wyman was playing. The man did nothing but play games, really. In truth, Griff didn't care anymore.

Wyman could believe what he wanted. It was no longer Griff's job to convince him of the true shape of the world.

His hand dropped away from his sidearm.

"May I go now, Mr. Vice President?"

Wyman still looked confused. He frowned, then waved Griff off as if washing his hands of him.

"You're a fool," he said, and stalked back to the protection detail.

Griff started for the gate. He figured he could have gotten at least two shots in when he had Wyman off by himself. Head and heart, for sure. Maybe even three, before the agents would have taken him down.

He wasn't convinced Wyman didn't deserve it. It was still possible the little worm was dangerous and needed to be stomped flat before he could do real harm.

But the worst part was, Griff didn't feel like it was his job anymore.

FORTY-SEVEN

Helen went to the office after the emergency room, even though it wasn't yet five a.m. Ken tried to help her into her chair. She shook him off irritably. She was not in a good mood. Despite the painkillers and two pints of blood pumped into her, the stitches in her neck hurt like hell.

Cade must have tripped the alarm on his way out, because Ken was in her apartment before she could bleed to death. He took her to the closest hospital just in time. Unfortunately, it was not the Company-controlled clinic. Her black ops status was useless when dealing with bureaucracy. She spent six hours stuck behind a curtain as gunshot wounds, drug ODs and heart attacks were treated all around her.

Around three in the morning, the cops showed up at the ER to question her about her possible "suicide attempt." Her badge was finally useful; she was able to flash it at the officers and get released.

Ken took her home, then back to the office. She didn't know what she was going to do. Cade was still alive. Which meant she was fucked. Konrad would never give her the Elixir now, would never trust her to deal with Cade again.

Her phone kept ringing. Ken finally answered it.

"Reyes," he said, after he'd hung up. "Says he's got some good news for us."

"Isn't that fucking peachy."

Ken shut up after that.

A few minutes later, Reyes entered the office. He looked at the gauze on her neck, but knew better than to say anything.

"Well?" she asked.

"We have the kid," he said.

Helen's jaw unclenched. Maybe the painkillers were working after all. Things were looking up.

HELEN ENTERED the interrogation room, where Zach was shackled to a chair behind a table, both bolted to the floor.

He'd fallen asleep, facedown on the wood, like a freshman pulling his first all-nighter.

"Morning," she said cheerfully.

He sat up quickly, blinking. He looked at the bandage around her throat. "You must have had a fun night."

Helen smiled even wider. "Nothing compared to the fun we're going to have today. Coffee?" she asked. She had two cups in her hand from the kitchen on the second floor.

She put the cup in his shackled hands. He had just

enough play in the chain to bring it to his lips. Then stopped. He looked at her, and set the cup down.

"No, thanks," he said.

So. Not as dumb as he looked. Or as any of his actions up to this point would indicate.

Helen sat down at the table and sipped, taking her time.

"Don't I get a phone call?" he asked.

"Zach," she said, a scolding tone in her voice. "You're not under arrest. In fact, you're not even here. You don't exist."

She leaned back, let that sink in. "And if you don't exist . . . well, who would you call? You can see the problem."

Zach glared. "You can't do that."

"Oh, poor baby. We already did. You're an enemy combatant, Zach. None of the rules apply to you."

"I work for the President of the United States—"

"That was back when you existed."

Zach closed his mouth and glared at her.

"Where's Cade?"

He shrugged. "How the hell should I know? I don't exist."

"You are adorable. I have such fun talking to you."

"Yeah, me too. Shame you tried to kill me."

"The bomb? You're taking that way too seriously."

"I'm funny that way."

"You've been keeping bad company. If you weren't hanging out with Cade, you never would have been in danger. I told you, you're on the wrong side."

"Oh, I see. You tried to blow me up for my own good."

"You're safe now."

Zach looked down at his cuffed hands, then at the locked steel door. "Yeah. I feel safe."

"Don't call me a liar, Zach," Helen said, her voice flat. "There's nothing to stop me from putting your brains all over that wall. You're safe as long as I say."

Zach stared at her like he was trying to see the inside of her head. "Who are you people anyway?"

"We keep everyone safe. That's all you need to know. But in order to do that, we need you to tell us where to find Cade. We need your help. I need your help, Zach."

Zach shrugged. He was breaking down. She could feel it.

He reached for the coffee. Brought it up to his lips.

Helen smiled.

He threw the cup at her, aiming for her eyes.

She was faster, of course. She was out of her chair as soon as he twitched, and, anyway, the coffee had cooled. All Zach managed to do was splash her suit jacket.

Her *brand-new* suit jacket.

Her pretty face twisted into a feral snarl. "You little shit," she hissed. She reached for her pistol, drew it back, ready to beat him across the face with it.

Then she froze. Remembered the cameras in the ceiling. Thought about Control, how he could be watching, even now. She tamped down her rage and considered her options.

Zach, still alive, and still a threat if he got back to D.C.

And even more of a threat if someone higher up came to question him. She couldn't let him go, couldn't keep him.

Cade. Still out there. Konrad would never meet his end of the deal if he found out. And he would find out eventually, because Cade was a fucking mad dog, he just wouldn't stop. He'd be back on Konrad by nightfall, if he wasn't at the doctor's house already.

The very existence of Zach in this room, the continued survival of Cade out in the world, they were evidence of her betrayal of the Company. She couldn't let them live. But she couldn't kill Zach, not without bringing down the wrath of both the Company and the White House. And without the Shadow Company's resources, she had no hope in hell of destroying Cade.

Then there was Reyes and Ken, and they knew everything she'd been doing. Control would find out she'd triggered the bomb at the safe house, despite his orders.

Too many loose ends; the slightest tug on any of them, and everything would unravel. It wasn't supposed to be like this. She was supposed to be immortal by now.

Instead, she was trapped.

Then it came to her: she had the solution, right here, in this building. A way to tie it off, staunch the bleeding long enough to get her reward. It would work. It had to work.

Abruptly, she holstered her pistol again, and left the room.

She found Reyes and Ken still sitting in her office.

She snapped her fingers at Reyes. "You got his phone."

He nodded. She waited half a second, then snapped again. "Well, give it to me."

He fumbled it out of his jacket, handed it over.

"Get out," she told them.

Ken hesitated. "What are you going to do?"

She began dialing. "I'm finishing this."

FORTY-EIGHT

Tania checked her watch. Just after six. Sunrise was supposed to be an hour away, but already the sky above was turning pink. In less than sixty minutes, daylight would start burning over the horizon.

The skylight would focus those rays down into the room. There was no corner they wouldn't reach. She might be able to delay the inevitable, but as the sun progressed across the sky the whole room would eventually be illuminated.

Then she would die. The blood in her body would solidify. Her skin would wither and crack, and draw about her like a vise. Her eyes would turn to dust. Her bones would split like dry kindling.

She would feel every second of it.

She was going to die in agony.

The door to the atrium snapped off its hinges.

Cade stood there, perfectly calm.

Tania felt the urge to rush to him, to put her arms

around him, almost like she was the silly little girl who'd first met Cade decades ago.

Then she remembered the collar and stayed put.

"Good timing," she said, pointing to the skylight. "I thought you might put the grave robbery together with me if I just chose an appropriate body."

"What are you talking about?" Cade asked.

"I . . . Bela Lugosi's grave. I thought you would—"

"I didn't come here for you," Cade said. "Whatever you did, I didn't hear about it."

Tania's mouth dropped open. She closed it quickly. Of course he hadn't. Stupid of her, to expect him to come charging to her rescue.

He never had. He never would.

"Where is he?" Cade demanded.

"Wish I knew," Tania said. "He left me here to burn. I would gladly watch you pull his intestines out."

"Why didn't you do it yourself? It's not like you to be so reluctant."

She flicked the collar with one fingernail. "Six ounces of plastic explosive. It's actually really humiliating, but he—"

Cade crossed the room before she could finish. He reached his hands to her neck, and while Tania was still frozen with shock, snapped the collar in two.

Tania winced for a moment, waiting for the explosion.

Nothing. The two pieces of the collar, broken cleanly at the lock, sat on the floor. Harmless.

"He lied," she said, her eyes wide.

"It's what he does," Cade said, already walking away.

She caught up with him, feeling the empty spot around her neck.

"How did you know?" she asked.

"I didn't."

She stopped. "You didn't."

He realized she wasn't moving, so he turned back to her, completely calm.

"There was no alternative. Either you would have died with it on or died taking it off. Seemed like the best thing to do was get it over with."

"And you would have made that decision with your own neck on the line?"

"Of course," Cade said, still damnably calm. "The alternative would be to become Konrad's slave."

She glared at him. Unperturbed, he walked away.

Tania considered the facts. Cade was right. And he wasn't lying. He would have torn the collar off as soon as it was placed around his neck.

She understood, suddenly, why Konrad had said Cade never would have let it happen to him.

Cade was already out of the building. She hurried to catch up.

OUTSIDE THE CLINIC, Cade looked to the sky. He didn't have much time. He might be able to make it to Konrad's house if he hurried.

His diversion with Tania had cost him valuable time, but he justified it to himself by pretending there was a chance Konrad would be at his clinic.

Laughable. He had to admit it now, even if he couldn't tell her he'd figured out her message. Holt had outplayed him. Now he was reduced to breaking down doors, looking for Konrad like a blind pig rooting for slop.

His phone rang. The call was from Zach. The boy must have been back in D.C. by now.

"This is not a good time," he said.

"Someone simply must teach you how to answer the phone."

It was Holt. Alive. And one step ahead of him, again.

Cade didn't bother asking how she'd gotten Zach's phone.

"Where is he?"

"I'm fine, thanks for asking," Holt said. "Even though you ran out on me. A girl could start to feel rejected, Cade."

Cade was in no mood. She'd timed the call just right. Sunrise in a short while. No chance of finding her before then. "Where is he?"

She dropped the flirty tone. "Nothing for nothing. We want you to come in. Quietly. Your ass for his."

"Where?"

"Do we have a deal?"

"Can we drop the charade? Tell me where he is. And I will be there. I know you will try to kill me. And you know nothing will stop me from coming for you."

"Such a suspicious mind," Holt said. But she gave him the address: the Federal Building, on Wilshire.

"Be here at sundown. Or we'll send your boy back to the White House in a box."

Cade hung up. He had no more time. He needed to find a place in the dark.

Tania spoke from behind him. “You look like shit, you know.”

He faced her. She stood there, waiting.

“Why are you still here?”

She thought that over. “Ask me again later.”

He started walking, tried to brush past her. “I’m working,” he said.

She put out a hand, gently, and stopped him.

“Wherever you’re going, you won’t make it,” Tania said. “Almost sunrise.”

Cade hesitated, unsure of what to do.

“And you’re exhausted,” she added. “You have a place to stay?”

Cade shrugged. “I’ll find a spot in an underpass somewhere,” he said. “Plenty of those around.”

Tania gave him a look. “I think we can do better than that.”

FORTY-NINE

Helen smirked as the phone went dead. She was starting to get the idea that Cade actually disliked her. Whatever. It wouldn't be her problem much longer.

She buzzed Ken and Reyes back into the office.

Konrad didn't know Cade wasn't dead, and there was no one who would tell him. She might still be able to pull this off.

As for Cade and Zach, she had her own blunt instruments to solve the problem right here, sitting in the chairs across from her.

"Cade will be coming here," she told Ken and Reyes. "Tonight. I'm depending on you to eliminate him."

Ken just nodded. Reyes's face didn't betray a single thing, but in his eyes Helen could see the panic. He wasn't as dumb as he looked, she reminded herself.

"We have the tools," she said. "You will be able to take him out."

She took out the weapons she'd ordered made when Konrad first told her that she'd have to eliminate Cade. R&D said they might work. Maybe. During the day, with a lot of luck.

But Ken and Reyes didn't need to know that.

She handed them across the desk to the men.

"Here's how it will go down," Helen said. "Ken, you will engage Cade first, with the holy water."

She pointed to the plastic pump-spray in Ken's hands now. It would shoot a jet of blessed water, taken directly from the font of a Catholic church. Vampire tear gas.

"While he's distracted and in pain, Reyes, you will approach from behind and fire the punch into Cade's back, staking his heart."

Reyes's weapon was only slightly more sophisticated. A blank shotgun shell would fire a bolt from the barrel. The bolt was tipped with a hardened graphite point—basically, it would be like stabbing Cade with a wooden stake moving at the speed of sound.

Reyes looked at the bolt-gun, then at Ken, then back at Helen. "Question?" Helen asked him.

"Yeah," he said. "Are you fucking kidding me? You want us to go up against that thing with a squirt gun and a sharp stick?"

"You questioning my orders?" Helen's voice was cold.

"Come on, Helen, this is just nuts—"

"Are you requesting reassignment, Agent Reyes?"

That shut him up. "No. No, Agent Holt."

"Good. Get some rest. Cade will be here at sunset. You'll want to be sharp."

"How are we supposed to know when he's here?" Reyes asked, still surly.

"Man the security cameras. Wait for the bodies to pile up," Helen said. "Cade's not particularly subtle." She stood.

"Wait, what are you going to do?" Reyes demanded.

It was over the line, but Helen figured she'd already pushed him pretty far. "I'm going to deal with the problem in the cell downstairs. Ken? Come with me."

Reyes sat in his chair and sulked. But Helen knew he'd follow orders. What the Company could do to him was scarier than Cade, at least for now.

SHE AND KEN WALKED to the elevators, down to the subbasement.

Cade would kill Reyes and Ken tonight, she had no doubt. If, by some miracle, they got lucky and the weapons actually worked, it wouldn't matter. Not to her anyway. Either she'd be long gone or her plan was blown anyway.

That only left Zach. The annoying little prick. Still in the interrogation room. On camera, and in the Company's records now. No way to change that.

Fortunately, she had a much simpler answer for him: Ken.

Ken was strange. Even Helen could see that, and she was well aware of the kinks in her own personality. On the surface, he was perfect. Tall. Broad shoulders. Blue eyes. Good hair, white teeth, clear skin, the whole package.

But if you spent enough time with him, you'd swear you could hear an echo. There was an emptiness where the rest of a human being was supposed to be. He smiled at jokes, but you always wondered if that was just a learned reflex.

On paper, Ken was equally perfect. Upper-middle-class family, decent grades in college, accepted into CIA in a heartbeat. That's where he met Helen.

He locked onto her the first day of training. She noticed him, too, but she could admit it was just animal lust for such a healthy specimen.

Ken was old-fashioned, like he'd learned to date from watching movies. He sent her flowers, for Christ's sake.

Underneath that, there was something more robotic. He seemed to regard her as a missing component, and he was going down a checklist to procure her.

Helen figured out a way to use that, of course.

She spent most of the training course just out of his reach. Then, right before graduation, she stole into his dorm room at the facility and fucked his brains out.

He called, sent e-mails, even letters. She didn't answer a single one.

But when she joined the Shadow Company and was given her own team, Ken was her first choice. She kept him at arm's length, never explaining, never mentioning their history.

He'd follow her anywhere; do pretty much whatever she asked. When he got too frustrated, she would arrange for some relief—but only enough to keep him loyal.

She'd pretty much broken him. Whatever emotional

deformity he had inside, Helen fit into it perfectly. Someday there would be a bill to pay for that, but for now, he was a good tool.

They stopped outside the interrogation room. She gave Ken a look.

"This is important to me," she said. "Do you understand? I absolutely do not want him harmed. He's special."

Ken nodded, even though she could see the confusion in his eyes.

They entered the room together.

Zach lifted his head off the table but didn't speak.

Ken took a position by the door. Helen walked around behind Zach.

"Zach, I have a few errands to run, so I'm going to leave you in the hands of Agent Blaylock. He's going to ask you a few questions. I want you to cooperate with him."

"I'll have to check my schedule," Zach said.

She laughed, and let her hand linger on Zach's shoulder.

Ken focused on that, then his eyes flicked away.

Good.

"I know you're going to do the right thing, Zach. There might even be a place for you on our team," she said.

Zach glared. "I'm positively moist with anticipation."

Anger clouded Ken's chiseled features. Helen just laughed again and tousled Zach's hair.

"Aren't you cute?" she said. "Be smart, Zach. You want to be on the winning side."

She walked back to the door. From the corner of her eye, she saw Ken's attention was completely on Zach now.

She leaned in and whispered into Ken's ear, just loud enough for the hidden mikes in the room to pick up, "Remember: do not harm him."

Ken gave her a slight nod.

Helen walked out of the room and went to the security station down the hall.

Inside were monitors for all the cameras in the holding cells. She checked number four, Zach's room.

She was just in time to see Ken unplug the camera from the wall. The screen went dark.

Helen smiled as she left the building. Ken would do just as she expected. God, what a big dumb animal.

Unfortunately, Konrad wouldn't be as easy to fool. She just hoped Cade hadn't gotten to him first.

FIFTY

The opulent room was so far removed from the cheap motel Cade and Zach used as to be on another planet. The bellman saw they had no luggage, saw the difference between Tania's designer clothes and Cade's rags, and gave them a knowing wink and smile.

Tania paid for all of it with a black AmEx card in someone else's name. The desk clerk was perfectly obsequious as he handed over their keys.

Tania pulled the blackout drapes, sealing the room completely. It could have been high noon or midnight outside. There was no way to tell.

Cade felt better instantly, out of the light.

So did Tania, clearly. A layer of tension and irritability dropped off her like a cheap coat. The approaching daylight had been getting to them both.

She stretched back on the fifteen-hundred-thread-count sheets of the bed, revealing the tight band of pale, flat skin at her navel.

There was an inevitability gathering in the air, like smoke. Hanging there between them.

She rolled to one side, her hair hanging slightly over her face. "You want to sleep? Or shower?"

Cade thought about it. "No," he said.

MOST VAMPIRES do not have sex. They consider it human and therefore degrading. But Cade and Tania weren't like most vampires. They still remembered some of the good parts of being alive.

He pulled off his cheap T-shirt and went to her. She peeled off her top and arched her back up. He pinned her arms above her head.

She locked her legs around him and bit him, hard, on the neck. He pulled free, his blood spilling over her breasts. He lapped it up, licking the salty taste from her nipples, her skin. She latched again, sucked hard, pulled more blood from the wound, let it run out the sides of her mouth and down her neck.

She pulled him down closer to her and then flipped him over onto his back, yanking away his pants.

Then she clasped her legs around him again, hips rocking back and forth, riding him down to the bed.

Cade's body tensed and shook like he was plugged into high-tension wires. He ran his hands over her, greedy for her feel, her touch. His fingers traced their way down, began working there.

She rode him harder. Her back arched. She tossed her head forward, her hair flying.

Cade's hand moved faster, thrusting upward, lifting her off the bed. Tania sat on top of him, still sticky with his blood, writhing like the sacrifice on an altar from some long-dead religion.

Their nerves, exquisitely tuned, thrummed and burned, back and forth between them, the moment stretching out, seeming like it would never end—

Until she sang, like a flock of birds moving swiftly by in flight.

Cade shuddered and bucked, and then they both stopped moving, suddenly as still as the grave. They lay there, piled on each other, instantly in the comalike state that passed for their sleep, dead to the sunlit world outside.

FIFTY-ONE

Zach never considered himself a tough guy—he would complain if a restaurant overcooked his eggs—but he'd always held a secret belief that he could hold up well under torture. He'd spent days on his feet, working with no sleep, eating practically nothing. In that place in his mind where he starred in his own action movies, Zach thought he could handle it, at least for a little while.

He was wrong.

Ken made a phone call. Reyes arrived in a few minutes. Together, they stripped Zach naked, barely looking at him.

Zach made a joke about how this was further than he usually went on a first date.

Reyes, with the same bored look on his face, punched him hard enough to make his nose bleed.

They went back to tearing his clothes off.

They found the duct tape Cade had wrapped over Zach's ribs and cut that away, slicing skin.

When Zach was naked, Ken cuffed his hands behind him and pulled them up to the level of Zach's shoulders. Zach doubled over from the pain. Ken yanked him over to the wall and hooked the cuffs over a peg. Reyes put a hood over Zach's head.

He stood there, his knees bent, his ass hanging out, his arms behind him and higher than his head.

He waited for another punch, or something worse.

He heard the door slam. They were gone.

He didn't know how long they left him like that. His legs began cramping immediately. His fingers went numb. His knees wobbled, but every time he started to lean forward, the pain in his shoulders brought him back up.

He tried not to make a sound. He really did. But after a while, he heard something. A low-pitched noise, almost like a growl of an animal in pain. For an instant, he wondered if they had put someone else in the cell with him.

Of course, it was him. He was singing out in pain.

The door opened, and light flooded back into his eyes as the hood was snatched away.

Zach blinked and looked up at Ken. Ken smiled back.

"That didn't take long," Ken said. He pulled the cuffs off the peg—Zach thought his shoulders would separate completely—and then dropped them. Zach collapsed on the concrete floor.

Tears of relief welled up in his eyes.

Ken gave him a full ten seconds of lying like that—the blood rushing back into his limbs, the nerves waking up with urgent messages of pain—before dragging him back to his feet.

Ken looked into his eyes. Zach blinked away the tears.

"I'm not going to talk," Zach said.

Ken laughed. "Who cares?"

He knocked Zach flat on his back with a hard slap.

"Let's get to work," he said, as he kicked Zach in the side of the head.

KEN NEVER asked him a question. Not once.

Not when he went to work with the Taser, shocking Zach over and over again on his bare skin.

Not when he beat Zach with the baton. Or when he poured a Diet Coke—a frigging *Diet Coke*—down Zach's nose, causing more pain than Zach thought possible, nearly drowning him in the process.

Or when he brought the dog in. Or when he just punched him.

He never asked a single question.

Zach offered. He offered whatever he could think of. Which wasn't too much, actually. But he thought, maybe if I can get him talking . . . And then he thought, Jesus Christ, only make it fucking *stop*.

It didn't matter. Zach didn't have anything Ken wanted to know.

So he just kept working, not saying a word.

He did whistle occasionally, however.

THE BOY TRIED to raise his head. Ken punched him hard, breaking the skin on his knuckles.

He put his hand in his mouth and tasted blood. The bleeding stopped. Ken hit the boy again.

Ken didn't think the kid had any info, but even if he did it wouldn't matter. He knew Helen wanted the boy to die in the interrogation room. She did the big lovey-dovey act just to get him in the mood. He wasn't that stupid.

He knew Helen was using him. He didn't mind. His whole life, he'd done what other people said, and it was boring. Sure, he was successful, but he'd always stayed within the proper boundaries.

When Helen recruited him, he thought it would be more or less the same. Then he learned that following her orders, he could do all kinds of things that had previously been forbidden. It opened new vistas for him. It changed the rules. He was free to be just as evil an SOB as he wanted, and he could consider it part of his duty to his country.

He felt Helen understood that, on a level too deep to talk about. He was sure they would end up together someday, and they would look back on these early years fondly. Like an extended courtship.

In the meantime, even without Helen in his bed, Ken was happy enough. He enjoyed the job.

He took his time with Zach. He wanted to make it last.

FIFTY-TWO

MURDERS DISTURB CALM WATERS OF LAKESIDE TOWN

BLAIRSTOWN, N.J.—Residents expected some pranks from the teenagers and staff at the newly re-opened summer camp on the shore. At worst, the local sheriff says, people worried about vandalism.

Instead, seven grisly murders have shattered the idyllic calm of the small town. Motives are unclear. The sole remaining survivor is in psychiatric treatment, her identity protected. One source close to the investigation said, "The girl is out of her head, talking about some boogeyman that sliced up all her friends."

State police referred all inquiries to federal authorities, who have assumed jurisdiction over the case. Special Agent William H. Griffin refused to comment, and the Federal Bureau of Investigation declined to provide any further details.

—*Newark* Star-Ledger, *June 15, 1980*

Griff went home and stayed there. He didn't know what else to do.

He sat in the Barcalounger in his living room and turned on the TV just for the noise. He looked at his creds and his badge. Like the gun, they hadn't taken them away.

But they might as well have. There wasn't a damn thing he could do for Cade or Zach. He was frozen out.

He looked at the photo on the creds. In his head, he could almost see it play out like time-lapse photography: a series of photos on all the government ID cards that made up his life. Starting with the photo the army took when he was twenty and in the Signal Corps, training in intelligence. A kid with a shaved head and a dumb-ass smile on his face. Then his first FBI badge—as a trainee, then as a special agent. Longer hair, sideburns. Glaring at the camera like it had done something. And then, year after year of the generic White House priority pass, the one that didn't have any department or title on it but still got him into every locked room. Growing fatter, balder and grayer in each one, until this last ID, which had an old man's face above his name.

He put the ID down and looked around his house. Mostly empty. Not much to show for a life. No wife, no children. With what he did, what he'd seen, it was hard to justify bringing anyone else into his world.

Fuck it, he decided. He got up out of the chair and went over to the liquor cabinet. His fingers traced dust on the knob. He'd stayed away from the stuff since his first diagnosis, over three years ago.

He got out the bottle of Bushmills—government salary—and poured a tall glass. He threw it back, felt the pleasant burn in his throat.

His doctor wouldn't approve. Fuck him, too. Sometimes, all there was to do was get tore up from the floor up. Like the kids would say.

He noticed the blinking light on the answering machine, but couldn't work up the effort to listen. Probably just a telemarketer anyway. Nobody called him at home.

He knew he was sulking. Knew that he should get off his ass and try something—anything—to solve the problem. Save the day.

But he was old and he was dying, and they'd managed to disgrace him on his way out. That hill was just too steep to climb tonight.

He settled in the chair, keeping the bottle with him.

FIFTY-THREE

Konrad took one look at Helen when she showed up, and he knew. He saw the bandage on her neck. That stupid little bitch. She couldn't do anything right.

Cade was still alive.

He was ready to unleash his full venom on her when she spoke.

"I want what you owe me," Helen said.

Konrad had centuries of practice at hiding his true thoughts, but, even so, he nearly laughed out loud. She was trying to lie her way out of her failure.

Unbelievable. He thought about slapping her. Or killing her with his bare hands. All his effort, for nothing.

But it was irrelevant, really. He was out of time. So was Helen. She just didn't know it yet.

He forced a smile. "Come in, my dear."

She stepped into his living room, over the stain on the floor where the pimp's body had rested. It was barely visible. Ken had sent the Company's cleaners, and they did a good job. Even with the really weird shit.

She sat down on the uncomfortable, low-slung couch. He went to the bar. "Do you want a drink?"

"I want what you owe me," she said again.

"The plan isn't yet complete," Konrad said. "Not until after the attack. We agreed—"

"I've done everything you asked," Helen said. "I don't want to wait until after the operation is over. It's time for you to meet your end."

He turned, a glass of champagne in his hand. "You're right."

Helen froze. "What?"

"You heard me," he said, handing her the glass. "I'm going to give you what you're owed. It's time."

She took the champagne with trembling fingers. "Is this . . . ?"

He smiled. "No. I thought you'd be in the mood to celebrate."

She downed the drink in one gulp and then threw it across the room. Before he could say anything else, she sank to her knees before him, already tugging on the belt of his slacks.

He grunted with satisfaction. "You know, you could have just said thank you."

EVENTUALLY, THEY MOVED to the bedroom. Helen woke up sore, and bruised, and hungover from the one drink she'd had. The blood loss had lowered her resistance to the alcohol, and Konrad had been as demanding as ever.

None of it really seemed to touch her. She was finally going to be free. Free of fear. Free of the worry of sagging, coughing, pissing, spitting up blood, all those sad biological functions that take over your life as you fade into a shrunken parody of yourself.

She was going to be free of death itself.

It was about time.

Konrad yawned and stretched. He was awake now, too. She checked the clock. Getting close to sunset. Time to go. Get the Elixir and then get out.

She rolled onto her side to face him.

"So what now?" she asked.

He laughed. "Getting a bit impatient?"

"I've been patient enough."

"Yes," he said. "You have."

He rolled over and reached for the bedside table, rummaging in a drawer there.

"Right now?" Helen said, voice trembling a little. "Now?"

"I keep my word, Helen." He turned, the needle in his hand, filled with a yellow fluid.

She started to get up, but he gestured her back to the bed.

"It's all right," he said. "Just relax."

She seemed worried. Perhaps this was too easy. Greed fought with confusion in her eyes. "What about the mission? You're still leaving the country next week, right?"

"Oh. That," Konrad said. "Yes, well. About that. I lied. The attack is tonight."

He plunged the needle into her neck.

Her reflexes were admirable. She slapped the needle away, knocking her fist into the side of his face. She almost got up.

The serum hit her bloodstream. Her body went rigid and settled back into the sheets.

Konrad watched as the paralysis spread. Her eyes darted at him, panicked, as she struggled to breathe.

"It's nothing you really need to worry about," he said.

He dressed in fresh clothes, then went to the bedside table and retrieved his watch.

Helen followed him with her eyes, struggling to say something.

"Why? . . . Y'din't haveto . . . dothis . . ."

Her speech was slurred. Konrad was amazed she could speak at all. The paralysis should have set in completely by now.

"Why? Oh, it shouldn't be that hard for you to figure out. Revenge. Not just against Cade. This whole, arrogant, adolescent country. The one that destroyed my home twice in the last century. That put a military base on the ruins of my family's castle. I want to see someone inflict the same pain on America that they brought to the Reich. I want to see their dream turn to a nightmare, like mine. I want them to wake up screaming."

Helen managed a small shake of her head. Konrad understood what she'd really been asking.

"Oh, you mean why did I do this to you?" he said. "That's actually much simpler: I don't like you, Helen."

She glared at him. It was all she had left.

"Bassard . . . Yyyyu prmssssd . . ."

Konrad smiled. "I kept my word. You won't age another day. You'll see."

The Elixir of Life. He'd made the serum from the bones Tania had brought to him. It was basically the same formula he'd found centuries before, the one that gave him his first step on the path to eternal life.

But, as he told the vampire, eternal life and eternal youth are not the same thing.

In its raw form, the Elixir was capable of animating dead flesh while making it stronger than leather and wood. Injected into live tissue, it froze all cellular movement. Helen would never age, true. She would also never move again, her metabolic processes slowed to geologic time spans.

He noticed the broken needle and syringe on the floor. She'd managed to snap it before all of the fluid made it into her bloodstream.

It didn't matter. There ought to be enough, Konrad thought. Still, he had to give her credit for trying.

He patted Helen on the thigh, picked up his suitcase and walked out the door.

FIFTY-FOUR

Tania parked on Wilshire, across from the Federal Building. The street was empty. Only the occasional car sped past, streetlights flashing briefly on their windshields.

"You think he's really here?" she asked. It was the first thing she'd said since they rose together and left the hotel.

"If he's not, someone will know where he is."

"They'll be waiting for you."

Cade shrugged.

"Why?" she asked.

"I have to," he said. "You know that."

She grimaced. "I suspect you would do it anyway. Even without your precious oath."

"We'll never know," Cade said, and opened the car door.

She looked across the seat at him as he got out. "I won't be here when you get back."

"I didn't think you would," Cade said, and got out of the car.

Cade strolled across Wilshire, straight toward the front doors. Just like any regular visitor.

REYES SAT IN HIS OFFICE, monitoring the security cameras through a hidden feed. He'd tapped into the lines, at Helen's insistence, so the team would always be able to see what the building's security force saw.

Which, right now, was a whole lot of nothing. But Reyes couldn't escape the feeling that this whole thing had gone foul.

Reyes was a lot of things, but he wasn't dumb. Sure, you could argue he'd made bad choices, but they were never foolish choices. And he always knew when it was time to cut his losses.

When he was twelve, he'd joined a gang. When he was sixteen, he saw what happened to everyone over thirty in the thug life: jail or death. He picked a new career: cop. At nineteen, he left the police academy and hit the streets in uniform. His old buddies didn't mind, because he fed them information. At thirty-seven, in plainclothes, working both sides finally caught up with him. He'd been one of a few dozen cops indicted in a wide-ranging scandal. Cops ripping off drug dealers, planting weapons, lying in court and murdering anyone who found out.

He was looking at a heavy prison sentence. Or a bullet in the eye if he flipped and turned state's evidence.

That's when the Company stepped in.

The Company had a network of dealers in L.A., selling drugs to fund a bunch of dirty little wars. Reyes had been asked many times to look the other way by guys with government credentials. But he went even further, getting prisoners released, losing evidence and passing information whenever it was necessary.

His indictment got shredded. He got a new badge, and a new boss: Helen Holt.

That was two years ago. Now he was feeling the itch again, like a target on his back.

Helen had been out of contact for hours. Down in the holding cell, Ken was losing it on the little *pendejo* from the White House.

Then there was Cade. Reyes looked at the bolt-gun Helen had given him earlier. R&D really thought this would stop a vampire? It didn't seem likely. Helen could have put a .50 caliber rifle with depleted uranium ammo in his hands—something powerful enough to punch a hole in tank armor. Or flamethrowers. Or white phosphorus grenades. Any of those would have had a better chance at killing Cade.

And Reyes knew if they didn't kill him at the first chance, that bastard would put them down a second later. No hesitation. He'd seen it in Cade's eyes.

He began to wonder if the Company would have even approved something this badly fucked. This began to smell like a setup to him.

So when he looked up at the security monitor and saw Cade strolling for the front door, the decision was easy.

He got up and ran for the back exit, not bothering to

hit an alarm. Sorry, Ken, he thought. See ya, wouldn't wanna be ya.

Reyes didn't worry about his soul, but he did worry about his ass. And he decided it was time to get it out of there.

VIDEOTAPE SUMMARY OF EVENTS, FEDERAL BUILDING

23:19: Lobby camera shows UNSUB INTRUDER at front door. UNSUB INTRUDER is male, approx. 20-30 y.o., wearing T-shirt, sweatpants and flip-flop sandals.

23:20: Front doors shatter, triggering alarm. Unknown if UNSUB used some form of explosive device to break down doors. Doors were composed of Lexan-layered glass, with titanium-reinforced frames.

23:20: UNSUB loses flip-flop. Walks across broken glass barefoot.

23:21: First security officer on scene, W. ELLIS, engages UNSUB, gun drawn. UNSUB picks ELLIS up bodily and hurls him into lobby wall, breaking his sternum and four ribs. (See appended CASUALTY REPORT.)

23:22 Corridor Camera One shows UNSUB enter main corridor. Three more security officers—C. GAGE, D. COOKE, S. KURTZ—arrive, guns drawn. No man is able to fire a shot before UNSUB physically attacks. Each man is left with several broken bones and injuries.

23:23: DHS LIAISON KENNETH BLAYLOCK enters from stairwell, carrying what appears to be a squirt gun.

23:23:30: The final security officer on shift, G. MORRISON, arrives from opposite hall entry, gun drawn.

23:23:35: Security officer MORRISON fires three shots from his sidearm. UNSUB is visibly hit. However, he does not fall. UNSUB assumed to be wearing body armor.

23:23:37: UNSUB knocks MORRISON unconscious with a blow to the head.

23:23:38: BLAYLOCK pulls trigger on squirt gun.

23:23:40: UNSUB reacts with extreme pain. Smoke rises from his arm. (Note: DHS has been questioned what chemical BLAYLOCK used on UNSUB. No answer yet.)

23:23:50: Blaylock moves in closer to UNSUB with squirt gun. UNSUB is on his knees at this point.

23:23:51: Despite repeated viewings, what happens at this point in the recording is unclear. In one frame, UNSUB is kneeling on the floor. In the next, he is simply not there. Several seconds must be missing from the recording. Diagnostics ordered for camera equipment and digital recording device.

23:23:52: UNSUB reappears in view, now behind BLAYLOCK. He knocks the squirt gun from BLAYLOCK's hands, and physically seizes the agent.

23:23:53: UNSUB pins BLAYLOCK to the wall, holding him one-handed by the throat. (UNSUB might have used PCP or other drugs, resulting in increased strength and ability to ignore pain.)

23:23:57 to 23:25:49: UNSUB and BLAYLOCK appear to talk. UNSUB holds BLAYLOCK against the wall for the entire time. No audio is available; Corridor Camera One is not equipped for sound pickup.

23:26: UNSUB and BLAYLOCK finish speaking. UNSUB pulls BLAYLOCK from the wall and pushes him toward the stairwell.

23:26:15: UNSUB and BLAYLOCK exit into the stairwell.

Camera coverage ends at this point. DHS LIAISON BLAYLOCK was later found in Lower Level 3. (See appended CORONER'S REPORT.)

A GUARD DOG SAT at attention in the corridor leading to the holding cell.

As Cade got closer, it began snapping and barking, straining at its leash.

He could smell blood on its muzzle. Zach's blood.

Cade had liked dogs when he was human. But they knew what he was, instinctively.

He shoved the Company man forward, was about to tell him to hold the dog, when Ken dove forward and unclipped the leash.

He went into a crouch, and screamed, *"Töte! Töte!"*

"Kill" in German.

The dog sprung toward Cade—and then ran right past him, tail between its legs, a black-and-tan streak down the corridor.

Cade grabbed Ken by the hair and dragged him back to his feet. He was already annoyed by the holy water upstairs. That burned. Now he was angry.

"I'm sorry," Ken said. "I'm sorry, I thought—"

"I know what you thought. Dogs aren't stupid," Cade said, pushing Ken toward the cell again.

"Any more surprises?" Cade asked.

Ken shook his head furiously. "No," he said. "I swear. Just remember. I had nothing to do with what they did to him. Nothing. Remember that."

"Open the door," Cade said.

His hands shaking, Ken put the key in the lock and swung the door open.

Cade saw Zach in the gloom, on the floor. His chest and groin were covered in scratches from the dog, and his inner thigh had a bite that was still bleeding. Burns on his skin from Taser shocks at close range. Bruises. A black hood covered his head.

There was more, but Cade had seen enough.

He reached for Ken.

"I swear, I had nothing to do with it—" Ken screeched.

Cade snapped his neck with one hand.

The body dropped like a pile of dirty laundry to the floor.

Cade entered the cell and removed the hood.

At first, Zach didn't know it was him. His eyes were screwed shut. When Cade tried to lift him, he struggled, until Cade spoke.

"It's all right now. You're safe," Cade said.

Zach looked at him, peeking almost, as if afraid to see if it were true.

He looked past Cade, at the body of Ken in the hall, his neck twisted halfway around.

"Did you do that?" Zach asked as Cade helped him up.

"Yes," Cade said.

Zach kept looking at the body.

"Good," he said.

IT TOOK A WHILE to get Zach's clothes together—Cade found them in a burn bag outside the cell. Zach dressed slowly, assembling as much dignity as he could.

"What now?" he asked.

"Now we get Konrad."

"Konrad?" Zach said.

"You have a better idea?"

"Yes," Zach said, looking at Ken's corpse again. "I'd like to kill every one of them."

"A little bloodthirsty, now?"

Zach looked at him with rage in his eyes. Then it broke, and a warped smile took its place.

"That supposed to be vampire humor?" he asked.

"I just want you to remember our priorities."

Zach nodded. "All right. Let's go."

The boy carried himself forward, limping, waving away Cade's hand. Cade felt moved to add something.

"Don't worry," he said. "If we go after Konrad, I'm sure his friends will be close by."

Zach didn't respond right away. As they made their way down the corridor, past Ken's body, he said, "'Bloodthirsty' . . . That was funny. You know. For you."

Cade's mouth twitched. "I have my moments."

TANIA WAS STILL WAITING outside the building when they exited. She leaned against her car.

Zach looked her up and down. "You brought a date?"

Tania flicked her eyes over to him, and Zach felt a shiver of the same revulsion that had gripped him when he first met Cade. He knew what she was. Her eyes went back to Cade, utterly uninterested.

"You were right," she said to Cade. "He is funny."

She looked Cade over. "I put a change of clothes on the front seat for you."

Cade saw the clothing, neatly folded. All black. Designer labels.

"I bought them while you were sleeping in the hotel. The gift shop had some very fine stuff."

"Why are you doing this?" Cade asked.

"I decided you've looked like an idiot long enough," she said. "You have just enough time to change. Konrad is meeting a cargo ship tonight at the port. Dock 29. I heard him while he was keeping me locked up."

She threw the keys, and Cade snatched them from midair.

"Better hurry," she said.

Zach snapped to attention. "Cade, that's the container," he said. "It has to be. Konrad is going to—"

"I know," Cade said. He stayed where he was. "I asked you a question, Tania. Why are you helping me?"

She looked directly into Cade's eyes, then grabbed him and pulled him into a deep, deep kiss.

It was a human gesture. It caught him by surprise.

She shoved him back and gave him a defiant look.

"Because I'm not afraid of you," she said.

She turned and ran. She was gone in a matter of seconds.

Cade stood and watched.

"Dude, your girlfriend is weird," Zach said.

FIFTY-FIVE

Dylan waited. The smell was starting to get to him. They had grabbed the cadaver parts before embalming. The feces and food in the bodies' intestines reeked. The stink seeped under his skin, worked its way into his brain. He wondered if he'd ever smell anything else.

He'd reached his destination a few hours earlier. The pills had worn off, but he had sheer terror keeping him awake now. No way in hell he was falling asleep in the back of the truck. Not with these things in here.

The corpses. Patchwork men, fitted together at the joints with a metal compound that looked like a shiny kind of mold. Their muscles burst from rotten skin, engorged and too large. They had turned a rainbow of greasy colors as decay set in.

The soldiers were still missing the heads—that was Khaled's job, to bring the heads. But they looked formidable enough, even decapitated.

They lay on metal racks, wires and tubes running from

their bodies into chairs, one at each soldier's side. A bank of equipment filled the rest of the truck, waiting for someone to throw the switch.

According to Khaled, the yellow fluid in the tanks behind the chairs would bring the soldiers back—even stronger than before. Stringy, dead muscles would turn into something like steel cable. Bones would become harder than cast iron.

Dylan wondered how it was supposed to work. Then he checked himself. He wondered if it would really work at all.

Throughout all of this, he'd thought it was a little crazy. But he wanted the money, so he figured, hey, if Khaled thinks it will work, let him, just so long as the final paycheck didn't bounce. . . .

But a bad thought kept rattling around the back of his brain. What if—and, yeah, it was crazy, sure—but what if it was all real?

He didn't want to believe it, but there was a stink in the back of the truck worse than the bodies. The whole setup reeked of—there was no other word for it—evil. He could sense it. This wasn't a scam. There was power here. Something tensed and waited, as if just outside the truck, ready for the moment when it could come inside.

Khaled believed. Dylan had assumed it was just in the standard raghead Jihad stuff he was always going on about. But what if there was more to it?

Suppose he believed in something even worse?

And what the hell were those chairs for anyway?

Dylan began to hope Khaled would get stopped at Customs. Maybe even if it meant he wouldn't get paid.

THE THREE MEN, dressed in medical scrubs and carrying a large cooler between them, stepped off the chartered jet.

Customs moved quicker than usual, because of the big stickers on the sides of the coolers: HUMAN ORGAN FOR TRANSPLANT—HANDLE WITH CARE.

The TSA inspector working security that night was named Scot, according to his name tag. He scratched himself behind the ear with the antenna of his walkie-talkie as he stopped the men.

"Sorry," he mumbled. "I gotta look inside."

The dark-skinned man in the lead frowned, but placed the cooler on the table.

Scot opened the cooler and peered through the mist as the cold-packs inside hit the air.

He jumped back, fully awake.

"Jesus Christ," he said.

"Satisfied?" the man asked.

"What kind of operation you guys doing?"

"Brain transplant," the man said.

Scot looked at him for a moment. What the hell, he figured. The paperwork was in order.

He waved the man through the line. His two companions followed.

A rented ambulance waited for them at the curb. The

airport police were polite enough to let it idle there until the men cleared Customs.

The ambulance pulled away from the airport, sirens wailing.

In the break room later, Scot sat down next to one of his coworkers, who was nursing a Diet Coke.

"You are not going to believe what I saw tonight," Scot said, grinning. "No shit: a human head on ice."

His coworker grunted and drained the rest of his soda. A human head. Yeah. Right.

FIFTY-SIX

It was so easy. That should have been Cade's first clue.

Konrad had been obliging enough to drive his Ferrari to the port and park it in plain sight. The ship in harbor was plainly marked with the Kuwaiti flag and the logo of KSM Holdings, Inc.

Konrad was standing at a shipping container. Cade saw him clearly from three hundred yards away. He was talking to several Arab men, all wearing jackets that didn't do much to conceal the weapons underneath.

"Stay down," he told Zach, and slammed the BMW's pedal to the floor.

Zach ducked below the window as the car executed a perfect bootlegger turn, sliding to a halt a dozen feet from Konrad and his thugs.

Cade rolled out of the driver's side. The Arab men—four of them—were still gaping at the car. Cade moved through them like a thresher. Only the last one managed to touch his gun before Cade knocked him into the side of the ship.

They were on the ground like fallen branches when Cade turned to Konrad. He smirked and held up his hands.

"I surrender."

Cade hit him anyway.

Konrad went down, and Cade pulled him up again by the lapels of his elegant suit.

"Where are they?"

It took Cade a moment to recognize the sound coming from Konrad, a kind of snuffling through the blood streaming from his broken nose.

He was laughing.

"Where are the *Unmenschsoldaten*?" Cade asked, shaking him. "Where?"

"Sehen Sie für sich selbst," Konrad said, smiling with hate.

Cade dropped him to the ground and stalked over to the container.

Zach stood, peering over the BMW's roof. He had a bad moment of déjà vu, back to the moment at the Baltimore shipyard, just a few nights before.

"Get back in the car," Cade ordered. Zach did.

Cade pulled on the handle of the container door. The chain and lock tore like paper.

There were no corpses inside.

There was nothing inside at all.

Konrad's voice mocked him from behind. "Did you really think I'd plan something so slapdash, so amateurish, as to have a container fail right when your Customs service would discover it?"

Cade turned. "You wanted me to find the first container?"

Konrad spat. "You came running, didn't you? Such a good little bloodhound."

Cade tried to make sense of it. "This was just a lure? A trick to get me out here so you could try to kill me?"

"It was worth a try. Helen seemed quite convinced she would be able to deal with you. Impetuous youth."

Cade still didn't understand. "So there never were any *Unmenschsoldaten*? This was all about me?"

Konrad shrugged, smiling. "Did I say that?"

Cade went into the container. At the back, he stopped, scanned the metal wall—and found something.

He pulled at a lever, almost invisible in the seam of metal where the corners joined. The back of the container swung forward, revealing a hidden compartment.

It looked like the cabin of a luxury cruise liner—cramped but still lavish. A compact bed and desk. Lights built into the walls, along with vents for air. A chemical toilet and a minifridge, running off a rack of batteries.

A perfectly hidden escape pod, built to bypass Customs, metal detectors and cameras.

It all fell into place.

Oh, Lord, forgive me once again for my arrogance, he thought. I've been so blind. So stupid.

All this time, he thought the *Unmenschsoldaten* were on their way to Konrad.

They weren't. They'd already been here and gone.

Cade stalked out of the container. He lifted Konrad from the ground again.

"Where?" he demanded.

Konrad looked as calm as ever. "Where do you think?"

For a moment, Cade wanted to rip his lungs out. It must have shown, because Konrad finally looked scared.

"They're in Washington, D.C. Right now. They plan to attack the White House. It could be any moment."

Cade knew that he was telling the truth. He knew, because he felt it in his bones, felt his sworn duty pulling him away.

By this blood, you are bound . . .

He had to go. Cade knew he literally could not waste another second.

Konrad knew it, too. The smile returned.

"You should let me go. You've got more important things to do."

. . . you are bound to the President of the United States . . .

Cade dropped Konrad, cursing himself.

. . . and to the orders of the officers appointed by him . . .

Cade was behind the wheel before Zach saw him move.

Through the windshield, Cade saw Konrad picking himself up off the concrete. The scientist was smiling.

"We're just letting him go?" Zach screeched.

Cade had the BMW in reverse, then spun it around in a tire-smoking 180.

"Cade, talk to me. What's going on?" He hurried to get his seat belt fastened as Cade floored it.

Cade's face was grim. "Konrad was leaving the country. The *Unmenschsoldaten* aren't here."

"So where are they?"

Cade looked at him, and it finally clicked for Zach, too.

It was the container that had to get to Konrad. But the spare parts—the spare parts were exactly where they were supposed to be.

In Washington, D.C.

"The White House?" Zach asked.

Cade nodded. "Call Griff. Tell him to get the president out of there. Do whatever it takes. Then call Edwards."

"Who?" Zach asked, trying to dial as the car, engine screaming, lurched in and out of the late-night traffic.

"The air force base," Cade said, snapping off every word. "We need to get back to Washington as fast as possible."

Zach looked at his watch. Just past one. Which put D.C. at just after four a.m.

"There's no way we'll make it, it's going to be morning there before we land."

"God damn it, do as you're told," Cade shouted.

Zach realized, suddenly, they were in the oncoming lane of traffic, headed straight at an oncoming SUV.

Cade sliced back into the opposite lane, inches ahead of a slow-moving Ford.

As soon as they were clear, Cade stomped on the gas again, sending the tachometer back into the red. Horns blared after them.

"Make the calls, please," Cade said, quieter now.

Zach didn't ask any more questions. He did as he was told.

FIFTY-SEVEN

Konrad watched Cade's car disappear around a corner of the shipyard. That had actually been a little too close.

He looked at the security men, scattered on the dock around him. They had been part of his deal with the so-called terrorists: armed bodyguards. He'd thought they might get lucky, maybe damage Cade if all else failed.

Predictably, he'd expected far too much. Konrad suspected the little Arab snot had paid bargain rates.

The man on the ground closest to Konrad groaned. Konrad nudged him with his toe, and the man's eyes opened.

"One of you still needs to get my container loaded," Konrad told him. "The man who did this to you—he's almost certainly going to be back. And I don't want to be anywhere he can find me."

The man's head lolled back, and he closed his eyes again.

Konrad looked to the sky. It was just so hard to find good help these days.

FIFTY-EIGHT

Dylan checked his watch again. Khaled and the others were late. Maybe they got stopped. He didn't know what he was supposed to hope for now.

Then he heard the booming sound of a hand pounding on the back of the truck.

He swung open the door.

Khaled stood there with two of his pals, Gamal and Tariq. All three wore medical scrubs. Khaled carried the cooler. He hoisted it inside the trailer, then reached out his hand.

Dylan hauled him up. He stared at the cooler. "That can't be them."

Khaled grinned. "It is. God really wants this country to fall."

Dylan couldn't believe it. He opened the cooler, then swore to himself.

Dry ice smoked around four severed heads. They looked like nothing human, not really. They were gray and wrinkled and swollen, the flesh hanging off them like poorly wrapped shopping bags. One eye stared at him, dead as a marble.

Dylan stepped back. The lid fell closed.

Khaled, meanwhile, surveyed the interior of the truck. He nodded.

Everything was there, as Konrad had promised. The tubes and the machines, which sat like waiting insects, ready to buzz into life.

He looked back at Dylan. "You've done well. You'll be rewarded."

Dylan finally started to figure it out. There was no payday coming.

"Hand me those," Khaled demanded. He meant the heads.

Dylan nearly vomited, touching the dead skin as he passed them to Khaled. Khaled placed them in the empty metal sockets at the neck of each corpse.

Any hope Dylan had that this was just a crazed fantasy had evaporated. He knew, just as sure as he was holding the heads of corpses while Khaled tightened the bolts.

In the meantime, Gamal and Tariq were strapping themselves into the chairs, hooking up the electrodes to their skin.

It began to dawn on Dylan, something he'd heard long ago in one of those science classes he flunked, you can't get something for nothing. . . . Whatever was going to run those corpses had to be kick-started somehow.

He knew it now. This was real. All of it was real. This

would work. He had helped to place these things on the Earth.

And he was going to die.

Khaled waited, unmoving, somehow communicating his impatience with just a stare. Gamal and Tariq were strapped down, faces tight with anticipation.

Khaled tightened the screw at the neck of the last creature. He was done.

Dylan glanced at the back of the truck. He had a clear shot at the door.

Now or never. Run or die.

He ran, sprinting for the door. He had it up and was scrambling out, diving like a swimmer for the pavement.

He hit hard and rolled. He could hear Khaled cursing him as he got up.

Dylan kept running. He didn't know where he was going, and he didn't care. He was done with this nightmare.

He was gone.

FIFTY-NINE

Griff almost didn't wake up for the phone.

Between the whiskey and his meds, he was pretty out of it. He reached out a hand, knocked the phone over, cursed and then held it to his face.

Zach was on the other end, talking a mile a minute. Griff's relief on hearing the kid's voice didn't last long.

He listened. Then he hung up, pulled on his suit jacket and moved as fast as he could for the door.

He choked back the nausea, the booze and the shame all rising in his throat at the same time. He could feel that later, if there was time.

Right now, he had to get to the White House.

FORTY TERRIFYING MINUTES after they started—Zach glanced at the speedometer once and kept his eyes shut tight after that—the car screeched to a halt on the tarmac of a runway at Edwards.

Zach got out of the car on slightly wobbly legs. There wasn't an aircraft, or a person, anywhere in sight.

"Move," Cade growled, and Zach wasn't sure where he was supposed to go.

Then he saw the plane.

It was stark black, unlit, almost invisible against the night sky and the black asphalt. It looked like a flat triangle. But it was hard to see—physically, it was hard for him to focus on it. His eyes seemed to slide off its rounded corners.

A door opened in its belly, and Zach suddenly realized just how big it was—they were still more than a hundred yards away.

A tall, gangling man in a flight suit waved at them impatiently from the hatch—a normal-looking guy surrounded by flying-saucer tech.

"Come on," he called. "Meter's running."

Cade turned to Zach. "Stay here," he said. "You'll be safer."

"Fucking what?"

"I said—"

"I heard what you said," Zach snapped. "You think I'm going to bail out now?"

"I won't be able to look after you, and I don't have time to argue," Cade said, impatience putting an edge in his voice.

"Yeah? Well, that's fine, because this won't take long,"

Zach said. He wasn't sure where he was getting the balls for this, but he tumbled forward anyway. "I'm going with you, Cade, and if you don't like it, tough shit. Because that *is* an order."

There was no change in Cade's tone or facial expression. But somehow, Zach got the unmistakable sensation that the vampire was proud of him.

"Good," Cade said.

Within a few minutes, Zach was strapped into a half-egg seat, filled with foam that molded itself to his body.

The pilot—the name on his fatigues read AHREN—handed him a mask and helmet. "Put that on," he said. "Try not to puke into it."

A copilot turned and checked on Cade, who was already strapped in. Cade had obviously made this run before.

"We don't have time to put you in the case, sir," the copilot said. His tag read GRAHAM. Neither of them showed any rank, but they both wore identical patches. A black circle, outlined with red letters, some kind of Latin: *"Si Ego Certiorem Faciam . . . Mihi Tu Delendus Eris."*

"We are going to get a little sunlight when we reach apogee," the copilot said, like an airline captain pointing out the Grand Canyon to passengers.

"I'll be fine," Cade said. "Let's go."

The pilots sat in their own chairs, which were more like recliners with a series of wires and tubes. Zach could have sworn he saw one of them insert a computer cable directly into a slot under his jaw, but that had to be an optical illusion. Both pilots zipped up and strapped on large insect-eyed helmets, then began flipping switches.

There was almost no sound—just a persistent humming that Zach felt in his bones. It took him a minute to realize they were moving.

They were moving very fast.

The pilots didn't have any of the usual preflight chatter or speak into their radios.

Zach, positioned directly behind them, could only see the edges of what was going on out through the cockpit windows.

The wing-shaped craft was at the edge of the runway in a fraction of a second, and then Zach's stomach lurched as they reared back at a ninety-degree angle.

"Approaching delta," one of the pilots said. Zach heard it through his helmet. He retched a little as his insides kept flipping.

One of the pilots must have heard him. "Don't worry," he said. "This is the worst of it."

"Well, unless we explode," the other said.

"Explode?"

Both pilots laughed.

Zach didn't have time to worry. In front of them, the sky went from black to purple to another, deeper black—but one lit up as if by halogen bulbs.

The craft stopped in midair, and Zach got one uninterrupted look out the windows as they spun upside down.

Zach saw blue again, a wide curve in the corner of the windscreen, and realized what he was looking at.

They were above the Earth—in orbit.

"We are at apogee," the copilot said. "Thirty seconds and counting."

The craft hung there at the edge of space, while the Earth spun below them. Just over the blue curve, a bright, glaring light appeared.

Sunrise, on the far side of the world.

"My God, what is this thing?" Zach asked. He realized he was floating against his harness. Even inside the plane, he could feel the cold of space clinging to it, sucking the warmth away.

"Near-Earth orbital reconnaissance plane," the pilot said, a little pride in his voice. "TR-3B Black Manta. Modified for passengers, of course."

"Unbelievable. I didn't know we had anything this fast. . . ."

"Not fast enough," Cade said. Zach couldn't see him behind the helmet, but he could hear the pain in his voice.

The pure, unfiltered sunlight stabbed at Zach's eyes, and he realized what this must have been doing to Cade.

"Hang on, sir," the copilot said. "Almost ready for reentry."

Cade didn't reply, his fingers in a death grip on his armrest.

"Cade, we're almost out of this. . . ."

"Not what I meant," Cade said. "I wasn't fast enough. I should have put it together. Now we're three hours from sunrise when we land. And they're already down there. We're out of time. Because I was too slow."

Silence.

"Three forty-four a.m. local time, sir," the copilot said. "Starting descent."

"We're going to make it, Cade," Zach said, without thinking. He was reassuring a vampire.

Again, Cade didn't respond.

The plane dipped, and all of Zach's weight returned. Velocity and gravity caught up with them again, and every muscle in Zach's body strained against the harness as the plane hit the atmosphere.

They fell below the burning sunlight and then went screaming back into the dark.

SIXTY

The fanatic is incorruptible: if he kills for an idea, he can just as well get himself killed for one; in either case, tyrant or martyr, he is a monster.

—E. M. Cioran

Khaled watched Dylan run into the night from the back of the truck. He thought about giving chase. He'd intended for the American's body to provide the raw fuel for the fourth corpse. But the idiot had some instincts for self-preservation after all.

He rolled down the truck's door before anyone noticed what was inside.

Perhaps the fourth corpse would not rise up. Perhaps none of them would. He would still go forward as planned. As with all things, Khaled knew it was in the hands of God.

Khaled's God was not merciful. He was cruel, and he was vicious, and he was powerful. He delivered pain and rage and destruction. The world was full of those things, which meant God was winning.

That's why Khaled worshipped him. That was the God he wanted on his side.

At the center of the truck, in the middle of the console of Konrad's equipment, was a large knife switch. It was within reach of the chair Khaled had chosen. Once they were all seated, he only had to pull that and their lives would be drained into the creatures.

Life requires death, Konrad had said to Khaled a long time ago when they first met. And death will consume life.

He strapped himself into his own chair, leaving only one hand free.

He gave one last look to Gamal and Tariq. Gamal nodded. Tariq's eyes were closed, his lips moving in prayer.

Khaled pulled the switch. His whole life distilled itself into this one moment. He was at peace.

The pain began a second later, but his smile never faded.

THE MOVIES GET IT WRONG, every time. There is no lightning, no boom of thunder. The flash is between neurons, life returning to bodies that should have been under the ground.

Slowly, three *Unmenschsoldaten* began to move. The restraints holding them snapped like tissue paper as they rose.

The fourth corpse got up last. It moved slowly, but it moved.

The *Unmenschsoldaten* lined up and began walking. As soon as they left their platforms, a pressure-sensitive switch activated the rear door, pulling it open again. Konrad had thought of everything.

The rear of the truck pointed the *Unmenschsoldaten* directly at their target.

Framed in the doorway, gleaming white in the darkness, it was the only thing their limited senses could detect.

The White House. Shining like a beacon across the flat green plain of the South Lawn, as if summoning them.

The dead began to walk.

SIXTY-ONE

They are neither man nor woman—
They are neither brute nor human—
They are Ghouls:—

—Edgar Allan Poe, "The Bells"

The president wore a shirt open at the collar and khakis that still had a knife crease in the legs. It was the most disheveled Griff had ever seen him.

Still, he didn't look pleased to be up at this hour.

Wyman was there, too, a pajama top stuffed in his blue jeans under a blazer. On his feet, those damn moccasins again. He'd come running from his residence at the Naval Observatory when he got the summons from the president. He actually looked happy because Griff was in trouble.

Griff's ID and reputation were enough to get him inside the White House, despite the cloud over him. They were not, however, enough to get anyone to hurry. Close to an hour was wasted while Griff told his story to the Secret Service, who roused the president, then again to the man himself.

Even now, however, the agents in the room—two from Wyman's detail and three from the president's—looked at him with suspicion.

"Sir," Griff said to the president, "you have to get out. Now. We're wasting time—"

"Agent Griffin," the president said, his tone clipped, "you have to do better than that. I need facts, I need information. If there's a threat, I can't just run—"

"Yes, you can, damn it, if you want to live," Griff shouted, knocking over his chair as he stood up.

Two of the Secret Service men, Patterson and Haney, were veterans. They knew Griff from three administrations. But they still moved between him and the president, hands on their guns.

Griff drew in a deep breath, struggling for control. Then he blew it out.

Patterson's nose wrinkled. "Griff," he said, "have you been drinking?"

Terrific, Griff thought.

Wyman smiled as if the only thing he was missing was a big tub of popcorn.

"Sir," Griff said again.

The president held up a hand, and Patterson and Haney backed off. He seemed to call up his last reserve of patience.

"Griff," he said, "I have trusted you and Cade on a lot of things. Things I never would have believed. But this threat—whatever it is—is not just aimed at me. If something is coming toward D.C., I can't leave unless I know I've done everything possible to—"

"Never mind," Griff interrupted.

Everyone in the room looked taken aback. They thought Griff was committing career suicide right in front of them.

"It's too late now," Griff said. He pointed.

Everyone turned and looked out the windows toward the Rose Garden.

In retrospect, Griff couldn't blame them for freezing.

No one is prepared for their first contact with the Other Side when it breaks through. No matter how many zombie movies you've seen, somewhere deep inside you know that it's just actors and makeup. But out in the real world, your mind rebels. It says, this cannot possibly exist. And yet, there it is. Walking toward you.

Dead men, some still wearing the wounds that killed them. Absolutely, irrevocably dead.

And yet, still moving. Still walking toward the Oval Office, through the Rose Garden, one easy step at a time.

Four of them. Cloudy eyes staring, fixed right through the windows at the men in the office. One of them put a decaying foot down on a rosebush and left a scrap of flesh behind.

Even the president was awestruck. Horrified.

That's the thing about horror. It freezes you up. Makes you stupid. Makes you prey.

Fortunately, Griff had a lot more experience with it.

He shoved past the agents and found the button on the console on the president's desk. The one hooked up after 9/11. He pressed it.

Hardened security screens composed of rolled homogeneous armor slammed into place over the windows. They would take anything up to a direct hit by a Hellfire missile.

Griff hoped they'd be enough.

THE AGENTS IN THE ROOM looked to Haney, the most senior man on shift. They were anxious, confused—and scared. They were trained to deal with every possible threat to the president and they were scared.

Outside the Oval Office, an alarm began to wail. The White House was never left undefended. A Counter-Assault Team was on duty at all times. They carried enough weaponry to repel a full-scale terrorist assault.

Griff knew they didn't stand a chance. The dead men would keep coming. It was built into them. They would find an entrance and seek out the life inside the building and snuff it out. It was all they knew.

Gunfire echoed through the building. The Oval Office's walls shook as someone fired what sounded like a grenade launcher.

On the other side of the room, Haney was speaking into the mike at his cuff. He was trying to be quiet, but Griff could hear him well enough. Sheer panic.

Then something came over Haney's earpiece, loud enough that the agent had to tear it out of his head. The other agents, all tuned to the same channel, did the same.

A very tiny scream wailed from the earpiece as it hung from Haney's collar. Then it died away completely.

Haney picked up the phone, trying to reach someone outside to get a report.

He shook his head. No answer.

The sound of splintering wood and tortured metal reached them from downstairs.

They were inside.

Both Haney and Griff looked at the Oval Office door. It did not have the steel shutters. The thinking was, if someone got that far, the president would already be long gone. It had heavy bolts to keep it shut. But they wouldn't last against the creatures.

Haney turned to Griff. "What's the plan?"

Griff noticed he'd gone from a lunatic to a prophet in less than five minutes. And Wyman didn't look at all happy anymore.

"Stay here. Wait for Cade," Griff said.

Agent Haney looked to the president. "Sir?"

Curtis took a long moment. Griff could see the struggle in his face. He knew, as well as anyone in the room, that going out to face those things was as good as suicide.

But his family was on the other side of the screens.

He addressed Griff. "There has to be a way to stop them."

"Not by us, sir. This is way above our pay grade."

Curtis thought for a moment. He looked at Haney.

"Bob," he said. "I'm going to ask you something. It's not an order. It's a request."

"You're not leaving this room, sir," Haney said.

"I need to make sure my family is all right."

"No, sir. You're not going."

"God damn it, Bob—"

"But I am."

They heard more glass and wood breaking. Above them, the ceiling shook as if the building was hit by a quake.

Haney pointed at the other agents. "Patterson, Roy, Spencer, you're with me. We'll run for the weapons cache, then into the Residence," Haney said. He looked at Griff. "You're not fast enough. No offense."

The ceiling shook again, and plaster dust rained down on them. "None taken," Griff said.

"You stay here with Terrill." Haney turned to Terrill, the youngest man in the room, a rookie agent. "Terrill, the president's life is in your hands."

Haney took his backup piece from an ankle holster, as well as his spare clips, and gave them all to Griff.

Patterson and the other agents formed up on Haney and prepared to head out the door.

Wyman noticed. "What are you doing? You're not leaving us?"

"Mr. Vice President, you're safer here," Haney said.

"You can't leave us," Wyman said. "You have to stay and protect us!"

"You've got Agent Griffin and you've got Agent Terrill," Haney told him.

Wyman wasn't listening. He clutched at Haney's arm as the agent turned to go. Haney looked down at his hand.

President Curtis peeled him away.

"Bob," he said again with a quiet force. "I cannot ask you to do this."

Griff could practically feel the weight of the president's gaze.

"You don't have to, sir," Haney said. He shook the president's hand. "It's been a pleasure and a privilege."

Then he sprinted out into the hallway, along with the rest of the agents.

Griff slammed the door shut and then threw the security bolts.

It wouldn't be enough. Griff grabbed a heavy chair and laid it down at the doorway. Then a table, then another chair.

"Give me a hand," he said to the rookie. "My back can't take what it used to."

Terrill jumped up and took the other end of a couch that was a favorite of Lady Bird Johnson's. He and Griff dragged it onto the makeshift barricade.

"You think this will stop them?"

"Hell, no," Griff said. "I'll be happy if it slows them down."

The look on the rookie's face told Griff that wasn't the answer he wanted.

THE MARINE LOOKED UNCOMFORTABLE. "Sir, I'm sorry. I haven't gotten any clearance from the White House."

He stood in front of Marine One, the presidential chopper, on its pad at Andrews Air Force Base. Fueled up, ready to go at a moment's notice. Currently not going anywhere, because the guard blocked Cade and Zach from getting inside.

"Look, you know who we are, just get us off the ground and radio ahead for permission," Zach said. "I am a deputy director at the White House—"

Zach reached for his credentials in his suit jacket—and then remembered they were probably in a Ziploc baggie near the holding cell in California.

"I've got orders to keep you here, sir. I'm sorry."

"Orders? From who?"

"Wyman," Cade muttered. The marine didn't hear, or didn't care if he did.

"I have my orders, sir. Please step back."

The marine's face was a blank wall. Zach had no idea how to get around it.

The marine's radio snapped to life. "We have a call from the White House, something's going down, prepare the chopper . . ."

Zach was going to say something to the marine when Cade ended the debate. He reached across Zach, grabbed the marine by his belt and flung him backward.

Cade was in the pilot's seat by the time the marine landed a dozen yards away.

"Get in," he ordered Zach.

Cade flipped switches, and Marine One's engines began to spin up. In the distance, the guard struggled to his feet, fumbling for his sidearm.

"Cade, he's getting up."

"Marines are tough," Cade said.

"Cade . . ."

Cade ignored him, still working at the controls.

"Cade, do you know how to fly this thing?"

Zach was answered with a lurching takeoff just as the marine began shooting.

If he hit anything, Zach couldn't hear it over the engines and the rotor.

The marine was still shooting as they turned away into the night, gaining speed.

SIXTY-TWO

It was only thirteen miles from Andrews to the White House, so Zach knew the chopper ride couldn't be taking as long as it seemed. Voices over the radio shouted at them. Then other voices shouted over those.

"Four, repeat, we have *four* confirmed intruders at the White House, we're trying to—holy shit, that can't be—holy *shit*—"

A scream, then static.

Cade switched it off.

Zach saw the White House through the windscreen, bright and tiered like a wedding cake in the lights. It looked strangely peaceful.

Cade put the chopper into a steep dive.

Zach looked over at him. Cade's lips were drawn back, his teeth exposed. His eyes were bright. It took Zach a split second to recognize what he was seeing.

His guilt was gone. This is what he was made for, Zach

suddenly realized. On the hunt, up against something that might present a challenge.

Off his leash. Kill or be killed.

Cade was happy.

THE AGENTS GOT down the stairs and into the Secret Service room. More gunfire erupted, this time closer. Then screams and then sounds that were sickeningly wet.

Haney and Patterson overturned a file cabinet and opened a panel hidden in the wall, revealing a steel door behind the clean white wood. Haney's hands shook as he entered the combination into the keypad.

It took two tries before the locks disengaged with a heavy thump.

The agents began sorting through the cache. Kevlar vests—no time. And those things didn't have guns. Automatic weapons—M16s. One each. And two AT4s. Shoulder-fired anti-tank rockets. These were the CS versions, specifically designed for close-quarter, urban warfare. They came with only one round apiece.

It would have to do.

Haney took the incendiary and its firing tube, a deceptively small, light cylinder. He handed the other to Patterson.

"I'm going to the Residence," he said.

Patterson frowned, but nodded. No time to argue. The other agents were checking their rounds, stowing their spare ammo.

Patterson and the other two agents headed toward the West Lobby. Haney, alone, ran past the press corps offices, toward the main residence.

THEY LANDED HARD ENOUGH to send Zach halfway to the ceiling of the chopper. The seat belt yanked him back down again. His ribs and his other injuries screamed in pain.

Cade was moving, unlatching himself.

"Cade," Zach said.

"The president's family," Cade snapped. "Go. I don't have time."

He was out of the helicopter then, sprinting for the buildings.

Zach, moving much more slowly, unstrapped himself from the restraints and got out, jumping several feet to the ground. His body reminded him of every injury as he hit the manicured lawn.

Cade was at the West Wing already, not looking back.

Zach thought about the president's family. And he thought about Candace.

He forgot his pain. He turned and ran as fast as he could for the White House.

SIXTY-THREE

Cade smashed through the rear entry of the West Wing's ground floor—directly into the Secret Service office.

The White House stank of rancid meat. It overwhelmed his senses, muddled everything like a fog would hide a landscape. Too much death, too much fresh blood.

Cade had to rely on his ears. He could hear footfalls on carpet despite the other sounds.

The lobby.

Cade was there in seconds. The marine guards who ordinarily stood watch at the door were already dead, their dress uniforms in tatters, their blood painting the floor and walls.

Three Secret Service agents were doing all they could against the thing that had killed the guards. They had their weapons up, firing round after round.

It all seemed to happen underwater to Cade. His perceptions were working as fast as possible. The bullets looked like lazy bumblebees, floating in the air.

The bullets didn't even pierce the creature's hide. The bullets kept coming, the agents firing wildly, until, one by one, their guns clicked empty.

The creature still stood. It then moved its mismatched limbs and overgrown torso and advanced on them. Dead eyes fixed on the agents.

It was within a dozen feet of the stairs to the Oval Office.

Cade leaped, hurdling over the heads of the agents in one move, hitting the creature as hard as he could.

It rocked back but not very far. Then it swung at him, nearly tagged him.

He barely rolled clear. Its fist left a crater in the floor. Faster than he remembered. Konrad had installed upgrades.

The agents were behind him now, staring, frozen in place.

"Humans, *out!*" Cade bellowed.

Their leader—Cade knew his name, it was Patterson—seemed to wake up. He shouted the order for retreat.

"Get out!" he screamed. "Go! It's just the monsters now!"

Cade almost smiled at that.

He steeled himself and then threw himself back at the creature.

SIXTY-FOUR

Zach collided with the Secret Service man as he entered the Residence.

The agent put a gun to Zach's face but didn't fire. His eyes went wide with recognition.

"Barrows? What the hell are you doing—"

That was as much as he got out before the doors behind them blew apart.

Another one of the things. Dead skin hanging off overstressed muscles, the corpse barely able to contain all its power.

And they moved a lot slower in the movies, Zach thought sourly.

He and the agent—Haney, that was his name—ran.

Zach slammed the doors of the Diplomatic Reception Room.

"Where the hell are the CAT teams?" he yelled.

Then they both looked around and saw the answer.

Corpses. But these ones weren't going to get up again.

They looked like they had been ripped apart. The hall where the president greeted foreign leaders had been turned into an abattoir. Bits of human flesh and blood spread out over the wallpaper selected by Jackie Kennedy.

"We have to get out of here," Zach said, pulling at Haney's arm.

"You go," Haney said, slinging a metal tube off his shoulder. "I've got to get the president's family."

"No, listen—"

"Go ahead and run, Barrows," Haney shouted at him.

Zach wanted to scream back, *That's not what I meant . . .*

Then it was too late.

Because Zach was right. The creature behind them couldn't have done all this. It was headed in the opposite direction.

There was another one. And it was in the room with them.

SIXTY-FIVE

Lance Corporal Ryan Garcia wondered idly if he was in Hell.

His last clear memory was of kneeling in front of a video camera while some Jihadi asswipe screamed at him. He'd known what was coming. He'd known since he and the other members of his patrol were taken from their vehicle after the IED went off in Sadr City.

More screaming. Garcia had been heavily sedated to ensure he wouldn't ruin the terrorist's home video. All he felt was irritation. He just wanted the guy to shut up.

The screaming reached a crescendo. He understood the words "Death to America!" Then: nothing.

Now he seemed to drift in and out of consciousness, like waking up to the blare of the clock radio only to hit the snooze button again. Something like that.

His body—well, it didn't feel like *his* body, but it seemed to carry him—was moving. There was pain. A lot of pain.

It only eased when his arms and legs lashed out against the dim figures in his path.

Again, he didn't feel like he was doing any of this. Like a dream, it was just happening to him. He could feel the pain as it coursed through his head, but everything else was like grabbing at shadows.

He knew, in some sort of abstract way, that there was a large white building in front of him and he was headed toward it. It felt like he was on rails. None of this seemed to have anything to do with him. Not really.

The shadows kept getting in his way, but they didn't slow him down. He was sort of curious what kept happening to them.

That was all he got before he sank back down into the dark.

In the West Wing, Cade watched as the creature moved toward him. Still headed for the stairs.

He'd already hit it as fast and hard as he could. It had barely staggered.

Weapon, Cade decided. I need a weapon.

Nothing nearby would work. The creature was too durable for small-arms fire. Anything he could tear from the walls wouldn't be any better.

It came to him, and he wondered why it took him so long.

The creature was a few feet away. Cade braced himself for the blow. The creature flung out one of its fists, aiming for the annoying thing that wouldn't break as easily as the others.

Cade caught the arm, turned and twisted it, in a move that looked like judo. Only instead of flipping the creature, the move tore the arm free at the shoulder, ripping out the joint.

The creature stopped. Cade wondered if they felt pain.

If so, then this was going to hurt. A lot.

He swung the arm like a baseball bat. Infused with whatever miracle potion Konrad had made, it was just as strong as the creature.

It cracked across the *Unmenschsoldat*'s skull, twisting it at an unnatural angle.

Unable to see straight, it began to walk in a small circle.

Cade swung again. And again. And again. And again.

THEY COULD HEAR the unholy din from the floor under their feet. The sounds of gunfire, then noises like Griff imagined dinosaurs must have made while fighting.

Through it all, the men in the Oval Office remained quiet.

The young agent—Terrill, Griff reminded himself, the kid's name was Terrill—stood, panicked, by the president. As if he could shield Curtis with his body alone.

Curtis sat in his chair, lost in thought. Ostensibly the most powerful man in the world, he could do nothing to save himself or his family.

Wyman sat in one of the couches, muttering to himself, shaking violently. Griff wondered if he was having a seizure. He walked over to the vice president.

A few steps closer, he could hear what Wyman was saying, over and over.

"This wasn't supposed to happen yet . . . This wasn't supposed to happen yet . . . I was supposed to know . . . It wasn't supposed to start . . ."

Wyman looked up and stopped babbling. A new kind of fear came into his face when he saw Griff.

"What was that?" Griff said quietly.

Wyman gulped. An expression crossed his face that Griff had previously only seen in cartoons.

"I—I just—things like this can't happen," he said. "That's what I meant. It's not possible."

There was the sound of more gunfire from somewhere else in the White House. They all looked up in response. Closer to the Residence. Curtis looked at the window, as if he could see through the metal shields by force of will.

Griff looked back at Wyman, who had, by some great physical effort, gotten himself under control. Griff knew this wasn't the time.

He put a finger in Wyman's face. "Later," he said, "you and I are going to talk."

A little of Wyman's old arrogance seeped back. "That's presuming there is a later, Agent Griffin."

Griff walked back to the door. Man had a point.

SIXTY-SIX

The things were strong, and fast, and seemingly impossible to hurt, Zach thought.

But, thank God, they weren't very bright.

The two corpse-soldiers stood facing each other across the bodies of the CAT team. They seemed confused.

Zach pulled Haney into the China Room, just off the Reception Room, while they stood there, confused by each other.

"Jesus Christ," Haney hissed.

"Stay quiet," Zach hissed back. He didn't know how the *Unmenschsoldaten* found their victims—he suspected they stumbled across whatever moved and then killed it—but he didn't want to take any chances.

Zach looked at the other door to the China Room. They could get through there into the Center Hall, and from there head up the stairs to the president's rooms. Maybe get to his family, get them out.

Haney was looking in the same direction. He nodded.

Carefully, they crept out into the hall.

Then Patterson and the other two agents showed up.

"Hey!" Patterson shouted as he spotted them.

The agents ran toward Haney and Zach. Zach waved his arms frantically, but it was not a lot of ground to cover. They were at the door of the reception area in no time.

They were loud. Leather shoes slapping on the floor. Guns and ammo rattling.

The first creature stepped out just as the first agent passed. With one hand, it plucked him from the floor like a flower.

The man didn't have time to scream. One second, and there was just blood and broken bone where his skull used to be.

Patterson and the other agent skidded to a halt.

Haney ran toward them, firing his sidearm into the back of the creature's head. It didn't even turn around.

The dead agent dropped to the floor. His heart still pumped blood.

The second agent skidded in the blood. He went down on one knee.

With a backhand slap, the creature cracked the man's neck like dry kindling.

Patterson aimed his M16 and fired.

Haney kept shooting, replacing clips one after the next.

The creature slowed, the bullets pinging off its skull.

Patterson dropped his rifle and slung his AT4 from his shoulder. He extended the tube and lined up the sights.

He waited one second too long. The other creature

emerged from the Reception Room and grabbed him by the chest.

He struggled. It should have been easy to pull away, but he couldn't. The creature's fingers dug in. Patterson cried out, but the breath left him immediately.

The creature squeezed, pulled more and more of the man's chest into its hand, like it was wadding up a sheet of paper. The agent's white shirt leaked blood. The creature's hand crunched through the rib cage, through the meat of his organs and into the spine.

The agent stopped struggling. His upper body was now just a mess in the creature's fist.

Someone was still screaming. Zach realized it was Haney, firing his bullets at both creatures, screaming with impotence and rage.

The first creature turned and tore the great oak doors leading into the Reception Room off their hinges.

It swung them about like flyswatters.

Haney managed to duck, almost in time to do any good. The door only clipped him.

It sent him skidding down the hall, all the way back to Zach.

Zach grabbed Haney and dragged him into the China Room. The man's bones seemed to be gone; it was as if his insides had been turned to jelly.

The agent gritted his teeth when Zach leaned him against the wall. "It's okay," Zach said stupidly. "We'll get you out of here."

Haney laughed at that. Fresh blood bubbled from his lips.

"Sure," was all he said.

Zach felt like slapping the man. "What the hell do you want me to do?"

"Here," he said, voice rasping, pushing the tube at Zach. "Army made these things idiot-friendly. Line up along the sights. Disengage the safeties. Cock the pin. Press the button."

Zach had held a gun precisely once in his life. A bunch of guys from the NRA took him out for drinks, and they ended up at an all-night shooting range. Now Haney wanted him to fire a grenade launcher.

He blurted out the first thing that came to mind: "You have got to be kidding."

Another cough. "You see anyone else here, Barrows?"

He must have not liked the answer he saw on Zach's face. He grabbed Zach's hand. "Do it, Barrows. Kill those fucking things."

Zach finally nodded, and picked up the tube. Haney seemed to relax against the wall. The fight left his eyes.

Zach headed back out the door that led to the Center Hall. He took a deep breath.

"Barrows," Haney said. He sounded like he was gargling, his throat filling up with whatever was crushed and broken inside him.

Zach stopped.

"Don't fuck this up."

Yeah, Zach thought. No pressure.

CADE KEPT HITTING the creature long after it stopped moving. Long after the body was reduced to slag and ground meat.

If it wasn't dead, at least it wasn't going anywhere.

He looked over at the stairwell. No way to the Oval from there.

He heard something from the Residence. The grinding noise of dead flesh as it moved.

Two more of them.

His club was done; it flopped uselessly, as shattered as the mess on the floor.

He dropped it.

He ran in the direction of the White House's Center Hall. He was going to have to improvise.

ZACH ENTERED the Center Hall cautiously. He half expected one of the things to be waiting for him, ready to kill him as soon as he poked his head out the door.

But they were both moving away from him, toward the stairwell.

They were going for the president's family.

Zach wondered what he was supposed to do to stop the one he couldn't shoot. Or if he missed completely.

His head bobbled back and forth like he was watching a tennis match. Which one? Eeny, meeny, miny, moe . . .

Screw it, he thought, and put the tube on his shoulder, the cone-shaped grenade pointed at the closer of the things.

Somehow it knew. It sensed the threat. It turned toward him, and began walking.

Zach lined up the sights. Just like he was told.

Then the doors at the other end of the Center Hall opened, and Zach nearly dropped the AT4.

Cade.

The other *Unmenschsoldat* stopped mid-stride and turned toward him.

Cade stood there, taking in the situation as calmly as if he were waiting at a crosswalk.

Zach brought the AT4 to his shoulder again. Cade was here. He could handle the other one. Another deep breath. Sights on the creature. Disengage the first safety. Done. Disengage the second. Done. Cock the pin. Keep the sights up. Press the button.

"Wait," Cade shouted at Zach. "Don't fire yet."

Zach felt an absurd burst of irritation.

"Are you shitting me?" he shouted. The thing was closing fast on him.

"Do as I say, Mr. Barrows."

Right. Just let the nice monster turn him into paste.

But he waited.

Cade danced in front of his *Unmenschsoldat*. The creature took a step left to block him. Cade spun about again. The creature took another step.

In a few moves, Cade had the two *Unmenschsoldaten* lined up, single file.

Cade was stuck between them.

"Shoot," he told Zach.

"But you're—"

"Aim for the head."

Zach grit his teeth. Always another thing to do.

"Do it. *Now!*"

The *Unmenschsoldat* was right on top of him now. The thing's face sat right in the center of the sights. Staring horribly, skin gone from the cheeks, dead rictus of a grin.

Now or never, he decided.

He pressed the button.

CADE HEARD the trigger button click. Dodged the meaty swing of the creature's arm and jumped clear. Crawling as fast as he could, away from both of them.

FOR AN IMPOSSIBLY LONG MOMENT, nothing happened. Then Zach heard a hissing sound that grew to a roar, the tube kicked in his hands, and the rocket shot toward the creature.

In a moment of pure amazement, he watched it tear the thing's head off. Direct hit.

The rocket exploded an instant after that. Zach caught a glimpse of both of the *Unmenschsoldaten*, burned into his retinas in the glare of the fireball.

He was blown back as the shock wave broke every mirror and stick of furniture in the hall.

EARS RINGING, Zach got to his feet.

The Center Hall was in ruins, half of the ceiling down,

revealing the steel infrastructure beneath. The walls burned in places. Smoke everywhere. Fire sprinklers doing their best to soak it all.

Despite the destruction, he could see the remains of the *Unmenschsoldaten*. Blown into large chunks. Heads gone.

Zach had never been so proud in his life. Even his damn ribs stopped hurting.

Cade crossed the rubble, covered in plaster dust from the ceiling, dripping with water. "Well done," he said.

Zach kept a death grip on the AT4. Still couldn't believe he'd managed it.

"The head is like a control panel for them," Cade said. "Take it out, they won't get up again."

Zach nodded dumbly. He realized Cade was pulling him along.

"Where are we going?"

"There's one left. I have to find it."

"Whoa," Zach said. "Wait a second."

Under the rubble, something moved.

A torso and an arm rose from the wreckage, headless, half burned, like it was doing a push-up. It reached over with the one arm, snagged a severed limb from the other creature.

Cade turned, saw it, too.

"I thought you said that would kill it," Zach said.

Cade made a noise.

The limb, a ragged leg, went into the creature's empty arm socket with a solid thunk. It cast about again with its arm, came up with an elbow joint. Another hand. Both went into empty spaces on the torso.

"Cade, *you said—*"

The creature levered itself upward. Blind, fingers grasping feebly from the hip cavity. It leaned like a tripod on a stump of an arm, a leg and another arm.

"Upgrades," was all Cade said.

It began to crawl away from them, like a giant roach, moving toward the rear stairs.

Then it picked up speed and disappeared around the corner.

Cade turned to Zach. "Run," he said.

Zach didn't have to be told twice. He sprinted up the staircase, into the family residence.

SIXTY-SEVEN

The roach-*Soldat* turned out to be much faster on three legs than it was on two, Cade observed.

It was hop-stepping its way up the far stairwell to the family residence, leaping the stairs two and three at a time.

It passed the first floor and kept going, with Cade right behind.

Cade headed it off. He jumped, clearing the upper railing, and met it at the second-floor landing.

It stopped, suddenly cautious. Cade had no idea how it was still navigating without eyes. But it must have known he was blocking its path.

They stood there, facing each other. Waiting for the other to move.

Zach made the second-floor landing a moment later, gasping.

The roach-*Soldat* angled itself toward Zach, as if looking for an easier opponent.

Cade turned to him. "Get out of here."

The creature tensed, prepared to spring.

Zach scrambled into the entrance hall of the second floor, away from both of them.

The creature hopped like a spider, rising into the air, trying to go over Cade and get Zach.

Cade jumped and tackled it in mid-flight. They hit the floor hard enough to crack the boards under the carpet, Cade on the bottom. He was stunned for a moment.

The misplaced hand caught at his throat. The other limbs flailed and kicked at him.

From behind, one of the arms grasped his neck. He was caught. It wasn't as strong as it had been when it was whole. But it was strong enough.

The roach-*Soldat* had his head firmly in its grip and it began to twist.

ZACH DOVE as far as he could into the entrance hall. Some instinct told him to stay down.

Nothing happened.

He peered up from the floor.

No one around.

Behind him, still on the stairwell, he could hear the sounds of Cade thrashing with the spare parts.

Just as Zach was beginning to haul himself to his feet, footsteps pounded behind him. A sharp kick took out his leg at the knee, and he went down again, face-first.

He was about to protest, but someone had a gun at his ear.

"Tell me why I shouldn't pull this trigger," a quiet voice asked.

Four days ago, Zach would have been scared shitless. Now he was merely annoyed; this didn't even rate in the top five recent threats to his life. "Is there any good answer to that question?" he asked.

Another voice, above and behind the one with the gun. "Let him up, you assholes, I know him."

Candace.

"Miss Curtis, you really have to get back, we're handling this—"

"Fuck you," Candace said, and pushed past the Secret Service men who had Zach on the floor.

They seemed at a loss as she helped him up.

"Zach," she said. "What the hell is going on?"

Another loud crash from the landing. Cade hadn't won yet, apparently.

"It's a long story," he said. "Your mom, your brother, they're okay?"

"They're fine," the first Secret Service man said coldly. "They're in the panic room, where Miss Curtis should be."

"And you would have shot one of my dad's staff people if I wasn't here."

"He could be involved," the other Secret Service man said.

"Candace, he's right," Zach said. They all looked at him like he rode the short bus to school. "Not about me being involved," he corrected quickly, "but about you getting out of here. There's some truly weird shit going down—"

"What about my dad?" she said, and in that moment her toughness, the veneer of the party girl manufactured for the press, dropped away. She looked scared and lost.

"We're trying to help him. But you really have to get out of here—"

As if to emphasize Zach's point, a scream of inhuman pain came from the landing, as if torn from the throat of some long-extinct animal.

Only Zach recognized the voice.

Cade.

He grabbed the gun from the hand of the nearest Secret Service agent—the man was still in shock from the sound—and ran for the landing.

"Stay here!" he told them. They didn't show any inclination to follow.

He couldn't blame them.

THE ROACH-*SOLDAT* was going to twist his head off. It was gradually ratcheting up the pressure, increasing the tension on Cade's neck. He struggled, but every movement only gave the creature a little more leverage.

He tried to heave himself up off the floor, but all that did was give the roach a chance to dig clawlike fingers into the skin of his face.

He turned, but it was too late. The roach-*Soldat* pulled hard, and half of Cade's cheek peeled off his skull.

He screamed. He had not been hurt like that in years.

The two limbs on his neck tightened even more. This was it. Decapitation.

He thrashed and kicked, the words of the oath burning in his brain, the need to protect the president hitting him like a cattle prod. He even bit, using his fangs to tear chunks out of the decayed flesh wherever he could.

None of it did any good. The only blood spilled was his own.

Cade was going to die. Forever, this time.

ZACH SAW CADE TANGLED in the mass of limbs, like a wrestling match with a Dalí painting. He didn't look like he was winning.

Zach took the agent's pistol and jacked a round into the chamber.

Which immediately caused the gun to eject the round that was already in the chamber.

Real smooth, Zach.

He tried to remember everything he'd learned with the boys from the NRA. None of it was coming back to him.

He didn't know if bullets would do any good on this thing. It took a rocket to the face and crawled away.

Then Zach saw an open wound on the thing's back, revealing sinew and gore underneath. Damage from before.

He'd have to get close. Really close.

Ah, hell. He'd fired the rocket launcher. This couldn't be that much tougher.

Zach walked over to the creature and put the barrel

of the gun to the wound. He didn't take time to think about it.

He just pulled the trigger, over and over, fast as he could.

THE ROACH-*SOLDAT* reared up off Cade. The pressure slackened around his neck.

Dimly Cade connected it with the sound of a gun firing, but he didn't dwell on the cause.

He had a chance now.

Cade pistoned one of his legs up, got his hands between the creature's limbs and his neck and kicked as hard as he could.

The roach-*Soldat* flew into the air, smashed off a wall and bounced into the Treaty Room.

Cade regained his feet, stretched his neck side to side, heard the vertebrae crunch back into place. He pushed the loose flap of his cheek onto his face again.

Zach stood there, looking stunned as usual, a smoking gun in his hand.

Cade was a little surprised himself.

"Thank you, Zach," he said.

He took the stairs in one leap and went into the Treaty Room after the roach-*Soldat*.

ZACH STOOD THERE STUPIDLY, watching Cade go after the thing, which was not dead despite the dozen or so bullets he'd pumped into it.

But that wasn't what surprised him.

Cade had said "Thank you." Even more amazing: he'd called him "Zach."

DIRECTLY UNDERNEATH Cade and Zach, the *Unmenschsoldat* carrying the head of Corporal Garcia walked steadily past the White House theater, past the empty visitors' foyer.

With the Secret Service and CAT teams dead, there was nothing to attract the *Unmenschsoldat*'s rudimentary senses. The offices were closed for the night. It was late enough that even the most die-hard staffers had gone home.

Garcia could feel, rather than see or hear, the commotion above him. But it didn't call him the way the glowing light on the other end of the building did.

The light was life. He could remember that much.

He didn't make any conscious decision to go toward it, but the *Unmenschsoldat*'s body went in that direction anyway. As if called.

Garcia was more or less just along for the ride.

THE ROACH-*SOLDAT* WAS WOUNDED. It cringed in a corner of the Treaty Room, scrabbling madly at the wall.

Cade wasn't taking any chances.

He scanned the room and found what he needed.

The Resolute Desk. An authentic piece of history. Made from the timbers of the HMS *Resolute*, a gift from Queen Victoria to the United States. It had been in the Oval Office of a dozen presidents. Roosevelt had ordered it modified to hide his wheelchair. Kennedy's children played under it. Reagan had it raised to accommodate his favorite chair. But Curtis had chosen a different desk, so it went back to the Treaty Room.

Of all the trivia about the Resolute Desk, however, Cade cared only about one fact: it weighed over a thousand pounds.

Cade hoisted it up, as high as he could balance it. He kicked a couch out of the way.

The roach-*Soldat* turned, limbs churning, trying for escape or counterattack, Cade didn't know.

He slammed the desk down as hard as he could.

The creature went flat, with a hollow crunching noise as its bones shattered.

The Resolute Desk broke into pieces. There was still enough left of the surface that Cade could smash the roach-*Soldat* again.

This time the desktop shattered completely. The creature twitched one leg, then stopped moving forever.

CADE EMERGED from the Treaty Room, panting. He realized, in a distant way, that he was exhausted. He shouldn't be this tired. Not even after all the punishment of the last few days. All he wanted to do was sleep.

He looked up.

He saw the answer in the skylight above. The night above was fading to a bright gray.

The sun was coming out.

Zach was still standing in the hallway, gun in his hand.

"Please tell me we're done."

Cade shook his head. "That's three," he said. "There's still one left."

Cade remembered he was still holding a chunk of the Resolute Desk. He dropped it, put his hands on his knees and fought the urge to sleep for a week.

"Cade, you don't look so good."

Cade had no response. He was running out of time, running out of strength. He'd used every trick he knew, and there was still one more *Unmenschsoldat* out there.

It was getting hard to think. He forced himself to focus.

"Cade?"

Like that, he had the answer.

"I'll be right back," he said.

He was halfway down the hall when Zach yelled at him.

"What? Where are you going?"

"Go to the Oval Office," Cade shouted back, over his shoulder. "I'll be there as fast as I can."

"What am I supposed to do?"

"Improvise," Cade shouted, and then he was gone, down the stairwell.

ZACH STOOD THERE for another moment, watching the space where Cade had been.

"Oh, *come on!*" he shouted, when he realized Cade wasn't coming back.

He heard something. Above him, at the entrance hall, the two agents stared at him. Candace was behind them.

"Zach?" she said. "Are you all right?"

Zach nodded. "Super." He looked at the agents. "I need more bullets."

They looked at each other, then one shrugged and tossed him a spare clip.

He caught it, ejected the empty clip and reloaded. Almost like he knew what he was doing. The boys from the NRA would be proud.

"Get her back in the panic room."

The agents didn't tell him to go screw himself. Zach guessed that fighting a multilimbed horror bought him a little respect.

They took Candace's arms, gently, and started pulling her back.

"Zach," she said, "what are you going to do?"

"It's okay, Candace," he said. "I'm going to check on the president."

She still looked unsure. But she let the two agents guide her away.

Zach was glad she was gone before the adrenaline shakes started. He ran like a spastic toward the West Wing, with 99 percent of his brain totally convinced he was going to die.

Still, that remaining one percent—the idiot part of him, probably—knew that if he wanted to, he could have Candace back in the Lincoln Bedroom anytime he wanted.

He'd just have to survive this first.

SIXTY-EIGHT

There are times when the defense of liberty requires the unleashing of monsters.

—President Andrew Johnson, private journal

It had been quiet in the Oval Office for several minutes now. They heard the explosion, muffled by the heavy steel panels. Then nothing.

Griff stood at the door, listening, gun drawn. He wasn't sure what was going on. It could be the fight was over already. Could be that Cade had lost. He didn't know.

Wyman, on the other hand, appeared to have reached a decision.

He stood, trying to straighten his blazer and pajama shirt as well as he could. He walked over to Griff.

"Agent Griffin," he said. "Open the door. I'm leaving."

Griff didn't think anything could make him laugh at this point. As usual, he underestimated Wyman.

"You're not serious," Griff said.

Wyman nodded. Of course he was. Griff could see now his chin was trembling. Wyman was barely holding it together. Somehow, he'd decided this was the plan. He'd just walk out.

"Mr. Vice President—"

Wyman cut him off. "I'm giving you an order, Agent Griffin. You will follow it. You will follow my order and open that door."

The president looked over, puzzled. "Les," he said. "Sit down."

Wyman ignored him. "Agent Griffin, I am not supposed to be here. I am not supposed to be here and you will open that door."

His voice pitched toward screeching at the end.

"None of us should be here, Les," the president said, his voice calm. "Just sit down."

"You don't understand, I am not supposed to be here! Now, open the fucking door!"

He rushed Griff. Griff stopped him easily, even as weak as he felt. He stiff-armed the vice president, holding him away.

Wyman struggled as hard as he could. Griff kept him back.

"Open the door!" he shouted.

Griff was sick to death of him. He pushed him back into his chair. Hard.

"Sit down, Lester," he ordered.

Wyman's eyes shone with tears, but he stayed put.

That's when they felt the impact of the first blows against the door.

DOWN THE STAIRS, into the P-OCK and through the tunnel. Underground, Cade's full speed returned. The wound on his cheek healed as he made the mile back to the Smithsonian in record time.

Cade opened the locker where Griff had secured the metal case from Kosovo. He flipped it open, wincing slightly.

In the gloom of the Reliquary, the object glowed softly with a gentle white light.

This was not an object from the Other Side. The Vukodlak had grabbed it from the U.S. Embassy, where it had resided since being saved from an Eastern Orthodox monastery bombed during the Kosovo conflict.

It was a human hand, perfectly preserved, encased in a metal gauntlet. The gauntlet dated from at least the fourteenth century. The hand was much older.

It was the hand of John the Baptist. Supposedly. The hand that had been touched by an angel and then touched the head of Christ. The relic was believed to have the magical ability to heal, even to return the dead to life.

Supposedly.

All Cade knew for sure was that it hurt him, more than the cross on his neck. It had power.

He just hoped it had enough.

He slammed the case shut and ran back into the tunnel that led to the White House.

ZACH FELT THE WALLS SHAKING. He rounded the corner, and saw the last *Unmenschsoldat* pounding at the door of the Oval Office.

He stopped.

The door began to crack, to tear free of its frame.

The thing kept pounding.

Zach aimed the gun and fired.

Stupid. Without a convenient open wound, the bullets didn't have any more effect than on the other creatures.

He emptied the whole clip, and nothing happened.

Zach screamed in frustration. He flung the empty gun at the creature's head.

It bounced off, again with no effect.

Actually, there was some effect.

The creature's head spun 180 degrees and stared at Zach.

It stopped pounding on the door. Its body swiveled to face the same way as its head.

It began walking toward Zach.

Oh, good, Zach thought. *I've managed to piss it off.*

CORPORAL GARCIA DIDN'T KNOW why he was trying to get inside the locked door. It seemed pretty urgent, but it wasn't up to him. It was the body, moving on its own. And the body hated whatever was on the other side of that door. It was like there was a high-pitched dog whistle in there, and the body under him would do anything to shut it off.

There was a slight feeling at the back of his head. Garcia turned, the first thing he'd done for himself in this nightmare.

He saw a young guy in a suit. The kind of wiener he

never liked in high school, actually. Student-government, college-bound, stuck-up, rich prick.

He didn't decide to move. The body spun around and started for the little jerk. Garcia could feel it now, the high-pitched whistle. It was coming from the guy in the suit.

It was annoying as hell. And he understood, suddenly, the impulse to snuff it out completely.

INSIDE THE OVAL OFFICE, the sudden silence was more unnerving than the steady pounding, or the splintering of the door.

President Curtis stood. Agent Terrill moved between him and the door, but the president edged the young man out of the way. He wanted to see for himself.

Griff didn't know what it meant. He'd heard gunshots, but there was no way bullets had brought the creature down.

Wyman was a great deal more optimistic.

"It's gone," he said, a grin breaking out on his face. "We can get out of here."

"Not a good idea," Griff said.

Wyman turned to the president, a petulant look on his face. "Sam, we have to go now. We have to get out. This could be our only chance."

The president looked at Griff.

"Agent Griffin. Is there any way to tell what's happened?"

Wyman rushed toward the president, blocked at the last

moment by Terrill. "Damn it, listen to me," he pleaded. "Don't waste any more time. Open the door."

The president looked at him, then back at Griff.

"Don't do it," Griff said. "We have to stay here, sit tight until—"

Wyman lunged past Griff and yanked at the lock. Steel bolts slid back.

Griff wasted a precious second on pure shock.

Wyman had opened the door.

ZACH STOOD THERE, trying to figure out something to do. Maybe if the thing chased him, it wouldn't go into the Oval Office. Maybe he could sacrifice himself to save the president.

There had to be a better plan than that.

But he couldn't think of one, and the *Unmenschsoldat* kept walking right toward him.

He heard a thudding noise. The door to the Oval Office popped open. The creature's blows had mangled a steel bolt, so it stuck in the frame, but there was a good foot or so of clearance.

Wyman came struggling out.

Zach almost couldn't believe his eyes. Wyman was squirming hard, pressing his body as flat as possible to get out of the jammed door. He was so frantic he didn't even see the creature.

But it saw him. It rotated its head again, locked onto the furious movement of the vice president.

It hesitated. Zach knew it could get inside the Oval

Office now. The door would fly open with one good blow from that thing.

He didn't relish the thought of dying to save Wyman, but he supposed it had to be done.

He picked up a piece of broken wood from the floor, ran at the creature and swung with all his might.

CADE ENTERED the West Wing hallway in time to see the whole thing, frozen in perspective. First Zach, with his makeshift weapon. Then the *Unmenschsoldat*, already turning back to the Oval Office. Then Wyman, stuck in the door, wriggling, his eyes wide with fear.

Cade didn't have time to open the case. He dropped it, grabbed Zach by the collar and yanked him out of harm's way.

Then he leaped on the creature himself.

GRIFF GOT HOLD OF Wyman's jacket and began hauling him into the room. Wyman kicked and braced himself against the toppled furniture on the barricade. It would have been funny, pure slapstick comedy, if only Wyman hadn't effectively just killed them all. Griff pulled harder.

Out of the corner of his eye, he saw Terrill move to help him.

"Stay with the president," he ordered, and the kid stood fast. Finally, Griff thought, someone who does what he's told.

Suddenly, Wyman stopped pulling and began pushing back. He was stuck. And he was trying to get back inside the office.

Griff took a look through the space in the door. He saw Cade grappling with the creature. And both of them stumbling and smashing their way down the hallway, right toward the door.

He pulled Wyman free just in time.

CADE AND THE MONSTER smashed through the door, the remaining bolt snapping cleanly.

They shattered the furniture in Griff's makeshift barricade, wood breaking like toothpicks, and hit the floor of the office, right in the middle of the presidential seal woven in the rug.

Agent Terrill shoved the president out of the way. To Cade, he looked as if he was frozen there, stuck in time. The creature's fist cocked back to throw another punch at Cade, and its elbow connected with the young man's head. Terrill's neck snapped with a hollow pop. His arms and legs went rag doll as he fell to the floor.

Another pointless death. For a moment, Cade saw nothing but rage, even as he dodged the creature's fist.

He bared his teeth and raised both hands above his head, jumping, bringing his arms down as he fell, using every bit of his strength, everything he and gravity could muster, and slammed his fists into the creature's skull.

It paused, shrugged, then kept coming at him.

Cade could see the first light of dawn. He had only minutes left.

One chance.

"Zach," he shouted over his shoulder. "Throw me the case."

ZACH HAD JUST GOTTEN UP from the floor where Cade tossed him. He could see clearly down the corridor into the Oval Office.

He heard Cade's command and saw the case sitting in the hallway, just a few feet away.

He ran forward, picked it up and hurled it through the door.

It pinwheeled through the air toward Cade's outstretched hand.

Griff knew: Cade wasn't going to make it.

In the moment that the vampire turned and called for Zach, in that second Cade had his back turned, he had left himself open.

That was all the creature needed. It was already reaching for Cade, prepared to rip his head off with one inhumanly strong hand.

Griff knew the president's life rested with Cade.

It wasn't a very hard decision to make, when you came right down to it.

He put every last ounce of his strength into his legs and pushed his way between Cade and the creature.

CADE SNATCHED THE CASE out of the air. He turned in time to see the creature put its hand through Griff's chest.

Griff's face was lined with pain, his eyes full of shock.

The creature flicked its wrist, like it was removing something distasteful from its fingers, and Griff went flying across the room.

For the first time in decades, Cade hesitated. He spent the moment Griff bought him in grief.

The creature turned toward the president.

CORPORAL GARCIA WAS BACK. He didn't know where he'd gone, but he was tired of this. Tired of this strange nightmare, tired of the pain. He was standing above a man—a man who looked familiar, someone he'd seen on TV—and his hands were moving again, prepared to grab that man and do something awful to him.

He was tired of doing these things, but it wasn't really him. He couldn't stop it, because he wasn't the one in control.

Everything was blurred. Everything hurt even more. The high-pitched noise was screaming now, and it seemed to be coming right from that man. He wanted very badly for this to end, and the only way to do that was to stop that noise.

Then he recognized the man. It was the president. What was the president doing in his dream?

He stopped. It took some conscious effort, like waking up from a deep sleep, but he stopped the body from moving, too.

Garcia just stood there, not knowing what to do next.

This was wrong. He didn't know what was happening, but he knew this was just *wrong*.

THE CREATURE PAUSED. Cade hissed a small prayer. He had time.

He moved between the monster and the president, knocking Curtis back into the wall. As he prepared to unlatch the case, he noticed something.

He looked into the creature's eyes. Saw pain, and confusion, and the dawning awareness of something—some*one*—desperately searching for answers.

Cade saw something human in there.

He opened the case.

The glow from the Baptist's hand bathed the creature in its light.

The effect was instantaneous. The spark in the eyes of Cpl. Ryan Garcia went out as his unnatural resurrection abruptly ended. The limbs went slack next, dropping and falling off. The body hit the floor.

Dead again. Returned to what they should have been, what they should have stayed: the empty parts of men long gone from this life.

The Oval Office was suddenly as quiet as a grave.

SIXTY-NINE

Cade heard the faintest rasping of breath. He shut the case and went to Griff.

The older man lay like a bit of wastepaper that had missed the basket. Blood pumped from the wound in his midsection, but slowly.

He didn't have much time left.

Cade leaned down, though he didn't have to get closer to hear him.

"The president?" Griff whispered.

"Safe," Cade said. "You did well."

Pink foam poured from Griff's nose and mouth. "It's bad."

"I don't know how you're breathing now."

Griff coughed, as close as he could get to a laugh. "Thanks." More pink foam.

Cade held the case before Griff's clouding eyes. "This could save you."

Griff looked pained, and it wasn't the agony from dying. It was disappointment. Shook his head, as much as he was able. "Not right," he said. "You know. It's time."

"It doesn't have to be."

Griff convulsed once, began trembling. It took long seconds for him to speak again. "Cade . . . Good . . . Bye."

Cade put the case down. He took Griff's hand in both of his, shook it formally.

"Tired," Griff said. Then his jaw went slack as the life went out of him.

ZACH ENTERED THE ROOM, saw the creature's remains on the floor spread over the presidential seal. He saw Cade, kneeling over Griff.

"Did we win?" he asked.

Cade reached down and closed Griff's eyes.

"We didn't lose," he said. "That's enough."

Zach looked down at Griff and realized what had happened. His breath caught in his throat.

From behind the desk, the president lifted himself off the floor. He shook his head, as if to clear it.

Cade went to him and helped him stand. The president looked over at Zach, then at Griff's body.

"I'm sorry," the president told Cade. "He was a good man."

Cade nodded.

The intercom beeped, a surprisingly mundane noise. Curtis answered. "This is the president."

On the other end, a new Secret Service agent babbled with relief. Communications lines were back up. Reinforcements were here, along with the army.

Curtis cut him off, his voice smooth and easy with command. "Keep the airspace around the White House clear. Establish a perimeter on the street. And bring in medical attention. We have wounded."

"Yes, sir, Mr. President. Are you all right?"

He clicked off the intercom for a moment and looked at Cade and Zach. "My family?"

"We just left them," Zach said. "They're in the panic room. Not a scratch."

The president gave a long sigh. He pressed the button again.

"I'm fine," he told the agent.

There was the sound of furniture moving. Cade assumed a battle stance, then relaxed. A second later, Wyman popped up from under a broken couch.

He surveyed the office as if measuring for drapes. Looked around at the destruction. The bodies. The blood on the floor.

He smoothed down his hair. He looked at Cade, and Zach, and then the body of Griff.

"I suppose you'll want to say 'I told you so,'" he said.

Cade was prohibited, by his oath, from doing what he wanted to do to the vice president.

Zach wasn't. He swung a hard right fist into the man's face, knocking him flat on his ass.

Wyman sat there, stunned, on the Oval Office carpet, blinking back tears.

"Not another word," Zach warned him, his fist drawn back to hit him again. "Not one more word. *Sir.*"

Cade, despite himself, felt a small grin on his face. For the vampire, this was the equivalent of falling down on the floor laughing.

Sunlight began to pour through the windows. They could already hear the soldiers and Secret Service men downstairs, the sounds of panicked voices and barked orders. Sirens outside. The media wouldn't be far behind.

Cade turned and headed for the elevator, back to the P-OCK and the tunnel out.

Zach looked to the president, who nodded. Time to go.

He followed Cade to the elevator. Wyman was still yelling at them as the doors closed.

EPILOGUE

CIA HEADQUARTERS, LANGLEY, VIRGINIA

"No, sir," the man in glasses said into his phone. "The White House managed to keep a lid on all of it. They're calling it an attempted suicide bombing. No evidence of the *Unmenschsoldaten* will ever reach the general public. Curtis's approval ratings have even gone up."

CNN, on mute in the background, played the same animation over and over: a graphic that said ATTACK ON THE WHITE HOUSE, which then exploded into a flare of light that filled the screen.

Angry words came from the phone. "Yes, sir," he said. "I know this isn't funny."

More sharp words. He listened. "In my defense, sir, Agent Holt behaved exactly as expected. She did everything she could to help Konrad, and she believed it was her own idea."

That didn't go over well. He listened to the abuse again. He could be eliminated on the basis of this failure, but he'd learned to live with that. It wasn't like they would tell him if it was coming anyway.

"Yes, sir," he said. "I apologize. I was wrong."

His superior hung up, leaving him listening to the sudden quiet in the office. Dimly, he realized that it was past midnight, and he was the only agent working in this section. Everyone else had gone home hours ago. Again. His wife was going to kill him.

He sighed. Was it too much to ask for a little gratitude? He'd done his job. Nothing could be traced back to the Company. Holt never knew the real plan, or how he'd manipulated her into moving it along. Using her obsessive fear of aging and assigning her to Konrad, he'd almost been able to fulfill one of the Prophecies.

The really annoying thing was, it should have worked. And it would have, if Konrad hadn't involved Cade. It was possible the vampire was becoming a serious threat. He'd have to run a cost-benefit analysis later.

The man in glasses sighed, and turned to his computer. With a click of his mouse, he opened his TO DO list. Moved "Dead Rising from Graves" back into the action items column, right before "Sky Turns Black" and "Moon Becomes Red as Blood."

He wondered who'd killed Holt—Cade or Konrad? It didn't really make much difference to him.

Ah, well, he thought. Back to the old drawing board. Armageddon isn't going to happen by itself, after all.

EXECUTIVE OFFICE BUILDING, WASHINGTON, D.C.

President Curtis sat behind Wyman's desk. The attack on the White House left him without an office, but not without work.

Wyman entered without knocking. Curtis gave him a sharp look.

"Sorry," Wyman said. "Still used to thinking of it as my office. Forgot something. Be out of here in a minute."

Wyman's left eye looked even worse now, swollen with a truly magnificent shiner. They blamed it on the terrorist assault, part of the cover story, but Curtis stifled a smile as he remembered the punch. Who knew Zach had such a mean right hand?

"It's fine," Curtis said. "While you're here, there was something I wanted to ask you."

Wyman stopped at the door. Was Curtis imagining it, or did the man seem nervous?

"What did Griffin say to you? When he pulled you aside."

Wyman's face was blank. Then he seemed to remember. "Oh, that. He just told me to calm down. Not to panic. I believe his words were, 'Show some balls.'"

Curtis looked at the vice president for a moment. "Nothing about the traitor?"

Wyman hesitated, then frowned. "Traitor?"

"Someone had to give up the location of the safe

house," Curtis said. "I think we can agree it wasn't Griffin. I had hoped he might have said something to you."

"Oh," Wyman said. He shrugged. "No. Nothing like that."

"Unfortunate," Curtis said.

"Yes," Wyman said. "Tragic."

Curtis turned back to the papers in front of him.

Wyman turned to go.

"That means we'll have to keep looking for him," Curtis said.

Wyman stopped.

"The traitor, I mean," the president continued. "Of course, now that we know he exists, he'd have to be fairly stupid to try anything again."

Wyman nodded. "Or very determined," he said.

Curtis stared at him; saw nothing but a perfectly blank expression.

"Good night, Les," he said after a moment.

"Good night, Mr. President," Wyman said, and left.

Outside Islamabad, Pakistan

Konrad's guide, a sullen young man in full beard and robes, showed him to the hut where he'd be working.

It was the most advanced facility in the small camp. It didn't have a toilet or running water. A kitchen table, badly scarred and worn, stood in the center of the room on a floor of linoleum on top of dirt.

Konrad's first lab, which had been in a medieval castle, was more sanitary than this.

This wasn't the deal, but now Konrad had little choice. The facility he'd been promised in Dubai—within walking distance of luxury shops, malls and a five-star hotel—was now far too public. After the attack on the White House, the U.S. military was chasing down every possible lead to Khaled and his group. Banks froze their accounts. Khaled's associates had been forced to retreat to the last safe haven—Pakistan. And Konrad had been forced to join them.

Well, Konrad could make it work. He'd done more with less.

Konrad surveyed the room and turned back to his guide. "So that's the lab. And where will I stay?"

The young man stared at him blankly. Konrad spoke no Pashto, and his guide's English was limited.

"Sleep," Konrad said sharply. "Where will I sleep?"

The young man nodded, and pointed with his AK-47 to a corner of the hut. A cot with an old blanket sat there.

"Of course," Konrad said. "Absolutely bloody charming."

He dropped his bag on the cot. Lice began crawling on the blanket.

Oh, Cade would pay for this. He would pay.

Los Angeles, California

Reyes knew he'd made the right move, especially once he saw the news. Almost buried in the panic over the attack on the White House was an item about a dead federal employee: Ken. Something about a mugging, miles away from the Federal Building. Yeah, right. He saw the Company at work there.

Well, tough shit, buddy, Reyes thought. You should've gotten out while you could.

He was packing a bag. The itchy feeling between his shoulder blades hadn't gone away. It had only gotten worse. It was time to visit Mexico. Maybe explore his roots. Or go even farther south. Someplace without an extradition treaty, where even the Company would have trouble finding him. He'd heard good things about Venezuela.

He stopped folding his shirts. He thought he heard something.

Reyes was taking no chances. He took out his pistol, turned around and crept toward the front of his apartment.

He saw someone there. He fired.

The bullet went wide and tore through the arm of the intruder.

She didn't even flinch.

He saw the gun. It was silenced, the wide barrel of the noise suppressor a black hole in front of him. He dropped his own weapon and raised his hands.

Only then did he notice who was holding the gun.

Helen Holt. But something had happened to her. She held the gun in her left hand, not her usual stance. The opposite side of her face was frozen, expressionless. In fact, her entire right side seemed . . . well, dead.

Maybe she'd had a stroke, Reyes thought.

"What happened to you?"

Only half of her face scowled.

She fired one shot. It hit him in the foot, blowing off a toe.

He fell back into a chair, mouth open to scream.

She shoved the barrel between his teeth. He got the message. He stayed as quiet as he could.

"That's a question you're going to learn not to ask," she said, words slightly slurred.

He sat down. Tried to not to look at her right side.

"Did the Company send you?" he asked.

"I don't work for the Company anymore," she hissed. "And neither do you. You're working for me now."

Reyes was confused. "So what are we doing?"

Half of Helen's face smiled. The other half remained expressionless. Cold.

"Oh, we have a lot to do," she said. "More than you can imagine."

Reyes noticed the bullet wound he'd just given her in the right arm. On her frozen side. It looked like a gash in a piece of furniture.

It wasn't bleeding.

Once again, Reyes had to admit: he was more scared of Helen Holt than he was almost anything else.

The Reliquary, Washington, D.C.

"What do you feed that thing anyway?"

Zach was pointing at the Allghoi Khorkoi, in its glass case.

"It prefers human flesh," Cade said. "Griff got it to take hot dogs."

After the attack, Zach showered the blood off, had his wounds stitched up and called his mother, who was frantic, watching the news about the terrorist assault. He told her he was fine. Then he hung up and went home and slept for twenty hours.

When he woke, he spent the day in bed, watching the breathless coverage on CNN. "A miracle that the president and vice president were not killed" is what the talking heads kept saying.

Underneath the constant yammering, the crawl ran a list of the Secret Service and White House staff killed in the attack. Every two minutes or so, Zach saw it scroll past: Agent William Hawley Griffin.

Some kind of miracle, Zach thought.

At dusk, his phone rang. Cade. Telling him to come to the Smithsonian, with instructions on how to open the hidden door.

He picked out another suit, put on his favorite tie and drove to the museum.

Now Cade was looking at him, his eyes measuring Zach.

"So what's your answer?" Cade asked. "Are you taking the job or not?"

Zach was mildly surprised by the question. "I thought I didn't have a choice."

"There's always a choice," Cade said. "No one is ever a slave."

"Griff said I'd have this job until I retired or died. He said turning it down wasn't an option."

"That's not what he told you," Cade said. "He asked you if you thought you'd be able to walk away. The question stands: can you?"

Zach knew the answer without thinking: "No."

"Good," Cade said. "Training is over. We have work to do."

He turned away, walking toward the computer. Zach had another question, however.

"Am I going to end up like Griff?" he asked. "Is that how this ends?"

Cade stopped. "There are worse ways to go," he said. "Does that change your answer?"

"No," Zach said.

"Then why are we still talking about this?"

"Griff's funeral is tomorrow at Arlington. I just thought—"

"Griff is dead."

Zach felt a flash of irritation. "I'm sorry, did you have something else planned for us?"

"Yes," Cade said. "We have one loose end."

"And I bet we're going to tie it off."

"No," Cade said. "We're going to sever it."

ONE WEEK LATER, ACAPULCO, MEXICO

Dylan sat in his family's condo and drank beer.

All was forgiven. He'd gone home to his father and apologized. He told the old man about his trip to Kuwait, where he worked for the army. Dylan's father actually seemed proud of him. He was just glad Dylan wasn't hurt, he said.

After a year like that, Dylan needed a vacation, his father said. He gave him a plane ticket and the keys to the condo in Acapulco.

Dylan went back to the sun and the sand and the babes and the beer, but it didn't feel the same. He watched the TV coverage about the White House attack and saw the faces of the men and women who'd been killed. Khaled had almost done it. He'd almost taken out the president. Dylan couldn't believe he'd gotten away clean.

In the mornings, when he woke up hung over and faced the brilliant Mexico daylight without any chemicals in his system, Dylan thought about what he'd done. He tried to tell himself he was the real victim here. He was just along for the ride. Khaled was the bad guy. If Dylan hadn't helped him, it would have been someone else, right?

And he didn't get paid, either.

It usually took several beers for any of that to sound convincing, even to him.

He was tired from hanging on the beach all day. Too much sun. He decided to stay home and watch TV.

Still, he couldn't lose the feeling that something was wrong.

Maybe it was the guy. There'd been some guy, some snot-nosed punk in a suit, hanging around the resort all week. He seemed official, somehow. Asking questions. But then he'd gone, and he never even talked to Dylan.

So why was he still so jumpy?

He drank more beer. Flipped channels.

The screen popped and went dead as all the lights went out in the apartment. Dylan dropped his beer. The power had been cut.

That wasn't too unusual in Mexico. He stood up anyway. His heart was slamming itself against his rib cage. His hands and legs shook.

He heard something on the patio. When he went to check, the door was open. He knew he'd closed it.

That was enough. He'd seen plenty of horror films, and the victims always made the same mistake: they waited around to find out what was going to happen.

Well, screw that. He ran for the apartment door.

He stumbled. Tripped over a coffee table. Then bounced off a wall.

Only it wasn't a wall.

Someone else was in the room, in front of him, blocking his path.

He was dressed all in black.

Dylan tried to push past him. The man shoved him, spilling him over the couch.

"You're not supposed to be here," he sputtered. "This is my family's place, you're in big trouble—"

The man spoke, in a voice as cold as anything.

"Dylan Weeks," he said. "My name is Nathaniel Cade. You are guilty of treason."

"No," Dylan said, struggling to his feet. "You got the wrong guy, I never—"

"You violated the bodies of the dead. You broke their trust. And you betrayed your country."

Cade was suddenly right in front of him again. Nothing human could move that fast. Dylan was knocked back down to the floor.

"I'm not here to argue," Cade said.

Dylan didn't like how that sounded. He got on his knees. "Please. I didn't know. I'm sorry."

Cade looked amused.

"Sorry?" Cade said. "You're sorry?"

Dylan nodded. "I swear. I had no idea."

"That changes everything."

For a split second, Dylan thought he might be off the hook. Forgiven.

Then he saw Cade smile and saw the fangs.

Dylan tried to scream.

Cade didn't let him.

ACKNOWLEDGMENTS

These people gave their time and effort to make this book better than I could alone. Many thanks are due:

Alexandra Machinist, my peerless agent, who also has the coolest name in the literary world; Rachel Kahan, both for her sharp edits and the inordinate amount of faith she showed in the manuscript; Lauren Kaplan, Ivan Held, and all the people at Putnam; Kris Engskov, former personal assistant to President Bill Clinton, for his help with the interior of the White House and its security procedures (I've taken liberties with the actual layout, and, of course, Mr. Engskov did not reveal the existence of a presidential vampire to me. I assume that would be classified); Claire Dippel (no relation to Konrad, at least as far as I know); Elizabeth Pontefract; Bryon Farnsworth; Amanda Rocque; Britt McCombs; John Rember; Ahren Heidt; Randal Eymann; William Heisel; the whole sick crew at Big Action! and, of course, my first reader and one true love, Jean Roosevelt Farnsworth. I should also thank my daughter, Caroline, who tolerated her father typing at the keyboard while she waited with wet diapers.

The true story of Andrew Johnson's pardon of a vampire

can be found in *The President's Vampire* by Robert Schneck, which investigates the facts first turned up by Charles Hoy Fort in *Wild Talents.* The Washington Prophecy is based on a story from *Oval Office Occult: True Stories of White House Weirdness* by Brian M. Thomsen.

KEEP READING FOR AN EXCERPT FROM
THE NEXT THRILLING NOVEL
BY CHRISTOPHER FARNSWORTH

THE PRESIDENT'S VAMPIRE

COMING SOON FROM G. P. PUTNAM'S SONS

Near Parachinar, Pakistan, November 29, 2001

Nathaniel Cade watched the men from his hidden perch as they walked up the narrow mountain path.

One was clearly in pain. He stooped, despite his height, and a younger man helped him along, at times almost carrying him.

To the south, the bombing at Tora Bora continued. The ten-thousand-pound Daisy Cutters slammed into the caves, one after another, the impact felt more than heard as earth and sky shook with each explosion.

It would have been impossible to block all the treacherous, winding paths out of the area, but the Americans had not even tried. That job went to the Pakistani military and a few warlords who switched sides only weeks before the invasion.

At least, that was the cover story.

Cade recalled how the general swore when told to

keep this escape route open. Cade had been alive a long time, but the general managed to surprise him with the inventiveness of some of the obscenities.

The order came direct from the president. The general probably assumed it was a political deal with the Pakistani military—a chance to prove themselves in the War on Terror. And a chance to conveniently forget all the help they'd given to the bad guys in the past. The general could not imagine they were actually going to let the target leave.

And yet, Cade watched as the most wanted man in the world simply walked away. Stumbling and weak, but still walking.

Osama bin Laden was almost free.

IT HAD TAKEN some doing to convince the president. Seventy-two hours earlier, in the Presidential Emergency Operations Center below the White House, Cade did not think it would happen.

"Gonna cost me the damn election," the president said, his face pinched with anger. He'd already been stewing about reports that questioned his absence on September 11—fleeing from one secure location to the next, while the wreckage still burned in New York and D.C.

Griff, Cade's handler, sat across the table. He'd been on the receiving end of many presidential tantrums in his career. He was used to it.

"Sir," he said. "You want to use Cade. This is the only way we can do it."

"We can't at least, I dunno, bring back the sumbitch's head, or something?" the president asked.

"All missions related to Mr. Cade are above top secret. You know that," the vice president reminded the president.

The president gave him a look.

"Sir," the veep added.

"I just want people to see what we do to the bastards who do things like this to us," the president insisted.

"Believe me, so do I, sir," the veep said. He stood and placed a hand on the president's shoulder. "But there are things here . . ." He paused, looking for the right words. "Things here are complicated. There are things it's better for you not to know."

The president squinted. "You mean that spooky shit, don't you? I don't like that."

"Which is why Mr. Cade will handle this."

The president appeared to waver. Then the vice-president spoke again. "Besides, George—there might be advantages to always having bin Laden out there. Nice to have a boogeyman whenever you need it."

"Yeah. All right," the president said. "Do it."

He walked to the door, still grumbling. "Gonna cost me the damn election."

At the door of the PEOC, he stopped and turned. He addressed Cade directly—something he rarely ever did. "Least you can do is make it messy, right? You make the sumbitch hurt."

Cade nodded. He could do that. It would be little enough payment for the wounds inflicted on the United

States. He was still a patriot. Even if he was no longer human.

CADE LOOKED DOWN at the Arabs again. At this rate, they would take another fifteen minutes, at least, to reach his hiding place at the crest of the ridge.

Cade shifted, feeling the wound in his gut. It was healing, but it hurt. The only thing keeping his intestines inside his body was a heavy-duty neoprene sheath. Of course, anyone else would have been killed.

Cade had spent most of the day of 9/11 in an underground parking garage, pinned to a concrete pillar by a sword driven through his torso.

He was still annoyed by that. He decided he'd waited long enough.

With one leap, he was out into empty air. He fell the length of three football fields and landed on his feet without a sound, directly in front of the man in the lead.

The man's reaction time was admirable. He was one of the elite of al-Qaeda's fighters, assigned as bin Laden's personal bodyguards. He had been hardened by years of combat, first against the Soviets, then against other warring tribes. Now, he had taken the most punishing bombardment the greatest military in the world could dish out—and lived.

Still, he barely touched his rifle before Cade pulled out his larynx.

The second man didn't waste time trying to unsling his rifle. He had a knife in his hand before his comrade fell, and he stabbed Cade in the side. It was a perfect strike—it should have driven up, between the ribs, and into Cade's heart, ending him.

That is, if the knife's point had not skidded off Cade's skin, which was tougher than Kevlar weave.

Cade twisted the second man's head completely around. His body fell nerveless to the trail.

Now he faced bin Laden himself, and his supporter. He shoved them to the ground, not wanting the man dead.

Not yet.

The fifth Arab used the clear shot at Cade to unload half a clip from his AK-47. Several of the rounds tore through Cade's wrapping, opening the wound again, and he nearly doubled over from the pain.

But he didn't drop. The fifth Arab's eyes went wide as Cade took the rifle from him. He whispered the start of a prayer and choked on his own blood as Cade drove the rifle through his chest.

The man supporting bin Laden was the youngest of the group—a boy, really, perhaps seventeen at the most. Despite what had happened to the combat veterans on each side of him, he did not hesitate to protect his leader. He reached for the grenades strung on the belt around his chest.

Cade snatched the belt away from him and tossed it to the ground before the boy could blink. Then Cade flung him into the abyss over the side of the trail. For a second, his arms scrabbled at the empty air as he began to drop. It would take a long time for him to hit the bottom.

Less than two minutes after it started, the fight was over.

Cade turned to bin Laden.

The most feared and hated man alive did not look particularly scary, especially when compared to Cade. He had been injured in the bombing, it was obvious—one side of his robes had fresh patches of red blood, and he panted heavily, struggling for breath. Cade could smell disease in him as well. This weak, sickly creature had brought the whole world to a halt, if only for a little while.

Bin Laden seemed to know he was no match for Cade. He remained on his knees, glaring. Cade wasn't about to kill him. He had questions.

Due to a number of chemical and psychological causes, Cade's memory, like every member of his kind, was perfect. He did not forget. Time did not dim his recall of anything. He could play it back with perfect clarity, even reliving scents and feelings.

Touching the wound in his abdomen, he was there again.

LATE AT NIGHT on September 10, he followed a target into a parking garage. He'd been tracking the man for weeks—it should not have been so difficult, and that should have tipped him off. He was searching the lower levels of the underground garage. He saw nothing. Then the man appeared as if from nowhere, moving faster than even Cade could see, and impaled him with a sword, driving it into a concrete pillar.

It shouldn't have been possible. No one was supposed

to be that fast, or that strong. No one human, at any rate. But Cade didn't waste shock on that. He was more concerned with the weapon that pinned him, like a moth to cardboard.

The sword was on fire.

Nobody believed him on this—not even Griff. But Cade's memory was perfect.

The sword burned with a blue-white flame until he finally managed to pull it free from the pillar, and from himself. It had looked ordinary then, a piece of forged steel, but he knew: the blade was on fire when it stabbed him.

It turned out he'd deliberately been kept out of the action. Someone had wanted him out of the way so the hijackings could succeed and the planes could hit their targets.

Whoever had enough resources to know about Cade's existence—and then take him out of the game—was more dangerous than a hundred al-Qaeda fanatics with a backpack nuke each.

That meant bin Laden had a great deal to answer for.

BIN LADEN stared at him; he was on his knees, but his face was still a mask of contempt.

"Who is the man with the sword?" Cade asked, voice perfectly level.

Bin Laden spat on the ground, replying to Cade's English with Arabic: "I will not foul my tongue with the language of the Great Satan. I am at peace with God. Do your worst. Know this, though: you are sending me to Paradise. I welcome death with open arms, for I am—"

Cade grabbed his face and squeezed. Bin Laden's voice died to a strangled little yelp.

"I do not believe you," Cade answered, in perfect Arabic. "I believe you know where you are going. And it is not to Paradise. I want answers. Who is the man with the sword?"

He released bin Laden, so the man could reply. "The sword is the sword of righteousness," he spat. "God's will is the fire in which it is forged, and your disgusting perverted nation will be split open . . ."

More gibberish. It appeared bin Laden did not know any more than his own part in the operation. He thought himself to be the center.

Then Cade realized bin Laden had stopped talking. He looked at Cade, his eyes dancing with a hidden joke.

"I know what you are," he said. "I did not believe they would send you. But they did."

Cade grabbed him again, pulling him close. "Who told you this? How do you know me?"

"You are not the worst thing this world has to offer," he said, grinning. "I know the truth. The sheep cannot hear it, but I have known for years. There is no God. Mohammed was not His prophet. My master will show you. This world belongs to him."

Cade usually never showed any emotion. He usually didn't feel any. His face was almost always an impassive mask, as still as the body in a funeral-home viewing.

But now his mouth narrowed to a thin line as he scowled.

"Belongs to who?" he asked.

Bin Laden's grin only grew wider. Cade was ready to do whatever it took to get answers. But bin Laden did know who—and what—Cade was.

He proved it by removing a small cross from inside his robes and jamming it against Cade's face. It felt like a railroad spike between his eyes.

Cade's lips peeled back as he screamed, and his fangs jutted out from his mouth. His human veneer dropped away. Cade already wore one cross around his neck as a ward against the thirst that constantly haunted him. The pain of another on his skin was almost unbearable.

"Vampire." Bin Laden laughed at him, shoving the cross forward again.

Cade recoiled involuntarily, giving another few feet of distance and another few seconds of time.

That was all bin Laden needed.

The Saudi curled in on himself. Cade hesitated, not sure what was wrong with him. He wondered if bin Laden's illness was about to claim him.

In a split second, Cade realized his mistake.

Bin Laden wasn't sick. He was *changing*.

His head and jaw jutted forward as black bile dribbled from his mouth. His skin shredded as muscle and bone moved beneath it like snakes under a tarp.

He locked eyes with Cade, and Cade saw his pupils had become diamond-slitted. His mouth gaped like a fish, revealing dozens of cruel, piranha-like teeth. The new flesh under his torn skin was dark green, almost black, and covered in scales.

Bin Laden's hands whipped out from under his robes, grabbing at Cade. But they weren't hands any longer.

Now they were long, yellow claws.

Cade barely had time to scramble away.

A harsh, snake-like hiss escaped bin Laden's throat. To Cade it sounded like laughter.

Cade lost his footing as he nearly tumbled over the edge of the path. Bin Laden pressed his advantage and slashed again with his claws. He caught Cade's wound, tearing it open further. Cade began to lose blood.

Cade flung one leg out in a desperate kick, but bin Laden had been walking these mountain trails for years. He was even more nimble now, scrambling around on reptilian feet. He dashed up the side of the cliff and came down behind Cade, claws darting, tagging Cade on the side, costing him more blood.

Cade spun, threw a punch, and missed. His momentum nearly took him over the edge again. He managed to avoid the fall, but only by landing in a tremendous belly flop on the path.

Bin Laden didn't let up. He leaped on Cade's back and began shredding him. Cade rolled over and tried to get his hands around the al-Qaeda leader's throat.

Bin Laden locked his claws around Cade's throat at the same time. His snake-like head darted forward, snapping jaws inches away from Cade's face. His neck seemed to extend like a spring. It took all of Cade's strength just to hold him back.

The bleeding got worse. Cade could feel the power draining out of him. He was not prepared for this. He didn't have much time.

He made a decision. He released bin Laden with his left hand while still fending off the jaws and teeth with his right. He began scrabbling in the dirt with his free hand.

Bin Laden never looked away. He was enjoying Cade's humiliation. He let loose with the same hissing laughter as before.

Cade's fingers found what he'd been looking for—right where he'd dropped it on the trail.

The belt of grenades he'd taken from the boy.

He managed to pull one into his fingers.

His arm trembled. Bin Laden redoubled his efforts. He was nearly at Cade's throat now. His teeth clicked only a few millimeters away.

Bin Laden saw the desperation in Cade's eyes. The al-Qaeda leader spoke.

"This world is his. But you will never see it, vampire."

Cade's arm bent, just a little more.

Bin Laden lunged, jaws wide, ready to latch down on Cade's neck.

And before bin Laden could stop him, Cade's left hand brought up the grenade and stuffed it in his mouth.

In the same moment, he kicked with both feet and sent bin Laden flying.

The pin to the grenade stayed where it was, hooked around Cade's finger.

Bin Laden's body spun out into the empty air over the chasm. Then he exploded.

Green-black blood painted Cade and the rocks all around him. Bits of scales and skin fell in wet chunks to the ground.

Cade stood and tried not to think of the wasted opportunity. He'd had questions, and they would never be answered now. It was his own fault. His wound had slowed him down. And he'd underestimated his opponent. He'd failed.

Still, there was one small victory. He would be able to tell the president bin Laden's death was, in fact, very messy.

From #1 *New York Times* bestselling author

LAURELL K. HAMILTON

BULLET

The Mother of All Darkness believes that she is finally powerful enough to regain a physical body. But the body she wants to possess is already taken—it belongs to Anita Blake.

The "addicting"* Sookie Stackhouse books by #1 *New York Times* bestselling author

Charlaine Harris

DEAD UNTIL DARK
LIVING DEAD IN DALLAS
CLUB DEAD
DEAD TO THE WORLD
DEAD AS A DOORNAIL
DEFINITELY DEAD
ALL TOGETHER DEAD
FROM DEAD TO WORSE
DEAD AND GONE
DEAD IN THE FAMILY

Also available:

THE SOOKIE STACKHOUSE BOXED SET

A TOUCH OF DEAD:
SOOKIE STACKHOUSE, THE COMPLETE SHORT STORIES

"Great heroine and great supernatural adventures."
—Jayne Ann Krentz

"[A] delightful southern vampire detective series."
—The Denver Post

***The New York Times**

penguin.com

M128AS0110